Biscayne

A NOVEL

Barry Jay Kaplan

SIMON AND SCHUSTER

NEW YORK · LONDON · TORONTO · SYDNEY · TOKYO

Simon and Schuster
Simon & Schuster Building
Rockefeller Center
1230 Avenue of the Americas
New York, New York 10020

SIMON AND SCHUSTER and colophon are registered trademarks
of Simon & Schuster Inc.

Designed by Levavi & Levavi
Manufactured in the United States of America

10 9 8 7 6 5 4 3 2 1

Library of Congress Cataloging in Publication data

Kaplan, Barry Jay.
   Biscayne : a novel / Barry Jay Kaplan.
      p.   cm.
   I. Title.
PS3561.A549B57   1988   88-27483
813'.54—dc19   CIP

ISBN 0-671-62535-7

Acknowledgments

The author would like to thank the following people for their help before, during, and after the writing of this book: Ron Van Lieu, Murray Moss, Franklin Getchell, Alice Martell, Michael Korda, Laurie Lister.

Part One

1.

A hansom cab came to a clattering stop at the gangway of the massive steamer *El Paso*. Two stevedores scurried to remove a high pile of baggage. The horse pawed the cobblestones of the dock, exhaling great clouds of steaming breath. A woman and a young man emerged from the cab into the dark, heavy mist. Both wore the black of mourning: black wool over black crepe, the woman hatted and gloved, the young man in a black cape with the collar pulled up to his ears. The woman paid the driver, then she and the young man huddled together a moment, their heads bent in conference, and finally turned white, anxious faces up toward the decks of the great ship.

The woman's eyes were eager, though her gestures were measured and slow; the young man's face, which resembled hers, had a fevered, apprehensive look. He cast his eyes furtively behind him, then strained to peer ahead; he looked, in a word, pursued. As the woman took her companion's arm, there was a straightness to her posture that suggested not only pride but a bristling tautness, as if her true energy were being held in check. It was apparent, in fact, that it was she who guided the man and not the reverse.

Looming grand and magisterial above the dock, the *El Paso* framed these last two arrivals as they ascended the steep gangway, their heads bent close together, their pale faces now hidden. The audience above, leaning out over the railing for a better look, was frustrated, and though it could only wonder who had died and given cause for the black crepe, it was certain, by who supported whom, which one was ill.

With the steward's help, Clara got Harry undressed and into bed immediately upon reaching the cabin; he was asleep before the steward could return with his bowl of consommé and poached eggs. Clara stood at the porthole window, stealing glances at the harbor, alert for any sign that Harry might need her.

The steamer's final blast signaled that the voyage was about to begin. Clara started, checked Harry one last time, then made her way to the prow, where she stood with her back to the receding port as a tugboat of the McAllister Line guided them out of New York harbor. The wind was sharp and biting, and she was glad she had brought the shawl to wrap around her heavy coat.

She pulled the shawl tighter around her, wincing as the sea spray fell on her face and hands. Her thoughts drifted to the sight, carefully preserved in her memory, of the morning mist on the Miami River, that distant river of her childhood. She gripped the rail and leaned into the wind. She wanted to cut the traveling time in half by the sheer force of her will. She wanted to be there now. The sight of the vast expanse of ocean was enough to make the cold bearable. Soon, soon, soon . . . The future beckoned on each wave that broke as the waters were sliced by the ship's prow.

They could have taken a train, but it would have meant executing a series of perilously timed connections: once in New York, to the Atlantic Coast Line bound for Washington; there to the Mid-Atlantic Baltimore and Ohio for Richmond; then on the Savannah, Florida and Western Line, stopping in Jessup, Ways of the Cross, St. Mary's River, and Jacksonville, Florida, where they could finally get a schooner to Key West. Clara decided instead to take the train only to New York and a steamer south, but even the short trip from Union Station in Middleton to Grand Central was a two-day nightmare of cold, flying cinders, and enough dry cheese sandwiches to last a lifetime.

They stayed overnight on Astor Place, ate steak Diane at Delmonico's, and at Harry's insistence took a landaulet up Broadway under a light sprinkling of snow. Delicate flakes melted on her lashes and on the fur of her jacket. Street musicians were playing "She's Only a Bird in a Gilded Cage," and Harry leaned out and tossed pennies into their hats.

The world had held nothing but surprises since Cameron's unexpected death. His affairs were left in the kind of impeccable order she assumed they would be; to keep things going as they had always gone, there was nothing for her to do but sign papers. And despite her shock, the opportunity of her situation struck her forcefully. This was her chance to free herself from her old life and create a new one. Though her decision shocked her neighbors and caused her women friends to suggest that grief had made Clara not herself, Clara knew that she was, for the first time in her life, just becoming herself. Once Cameron was buried and a respectable amount of time had passed, there was no reason to stay in Middleton. The notion was at once simple and revolutionary. The Reade Ironworks held no interest for either her or Harry; Clara would be only too glad to assign its maintenance to its board of directors. And once the decision to go had been made, there was no reason not to go right away. Harry supported her in this; in fact, he was eager to go, and were it not for a bout of pneumonia that had kept him from attending the funeral, they might have gone sooner. The business was in good hands and the house was put up for rent. Once Harry was well enough, all that was left to do was make the travel arrangements and write to Quentin McLeod of the Biscayne Bay Company to tell of their arrival. Pack. Say goodbye. Go.

And now, as land dropped away completely and she faced the open sea, Clara could acknowledge to herself that these decisions had been lurking in the deepest pockets of her secret heart for years and years, that she was simply following through on plans made half a lifetime ago. She had been given a second chance, and this time she would not turn back.

The eggs and consommé sat untouched and cold on a tray next to Harry's bed. Clara rang for the steward and ordered the same again. As she closed the door, Harry stirred. Always a restless sleeper, she thought, and moved to his side. Though eighteen years old, in sleep he seemed only a boy, his face unlined and untroubled, a mask of innocence that she wished to maintain as long as she could. His innocence always made her feel hopeful about the future.

He turned his head in sleep, arched his neck off the pillow, and relaxed again. Her heart quickened, so fierce and tender and protective was her love. And to think that such sweetness had had to confront death in such a brutal way, for her husband had died in their son's arms . . . Yet she was obscurely glad for Cameron's sake that his last moments on earth were spent in the arms of his only child. Oh, but the poor child . . .

"Harry?" she whispered.

He was her bright spot, her angel, the reason that her life was not the unbearable stultification it might otherwise have been. Early bouts with scarlet and rheumatic fevers had left him housebound for long stretches of time, yet in her heart of hearts Clara could not complain about the care he had required. If he had been other than he was, he would have been out in the world and she would not have had him with her for those long periods—once a whole winter, another time an entire summer and fall. And now this pneumonia had weakened him once again. The sun, she thought; the sun will make him well.

She ran her fingers lightly over the curls at the nape of his neck. He had shaved closely before this morning's departure from the hotel and his throat was very white. Clara licked her finger and gently rubbed at a tiny drop of dried blood where the razor had nicked him.

She looked at herself in the mirror at his bedside. Cameron had always been so particular about the way she dressed, and though he was gone, she had unthinkingly maintained the habit of satisfying him.

She adjusted her high lace collar. How pale I am, she thought, knowing it was not simply grief—there had been rather little of that— or the weariness of her long journey. She felt as though some gradual diminution of her spirit had been taking place for years and years. If I'd stayed where I was—in that city, that house, that marriage—I soon would have had to resort to powders and rouges and kohl. Clara saw now, in what people had lately described as a maturing of her young good looks, that something was gone that had to do with neither beauty nor youth. Oh, I have come very far indeed from the girl I was, she thought ruefully, then pinched her cheeks lightly and ran her teeth over her lips to bring up the color. A few stray hairs escaped her careful set and she smoothed them into place. One caught the light, silver among the brown; not yet, she thought, and yanked it out.

"Mother, what *are* you doing?"

Startled, embarrassed, Clara turned to Harry. "Don't you want me to look nice?"

Harry shook his head. "You always look nice to me."

"I never heard of a son yet who didn't think his mother's looks were special."

"But yours *are* special," he insisted.

Clara shook her head again; men had been saying this her whole life long, but it meant little to her. The rosy roundness of her cheeks had gone, replaced by a sculptural quality, it was said, the modeling stuff living flesh. Her smooth high forehead was as yet unlined; her hair, pinned back with tortoise combs, was dark, deeply waved, unruly as a river. Her mouth, once full and pouty—Cupid's quiver, as society painter Petrus Flashman had once declared when drunk on champagne—with the years had settled into a firmer, more sinuous but less luxurious line, drawn in on itself, wry, wary of saying too much. Her eyes had always elicited the most comment: "naughty" Cameron had called them when he courted her, "arrogant" he said later as her mischief turned into rebellion. He had given up looking into her eyes directly and said he did not understand her. The light in her eyes had slowly become a cloudy sky—gray green, silver green, lit from within as if the sun were trying to burst through but didn't quite dare.

Clara smoothed the blankets over her son's chest. "Is there anything you need?"

Harry lifted his face to her. "A quick peck before you go."

She saw the pale purple veins of his eyelids as she put her lips to his cheek. "The steward is coming with some eggs." She leaned back and breathed deeply, then, resting her hand on his knees, said, "I need to ask you something." She hesitated. "You . . . you *do* think we've done the right thing?"

Harry squirmed under the blanket. "By leaving?"

Clara nodded. "Was it . . . disrespectful of us to leave so quickly?"

He shrugged. "You didn't love him."

"Oh, Harry." She sat up straight. "You mustn't say such things."

"I have eyes and ears, you know."

Clara turned her face away from him. "A husband and a wife . . ."

She lifted her hands and let them drop back in her lap. "There are other things—loyalty, fidelity, gratitude . . . "

Harry burrowed deeper into the pillows. "You can get all that from a cocker spaniel."

She shook her head. "You're making me very unhappy, talking like this."

"He's the one who made you unhappy."

Clara made no reply. He stroked her back in the absent way he had when she read to him on long winter afternoons.

"We hated that city, Mother. It was horrible. Iron works and black smoke covering the sky. Unhappy people doing work they hate. People shouldn't have to live that way."

"I know, darling. In your ideal society—"

"I meant everything I said about it. I still do."

"There's practically nothing there," Clara said with a helpless little laugh.

Harry smiled. "But we're going to make it . . . *something,* aren't we?"

She smiled at his persistence. "You've got my promise on that."

"I love you," he said.

She smiled in relief. Murmuring something she couldn't hear, Harry buried his face in the deep purple-black folds of her skirt. "What is it, dear?" She stared at his curls, at the pink downy ear, at the smooth curve of his jawline, shadowed faintly blue.

"I want so much for you to be happy," he said.

She sighed and gave the tender lobe of his ear a gentle tug, but she couldn't get him to turn his face up to her. "I will be. Do you want my promise on that too?"

He put his hand over hers and pressed it to his head. "I'm serious!" he exclaimed and tightened his grip on her hand. "I'll do anything to make you happy." His voice held a tinge of fear. "Promise you'll let me."

"Harry, what is wrong with you?"

"Promise!"

"You're hurting my hand . . . Yes. Yes, of course."

It was only then that he relaxed and let her go, first pressing his lips to her palm and finally turning his face to her, beaming. He was still her boy, still her Harry. Everyone said he had her beauty, the same small oval face and broad cheekbones and full-lipped mouth, the same finely sculpted nose, all slightly coarsened and made masculine by his father's pugnacious jaw. His eyes were his father's too: green and heavy-lidded and sleepy-looking.

A knock came at the door and the steward entered with the poached eggs and consommé. Clara and Harry were silent while the man set them down and backed out.

"Why don't you go for a walk?" Harry said. "I know you'd like that." He laughed at Clara's hesitation. "Go on. I'll be fine. I'll gorge myself on consommé."

Clara hesitated a moment longer, then pressed her cheek to his. "Thank you, darling," she whispered and was gone.

Harry sat up and looked at the cup of poached eggs. He pierced them with a spoon, stirred them around, watching with slight revulsion the yellow drooling into the white, then chopped the white into gelatinous chunks until the steam stopped rising from the cup and the eggs lay in the bottom, developing a shiny film as they cooled. He wrapped a blanket around his shoulders and took the eggs with him to the porthole, setting the cup down and opening the window. A chilling blast of sea air hit him in the face. He gasped, then tossed out the eggs, cup and all, and leaned out to watch them disappear in the cold ocean.

Back in bed, he sipped the consommé. He would honor the promise he'd made, but he would never tell her what had happened the night his father died, not of the true circumstances, not of his own participation. Not of his guilt. He had saved his mother from scorn and shame and despair, and he vowed now to continue to protect her for as long as he lived.

The morning of the second day dawned bright and cloudy, with a sea rippled and shadowed like endless bolts of undulating gray silk. After a hurried breakfast, Clara paced the deck, still wrapped in her heavy black coat and shawl. All day she moved restlessly from bow to stern and port to starboard, following the rise and setting of the sun. After years of living indoors, she wanted to keep it in sight at all times. She delighted in the subtle changes in sea and sky as the boat steamed south.

Some of the passengers spent the first cold days in the lounge, reading or playing whist or gossiping and miming pleasure at Caruso's unearthly screeches on the ship's primitive gramophone. A few approached her, but Clara felt overwhelmed by their murmured sympathies and fled outdoors, pacing the deck, trying to tire herself out. But she was too stirred up to rest. The blood raced in her veins; the ship felt to her as if it were only inching forward. All she had ever known of patience was forgotten.

She encountered no other passengers outdoors, only Harry bundled up in his deck chair. She stretched out on the chair next to his, covered herself with a lap robe, leaned back, and breathed deeply of the sea air. But no matter how she contrived to appear at ease, her heart raced with anticipation. A few moments of silence went by. She watched the steam rise from one of the ship's funnels and vanish in the sea air. A rope swung against an outside cabin wall with the regular beat of the waves against the hull. She hummed "She's Only a Bird in a Gilded Cage," clicking the toes of her shoes together. She found a loose thread on a cuff and pulled it free. She glanced over at Harry and saw that he was watching her.

"I'm anxious to get there," she said.

"I can see that," he replied.

"Are you laughing at me?"

"A little."

She shook his hand and held it between hers for a moment, and they both looked out at the ocean. At home they would have been looking at the park across the way.

"The first thing we ought to do is change the color of that ocean," Harry said.

"Too blue?" Clara asked.

"Too green."

"Absolutely," Clara agreed. "It clashes with your eyes."

"My thought precisely," Harry said. "Then we fill half of it in with dirt and plant azaleas and oleanders."

"And a banana tree," Clara said.

"Of course. Mustn't forget the bananas." They laughed and were silent again until Harry tapped her shoulder. "And nobody will have more than they need and nobody will have less. In fact, everybody will share in—"

Clara put her hand on his. "Let's not, darling," she said. "All this fantasy—"

"It's not fantasy," Harry said. "It's a new society." He was a little hurt that she did not understand him, but the expression on her face was so open, he could not keep his hurt very fresh. "Why don't you read Mr. McLeod's letter again?"

"Oh, Harry, shall I?" she said, and Harry knew he had said the right thing.

Clara kept it folded deep in the pocket of her skirt; with every step she took it pressed against her thigh, reminding her of her sole living connection to the bay and her girlhood home at the river's mouth.

"Quentin McLeod," Harry said, shaking his head. "Probably a grizzled old seadog with skin like an alligator's."

Clara laughed and nodded. "And mail-order clothes he patches himself."

"His pants are probably held up by a rope instead of a belt."

"Still," Clara said, "I have the feeling I'm going to like him."

"If he doesn't smell too badly from cigar smoke and fish."

"Listen, darling," she said as she smoothed the letter on her lap. "I'm listening."

Dear Mrs. Reade,
    So you are planning a trip to see the Miami River at last.

Harry laughed. "He sounds relieved. Now there'll be three of us instead of just him."

"Shh. Listen."

I am glad that you have decided to come down to the bay and see for yourself the house and land your parents left for you. Your mother and father loved the area as I am sure you must know. Their old house needs looking after or repairing or selling. I would leave that to you but advise that it is not likely to last another hurricane without some kind of repairs being made. I have arranged accommodations for you and your little boy at the inn at Palm Grove, where you will be comfortable for your stay. I will bring my boat the *Newport* to take you up the strait from Key West.

There were additional words of sympathy for her loss and of advice on what kind of clothes to bring, but Clara skipped over those. She let her hand fall to her lap and leaned back in her chair.

" 'You and your little boy,' " Harry said and put his thumb in his mouth.

"He misunderstood," Clara said.

Harry shrugged. "I'm still curious, though. Who else lives there?"

"Well, there's a couple called Rufus and Ida Finch. I think they've got the trading post on the south bank of the river somewhere. I'm sure we'll meet them soon enough. And there's a tiny community at Palm Grove. And there might be someone living in Fort Dallas. You'll hear plenty about the fort, I'm sure, and don't you believe half of it. The whole time I was growing up there, all I heard about was what went on inside that fort. The way people talked about it, you'd think the whole history of Florida happened right there. The fort could be gone altogether, though. We'll see. A building in the tropics might stand for years quietly rotting from the inside, then suddenly collapse in a heap of clay, to be lost forever in a web of strangler vines." Clara smiled to herself: *strangler vines,* I haven't said those words in over twenty years.

"You never talked this way at home," Harry said.

"We're on our way to our home," Clara responded emphatically. "It's as if I'm going back to a fork in the road, and now I'm going to travel the one I didn't travel before."

It rained the third day out, and though the *El Paso* had loomed awesomely powerful from the dock, its mass proved slight and yielding when confronted with the relentless pull of the sea. The cabins were either cold and damp or hot and stuffy, but the pitch of the waves left most of the passengers flat on their backs inside them, regardless. Clara was physically unaffected by the weather, though the confinement gave a claustrophobic edge to her restlessness. The rain came down continuously, monotonously, the sky and the sea nearly invisible; all outdoors seemed silvered. The only sound was the metronomic splash of rain on the decks.

The fourth day at sunset the *El Paso* dropped anchor for the first time. The city of St. Augustine—"The oldest in the whole country, Harry!"—seemed to Clara as she imagined Egypt might be, low and flat and burning with age and sun and religion. An orange glow hung over it as the sun went down; mist rose from the ground and softened the edges of buildings. She and Harry sat on deck and watched as scattered campfires were lit. Waltz music wafted faintly across the water from the old fort; huge sentinel palms did back bends in the breeze against the purple sky.

On their fifth and last dawn at sea, the sky was a buttery yellow-white, threatening a day of intense heat. Clara stretched in her narrow cabin bed and smiled: after twenty-five winters in Middleton, she welcomed the heat. Sea gulls were visible through the porthole, hovering over the ship as it came into port at Palm Beach. Clara watched with growing impatience the long parade of travelers as they disembarked in their summer whites. She wished she could fly on the back of a gull the rest of the way to the Miami River. Even as their destination neared, the trip seemed endless.

By mid-morning the *El Paso* was off again. Clara had finished packing the night before and now busied herself tucking last minute odds and ends in her steamer trunk.

Before they touched land, she had one thing left to do. She had prepared the large bundle the night before and now hauled it up on deck. The sea breeze whipped her hair around her face; she made no effort to keep it in place. She stopped at the stern, leaned the bundle on the railing, and stared at the churning water. With eyes half-closed against the wind, she could see the house on E Street riding the waves that swept out behind the boat. She could see the iron stove in her studio and the snowy avenue outside and the park across the way where Cameron had first held her. She could smell bread baking, see mist forming on the dining-room windows and Cameron lighting his pipe . . . and for a moment doubt and fear replaced the purpose and excitement she had been feeling just a few minutes earlier. She was suddenly overwhelmed to have left a routine of ease and comfort for a life of hardship and labor, to have deserted civilized society for a desolate, unpopulated wilderness, a comfortable house for a crumbling shack, a steady, formal, ordered existence for chaos, for the anarchy of an untamed, unknown . . .

Her heart beat fast as she undid the bundle, drawing out the heavy coat and shawl she'd worn on her first day at sea. She leaned over the railing as far as she could and let the heavy garments go. The wind caught the coat; its arms waved empty at her. The shawl sailed crazily upward for a moment, then swooped down.

Good-bye . . . good-bye . . .

She kept her eyes on them until coat and shawl were sucked into the boat's wake, scrambled in the white water and pulled under. The moment they disappeared from sight, Clara turned away.

She vowed to create a life that would put to shame the safety, the ease, the suffocation of the one she'd left.

The *El Paso* cut its motors and glided into Key West harbor.

2.

Clara had been to Key West only once before in her life; her missionary parents, who lived in peace and solitude 150 miles up the bay, thought it a wicked, worldly place. Now standing at the railing with Harry as the *El Paso* drifted into port, she saw little change: white houses perched on the coral shores, delicate as bird cages with their gingerbread trim. Lovely wide verandas swept around each home. She had spent many dark years in Middleton dreaming of sitting on these same porches in the balmy sea breeze. Brilliantly colored bougainvillea, alamanda, and oleander dripped down the sides of the buildings, just as they had in her memory. Clara opened her umbrella to shield Harry against the glare of the sun and dabbed her face delicately with her handkerchief as the boat docked.

The port swarmed with activity: schooners, barkentines, sailboats, canoes, and ocean-going steamers from all over the world bobbed in the calm waters. There was even a British military ship, the HMS *Vanitas,* anchored offshore. On the dock itself, manned platforms hoisted by elaborate pulley systems swung big bales of deep water sponges and Cuban cigars and crates of local turtle meat over the wharf and into the holds of northbound freighters. Sailors from the USS *Powhattan* were posing for photographers on board the flagship, hats doffed, grinning for posterity. The old Customs House, a sturdily impressive three-storied structure faced with dormer windows, stood at the dock's tip, looking out to sea. A spirited little auctioneer was positioned out front, selling off a huge pile of merchandise—weathered timber, dark red chairs and sofas scored with salt stains, a forlorn chest of drawers with no drawers, slatless deck chairs, huge skeins of fraying rope, battered steamer trunks, piles of tarpaulins—clearly the detritus of many a shipwreck.

Clara suddenly had the odd sensation of being watched. She scanned the bustling crowd, finally drawn to a pair of eyes that met hers fixedly. They belonged to the only man on the dock not engaged in some sort of hurried activity. His very stillness drew the eye to him. The man leaned lazily against a pier piling, holding his straw plantation hat on his head against the stiff sea breeze, his long legs and bare feet stretched out before him. His white suit seemed to shimmer in the sun. Slowly, he doffed his hat toward Clara, nodding, not breaking his steady gaze. The breeze riffled through his snowy white hair, which curiously belied his youthful face.

Slightly unnerved by the boldness of the stranger's stare, Clara turned her attention to Harry, taking his arm, supporting him carefully down the gangway. But she could not keep herself from casting a quick glance back to where the stranger reposed; his eyes were still on her. Halfway down she stumbled, clutching at the rope rail for balance as her open umbrella floated in slow motion over the side. She made a grab for it, missed, and to her acute dismay, watched as the man in the white suit dipped a bare foot into the water, grasped the umbrella handle between his toes, and flipped it into the air.

"Your parasol, ma'am," he drawled with what looked like a smirk, as she made her way to where he stood shaking her umbrella. He handed it back to her.

The *nerve* of him, she thought. "Thank you," she said stiffly. *With his toes!* He nodded again, a boyish lock of hair white as cornsilk falling into his eyes. Thinking he was waiting, expecting a tip, she fumbled for some change. "Oh, it's in my trunks . . . " She looked up toward the ship and saw to her astonishment that she'd left Harry behind. He was poised on the gangplank, motionless. "My son . . . " She gestured to the stranger. Harry proceeded slowly down toward them, none too steady on his feet. Suddenly he swayed as if struck, clutched the rope railing, and stumbled helplessly down to the dock, collapsing in a heap against a huge bale of arrowroot.

By the time she could push and struggle her way through the milling crowd to Harry's side, a seaman's jacket was already placed under his seemingly lifeless head, his tie removed, his collar loosened. An anonymous hand proffered a tin cup of water. Gratefully, Clara held it to her son's lips. His eyelids fluttered. Clara let the water run into his mouth; Harry sputtered and choked. Tears came to his eyes.

"It's just the sun, darling. Drink some more water."

An arm reached past Clara and gripped Harry, pulling him to his feet. Once again it was the man in the white suit. Clara sighed with a bit of impatience. Despite his help, the man was becoming a nuisance.

"Quentin McLeod," he said. "Mrs. Reade?"

Now Clara could only stare; he was not at all what she had expected. She felt somehow betrayed.

"Let's get him out of the sun," McLeod commanded, helping Harry to a bench. "I'm afraid we can't take too much time, Mrs. Reade. The breeze on Biscayne Bay don't wait. Not even for Northerners."

Clara ignored the jibe. "Our trunks . . . "

"I'll get 'em seen to," McLeod said and strode off.

Clara turned back to Harry; he was pale but his breathing had returned to normal. He broke into a weak grin. "Hardly the grizzled old seadog we imagined!"

Clara laughed, relieved. "Come on, darling. Let's get out of this sun."

McLeod rejoined them. "Bags are taken care of," he said and looked down at Harry. "The boy well enough to travel?"

"The 'boy' is well enough to speak for himself, thank you," Harry said, scrambling to his feet. "Just lead the way, if you will."

"Well . . . " McLeod looked unwilling to rely on Harry's estimation of his condition but finally shrugged. He signaled to the three Cuban boys carrying the trunks. Clara opened her umbrella, trying to muster the shreds of her self-assurance. Harry refused the support of her arm.

"Lead on, McLeod," he said.

· · ·

Harry was asleep in the tiny trunk cabin by the time the *Newport* caught the wind out of Key West harbor.

"Say good-bye to civilization, Mrs. Reade," McLeod said.

"I'm only looking *ahead* these days, Mr. McLeod," Clara replied as the bustling port receded in the distance. Its giant palms sank and sank until they were just a fringe on the horizon.

Clara sat beneath her umbrella on a huge crate of sorghum and dried beef bound for Finch's trading post. McLeod sat at the tiller, his bare feet propped on the *Newport's* rail. Clara undid the top two buttons of her shirtwaist and dabbed her chest and neck with a handkerchief drenched in gardenia water. Her skin felt unusually tingly and sensitive. Her hair, despite the tortoiseshell combs, refused to stay in place.

The sails filled with a breeze so fragrant—with brine and sweetness and sun-upon-flesh—and so familiar that it seemed to Clara only yesterday she had slept under its spell. "It's been twenty-five years since I've been here," she told McLeod.

"You won't find much changed," he said. "It's still sort of a secret. The few who come down here either stay and keep quiet or leave and don't talk about it. Not much to talk about. We got no roads, no bridges, no drainage canals, no schools, no real church, not even a plowed field."

"Why, Mr. McLeod, you sound like you're bragging!" Clara said.

McLeod smiled, despite himself. "I'm not bragging. But I'm not gonna paint a rosier picture for you than what actually is."

"Why, I wouldn't *want* you to!"

"Population grows by the tens every year," he said. "At most. I'm the census taker, and my last count for Palm Grove, Pineland City, both banks of the Miami River and all the keys but Key West was one hundred and twenty-four sweet souls. Not counting Seminoles, of course. Not that they don't count, but they don't like being counted. The way they see it, it's all theirs anyway. Most of 'em's been removed out by the government to Louisiana and Texas. The ones still here is out in the wetlands."

"What brought you down here?"

McLeod looked away from her and squinted in the sun. "Man I knew worked for the Biscayne Bay Company and asked me to come down

24   · *BISCAYNE* ·

and join him developing the area, getting people to move in." He shrugged. "I was just . . . starting out in life, so . . . "

Clara watched him closely. The muscles of his shoulders were all bunched up, and Clara wondered what had put the edge on him. With the sun behind him, she couldn't quite make out his expression, only the sharp thrust of his jaw and the strain in his long muscular neck. In silhouette his face had the strong, clean lines of a very young man. He hadn't shaved for a few days and the stubble was as white as the hair on his head. Was his white hair natural, she wondered, or was it the effect of the sun? As he turned to face her he looked much more aged; the sun had clearly done its work on his skin too, lining it and scoring it with fine wrinkles around his eyes and mouth.

"So . . . I come down and stayed," he concluded simply. Clara sensed there was more to the story.

A few moments later Clara spotted a lighthouse rising out of the water. McLeod craned his neck, newly alert. "American Shoals," he told her. "That's the first of twenty-four you'll see."

Clara kept her eye on it as they passed, thinking of the isolation of whoever lived there. What strong reserves of personal fortitude he must have to endure the harsh sun and storm all alone! And what will be required of me, where I'm going? she wondered.

An hour or so later another lighthouse came into view, taller and more elaborate in its gridwork than the first. "Sombrero Reef," McLeod announced.

"Does it look as lonely to you as it does to me?" Clara asked. McLeod shrugged. A distant look came into his eyes, and Clara realized her question had been too personal.

He stood up and cast an appraising eye over the water. "'Scuse me, Mrs. Reade. I got to keep a close watch now. The water coming up's lethal."

Clara turned her attention back to the water. Every once in a while a wave fell to reveal strings of teethlike coral ledges and shoals. They were lovely and fiercely dangerous at the same time. She remembered her girlhood lessons about Ponce de León sailing these waters and calling the reefs *los martires* because they looked to him like men in agony.

The *Newport* sailed smoothly, however, in calm waters. McLeod was perched at the tiller, binoculars at the ready, altering his course around marks that did not meet Clara's untrained eye. There was another lighthouse on Alligator Reef. Inside the framework was the white-washed residence of the keeper and above, at the top, a huge set of arc lamps. The lighthouse appeared to rest directly on top of the water, but Clara knew that this was what was so cunningly deceptive about the reefs: they hid beneath mere inches of water that looked smooth and deep. When she looked down, the water was so shallow and so clear she could see the coral and seaweed and even the sandy bottom alive with turtle and crawfish.

The air was clear, the sky a dense azure blue with powdery white clouds, the breeze warm as a smile. In the distance were low green islands that seemed to be floating, stacked one on top of the other. Gulls and herons glided lazily overhead, making an occasional dive for a fish.

Once, late in the day, as they approached the Carysfort Reef light-house near Key Largo, Clara saw the wreck of a four-masted schooner tipped halfway over and bobbing not a hundred yards from the light-house itself. They passed it on the near side of the reef, and she could see the hole ripped out of its bottom. The sun was setting behind its hull and Clara was glad when McLeod took in the sails and dropped anchor for the night.

Harry was feverish and sleepy, though he'd slept the whole day. His limbs felt heavy and unmovable to him, and the air in the small cabin seemed as close as a crypt. Long moments went by as he tested his breathing: deep breaths in . . . holding for a count of three . . . then slowly exhaling through his teeth, to see if he could detect any conges-tion in his chest. He had to get well! He was determined to be well, to leave illness and weakness behind him in Middleton.

He had longed to escape from there even before his father's death gave him and his mother—for entirely different reasons—the perfect, unquestioned, reasonable way out. If he had been able to bluff his way through pneumonia, they could have gone as soon as business affairs were settled, but he had been very ill, and he shivered now in the stupefying heat to think of just how close that delay brought him and his mother to total exposure. Another few weeks and word would have spread . . .

He put the palms of his hands against his eyes to rub out the images that began to form of that night. As long as he could get his mother away from Middleton, he knew, they would be safe and he could force Middleton to become only and forever the past.

If they had stayed, there was the danger that someone would reveal something that would hurt and shame them, that would tear apart the fabric that bound them to society and expose the personal horror beneath. Harry's fear was so vivid that he would pull it over him like a blanket and wrap himself in it at will; it would float down upon him unbidden at the thought of a certain street corner in the mercantile district, at the sound of a Sousa march a girl had hummed, at the sight of a particular shade of Prussian blue silk. If they had stayed in Middleton they would be prey every day to the eyes and leers and insinuations of the town's good people. And even if no one, by word, deed, or implication, suggested that the knowledge was public, Harry knew himself; it would take many miles and many years to make him forget his part in the nightmare.

It had been his mother's night at her Ladies' Great Books Circle, and so absorbed had she been in last-minute annotations of *The Mill on the Floss,* she scarcely noticed Harry's reluctance to spend this evening with his father, who looked forward to introducing his son to his club on the occasion of Harry's eighteenth birthday and ascension to that sphere of adulthood where men, behind the hallowed portals of that fifty-year-old institution, eschewed the company of wives and mothers, sisters and sweethearts, and were "men among men."

Harry had hoped for a different sort of initiation—one of his classmates had had just such a one and regaled everyone with explicit details for days afterwards—but his father, puffed up with self-importance at the approaching evening, would have brooked no such suggestion even if Harry had found a way to voice it. And the faint hope that his father would understand him, would put himself in Harry's place and imagine what he might want on this special day, was extinguished by his father's moist-eyed reminiscence of an evening identical to this one when he himself made the leap from boyhood to manhood in the company of his own father at the very same club they were off to now. Harry felt condemned to repeat history; desire would have to wait.

Sighing with boredom, irritation, and impatience, eager to get the evening going so its end could come as quickly, Harry kissed his mother good-bye and followed his father out. Bundled in astrakhan coats, under a beaverskin lap robe, they began the ride. The carriage was close and stuffy; the isinglass curtains were pulled down to keep out the snow, which had begun as they left the house on E Street. Earlier, his father had knocked at Harry's door and ceremoniously presented him with his own bottle of Knize eau de cologne, and now the shared scent hung in the air with heavy, unwanted intimacy.

In the club's oak and gilt Edwardian Room, his father's cronies, mustachioed and bald, portly behind starched shirts and waistcoats, toasted Harry's health, toasted his majority, and toasted the ladies they loved, and Harry, urged on by the atmosphere of camaraderie, matched them brandy for brandy, cigar for cigar until his head spun and he found himself veering wildly between an unbidden, woozy affection for these men who kept clapping him on the shoulders and calling him "my boy" and a swooning revulsion. That his father beamed with pride now irritated Harry more than he could say; how dare he take so much pleasure when he so misunderstands me! But such irritation was not new. Harry had always felt apart from this father who dressed in expensive suits cut to disguise a soft, overfed body and seemed a stranger in the house on E Street while reigning as its despot—a bully who inspired fear but not affection, a braggart who contributed to community charities but who operated an ironworks factory that fouled the air of that community with black smoke.

And now, seeing his father in his club, Harry was struck by an even greater sense of apartness from him: not for me, Harry thought, a life of factories and board meetings, of male sanctuaries and the exclusivity of clubs and brandy; I'll have a wife and family I'll love and not want to leave behind. And it suddenly struck Harry as the height of absurdity that this kind of men's club swagger, this brandied bonhomie, this self-satisfied preening and posturing supposedly defined an ideal of manhood. Unable to bear it a moment longer, his discretion and his fear drowned by the brandy, Harry slammed his glass on the bar.

"Is a man a man simply because he drinks whiskey?" he demanded to the now-attentive group of men. "Is he a man because he boasts of his business prowess, wears side-whiskers, and laughs heartily from the chest?" With all the superiority and contempt a boy of eighteen can muster to show his elders that he is their better, Harry assured them that a man was something different, that a man was something more. "A man's nature is passionate," he declared. "A man is someone who makes great gestures, who seeks the grand, the adventurous in life, who isn't afraid to know his animal side, to satisfy his desires."

In the ensuing silence, one of the men cleared his throat. "We can't all go around satisfying our animal desires any time we like, young man. That would breed social anarchy. The whole fabric of society would unravel."

Harry downed the last of his brandy and answered excitedly. "Would that be so bad? It seems to me that if you pillars of society would just loosen your collars for once and feel some fresh air on your skin, we'd all be—"

Harry felt a painful grip on his arm and looked up to see his father glaring at him. The others had begun to avert their eyes and now, shuffling their feet and clearing their throats, were going on to other, more convivial topics of conversation. Harry was not surprised that his father, nearly choking with embarrassment and rage, called for their cloaks and their carriage. The rite of passage was over, and Harry knew that once they were alone, the dressing-down would begin.

"As if you knew the first thing about being a man," his father said when the carriage had taken them away from the doors of the club. "Sniveling and whining aren't what make a man, I'll tell you that. Grandstand speeches won't do it either. Hard work and discipline are what make a man and you've never worked a day in your life! The nerve. Pampered and coddled . . . I never should have treated you like a man in the first place."

"By taking me for a night at your club?"

"When I was your age my father began the tradition and—"

"When you were my age!" Harry laughed harshly. For the first time he would not allow his father to put him in his place so easily. "Was it so long ago that you don't remember that a young man has appetites? That there's something he might want more on his eighteenth birthday than a glass of brandy and a Cuban cigar?"

His father turned slowly to him, and in the flickering light from the lampposts outside, Harry could see that his father was looking at him as if he'd never quite seen him before, as if the man beside him was unrecognizable as the boy with whom he'd begun the evening.

"Please, Father," Harry urged. "Let's have a real adventure."

His father's eyes darted away. "I've never . . . that is, I don't know of . . ."

"There's a place in the mercantile district," Harry said.

"Your mother wouldn't like this."

"This is between us men," Harry said. His father remained silent, and Harry gave directions to the driver, who was keeping a slower pace now that the snow had begun to accumulate. Excited, Harry laughed and clapped his father's shoulder, astonished at his own power, at how easily he had taken over.

The carriage soon came to a stop. Harry raised the isinglass curtain to let in revivifying cold air and saw Kalor's Brewery on the side street. They were near the river; he could smell the sharp tang of it and hear the slap of water against the pier pilings. A mist of powdery snow was illuminated in the cone of light at the corner lamppost. From far off came the muffled click of footsteps on cobblestones. The cold air and snow cleared Harry's head, and he felt a kind of recklessness buoying him.

In a gesture calculated to reestablish control of the situation, his father dismissed the carriage and driver, but once it had gone he could only look around with an air of bewilderment. He seemed diminished to Harry, old, a figure of pathos. The great man of industry, Harry thought with contempt, but for the first time in his adult life, he also felt a pang of love for his father and, on its heels, regret that it had come so late.

He started across the street toward a row of warehouse offices, his father lumbering after him, and approached a door that bore the painted sign French Imports. Harry tugged at the iron bellpull; the door was opened a moment later by a Negro in a powdered wig and silk breeches. "Ev'nin'," the man drawled. Harry gripped his father's elbow and piloted him inside.

In the small anteroom banked by high mahogany doors, the butler helped them off with their coats, then pulled aside a velvet drape to permit them entry. The room revealed was squarish, draped and fringed and lit by gas wall sconces of tinted milk glass that cast an amber glow over the thirty or so inhabitants and had the effect of making them look set in time, glacéed, ageless. They were standing at a long buffet table nibbling marzipan tarts or lolling tête-à-tête on overstuffed horsehair sofas or dancing with slow stateliness to the tinny sounds coming from an elaborately painted gramophone atop a lace-covered table. Potted palms loomed in corners; Boston ferns feathered out from pedestals. The walls were hung with paintings that Harry recognized as depicting the rape of the Sabine women, the ravishing of Leda by something half human, half swan, the abandonment by Jason of a distraught, bloody, and nude Medea. The men wore tuxedos, some of them, or stiff gray waistcoats and high collars with cravats and pearl stickpins. The women, their hair piled and ratted and curled and set off with multicolored feathers and glass trinkets, wore dresses of shiny materials; they arched back in their seats to show off the rosiness of shoulders and arms. The whole room was softened by cigarette smoke. The music from the gramophone imparted a certain wistful sadness to the people's conversations, as if they all were talking about their dreams.

"Don't look so shocked, Father," Harry said, delighted that the sight had elicited this response. Now who's the man, he thought, and steered his father's clumsy bulk across the room to a small sofa of tufted red damask. "Just like the ones in your club, eh, Father?"

Harry took a glass of champagne from a tray and pulled his father down beside him on the sofa. As he sipped, his lightheadedness left him completely and he saw everything as a marvelous, unbelievable charade, every bit as entertaining as a play in a theater. He was vaguely aware that next to him his father squirmed restlessly against the cushions as if trying to disappear in their depths, but then Harry forgot all about his father's uneasiness, for a girl across the room caught his eye and nodded in frank appraisal.

Harry's lips went suddenly dry; so this will be the one. Her image swam before his eyes; he was drunk again. He tried to focus on a single aspect of her appearance as she approached but saw only a haze of black hair and pale, pale pink. She stood in front of him now, hips swaying slightly. Harry's eyes locked on her hand, holding a slice of tangerine, as she brought it slowly to her lips.

"Care for a bite?"

Harry stared, unable to make his mouth work, as the girl bit into the tangerine and licked up a wayward drop of juice with a pointed tongue. Harry thought the gesture as clever as a feat of legerdemain. She had small, bright eyes and very white teeth, though she was older than she'd first appeared; Harry thought she might even be as old as thirty.

"My name's Gina," she said.

"Mine is—"

She leaned over, bringing the scent of mimosa and the sight of a deep, white bosom; she touched his hand to silence him. "Would you like to bring your champagne to my room?"

Harry clutched her hand and with her help rose from the sofa. He started to go, then remembering, turned to glance back down at his father: a great lumpy figure in stiff gray clothes, his neck so sunken into his starched shirt that his mottled skin folded over the collar. "A minute," Harry said to Gina, then looked around him and lurched to grab the arm of a dark-skinned girl in Prussian blue silk standing nearby, humming a Sousa march.

"My father," Harry whispered to her, indicating the man on the sofa. "Show him a good time."

The girl glanced at his father, took a breath so deep she might have been preparing to plunge into ice-cold water, and fell back smiling on the sofa, landing in a great whoosh of satin and jasmine. Harry watched the girl's fingers snake and wind and finally stop on his father's thigh.

"An adventure, Father," Harry said, and his father, though red-faced with embarrassment, forced a grin at Harry, as if to show what a good sport he could be.

He's old, Harry thought with a sudden, sobering chill, and felt as if it was a cruel trick to drag him here, to humiliate him this way. "Father, I . . ."

Gina was running her hand along his shoulder. "Mustn't let the wine go flat," she said as her fingers did tantalizing things to the back of his neck. Harry shuddered, yielding to pleasure, and left his father on his own.

Gina's room was on the third floor: "The longer you work here, the closer your room gets to the parlor." She proceeded him up the narrow staircase. Harry watched the sway of her pink satin dress; he had the urge to fall into it and lose himself in the undulating waves. "Some of the girls put on so much weight they can't even climb up after a year or two. It's those tarts and crullers Mrs. Poole lays out every night. A girl can't resist. And me with a sweet tooth!"

Her room—its smell of soap and disinfectant reminded Harry of his own house after a spring cleaning—contained a wide bed, a washstand piled with towels, and a painted dressing screen. Gina went behind the screen and Harry heard splashing water and the swish of silk. He sat on the edge of the bed and started to remove his shoes with fingers unaccountably thick and clumsy.

Moments later Gina stepped out from behind the screen; her wrapper was open down the front to reveal her white lace Lady Hamilton. Harry swallowed hard, staring. He cleared his throat. She came toward him. In a moment he would press his flesh to hers. His eyes were focused on the downy white smoothness in the shadow between her breasts. His breath came quick at the thought of burying his face there. He gestured toward the bed without taking his eyes from her breasts; there was a slight sway to them as she came closer, and he could smell her now, a perfume unlike any he'd known. He thought of a forest floor, damp moss, bread baking, and the sweet earthiness of raw yams.

From somewhere in the house below came the sudden piercing sound of a woman's scream, then doors being opened and shut and people bounding up and down the stairs. "Mr. Reade! Is Mr. Reade in there?"

The door flew open and a woman who might have been a member of his mother's book circle but for the brightness of her face paint rushed in and grabbed Harry's arm. As she maneuvered him out of the room, he passed through a small group of the girls, who were crying silently and biting their lips. "What is it?" Harry asked.

The woman didn't answer but rushed him down the hall, down the steps to the second floor. "I run a respectable house," she said impatiently. "I've never had any trouble till now. If they close me . . . and in the middle of the winter!"

She stopped at an open door and Harry looked in. The dark-skinned girl stood naked in a corner of the room, clutching her blue dress in front of her. Her mouth was trembling, and she breathed in gasps and sobs. On the bed was a dark satin quilt; the older woman motioned with her chin and Harry moved slowly toward it. Poking out from beneath the quilt was a hand; Harry recognized his father's club ring. He pulled the cover down. His father lay with his face averted, dressed only in his shirt. The white sheets were splashed with blood.

"He was on me," the girl in the corner was saying between sobs.

"Pumping away, you know, and all of a sudden he coughed . . . and . . . and I felt something hot running down my neck and into my hair and I touched it and it was blood and I looked up at him and it was pouring out of his mouth." She broke down again and the older woman held her hand tightly. "He collapsed on me . . . but his thing . . . his thing didn't go soft and I couldn't get out from under him and . . . oh God . . . he was dead, I knew he was dead and I couldn't get out from under him and . . . have I got blood on me still? Oh no! It's in my hair!"

Harry touched his father's hand; the fingers were hard and cold. His neck was arched, the mouth and eyes open. Harry closed the eyes, then stripped off the pillowcase and wiped the blood from his father's face and neck. He heard people talking behind him and turned to the older woman. "Don't call anyone."

"Not likely I will," she said.

The Negro butler helped Harry dress his father but would not carry the body any further than half a block from the front door. The door slammed with a hollow thud and the street was dense with quiet. It had continued snowing and high drifts had accumulated everywhere. His own labored breathing and the blood pounding in his ears were the only sounds Harry could hear. He tried to hold up his father's body, but it slipped down into a heap, and now all he could manage was to drag it through the snow. He was able to get it across the street and down the next block, only to collapse on top of it finally under the scant protection of the corrugated awning of Exeter's Barley Mill.

He used snow to wipe all remaining traces of blood from his father's mouth and neck and even where it had pooled and dried in the whorls of his ear. The weight of the body against him warmed him at first, but the wind drove the snow up onto their feet and legs as they lay under the awning, and he was soon shivering. He looked up and saw they had come but two blocks from the sign that said French Imports.

Harry did not blame Mrs. Poole, not then or ever, for not helping him more than she did. A death in a place that celebrated pleasures, and illicit ones at that . . . No, he understood the limits of good fellowship. He had protected his father from being discovered in that house, but it was his doing that his father was there in the first place, his sneering attitude that had driven his father to the girl in Prussian blue, his taunting that had been responsible for all of it, all of it, even unto death.

His mother must never know the circumstances. She must be made to believe her husband had met his end while he and Harry walked alone in the streets. Harry would confess in shame to drunkenness, and his mother would pity and forgive him. He had never lied to her before, but he would do anything now to spare her the disgrace of the truth, that he had driven his father to this untimely and ignominious end.

Late night wore on toward early morning. The snow soaked through Harry's shoes and melted in rivulets down his neck. He slept and wakened to brush the snow from himself and his father, then drifted off to sleep again. At some point he heard the muted clattering of horse carts in the streets and opened his eyes to see a horse's snout about to nudge him; the cart driver bending over him jumped back when Harry stirred.

"Thought you was both dead," the driver said breathlessly.

"No," Harry said. "Just . . . just my father . . ."

He told his mother a story both sad and painful, if not altogether true: he and his father had both had too much to drink and halfway home had gotten out of the carriage to clear their heads in the brisk night air. But they'd gotten lost as the snowfall obscured the street signs, his father's breathing turned to gasping, he'd clutched his chest, then . . . Clara had no reason not to believe him. But for the first time he was not the boy she thought he was. Nor had he ever been the kind of man his father urged him to be—dictatorial, ambitious, imperious: qualities Harry suspected were signs not of manhood but of weakness and fear. Father would want me to boast of my exploits, he thought now, yet it was his father—or rather the grotesque manner in which he had died—that had forced Harry to marshal heretofore unknown strength, the strength to harbor this secret. Its corollary effect was to construct between him and his mother a wall of silence. He did not fail to see the irony: only in death had his father accomplished this separation. And it was this perception, perhaps more than what had happened that night, more even than the burden of keeping it secret, that had taken him barreling toward early manhood.

His mother appeared, as if conjured out of his imagination, bringing the scent of gardenia perfume into the close cabin. "Mr. McLeod's made soup from a turtle he caught." She sat on the camp stool next to the bed and held the bowl in her lap, then dipped the spoon into the soup.

Harry sat up and looked down at the bowl. "Nothing still living in there, I hope."

"Come on, darling," Clara said with a little laugh. "Just a taste."

Harry shook his head. "I'll stick to beef jerky if you don't mind."

"You've got to eat, Harry. You've got to keep up your strength."

"I'm strong enough," he replied stiffly.

There was silence for a moment but she did not go away. Harry turned to look at her; she held the spoon stubbornly suspended midway between the bowl and her mouth as if she was about to demonstrate, as she had done when he was a child, how delicious the soup was by tasting it herself.

"Just leave it here," he said.

"Promise you'll eat it?"

"I promise!" Harry shouted. "All right? I promise!" He could hardly look at her after that outburst and sank back against the pillow. "I'm sorry," he said. "I'm still . . . tired."

"It's all right," Clara said and stood up, placing the bowl on the stool. She leaned over and put her cheek to his. "Have a good sleep," she said and was gone.

Harry stared at the ceiling. His poor mother. How could she know the enormous changes that had come over him in the past few months? She, who had been a barometer of his moods for his entire life, no longer knew him at all. That she had suddenly, and through none of her own doing, become a stranger made him feel that a part of him had been shut down. He wanted to put his head in her lap and cling to her as he had once done, but he was not the boy he had been and her comfort seemed out of his reach.

Her scent hung in the air, which now seemed to take on a weight of sorrow, for Harry realized that he no longer believed, as his mother still did, in his innocence. He would do all he could to protect her from such enlightenment.

Clara woke up on deck before dawn as McLeod was preparing the *Newport* for the day's trip. She stared straight up at the pale gray sky and watched it turn blue, bluer with the rising of the sun; the heat too came up quickly, before the breeze of the boat's movement could cool it. Clara's skin began to itch; she knotted her cotton shawl to the railing and rolled up her sleeves. A pail of fresh water had been placed on the deck for her to wash in and she smelled coffee brewing. McLeod nodded his good morning and went about his business. The coffee tasted strongly of chickory, and Clara sipped it slowly as the *Newport* glided through the shallows.

The breeze passed over her like long veils of perfumed silk; her skin tingled with the gentle touch of the sun, her cheeks hot despite the breeze. An easy smile played on her lips; her thoughts drifted. She was aware of her flesh as she had not been in years and years, as if the sun and the breeze and the tang of sea spray defined her.

They passed a settlement on Elliott's Key where she saw a family of five and a skinny white dog standing next to a dinghy. The stunted palms and coconut trees on the beach looked like an oasis, but instead of a desert there was water surrounding them. The family kept waving until they dropped out of sight in the sea.

Harry came up from the stuffy cabin, squinting in the bright glare of the sun, and opened the umbrella. He stumbled as the boat tacked sharply to starboard and flung himself down on a sack of pinto beans. He's in a mood, she thought, and determined to leave him be.

The rest of the day was bliss. Clara's sense of patience remained with her. The wind was high, the sky absolutely free of clouds; she had never dreamed such clarity and scope. To the west, Biscayne Prairie gradually came into view, sweeping out of the empty horizon like a broad grassy river. As they came slowly closer, it was more clearly defined by scalloped ridges of pines and palms and set off by every subtle shade and intensity of green. Large gulls swooped overhead, and at the shallows near the shore egrets and blue herons wheeled in to rest and dip their bills.

Clara and Harry spent the day under the umbrella, sipping the chickory-flavored coffee and eating McLeod's turtle soup and the last of the Louis Sherry chocolates they'd bought in New York. Clara kept her eyes on the shore and saw that except for pioneer homes scattered widely apart, the land seemed completely untouched.

In the afternoon, at the sun's peak, the bay was an open, gleaming sheet. Harry replanted the umbrella between two sacks of cornmeal and lay beneath it, eyes closed, a dreamy smile on his face; Clara ensconced herself in a place at the prow where she wouldn't be in McLeod's way. A warm breeze embraced her, caressed her neck and face, shaded by a hat made from palmetto leaves that she had found in the cabin. Her skirt was tucked around her knees, her blouse loose, the wind lifting it, billowing it along with the sail. She recognized the lighthouse on Florida Reef and then Bear's Cut, where the ocean was visible between and beyond the reefs.

Soon, soon, soon.

Ahead, the land was a thin strip at the very edge of the water, water so light and clear and still it was nearly the same color as the sky and that tiny strip of land was the thing that made one not the other. Clara felt giddy, all spirit and sensation, weightless, floating, dreamily awake. And an essential part of her, a quality of her beauty that had been hidden, grayed, muted, began its release, as if all it took was sun and the bite of sea air and the long-delayed, longed-for return to the place of her birth.

McLeod pulled the sail taut and tacked to port until the *Newport* caught a contrary breeze that took it skimming across the slick surface of the bay, barreling toward that thin strip of land. The land mass began to fill out, and Clara could now distinguish trees and leaves and roots, pointed and in clumps, the trunks brown and black and mottled ocher. Her heart pounded, the notion that this was home, a familiar sight, was suddenly lost, of no importance, compared to the physical sensation of coming in.

And the land, a moment ago a solid mass, revealed a tiny split, and the split suddenly opened up, widening, and they were approaching the mouth of the river. On either bank, palm trees shimmered in the breeze, their edges as delicate as lace borders. She could hear the rustle of palm fronds. She felt weak and dizzy, and something inside her gave way. She experienced a physical melting, a softening, that made it impossible for her to resist the river's power. One hand touched her parted lips, the other clutched her bosom. She moaned in her throat, feeling nearly faint now, lost to it, lost to the coursing of the river, hot under the sun that reddened her hands, lost to the pull, lost to the breeze, sucked into the river's mouth. She had the sense that the river was the pulse of the land and that on this land she would be transformed.

3.

The land had actually grown since she'd been there. Hurricanes had piled up shoals near the shore and the mangroves, always eager land makers, had been adding to it ever since: seaweed, broken twigs and branches, lost items from shipwrecks. The jungle had become too dense for the house to be visible, and if Clara had not felt McLeod's eyes on her, she might have cried out in dismay.

McLeod helped them haul their trunks off the boat and along the rickety slatted dock to the sandy shore, where a wagon with rusted iron wheels, one of them bent into an oval, was lying on its side. McLeod gave it a hard tug and it came up reluctantly, uprooting vines that had grown around it.

"You sure you don't want to stay at the inn in Palm Grove?" he suggested.

"We're already here," Clara said.

"You can have a real bed there," he said. "Who knows what—"

"We'll be fine right here," Clara said, trying to keep her voice steady.

"Don't go too far, darling!" she called out to Harry, who was taking tentative steps along the shore.

"It's no trouble running you over there," McLeod said. "You'd be better off."

"Mr. McLeod, I have no intention of starting off by pampering myself."

McLeod slapped a mosquito on his arm and flicked it off with his thumb. He looked from her to Harry to the overgrown path in front of them. "You don't look like you're going to last very long."

"I was born here, Mr. McLeod!"

"You haven't been here in twenty-five years! You're a city woman now. You're not used to this. No one's gonna take care of you; no one's gonna come running. And from the look of your son, he's not gonna do you much good neither." McLeod shook his head and looked at her quite openly. "There's no doctors at the Miami River. Did you ever think of that? There's a trading post and a passel of Seminoles and that's it. You could save yourself a lot of heartache and just go back where you come from."

"Middleton?" She was laughing, suddenly confident again. "Middleton's grand if you think a person's dreams lie in a sooty brownstone building or an office on Euclid Avenue or an ironworks by the river." And now it was her turn to stare at him. "Why is any of this important to you anyway?"

McLeod hesitated. "Let's just say I like the quiet."

"What makes you think I'll disturb it?"

"Oh, you will, Mrs. Reade. I've met women like you before."

"Women like me?"

"I know what comes next. You've got money to burn and you're just crazy about the ocean. You worship the sun and you hate the city and you're looking for some man of nature to make you happy."

Clara straightened her back and started gathering her bundles. "You make too many assumptions, Mr. McLeod." She turned from him and called out to Harry. She didn't ask for McLeod's help and he didn't offer any. In a few moments she heard the sound of his boat leaving. It was her anger that gave her the strength not to follow him with her eyes. She concentrated on getting their trunks to the house.

One trunk at a time could be balanced, albeit precariously, on the old wagon, and while Clara kept a steadying hand on it, Harry pushed.

"It's just up ahead," she told him with more optimism than she felt.

The path bore all the signs of years of disuse. Tree limbs had fallen across it, brown leaves lay in piles in various stages of disintegration, weeds and vines covered it completely in places; in the failing daylight, shadows on shadows made their route even more perilous. Harry caught his foot in the elaborately curling root system of a banyan tree and went sprawling into the embrace of a large, pale green yucca plant. The trunk and wagon tottered and remained, amazingly, upright; Harry brushed himself off and assured Clara, with some impatience, that he was unhurt. They continued on without further incident.

"The end of the path is marked by a pair of banana palms," Clara said. "I used to think of them as sentinels guarding the house."

When they reached them, however, one palm had disintegrated completely, its roots dry and gone to dust; the other was almost totally lost in the embrace of strangler vines. The yard had once been a large, roughly circular clearing of sand with patches of coral showing through in what Clara as a child had called bald spots. Now yellowed grass grew shoulder-high, though in some places it had been flattened down, suggesting that a large animal—a deer, perhaps, or wild boar, even a panther—had made the spot its bed. Harry set the wagon down. Clara took his hand. I will not cry, she vowed.

Time and the peculiarities of the tropical climate had worked their strange alterations on the house that for twenty-five years had glowed pure white in the sunshine of Clara's memories. The reality at the far end of the untended clearing was a shock to her. Though the intervening years had passed for her like a dream, the house had lived every single moment and bore the ravages of time and weather.

It had been constructed on stilts, four feet off the ground, to discourage termites; her mother used to scrub the pine floors and the stilts with a wire brush and lye to kill the ones that managed the climb. Spanish moss, which her father had had to clip with irritating frequency, so profligate was its growth, had advanced freely since his supervision ended and now draped one side of the house, completely obscuring windows and doors. The palmetto thatching above the porch had become home to birds, lizards, and tree frogs.

Even when the house was first built, it had had a ramshackle quality to it, rooms opening onto rooms without plan or design; simple necessity dictated when and where more space was added. A small assembly room with windows on the bay that was tacked onto the side had withstood the strong winds off the water, but the porch that had extended around it had partially collapsed and two wicker chairs lay in the pile of old and rotted boards. Her parents had used the house not only for living but for prayer meetings and as a classroom for Seminole children, anywhere from a half dozen to twenty at a time. Not that they'd been rewarded for such a labor of love. Even now Clara could hardly stand to think of how her parents had met their end and at whose hand. She remembered letters from her mother telling of the Seminoles whose children had been brought to their missionary school. All had gone well until a dispute arose in the county over a piece of reservation land the Indians claimed the government was taking away to force them deeper into the Everglades. Her parents had spoken up for the tribe, but the Indians stopped coming to their school and then some of their animals were slaughtered. A few weeks later her parents' bodies were found floating in the bay . . . A drowning was the official conclusion, but Clara didn't fail to see the connection between Seminole banishment and Seminole revenge; the history of Florida was scored with it. She felt safe now only because the Seminole had been driven by government orders so far inland.

As Clara moved toward the house, a fat rooster walked out of it and squatted placidly on the front steps; its solitary, composed presence was at once poignant and comically absurd. Seeing her, the rooster rose as if highly indignant at the intrusion and veered off squawking into the hammock of tall oak trees behind the house.

Clara turned to Harry, laughing. "Home, sweet home," she said. Before the sun set, they managed to find a few candle stubs and dusted as well as they could the two old straw mattresses. Clara only had the briefest impression of the inside of the house: decay and shambles and the smell of fetid rankness, as if animals had made it their home. She would attend to it in the morning; there was plenty of time to make things right. They lit one candle and sat together on the creaking porch steps. As darkness fell and the blue was drained from the sky, giving way to red to purple to black, the sense of solitude became immense.

"Wait till you see an orange grove," Clara said softly. "And the river. We'll have to take a boat ride up to the rapids. You should see the way the water churns up, you'd think—" She stopped and laughed. "Here we are, actually here, and I'm still describing it to you."

"I don't mind," Harry said.

All encumbrances were eliminated. She had her son; this paradise would return his health to him in a way that living in coal-heated rooms in a cold city never could. They would know other people who craved this kind of simple living. A vision of other houses along the bay came into her mind. Stores and streets and shops. A perfect, an Edenic spot to build a little town. She smiled to herself at the grandiosity of her imagination. But here, in this wonderful place, it was freed from its constraints and she would do nothing further to rein it in.

I will not miss anything of my old life, she thought, and the truth of this chilled her: that I could have been so long in one life and now have no regrets—not one!—at leaving it behind . . .

"Middleton seems pretty far away," Harry said.

"Sad or glad?" Clara asked, a phrase they often used to gauge each other's mood. In the flickering candlelight, she could see only the outlines of his face.

He hesitated. "Glad we're safe," he said finally. He looked down, his lashes throwing long shadows down his cheeks.

"Oh, Harry, you're exhausted!" She ran a soothing hand along his arm.

Harry stood up, his face going out of the light, only his hands visible by the candle's flame. "Don't fuss at me, Mother. I'm just relieved to be here."

Clara rose and stood next to him. She longed to embrace him but feared his skittishness. There was silence for a long moment. A bird cried out. Clara involuntarily clutched Harry's arm. He jumped back, and Clara gave a choked laugh. He smoothed his clothes, backing away from her into the house.

"Take the candle, Harry. You'll—"

"It's all right," he said as the darkness swallowed him.

"But you don't know the way. You're liable to hurt—"

His last words came from a great distance. "I'm all right!"

Clara stood alone. There was a high-pitched cooing sound. What was it? Oh yes, I remember, she thought: a chuck-will's-widow. She bent and picked up the candle to light her way to bed. Harry'll be himself in the morning, she told herself, but could not help thinking that he had not been quite himself since his father's death. She had certainly seen him temperamental and edgy before and had always found ways to excuse and understand. But this seemed different; it seemed like a man's coldness and not a boy's petulance, and Clara experienced a shudder of apprehension.

He had seemed eager to come at first, hadn't he? But perhaps he was simply eager to get away from the cold and gloom of another Middleton winter. She'd had no idea he would be so affected by his father's death. She'd been upset herself, of course, though she could not help but admit that she missed Cameron very little. Perhaps she should have missed him more or been guiltier that she didn't.

She had been wife and mother for so long, she had put aside her own self, her own impulses. And yet when she had first met Cameron Reade, she had seen him as noble and impressive.

Mr. Cameron Reade contributed generously to the Sisters of Mercy School in Middleton, where Clara remained after her parents' deaths. His first wife had been a scholarship pupil there, and in her memory he held an annual dinner for Middleton society, such as it was, to meet succeeding scholarship girls. It was a rather shameful event for the girls, for they felt themselves being displayed like a set of good works, with the wealthy coming to admire their pluck. Clara had never before seen such splendor as the Reade house on E Street, filled as it was with dark and magisterial Eastlake furniture. She made a distinct impression on its owner that first night, done up in a plain, inexpensive gown with no jewelry or decoration but for a green velvet ribbon around her throat that made her pale skin even paler. Her shoulders were covered, unlike those of the other ladies present, and also unlike them, she was uncorseted, a state that would have been considered brazen in an older woman but that brought out in Clara her health and innocence.

Clara had a simple, unadorned beauty, pale and faintly rosy, gray-eyed and soft-skinned; her head was held high, rounded chin up as if in challenge, and she walked with arms swinging, an outdoorsman's walk that was a charming contradiction to her hothouse complexion. Her direct simplicity of manner was startling in the formal company and lavish atmosphere.

Cameron Reade arranged to have her seated to his right at dinner and began his wooing with the oxtail soup, soliciting her opinion of Balzac's *Lost Illusions* as the roast was carved and served, complimenting her ability to listen to the ramblings of the dinner partner to her right while the champagne glasses were filled, and eliciting a genuine laugh as they concluded with baked Alaska.

But as Clara was later to discover, there was a reason for his admiring attentions that had nothing to do with affection or attraction or appreciation of beauty and wholesomeness and youth. Before she went back to the sisters, Cameron proffered an invitation to an opera performance and, while he helped her with her cloak, extracted a promise from her to think of him.

Clara could think of little else. Cameron Reade was tall and distinguished, and if not handsome, certainly masculine and proud. His very maturity was vital and appealing: he'd *done* things. She liked the smell of tobacco and bay rum and wool that came over her when he helped her with her cloak. She liked the thrust of his chest and the way his mustaches curled up at the ends. And that house! She could not deny the lure of that house and the change in her life an association with a man like Cameron Reade might effect. With her parents gone, she had neither a home to which to return or money to continue her education. Upon graduation, she would live on with the Sisters of Mercy and pay her way teaching Latin declensions until she could manage a marriage to a bank teller or a young law clerk and take up housekeeping.

The following day Cameron Reade came for her in a carriage; the sisters treated him with great deference and accepted a donation rather larger than was Mr. Reade's custom. He took Clara on a tour of his ironworks. The sense of his power, as reflected in the oversized machinery and doomsday noises, was to Clara a sign that Mr. Reade made a very distinct impression on the world. He told her too about the frail young wife who had died some years before, and Clara found herself astonished and moved by the depth of grief that the mere mention of the first Mrs. Reade called up in him. It bespoke a softer side, Clara thought, and she pitied him a little, a feeling that made her seem, at eighteen, not quite so young and Mr. Reade, at thirty-seven, not quite so much older.

"I revere the institution of marriage and I make no bones about it," he told her a week later as they sat in his box at the Opera House, whispering while Madame Butterfly wailed onstage. He patted her hands, which lay clasped together in the lush folds of her dress. "I'm not a romantic young man. Perhaps you'd be disappointed..." He hesitated; Clara looked at him. He's nervous too, she thought, and liked him for it. "Between us," he was saying, "it might not... be a bad proposition all around." He did not look at her but kept his eyes on the stage; Madame Butterfly was brandishing a blade. "I know my house must seem somewhat formidable. But the servants help to run it as smoothly as my factory." He essayed a laugh here, met with angry shushings from the neighboring boxes and anguished screams from the stage.

Clara hardly spoke when they were together—he had so much to say, she had so much to learn!—but Cameron seemed to take little notice, so full of plans for the future was he. The girls at the school wanted details. Did she love him? "I think so..." Clara groped for the words to describe the way her body shivered when he touched her arm or leaned close to open the carriage door, or the sensation of freedom she had going around the city with him, of the wide world opening for her, of standing on the edge of grand and glorious opportunity. "It's all happening so fast," she admitted to her school friends; her very confusion felt like love.

"You will learn to appreciate my qualities in time," Cameron told her on a walk among the elms across the road from his house. They stopped beneath a tree and, hidden from view, she closed her eyes and held up her face for their first kiss. Cameron put his hands on her shoulders; she opened her eyes and looked at him, puzzled by his hesitancy, then, not caring if she was being forward, pressed her head to his chest. As Cameron smoothed gloved hands across her back, she envisioned her final transformation into womanhood that would come through physical ecstasy.

In their stateroom on the steamboat taking them on their New Orleans honeymoon, they prepared for bed in separate dressing rooms, and when he joined her she was already stretched out, her hair in wild disarray against the pillow. She felt free and loose. "You look like a gypsy," he said and cleared his throat. Clara smiled secretively. Cameron blushed and looked away. He lowered the flame in the oil lamp and sat at the edge of the bed with his back to her. "My first

wife was so shy she wept," he said. "You needn't . . . We needn't . . . "
Clara breathed evenly, hardly hearing him, only feeling the heat of his
body near hers.

There was silence for a few moments. Clara saw the moon through
the porthole of their stateroom, heard the lap of the water against the
side of the boat; she was ready. "I won't weep, Cameron," she whispered. She reached for him. His shoulders stiffened. He hesitated, then
turned to her with a sigh. And in the moments that followed, her ardor
was so much greater than his that she felt ashamed.

Their marital pleasures thereafter occurred with biweekly regularity,
marked not by passion but by an urgency to produce an heir; in
retrospect, Clara saw that his speedy courtship had been impelled by
the same motive. With her pregnancy, their relations became sporadic
and perfunctory. Physical ecstasy did not occur and Clara watched the
hope of it slip slowly, regretfully, into the past. Cameron, recalling the
modesty of the first Mrs. Reade and priding himself on his sensitivity
to a woman's delicacy, eventually took a separate bedroom. For the
sake of her marriage, Clara assumed certain aspects of that delicacy.
Everyone said that, as a couple, the Reades were ideal.

Clara soon saw that Cameron had been charmed by her youth and
had evaluated her character as malleable material to be formed and
finished by him, the model apparently being the mourned, lamented,
and idealized first Mrs. Reade. In the early years of her marriage, Clara
was rarely allowed to forget this paragon. The first Mrs. Reade did not
wear such vulgar colors, he would say. The first Mrs. Reade spoke
sternly to the cook and did not fraternize with the help. But though
she bore some slight physical resemblance to Cameron's first wife,
she had little of that woman's personality; the evidence of their difference astonished and angered Cameron, as if Clara willfully persisted
in defying and disappointing him.

Not that Cameron was without his good points: he was direct, force-
ful, fair, high-minded, though impersonal, exacting, even hard. He had
a clear outline of the man he wanted to be and hewed to it with strict
accuracy. But he had no real belief in the innate possibilities of his
wife or his son.

Clara, with no theories of marriage to guide her and unwilling to
oppose her husband at every turn, allowed his vision of their marriage
finally to dominate, and so she became an adjunct to her husband,

defined by him. She was hostess to the social functions incumbent on a man of his business stature, consort to a man of society with a fondness for concerts and operas, sympathetic ear, espouser of correct ideas, supporter of charities, reflector of his success, planner of menus, house manager, advisor, nurse, confessor.

But where was Clara herself in all of this? Was she simply well trained? A life had been created for her, defined by its functions. Now that the functions had dissolved and she had escaped, she found, much to her continuing delight, that she was not lost, not anxious, not desperate or lonely or overwhelmed by impossibilities. Instead she felt filled with ideas and energy such as she had not experienced since she was a girl. Suddenly there was a future, an old home her new home, and the days ahead held limitless opportunities. She had feared Cameron's ambition sometimes, that if he sought a higher goal she might somehow be found wanting and be left behind. Yet when it happened, not through ambition but through death, she found in herself, lurking beyond her immediate grief, relief.

She found her way to her bedroom and undressed by the flickering candlelight, then climbed wearily into bed and sank back on the straw pillows. She looked around her. My parents lived here, died here. On the wall near the bed, illuminated by the candle's flickering flame, were pasted several large sheets of the *Florida Sentinel,* now yellowed with age and peeling in spots. One sheet contained an article written by her mother about her father: "Mr. Forrest Jones has made the first successful break since the Seminole Wars of 1840–41 in reclaiming the county from the primeval state into which it has relapsed. It is a little spot, an oasis in the wide water of unproductive country, but no one, seeing it, can fail to be convinced of the feasibility of the undertaking . . ."

$4.$

By daylight the house looked both better and worse, better for the glorious sunlight itself, worse for what that light revealed. The room Clara had slept in had been her parents' bedroom. Of the elaborately carved mahogany furniture, whose contours aping fruits and vegetables she had found so endlessly fascinating as a child, there remained only the bedstead and a highboy with tarnished brass pulls. The light coming through the curtainless, glassless windows was dappled by the oak trees. As she got out of bed, dust rose in the shafts of light. A chipped pitcher and bowl stood in a corner; Clara thought of the mornings she'd seen her mother fill the pitcher and the splashing and sputtering her father made at it. Apart from these things, the room was empty, and the daylight threw the shabbiness into glaring relief. The newspaper that her father had put up on the walls to keep out mosquitoes was yellowed and peeling. The gestures at prettifying by her mother—a framed print of a bowl of roses, ruffles at the window ledges, peacock feathers in a broken clay vase—had all been faded and withered by time. Clara felt a pang of sorrow that the house had stood so long untended and alone.

There was one other bedroom—hers as a child—where her own child now slept, and a central room that combined parlor, dining room, and kitchen; glassless windows spanned three of its walls. Shutters with broken slats hung askew, letting in shafts of light that cut up the room at bizarre angles. An odd mustiness, the scents of roses and sage, came off the purple horsehair sofa. The upright piano in the corner, used to accompany hymns on Sunday mornings, bulged and sagged, and when Clara ran her fingers from middle C to G, a flat dead sound emerged and two lizards darted out from beneath the cover.

Reluctant to disturb Harry, she rose and pushed the screen door open, advancing a few steps until she emerged from the shadow of the porch roof into the sunlight. She lifted her face to it and pulled her wrapper close around her; a shudder of pleasant warmth coursed through her. She stepped barefoot onto the parched grass and felt again a sense of familiarity; the touch of the earth beneath her feet was as familiar as if she'd walked this land yesterday. Burrs and leaves stuck to her wrapper as she walked around the yard. Above her the sky was a brilliant azure without a cloud. Around her, the trees moved with just the faintest rustling; Clara smiled to imagine that they were whispering of her return.

As she moved quickly along the path strewn with rust-colored pine needles, she could see an irregular oval of blue in the near distance and there was the bay, as fresh as if it had been spread out just for her. It was here, now, that she had her strongest sense yet of why she had come back: not for the house, not for the sad and sweet memories of her parents, but for the sight that showed itself to her now. The bracing tang of seawater was in the air, but as she approached, the lulling sound of a breeze rustling the trees was split by a loud banging.

"Careful!"

She turned to see Harry, in shirtsleeves, on hands and knees on the old dock, driving nails into the slats of splintery wood. Clara smiled and waved as if this were a morning like any other, and she felt a wild surge of hope, as if she'd been slapped unexpectedly by a blast of pure, reviving air.

For the first time in his life, Harry looked at his physical surroundings and saw that he might have an effect on them, that his relationship with the natural world might, in fact, be reciprocal, and that he would not be prey, as he and every other benighted citizen of Middleton had been, to the decisions of the few men in power. His father had been but one egregious example of the elite who did with *their* city what suited *their* ideas and pocketbooks. Harry's tutor, Kurt Gutman, a disciple of the great Henry David Thoreau, had taught him that such ownership was anathema to the notion of how free men ought to live. Gutman had espoused Thoreau's principle of retaining a landscape without owning it, and Harry had come to believe that that principle was right and just.

Already the sensory memories of his native city—the smell of industrial smoke, the needlessly polluted river, the noise and danger of traffic and new-fangled, man-eliminating machinery, the sight of slums and poverty and filth—were evaporating in his mind. Even the horrible night of his father's death, even "that night," had begun to fade from memory, and though Harry knew that he would never lose all sense of guilt and regret, at least he would not be faced with reminders of it on a daily basis.

For here they were, thousands of miles away and finally safe in their better world. For the first time he existed with the sun and the stars and the earth and was humble in the face of the natural richness around him. While he worked, Harry would glimpse his mother sweeping away the dried pine needles from the porch, hacking at branches along the overgrown path, dusting, washing, cooking—happy!—and know for certain that he had done the right, the selfless thing that night by telling her nothing, that no matter how heavy the burden of the guilty secret he held in his heart, he had at the very least saved his mother. He had proven to himself that he was no longer a boy who needed to be pampered or protected or consoled, whatever his mother might think; what irony and horror that he could not explain this to her, only recoil from her concern in anger.

His childhood illnesses had caused his mother to indulge him and even to encourage a streak of natural laziness, but now, without encouragement from her, he took upon himself physical labor and his body—fed by the sun, stimulated by clear air and sea breezes—rose to the challenges he set for it. At home in Middleton he might have been lying in bed well into the morning, dreaming through a snowy afternoon and reading *Walden* by candlelight past midnight. Here he drove his body until he could no longer hold up his head and fell into dreamless sleep at sunset. Kurt Gutman would be proud.

His color improved almost at once, and Clara was struck by how handsome he was becoming, a man now, not a boy. His young body quickly showed signs of the change: his arms, bared to the shoulder as he pulled vines from the roof or stacked firewood at the side of the house, took on muscular definition. His back and chest broadened from piling rotted furniture at river's edge and hauling great clumps of seaweed to use as mulch around the oak trees her father had planted long ago as saplings. She heard his first great burst of spontaneous laughter when he managed to drag the old piano out into the sun to dry, only to see all the keys dislodge and slide into a heap in the sand.

"Harry, I think we've done right—coming here, I mean. Don't you?"

"Yes, of course. Why do you keep talking about it? We're here."

She stood on the porch with a pitcher of lemonade squeezed from their own lemons and looked at his back for a long moment before joining him in the yard. She poured him a glassful. "I don't know why I keep on about it," she admitted. "But I do know that I don't want to just stay here and . . . " She sank to her knees next to him as he sawed away with a long-handled kitchen knife at a thick root. "I don't want to just get this house in order and then stand back in awe and keep remarking on how beautiful everything is." The face of Quentin McLeod appeared in her mind as the real adversary to whom she justified herself; she shook her head to dispel that image. "I want to belong here," she said. "I want to . . . to deserve all this."

She watched Harry struggle with the root. It was hard and unyielding; it squeaked as he sawed past the bark into the moist green flesh. "My God," she said as she looked from him to the yard around them. "One thing I learned from your father is that enormous and impossible things *are* possible. Take the ironworks! The sheer size of them! And they all started from an idea in your father's head."

"For someone who's got so much to do, seems to me you do an awful lot of standing around and talking." Harry looked sideways at her and laughed.

"Never thought you'd turn into such a hard taskmaster," Clara said. She knew that he was showing off a bit and she liked it. She took a deep breath and dug her hands into the soil to free up roots for him to saw. Often nothing had to be said between them, and in fact entire days would go by in which they hardly spoke at all; what needed to be done was apparent, and when a simple raising of an eyebrow was the question, a simple nod was often the answer. Harry was happy— she could see it in the ease of his movements, the lope of his stride, the unfurrowed brow—and once sure of that, she could think about her own happiness and the kind of life she intended to lead.

The sun was strong; she didn't know how long she could last under it today, glad at least that McLeod had let her keep the palmetto hat she'd found on his boat. Her plans had been general at first: leave Middleton in the worst of winter, return home to the South Florida wilds of her birth, and settle into her parents' old house. She had not allowed herself to plan beyond that, and her grand vision of a community, a town, remained at the level of fantasy. There were so many small details yet to be attended to! The house needed a coat of white-wash, the porch needed shoring up, screens needed mending, and furniture restuffing. And the yard looked hopeless, a long way from the garden Clara had her heart set on. She remembered her own mother digging and rooting and planting vegetables and grains only to see land crabs eat the seeds and then return for the tender sprouts grown from the ones they'd missed; how her mother had longed to grow tomatoes, only to have raccoons prove her nemesis. Her father had hired a few workers from Key West after several such failed attempts and had cleared a couple of acres of pineland and planted orange trees instead. The smell was delicious even now, though the grove itself was overgrown by the jungle and inaccessible. Harry wanted to clear out the tangle, pave a road, have a thriving crop. They were determined to be self-sufficient, not to send for help, but the thought of doing all this on their own was daunting, and her doubts mocked her original ideas of reviving her parents' old land and making it prosperous.

After a few hours of yard work, her light cotton shirtwaist dress— the first out-of-mourning one she'd worn—was soaked through at her back.

"I can just picture the expression on our neighbors' faces in Middleton if they saw us now," she said, looking at her hands, dirty with

Florida soil. She turned to hold them up to show Harry just at the moment he turned and held up his dirty hands to her. "Partners," she said with a laugh.

"Partners," he echoed, and they shook on it.

Harry's body ached that night, and he continued to feel flushed long after the evening cool had descended. His mother was afraid he was running a fever, but all she had to give him was chamomile tea and a warning not to spend so long in the sun anymore. She checked on him twice during the night, and his fever, if that was what it was, hadn't abated.

In his dreams he continued sawing and the roots continued to resist him. He woke with a start from this troubled sleep, with the sure sense that someone was watching him. The night was moonless and very black; a warm breeze stirred the curtains and created vague silvery shadows on the ceiling. My imagination, he thought sleepily, and tried to find a cool spot on the bed, yet the feeling of being observed would not leave him; in another moment he was fully awake and listening.

The breeze rustled the pine trees; a snake slithered through the grass with a susurrant sound; an owl hooted plaintively. But beyond these sounds was another, a human presence, a throbbing. He lay still and stared at the window as gradually his eyes grew accustomed to the dark and then . . . yes! A pair of eyes met his! He flung the bed clothes from him and scrambled to his knees.

"Who's there?" he said in a choked whisper.

A flame was lit and in its aura came visible the face of an old Indian. Pinpoints of light seemed to emanate from black eyes slitted like a cobra's. The features were crude and elemental as if carved from living copper. Shoulder-length black hair framed the wide, square face, rows of beads and layers of brightly striped cloths covered him to the neck. Frozen, in awe, Harry recognized the face as human, yet it also seemed to him animal, both ferocious and benign.

The flame died; the face was swallowed in the night. Harry bounded across the room to the window; outside all was blackness. He stood very still, held his breath, and listened; through the silence broke the rustle of the breeze in the pines, the distant lick of bay water on the dock pilings. All he could see were hazy shadows of blue and silver. He backed up slowly, disappointed, until he was at his bed, and so familiar was the feel of the sheets on his skin and the warm depression on the pillow where he lay his head that he wondered if it wasn't all just a dream.

A flush spread across his face and chest. He was suddenly dizzy, but even as he lay there in the dark he felt the apprehension about this fever lift from him. In a few moments, just as he dropped off the edge of consciousness into sleep, he knew that those eyes were on him again.

He dreamed he walked naked in the jungle and all manner of jungle life, animal and vegetable, was there to greet him, and though he did not understand their language, he knew they guarded him, embraced him and welcomed him to their bosom. Come to us, they said, come to—

"Harry!"

His mother's voice shattered his sleep, and the sense of alarm when she called him again—"Harry! I need you!"—had him out of bed and on the front porch before he was fully awake. The sun had barely crested the tree tops and Harry shielded his eyes. His mother stood on the top step, her shoulders rigid, holding the railing. Squatting at the far end of the yard was the old Indian. He was very still; only his hands moved, running lightly over the ground with as much tenderness as one accords a living creature. His back was to the house until Harry came out; then he turned his broad, serious face to him.

My friend, Harry thought.

Clara leaned toward Harry. "It's one of the Seminoles. I wish we had a gun."

"Don't be afraid, Mother." As he stared at the old man, Harry could not help but smile.

Clara took his arm. "But I am," she whispered.

The Indian stood up and walked bandy-legged across the yard toward them. His hands reached inside his long, multicolored striped shirt as he came to the base of the porch steps. Harry felt his mother's grip tighten on his arm. In one hand the Indian held a small leather sack, which he extended to Clara. "Your mother and father teach my family to read." He spoke in a whisper that seemed to emanate not from his throat but from his whole body. "Medicine bundle for boy. Soak herbs in water. Boy drink. Fever go." He smiled at Harry. "Too much sun." Harry smiled back. "I am Dr. Tiger," the Indian said with gravity, then indicated the yard. "When you are well, I teach you to plant garden."

Clara still held Harry's arm. "I wish we weren't so alone here."

"But he's going to help us!" Harry exclaimed and took the medicine bundle.

As Dr. Tiger had predicted, drinking the herb tea brought down his fever—"It would have gone down anyway," Clara insisted, still wary—and when the Indian appeared in the yard the next day, Harry was already dressed and ready for him to make good on his promise to help with the garden.

Getting the acre or so of yard ready to be seeded would have been a daunting prospect to anyone. But unlike Clara, Harry realized, Dr. Tiger did not only see the work to be done in the garden but saw too the vegetables grown, as if the future existed as tangibly as the present.

"Vegetables here," he told Harry, pointing to the ground, to the sky, to the seeds cupped in his palm. "We go to meet it."

He rejected the long-handled kitchen knife Harry had used and instead rooted around under the house until he found a can of kerosene and a short-handled hoe. It was with these that he and Harry spent the early mornings and late afternoons. The kerosene was pumped with a sharp-nosed funnel into recalcitrant roots, then the roots were burned out.

Clara, working inside, was overpowered by the stinging, dizzying smell that filled the house, and she'd hear the *thud thud thud* of the hoe coming down on a stubborn palmetto root, and she too began to picture the earth in flower, only to be brought to by the dull pain in her chest at the thought of her parents' bodies floating in the river. Most of the rocks Dr. Tiger and Harry unearthed were put to good use in shoring up the superstructure of the house, whose timbers looked splintery and felt soft; who knew how eaten away by termites they might be at their hearts? After that was done, Clara used the stones that remained to build a three-foot-high stone wall around the yard to discourage deer and rabbits from eating the vegetables.

Most of the time Harry and Dr. Tiger worked in silence, and it was only when they broke for a rest in the shade of an oak tree, with cool lemonade to quench their thirst, or when the Indian guided Harry on long slow walks through the hammock that Dr. Tiger would speak of the past. His people had been divided and divided again since the

56 · *BISCAYNE* ·

beginning of the century. He had been a boy in 1812 when the white man punished his tribe for giving sanctuary to escaped Negro slaves, a seventeen-year-old brave when Andrew Jackson led the attacks that burned their towns, a leader in the second war under the renegade Osceola, whose capture signaled the defeat to come, an old man when Congress passed the law to rid Florida of all its Indians that precipitated a third war. "We have no papers," he said mildly. "The white man has papers." Pushed farther and farther from the bay, the few hundred Seminoles that remained lived now on a protected reservation upriver, beyond the rapids, in the Everglades. His ultimate wish was to join his ancestors in the ancient burial mound by the bay. "I go with joy to the Great Spirit." The beatific look on his face as he spoke of it made Harry think sadly that such time would not be far away.

He knew that there were people in the area who suspected his tribe of killing Clara's parents, but he denied it to Harry. Clara's parents' very defense of the Seminoles had put them in danger with certain of their own people. Harry believed him implicitly. Clara was not so quick to accept this version.

"Most guilty people deny they've done anything wrong and try to put the blame on someone else."

"The same could be said of the white man, Mother."

Clara shook her head. "The Seminoles may even feel justified in what they did. They don't live under the same moral code as we do."

"But Mother—"

"You believe what you like, Harry, and I'll do the same."

"But there hasn't been any trouble between the Seminole and the whites for—"

"Good," Clara said and lowered her voice when she saw Dr. Tiger near them. "Let's hope it stays that way."

Harry treasured his time with the old man, knowing it was limited. He seemed to fill a space in Harry that had been left empty by his own father, replaced only temporarily by his tutor Kurt Gutman. His wisdom came not as his father's had through rigid discipline, not even as Gutman's had, through preaching and aphorisms, but through demonstrations of simple, pure knowledge of the land. He showed Harry how to look under the rifts of seaweed along the shore for crabs and worms to use as bait, then how to hold down a flailing fish with his foot and extract the hook. He showed him which roots and seeds and berries were edible in the hammock and which were poison, how to find fresh water pooled in leaves and how to tell where a wild peahen had laid her eggs.

Clara kept her distance from Dr. Tiger; she no more trusted the animal nature of his wisdom than she did any wild creature of this strange jungle, and in fact, his daily presence only served to remind her of how unpredictable the area was and how illusory her sense of safety.

"But he only wants to help," Harry said.

"Why? Have you ever thought of that?"

Harry shrugged. "To repay your parents for teaching his—"

"I know how his people repaid my parents!" Clara shook her head as she looked out the window; Dr. Tiger was sitting under an oak tree, eating mashed banana from a cupped hand.

"But no one knows for sure how they died," Harry insisted. "We're friends with the Seminoles now."

"I'm not," Clara said.

Back at work, the stone removal completed, the men had still more to do to make the ground arable. Old stumps that couldn't be hacked away or pulled out or burned out with kerosene were drenched and left to disintegrate to ash. Everything was raked then raked again, and every last bit of coral, root, and stone was picked out. The roots were piled by the side of the house to use in smoke pots, since the dense wood burned too slow for cooking fuel. Clara planned on paper a small fenced garden of hibiscus, phlox, and Bermuda grass with a border of periwinkle.

"When do we get to plant?" Harry asked Dr. Tiger as they sat back on their heels and drank from the pitcher of lemon water Clara had brought out.

"Two acres all one man plant here. Grow velvet beans in summer to feed soil. Rotate crop. Use fertilizer from cow."

"Haven't got a cow."

"Get one."

"But when do we plant?"

"Tomorrow," Dr. Tiger replied and fell to his labors again.

And the next day he was gone, gone as abruptly as he'd come, the only sign of him a small leather sack, left on the porch, that contained bits of minerals and bones, stones, powders, and dried herbs.

"His medicine bundles," Harry told Clara sadly and looked off to the jungle. His impulse to follow Dr. Tiger was stifled by the forbidding aspect of the hammock itself. There was no easy access without him, no visible path, no sign that told the novice traveler where to turn.

"I'll rest easier with him gone," Clara said.

All day they worked on their knees in the garden, planting the seeds Dr. Tiger had left: soursops, sugar apples, barbadoes cherries, peas, and beans. They dug long, shallow, parallel rows and dropped the seeds at regular intervals. But Harry could not seem to keep his eyes from the jungle wall and his planted rows became more ragged and out of plumb as the day wore on.

"Harry," Clara said finally, "I don't mean to criticize, darling, but you *are* making one fine mess. You have to watch what you're doing."

Harry sighed. "I know, I know, but . . . Well, it just seems to me that I am ignorant of just about everything worth knowing in this life."

Clara sank back on her heels and shook her head. "With your education!"

"I mean . . . " He searched for words and could find none adequate to express his feeling that all the true mysteries of life and death, all its clues and solutions, its beauty and sadness and wonder, were contained in their natural state. Gutman had led him to Thoreau, who thought so, and in his own way Dr. Tiger had taught him the same thing. But now, he felt, they had taken him as far as they could; if he was to know more, he would have to become his own teacher. He and Clara continued to gentle the soil over the seeds, water them, hope for the best.

He kept the medicine bundle by his bed when he slept. One night he dreamed that Dr. Tiger was standing at the jungle wall, was beckoning to him, was welcoming him to follow. The hammock wall seemed no longer so dense, seemed in fact to part for him. Then Dr. Tiger was guiding him through mottled shade into and out of pools of sunlight, introducing him to fabulous plants and flowers and trees and vines but always the Indian himself remaining just out of reach as Harry slogged heavily after him, arms outstretched, an unformed question on his lips, and always Dr. Tiger beckoning him wordlessly to follow, the light radiating from his cobra eyes implying that the answer lay one step deeper into the jungle. Harry woke up panting, heart pounding, in a sweat.

In the cool yellow light of early morning, he ran to the garden. His mother was chasing a rabbit away from the seedbeds with a swish of her apron. The rabbit scooted into the hammock and disappeared; a blink of an eye and Harry could not pick out the spot. Clara turned to him, wiping the sweat from her brow. "Sometimes I think the whole jungle's filled with rabbits and raccoons and I don't know what all else, just waiting for us to go to sleep so they can feast on our garden. Have to put up a high fence or something . . . "

Harry remembered the rooster that had appeared from the house that first day. And what about the deer he'd spotted darting back into the jungle and the quails who came to wash in the dust under the porch. He looked again for the spot where the rabbit had disappeared, and it occurred to him that indeed there were signs everywhere to lead him, signs as yet unknown to him but as knowable as the distinction he had learned to make between the swish of palm fronds and the rustle of stiff banana leaves in the evening breeze.

He worked the rest of the week on his knees in the garden, making sure the seeds were placed properly, according to Dr. Tiger's instructions. An excitement was building in him, an anticipation that a world was about to open to him, that he had only to yield to it, without fear, and it would welcome him. His eyes no longer darted to the hammock; he knew what he was going to do. And when the last seed was planted, he rose from his knees, brushed the dirt from his trousers, and, the image of Dr. Tiger's beckoning hand set firmly in his mind as his guide, entered the hammock. He told his mother he was going exploring.

Clara continued to tend the garden, watering, standing guard, watching, waiting. After a few weeks she learned that for most of the midday the sun was too intense to work under and that after a certain point, the straw hat no longer ventilated but kept the heat in. She whooped in victory at the first sight of the delicate green shoots, then worried that they would burn in such harsh sun. She worried that the rabbits would eat the ones that survived and so flew a signal flag on the dock, hoping Mr. McLeod or someone would see it so she could find out how to buy wire for a fence. Harry's absences had concerned her at first, but he came home each day, tired and happy—though he hadn't much to say—and she was surprised to find that she did not mind being alone so much as she might have thought.

One day after he'd gone, without thinking about it or planning a route, she found herself walking toward the riverbank and the place she used to come to as a girl, and she realized that she had wanted to do this from the first but that there was something about coming here that she wanted to keep private. Though she could not have explained what she wanted to hide, either to Harry or to herself, she was actually glad he was gone now, had, in fact, been in a half-conscious way waiting to be alone.

Once she reached the river, she began to pick her way through the dense mangrove roots that grew along the bank. The roots jutted out, arching over the water, then dropping down, doubling back, twisting in on themselves, wrapping themselves vinelike around other trees and branches and forming tunnels of interlocking roots and vines. Deep inside the weblike growth, Clara felt as if she were fourteen years old again and all that had happened between then and now had been parenthetical to her real, her true life here on the river. By gripping the high vines and stepping on the sturdiest ones, she managed to make her way, the river sometimes flowing beside her, sometimes, when she walked on the farthest-reaching roots, rushing only an inch beneath her feet. The smell was thick with earth and dampness and a kind of rich, heavy sweetness Clara had always associated with a multitudinous, riotous life. The breeze from the bay made quiet whistling sounds in the delicate, spidery vines, and tiny white orchids seemed to spring from the mature mangrove roots.

Only *I* have changed, she thought, her hands clutching a gnarled old root as she leaned over the river. And have I changed so much?

She was fourteen years old when they sent her north, come to the end of what her missionary parents could teach her and too quick and bright, they thought, to be satisfied with knowing only a little of what there was to be learned from books, not to mention from the experiences denied her in this remote, isolated place. There was just the bare beginnings of a community in Palm Grove, and they couldn't depend on it lasting long enough to do much for their girl. They spoke of her own good, of the benefits of education, of God's will and good works, of transcendence of the spirit. They had been called by God to bring the Seminoles of the South Florida wilds to grace. But the choice for their Clara was clear.

The schooner came, she was rowed out to join it and sailed down the strait to the harbor at Key West, where she boarded a seagoing steamer and landed in New York City. She marveled that a place could grow so harsh at the hands of men: steel towers, sharpness, ice and gray skies, shrieking, unhappy people, endless streets of filth and rot. A colleague from her father's seminary days met her at the boat and led the way to a hotel where she spent the night and where water came from a faucet. From there a railroad train transported her halfway across America to the Ohio city of Middleton, where she was to attend the Sisters of Mercy School and acquire the knowledge necessary to take her place in the civilized world, of which her home, her teachers insisted, was not a part.

But deep inside her private heart, no matter how many samplers she stitched and how much tea she poured perfectly, no matter how much French she spoke and how many piano scales she practiced, she remained moored to the land of her birth. She remained alien to the city, no matter that she lived there twenty-five years, married there, and bore there a city child.

She had lived in Middleton just three years when her parents' bodies were found in the Miami River near the wreck of their boat, their hands clutching Seminole beads, the only sign that it was not simply a storm that had killed them. Thus her link to her home had been severed. At the end of her final year at the school, it was decided by the sisters that the homeless girl might stay on as a lay teacher. Clara, hands clasped behind her as she listened to her future being imprisoned within the walls of the school, was frantic to get away. In her narrow bed, by the light of a street lamp on Maple Avenue, as snow flakes peppered the light so that the very walls seemed to stream with tears, she dreamed herself back home, floating over the land, but, to her increasing panic, she saw the murdered bodies of her parents in the clear water of the bay. And she hovered like a cloud, full of sorrow, as her home moved with heart-wrenching slowness into the distance.

Oh, how I've missed this, Clara thought now. But I'm back, I'm here, and this is all mine again, mine as it was meant to be. She found a spot to sit where the mangroves parted to give her a clear view of the gently flowing river and the expanse of bay beyond it. Behind her the bank sloped up toward her own garden. She lay back and the sun winked through the tangle of branches overhead, passing a warm gentle touch along her cheek, down her neck, across her chest, engirdling her waist.

She sat up after a moment, breathless, then rolled up the sleeves of her shirtwaist dress and opened the top buttons. Laughing to herself, she unlaced her shoes and peeled off her stockings and scooted down the bank to let her bare feet dangle in the water. Though the water was warm, the caress of the current on her ankles made her shiver. She laughed again at the next thought that came to her, though it was less a thought than an impulse she felt powerless not to act upon. With a quick glance behind her, she unbuttoned the rest of her dress and slipped out of it, tossing it behind her on the mossy bank, and did the same with the linen petticoat, deciding then and there never to wear one again as long as she lived by the river. Last came her chemise, and with a delighted shiver she slipped into the warm river. The muddy bottom was like silk between her toes. The water's embrace on her bare flesh was more delicious than she remembered. Had she ever done something so bold? Its flow defined the curves and swells of her body, touched her everywhere and left her unashamed. Have I gained weight? she wondered. Her body felt fuller, rounder. I don't care, I don't care. And I'll never wear a corset or stays again.

There was something splendid in the solitude, something noble and grand in being immersed in the river, watched over by sentinel palms and sapodilla, something glorious, something more religious than her father's God simply in floating, clinging to a mangrove root and confronting, wide-eyed, the endless span of the bay.

Later she dressed and lay on the bank, her hair spread out on her petticoat to dry in the sun, her mind empty, her body full and tingling. But something nagged at her, a sense of incompletion, of . . . loneliness. She squirmed against the grass, annoyed with herself for the thought. I don't really need anyone. But . . .

"Missus?"

Startled out of the silence, Clara scrambled to her feet, fussing at her hair and gathering up her petticoat and shoes. Two Negroes stood a bit above her in the clearing near her garden, dressed as for church.

"We be Edmund and Geneva Legitimus come from Pineland City," the man said. His voice was as light and high as a child's and made this simple sentence like a song. "Mistah McLeod he say you pay us two dollah a day. I work on house, on land. Geneva do laundry, cook, and clean."

Clara stood up and brushed the dirt from her clothes. "I'd like that," she said.

Edmund's face split into a grin; the good news made Geneva's expression even sadder. They began work that day, and as the weeks went by Clara often would come upon Geneva, paused in the midst of soaking laundry in a barrel or stirring up a steaming pot of plantain stew, staring out the window at the bay in the distance. "I miss it home" was her reply to Clara's inquiry, and that told Clara all she needed to know, though she expected that sorrow was really in the woman's nature.

Despite her wandering attention, Geneva proved to be a wonderful cook. She used guava syrup to sweeten her pies and cakes, since sugar was scarce. She made ash-baked sweet potatoes in the coals of a cook fire and a concoction she called Eleuthera stew which Harry loved and which Clara never told him was made with turtle meat. There was also Seminole squash and reef bean soup and coontie pudding and a plentiful supply of sapodillas, coco plums, and limes.

The seeds Clara planted came up in long, firm green shoots—"See?" Harry gloated—and in less than three months Clara and Geneva were to spend the morning snapping beans for one of Geneva's stews. If Edmund had a good day in the hammock with his rifle, there might be wild duck or quail roasted for dinner and served with sea grapes or custard apples.

Edmund and Geneva had come up from the Negro settlement near Palm Beach, a few miles north of the river, where Edmund's father and mother had come with other runaway slaves from Santiago de Cuba. There they had been part of a band of pirates led by Frenchman Achilles De Frou and had fought against slavery. Weary of battle finally, they fled to Key West and then north to Pineland to carve out a life for themselves. Their number swelled with Bahaman Negroes who made the hundred-and-fifty-mile boat journey across the gulf. Geneva was herself from Eleuthera, and when she spoke, which was rarely, she had a distinct British accent.

They constructed for themselves a one-room house of bamboo frame, covered completely in palmetto leaves, which Edmund stripped from the trees and Geneva picked over for the greenest and strongest; then they coated the house with a combination of plant oils and herbs and scented it with eucalyptus. Harry sneezed whenever he came near it; the smell reminded him of his sickroom in Middleton. The house looked to Clara like one of Harry's childhood drawings: the roof an inverted V, a boxy front door, one window. But Edmund was inordinately proud of his accomplishment. "On Eleuthera," he told Clara, "such a dwelling as this would be the most luxury. The most beautiful."

It was very neat inside with a rope bed in one corner, a cook stove in the opposite one near the window, and a large pine table in the center of the room with two stools secreted underneath. To keep the silverfish from devouring the fabrics she wove on her knee loom, Geneva kept a garter snake indoors; Clara watched her feed it bread and milk from a bowl.

In the woods near Clara's house, Geneva picked long, round blades of wire grass and set them out on the dock to dry in the sun. They turned a paler shade of her own coffee-colored skin and, when she sprinkled a little seawater on them, became pliant enough to weave. She made baskets and table mats by sewing the woven strands together with dried flowers and fig vines. She had made Edmund a hat braided of coconut leaves, and it lasted till the day a hurricane wind whipped it off his head.

A few weeks after they arrived, Geneva disappeared. Though they had been married for five years, Edmund had no explanation for her behavior, and his face was long in sorrow though he accepted her desertion philosophically. "Maybe she go back," he said, his eyes on the vast expanse of bay. But a few days later Geneva returned, leading a large spotted cow, a belated wedding gift from her mother. Harry used the manure in the garden, and Geneva was able to churn almost three pounds of butter a week, some of which she sold in the tiny Negro settlement of Lemon City for fifty cents a pound, and she made cottage cheese too, which she could sell for twenty-five cents a pound. She considered that this addition to her income made her a wealthy woman, and Edmund was delighted by his wife's industriousness.

With Geneva's help Clara had gotten the inside of the house fixed up enough finally to unpack the steamer trunks that had been sitting in stacks since the day they arrived. Edmund lugged them inside, and Clara began the job of setting things in order.

"Be careful, Mother," Harry jokingly warned her on his return from one of his long days in the hammock. "We don't want it looking like Middleton, do we?"

Clara kissed him, shooed him back outside, and began sorting through their things. She hung their clothes and used the bed linens, still smelling of flowered sachet, to make up the straw mattresses; her favorite vase she filled with hibiscus picked from the hammock, and other objects—a silver picture frame bearing a likeness of Harry as a baby, a silk coverlet stitched together by Clara herself from Cameron's old silk ties, Harry's pads and inks and colors and brushes, a gilt music stand with some sheet music of popular tunes and a few books of Chopin and Debussy and Brahms that were Clara's favorites—she placed around the common room and the two bedrooms.

Sometimes, late in the day, she would find a shaded spot along the bay and watch the water lap at the shore, pool and eddy among the fantastically twisted and intergrown mangrove roots. Boats sailed by and Clara stood up to wave. She saw nothing of Quentin McLeod in all these months. He had left them that first day with a box of provisions that carried them until Harry's newly acquired knowledge of the hammock's bounty began to yield other nourishment. She looked for the *Newport* and for his white-blond hair to catch the sun, but even if she could have seen him, she would never know if he could see her. He disapproved of her, and Clara suspected that he'd sent Edmund and Geneva because he believed she would not survive otherwise. On that score, Clara had already proven him wrong, and though grateful, she was the slightest bit offended at his presumption of her failure. That the man himself stayed away, Clara was, as Harry might have said, sad and glad.

The house had been washed inside and out, and while the mosquitoes could never be conquered, enough holes in the walls had been plugged up with pine tar that the netting stretched across the windows kept them from taking over. Edmund had stripped the leaves from some palmettos and used them to restore the pair of wicker chairs that had lain in a heap on the collapsed porch. He presented them proudly to Clara and Harry one morning and smiled as they sat and got comfortable for him. The path from the front porch to the bay was clear now; Harry and Edmund had gathered the fallen leaves, hacked and trimmed back the vines so that an aisle was formed of the palms and oaks that led to the refurbished dock and the clear expanse of the bay.

"It's just the way it was when I was a girl," Clara said with wonder, as if her son had created this miracle especially for her.

Harry shrugged modestly. "It's just the way you described it to me," he said.

Clara found herself for the first time wondering what next to do. Each decision she'd made thus far had seemed inevitable and the solutions, no matter with what difficulty arrived at, preordained. The land held great promise—there might be a city here on the bay, boats on the river, a harbor, a hotel—but the isolation fairly undid all of her dreams of transformation. Transportation was problematical at best; no matter how beautiful and desirable the area might be as a place to build a town, there was no easy way to get to it. The bay was too shallow to allow deep-water crafts—at least that was what McLeod had told her—and the roads seemed not to exist at all, save for a few old Seminole trails through the hammock that, according to Harry who had it straight from the source, Dr. Tiger had plowed himself.

"There's something I want to show you," Harry said one morning.

"What is it?"

"Something I discovered. A surprise. Just put on your best walking shoes and your worst dress."

"After the work I've been doing, they're all my worst dresses," Clara answered laughing, and they left the house to begin threading their way along trails that more often than not would simply run out, narrowing nearly to a ribbon, then stopping altogether at an impassable wall of jungle. They were familiar cul-de-sacs to Harry, and he usually knew how to backtrack and rediscover the route.

Tired out after a whole morning's walk, they stopped finally to rest in a small clearing next to a deep, dried-out creek bed. Exposed roots along the inner banks had grown thick as trunks and sprouted branches, which were wrapped in vines and which hosted, in turn, tiny white orchids.

"Dr. Tiger said that the hammock can digest a whole civilization in no time," Harry said. He unknotted the handkerchief from his neck and wiped his face of sweat. "There was a man once who came here looking for land to settle. An industrialist, I think."

"A Northerner no doubt," Clara said.

"Yes," Harry replied. "And as luck would have it, used to the city."

"As luck would have it?" Clara echoed wryly.

"I'm being perfectly serious, Mother," Harry said. "He came into the hammock on his own with a few days' supply of food and a map the conquistadores had left in Fort Dallas. When he hadn't come back in a week, his cronies went out searching for him. He wasn't hard to find." Harry picked up a dried twig and twirled it between his fingers. "All they had to do was follow the buzzards. They'd half devoured him by then. Couldn't even move the body for a decent burial, so they left him in the woods till the vines just grew over him. Who knows? We might be leaning on him right now."

"That is a perfectly disgusting and no doubt apocryphal story," Clara said and ostentatiously leaned back against a fallen oak tree, her head cradled on a bank of dry moss. She looked at Harry's mischievous grin; a startling stalk of tiny, delicate white orchids hovered over his head like a nimbus. She adored him.

"Nature mocks man every time," Harry said. "There just isn't a way to conquer it." He sidled up to sit near his mother. The jungle was cool, though some sunlight poked through the tangle above them to splatter delicate pinks on the rust-colored forest floor. There were few birds at this density of the hammock, and the quiet was wonderful and terrible too. As much as he wanted to run ahead and show his discovery to his mother, Harry also enjoyed stilling his impatience.

"I love the breeze," he said. His eyes were closed, his body stretching and bowing back against the jungle floor. "Especially where I've gotten burned by the sun. It hurts and then it's cool. Mmm."

Harry hadn't let Clara bring food, insisting instead that he had learned enough about the hammock to reap its natural bounty. After his first stumbling days in the hammock, Harry had begun to recognize the spots he'd passed the day before and, using these landmarks, branched out further, expanding his circle of familiarity. One day, as if in reward for his persistence, Dr. Tiger had reappeared and his tutelage resumed. Now Harry showed his mother what he had learned—how to bite off just the tender tip of the heart of the palmetto, how to find elderberries, their flowers like Middleton snowflakes, in the open glades edging old Seminole fences, even how to make a certain grade of pine sap serve as chewing gum. There were huckleberries and wild grapes too, but the purple-black palmetto berries were too bitter to eat, though the wanderers stuffed their pockets full for Geneva, who might make a passable pie if she goosed it up with guava syrup.

Sated finally, their thirst quenched with the juice of fresh limes, they continued through the hammock. "It's not much farther," Harry said.

"What isn't?"

"Dr. Tiger led me to it," Harry said. "You'll see."

And then they stepped through a clearing in the jungle and there were the orange groves her father had planted all those years ago, the trees in full fruit now with barely a space between each for the visitors to make their way. The waxy green leaves rubbed their clothes and faces, and the sense of abundance, of nature's bounty, was immense and gratifying.

"Like rows and rows of Christmas trees decorated with balls of gold," Clara said, and Harry was even moved to quote Goethe.

"Know'st thou the land where the lemon trees bloom,
Where the gold orange glows in the deep thicket's gloom,
Where a wind ever soft from the blue heaven blows,
And the groves are of laurel and myrtle and rose?"

Clara hooked her arm through her son's and pressed her face to his shoulder. "Have you grown taller, my darling? I think all this sunshine is doing you more good than I even dreamed it could."

Harry breathed deeply. "I feel like we've come to some ancient biblical land," he said in a hushed voice. "Where's the finger of God, Mother? Hasn't he pointed it here? Aren't we blessed?" There were sweet tears in her eyes; she felt protected in the lushness of the grove, nearly dizzy with its perfume, dazzled by the sunlight on the golden fruit that hung in such astonishing profusion. Harry pulled an orange from a tree, dug in his thumb and sucked out the juice, laughing, delighted. Clara laughed too to see him so pleased.

"And me?" she asked, tilting her head back to let the juice from his orange trickle into her mouth.

"Nectar of the gods, Mother," Harry said.

They were half-lost in the grove, too happy with each other, too

· *Barry Jay Kaplan* ·   69 sated with the pleasure of the scent and the juice of the fruit to notice how deeply they had wandered. "We can't be lost in God's grove," Harry said, and indeed, by simply following the sun, the sun that enriched the glow, that brought the oranges from green to gold, they made their way back, arm in arm, moving as one, full of plans for a wonderful future.

"What we've got to do now is harvest these beauties," Clara said.

"We can hire workers from Key West," Harry chimed in.

"We'll order some of those bean crates—"

"I figure that we can get two hundred oranges to a crate! Think of it, Mother!"

Clara was laughing again, pointing down the aisle of trees that seemed to go on into infinity. "Make a trail along the edge of the grove right to the river," she said, and plucked an orange from the corner tree. "Let's call them Reade Beauties."

Harry took the golden fruit from his mother's hand and kissed her empty palm. We are safe here, he thought. "I love you for this," he said.

Yes, yes, Clara thought. This is what I came here for, and she clung anew to her handsome, her beautiful, her adored son.

They sat quietly on the porch a few nights later, Edmund's repaired chairs creaking beneath their weight. The atmosphere was changing subtly around them; the light slowly faded, causing a barely perceptible softening in the hues of the leaves and the ocean and the sky. The light became cooler and the color was slowly drained from their world. Clara waited to light the candles until the last faint glimmer of day was gone, and even then, in utter darkness, she hesitated. There was no moon this night, and with the sun gone a faintly chilled mist came filtering down through the leaves and settled on their skin. Clara tasted the sweetness of a flower's scent on her lips, smelled the sun's traces on her bare arms. The night embraced them as an old friend, not a thing to be shut out or feared. New sounds came up, the low moans of frogs at ground level, high-pitched squeals of birds, the rustle of lizards in the tall grass, the muted clatter of palm fronds above their heads.

"Let's always be this happy," Harry said. Clara took his hand and he squeezed hers in return. "I wish this could last forever," Harry said. His voice came to her out of the darkness, like an emanation of his spirit, for their actual presences had evanesced in the night. They were two forces that existed side by side in the bliss and eternity of this place.

"It will, darling," she said. "I promise."

$$5.$$

Quentin McLeod was an enigma to most of the people he met. He was friendly enough, they'd all agree, an easy man to do business with and as fair-minded as a person could expect in as rowdy and rough a place as the South Florida frontier. If he took his own sweet time in answering a question, what he finally came up with was bound to surprise people in the way it cut to the heart of the matter. The man had no use for what was known as small talk, or perhaps he simply had no skill with it. His directness was sometimes taken for rudeness, especially by those pioneers from cities up north who were accustomed to bellying up to the bar with an acquaintance and matching each other shot for shot before the deal could be struck. McLeod had a two-room frame cabin up the Miami River and seven or so acres of hammock and pineland and would rather have spent his time fishing the Miami River and Biscayne Bay and tending his exotic crops—"Cuban mameys, he grows! Carambola from Malaysia! Winged beans from the Philippines!"—than trading tall tales with some Key West shipper angling for a better price on his Cayenne pineapples or Jamaica sorrel jelly.

He preferred solitude. If he wanted company, he'd sooner choose that of the early bay settlers than that of the prominent businessmen of Key West, though he could certainly best them in arguments on such topics as came up during the run of business. McLeod seemed to know something about everything, though he would become self-deprecation itself when explaining how. "I don't know most things but half well," he'd protest. "I don't know what that tells you about the other fellow who thinks I know a lot. Hell, when I came down to Biscayne Bay I knew, let's see, three sailor knots, one never-fail method of setting a fire, and the Australian crawl." He would laugh then, and how startling it was to see the square planes of that lean, handsome face break up into a grin, though his laugh, strangely enough, produced no sound at all. "Good thing I learned that crawl too, since I lost my boat on the Miami River rapids first week I was here."

First week? When was that, Quentin? He'd pause, the asker would wait, and finally there'd be an answer. "When I came here there was about as much civilization as you could balance on the end of a pine needle. No roads, no bridges, no canals, no schools, no churches, not a plowed acre anywhere." Quentin, when was that? Quentin? And that's when he'd get that look that no one could break through, and that's when business would conclude with a handshake. It was as if he had a private code that no one could decipher and a private sorrow that no one could console.

What people did know about him was a patchwork quilt—"A crazy quilt's more like it!"—of pieces of his past. He'd come down to Biscayne Bay fresh out of Harvard College. When? No one was exactly sure; it could have been as early as 1875. His looks were no clue: he had the kind of face that's old as a young man's and young as an old one's. And maybe it wasn't Harvard College either; maybe it was Yale, or maybe he never went to school at all. Some people said he was half-deaf, but that idea may have been the result of their own impatience with the slowness of his replies. He limped when he was tired, and a story went around that he had been a convict on a Georgia chain gang who got shot during a break; there were plenty of men on the run in Key West who said it, and it took one to know one, right?

Everyone knew him by that white-blond hair, and the ones that liked him were loyal to him till the day they died and did things for him a man in a frontier place only did for someone whose honesty was beyond doubt; they may not have known a lot about him, but they sure knew that much. They wanted him to run for mayor of Key West once—and Miami too, years later—but it was more of a wish on their part than a reflection of his own ambitions. McLeod preferred fishing and building boats—he designed a flat-bottomed skiff to trawl for turtles along the reefs—and sailing his schooner *Newport* to ports in the Caribbean and along the eastern ledge of South America.

As land agent for the Biscayne Bay Development Company, he admitted to negligence and with good cause. "Folks can't be sold land like this. They've got to want it. It's got to . . ."—and here his face took on a secret smile again and his speech turned nearly poetic—"it's got to sing to 'em."

He believed in the land—in its beauty, its pride, its wildness, and its integrity—and he didn't believe in Clara Reade. He'd ferried people like her before around Biscayne Bay. "Rich people with a purse full of boredom and a pocketful of cash," he said. "Tourists spoiling the air with their bright voices and fake perfume and bad ideas about what the bay ought to be." Mrs. Reade was, in his initial estimation of her, no exception. So convinced was he of her reasons for coming down to the bay—"dabbling in nature," he muttered to himself the evening he set her and her son ashore at the dock—that he hardly even noticed what she looked like. A Northern woman, a widow, brown hair, some secret in her eyes. He saw her a few times after that, though only from his boat, even felt a little sorry for her. She seemed such a tiny, pathetic figure, standing at the edge of the water and shading her eyes against the sun, that he sent her Edmund and Geneva. He didn't want a starved woman and boy on his conscience, and it gave the Negro couple a month or so of gainful employment. He had no doubt that any day now that small figure would be waving the red flag for help or that he would receive a frantic, breathless SOS from the sorrowful Geneva. He was prepared with a schedule for steamers going north.

Months went by, the rickety dock was shored up, natural debris along the path to the house was cleared away, and the only SOS he had was when Edmund paddled upriver in an old canoe with some dollars and Mrs. Reade's shopping list: whitewash, a box of nails, a length of mosquito netting, fence wire, new axe. McLeod filled the order at Finch's trading post in Palm Grove and, curiosity tickling him, delivered it himself.

The dock in front of her property was certainly a lot sturdier under his feet now. As he lugged the packages along it, though, it maintained a kind of sway, rising and falling with the beat of the current against its pilings. The old canoe lay bottom-up in the sand. Edmund was near it, crouching before a small fire, melting pine tar in an old metal pot. He grinned up at McLeod—"Hallo, Mistah!"—then dipped a stick into the steaming, gummy tar, slapped it on the back of a piece of bark, and set the bark on a worn spot on the canoe.

"The lady working you hard, Edmund?"

"Oh, she be tough on me, Mistah," the man replied, shaking his head in mock woe.

The pathway through the trees, so overgrown a few months ago, had been cleared, and as he walked, McLeod saw that what was once a nearly impassable bank of undergrowth and overhang was now a perfect aisle. Shafts of light penetrated the foliage, illuminating the footing of smooth pine needles on soft sand.

The yard had undergone the same kind of house-cleaning operation. A rusted machete leaned against a tree stump next to an axe whose handle had rotted in half. Could that be the son coming around from behind the house? In shirtsleeves, hatless, he looked too strong and healthy to be the pale, sickly boy of a few months ago, but it was he nevertheless; he strode across the yard and extended a work-roughened hand to McLeod.

"Hope you brought some real coffee," Harry said, eyeing the packages stacked around McLeod's feet. "I'm getting sick of Geneva's home brew."

McLeod shook his head, still surprised at the change in the boy. "I brought some wire," he said.

Harry shrugged. "Already made a fence out of young mangrove vines," he replied with a little laugh. "Those rabbits were awfully eager to get at our garden. We had to do something fast."

McLeod took a slow look around the yard. "You did more'n just something, Mr. Reade."

"Harry."

McLeod nodded. "Harry it is," he said as the boy hefted the wire and hauled it around the side of the house.

The house looked better too, though McLeod thought it would still not make it through the next hurricane; the roof wouldn't even keep the inside dry during a heavy rain. The whitewash he'd brought for her would go a long way toward prettying the place up, but a new roof was what it really needed.

As he crossed the yard, a woman appeared on the porch and McLeod stopped in his tracks. She wiped her hands on an apron, then leaned against the porch railing. It has to be Mrs. Reade, he thought, and yet the woman whose face emerged from the shade of the porch roof to be struck by a shaft of afternoon sun looked more like the pioneer women who lived in those isolated settlements along the keys than a city woman who'd been here such a short time. She was the image of the kind of woman whom McLeod pictured as settling the western lands, traveling endless miles in covered wagons, spinning cloth in log cabins, cooking over crude fires. She looked to him like all the women who ever traversed an American prairie and dug in to stay.

She saw him and straightened up; her woman's vanity made her hands automatically reach up to adjust her hair, then down to smooth her skirt. She waved and walked toward him now, with the confident stride of someone long used to being out in the open, working the land. Hadn't she said something to him about living here before? He hadn't paid that much attention. Wasn't she born here, in fact?

She certainly wasn't in mourning anymore. The dress she wore was white and as fresh-looking as if it had dried in the sun and just been snapped from a clothesline. The sleeves were rolled to the elbows and there were flecks of flour on her bare arms.

Each stride she took brought more detail to McLeod's eye. The white dress blew in the breeze and showed him the outlines of her body, round, uncorseted, swaying, slim to the waist with a nice swell of flesh below. Her hair, which had seemed vaguely brown to him on their first meeting, had come up gold and red in the sun and blew in wisps around her face and neck.

"I'm making elderberry pie!"

Her voice had a lilt to it that McLeod had always associated with Southern women, a kind of laziness to the words, as if the whole sentence were swinging in a hammock. McLeod set the bundles down as she stopped in front of him. When she moved her hands to draw the hair from her eyes, he saw they had roughened with work, and for a moment he was touched by her. The city woman on a tourist's vacation had all but disappeared.

"I guess you've got everything I want," Clara said as she checked the packages at his feet.

Her face was burnished around the nose and cheeks, the color of a russet apple, and was finer-boned than he'd remembered, though her full lips kept it from being delicate. And those eyes: gray under the shade of her lashes, lightening near to green as she looked up into the sun.

"Are you all right, Mr. McLeod?"

I must be gaping like a fool, he thought as she turned, axe in one hand, box of nails in the other, and started for the house. "I was just thinking you and your son might like to come to Sunday services today, Mrs. Reade!" he called out after her.

She slowed down and turned her head, and he saw she was smiling at him. Damn! McLeod hefted the mosquito netting and the pail of whitewash. "We'd love to!" she said and walked quickly into the house. "Harry! We're going to church!"

While McLeod waited on the porch, Clara changed from the white dress to a more formal one of blue the shade of a shimmering afternoon sky and put on a straw hat with a tiny owl feather she'd found floating down from an oak tree one dawn. Clara knew that something had changed in McLeod from the moment he'd come walking across the yard toward her—still barefoot, she'd noticed. There was the same frankness in his gaze—those blue eyes didn't miss a trick!—but that first time they'd met he had measured her and found her wanting. She could feel his eyes on her now as she and Harry settled in the stern and McLeod went about untying the guide ropes and taking the *Newport* out into the bay. His admiration pleased her but unsettled her too, for despite his previous treatment of her, she wanted his approval; in some way she could not quite articulate, yet which felt absolutely clear and sensible, she associated McLeod with the whole area. It was as if his simplicity and directness of manner personified the very best of the land. Even his disapproval of her had been accurately placed; she herself would disapprove of a woman like her if she hadn't known more than was apparent to anyone just meeting her.

He was protective of the place; she liked that. She reached for Harry's hand and smiled at him, glad he'd come, proud of how healthy he looked. He smiled back at her, his shyness with strangers already making his eyes a bit guarded; I'll never know him well enough, she thought, and wondered why she'd thought such a sad thing on such a happy day.

The fantastic, grasping mangrove trees, with their curved and twisted roots thrusting out into the bay, forced the *Newport* a good distance from shore. Clara could see, enmeshed in the sand and sea grass and mangrove leaves themselves, startling evidence of man's habitation: a long piece of torn white sailcloth braided through the roots, the staves of a barrel sticking up like teeth, a lady's red shawl that looked like an open gash. Yet all had become part of the system, all moved gently with the flow of the water; a breeze brought to her ears a groaning sound, as if the mangroves resisted the pull of the currents. Clara pointed across the bay to what looked like a long, low reef covered in mangroves and asked McLeod for some information on it.

"That? Well, we just call it the Beach. Actually it's the first of the keys. Once upon a time a man from the court of Spain lived there, Don Pedro el Biscaino. He held the title of Keeper of the Swans, though I don't guess there was much for him to do out there but fight off the mosquitoes and gators. Anyway, he stuck it out in the name of the king and the bay got named for him." Farther on McLeod pointed to a series of rocky bluffs along the mainland shore.

"The highest place on the whole coast," he said. "See how that one there's got a face on it?" Clara nodded. "Old Tigertail, the last of the great Seminole chiefs, was killed by lightning on that spot, and they say the stone took on his look." He glanced at Clara with a self-effacing shrug. "This place is full of stories like that. Believe 'em at your own risk."

From under the brim of his straw hat, Harry stole glances at his mother and McLeod. When had she ever looked at someone in that way, with such attentiveness, such fervor, such interest? Why, her whole face seemed changed, made young, charged and glowing with color, as if it were she and not the sun that gave off heat and light. Under his deep sunburn, McLeod blushed like a schoolboy, and the grin on his face was nothing short of silly. Harry felt an intruder on something not meant for his eyes and turned away, embarrassed and shy, to look with pretended interest at the mangroves, only to feel his mother's lips on his cheek a moment later and hear her high, delighted laughter as she took his arm and leaned against him.

"Oh Harry," she said, half out of breath. "Isn't it a wonderful day?"

McLeod took in the sails and the boat glided smoothly toward a long, narrow dock jutting out from shore where another schooner, shorter than the *Newport,* was tied up, along with three canoes and a flat-bottomed skiff. A gently sloping semicircular plot of land about a hundred by thirty yards had been cleared, then seeded for grass and manicured like a lawn. Clara marveled at the backbreaking man-hours of labor that must have gone into such an undertaking. Palm trees marked the perimeter of the area in a wide sweeping arc. Nestled tight against the hammock, cozy and protected from rain and sun by the leafy overhang of ancient oaks, were two whitewashed structures. The larger, two-storied one was wide and shallow with a deep porch stretched around three sides and a mustard-colored shingle roof reaching out to shade it. Bright white curtains, drawn out on the breeze, waved from the open windows and seemed to welcome visitors, a picture as homey and simple as a woman shaking out her apron. Connected to the house by a long narrow breezeway roofed in the same mustard-colored shingles was a smaller, squatter, windowless building, an offspring that hadn't reached adult height, but it stood as proud and chesty with its arched double doors and peaked roof, topped with a hand-carved weathervane of Christ on the cross; with the breeze coming off the river, Christ shimmered east toward Bethlehem.

Harry gave his mother his arm again, and they followed McLeod across the grassy sweep. As they did, voices rose up in song to greet them: "Onward Christian soldiers, marching as to war!"

Clara smiled and pressed Harry's arm, and her step quickened to the familiar melody. A piano without much power carried the tune through the verseless passages, and a sweet, piercing soprano led it to a rousing, if not exactly musical, finale.

"Looks like we've missed the service," McLeod said, as the congregation filed out of the darkness of the shack.

The three women emerging, squinting in the glare of the noonday sun, were plainly dressed in linen and bombazine and silk; a bit of lace at the wrist, a straw hat with a cluster of wooden cherries, a silk rose at the waist, a garnet brooch or cameo were their only ornamentation. Their simplicity was in marked contrast to the lushness of their surroundings, as if they had realized they could not compete with the purple bougainvillea for color, nor with the mangrove and palm for pattern and design, and so refused to try. The men followed, affecting a loose-limbed jauntiness as they ambled across the lawn. Some sported elaborate muttonchops and mustaches; most were clean shaven and red-cheeked. They wore straw boaters against the glare, tight jackets and white trousers, and carelessly knotted silk ties that blew in the breeze and looked like exotic birds perched on their shoulders.

But for the garden that contained them, Clara thought she might have seen any of these people in Colonel Moss Park on a summer Sunday in Middleton.

"Mother, you're crying!"

Clara shook her head and laughed; in her relief at escaping Middleton and finding joy on the bay, she had, without quite knowing it, missed the family of man. "I'm happy," she said and kissed his cheek, then turned to McLeod. "Thank you for bringing us," she said and hooked her arm through his as he took her and her son to meet everyone.

First was Flora Goram, a doll-like woman dressed in dotted silk, with a delicacy of feature and lightness of movement that was darting, birdlike. "Flora runs the starch mill over by the Arch Creek Bridge," McLeod said.

"Oh *Mr.* Goram's the one that runs it," Flora told Clara. "With five little ones I've got just time enough to draw a deep breath at the end of the day." She smiled modestly and handed each of them a lemon from a large basket balanced on her hip. "Today's a lemon social," she said, shooing away her children, who played tag around her full skirts. "Mr. McLeod, will you do the honors?"

McLeod sliced his in half and passed the knife to Harry. "Everyone puts in a penny for each seed," McLeod explained.

"Someday we'll buy Ida a new piano, God willing." Flora counted the seeds and collected the pennies and tossed the fruit back in the basket. "Lemonade for dessert," she said gaily and moved on to the next guests.

"She's the one that runs things," McLeod told them once Flora was out of earshot. "Her husband spends his time writing 'uplifting' essays for a Utopian magazine called *The Simple Life*. An unregenerate idealist, poor soul."

A dozen or so yards in back of the house Clara saw a man in overalls standing red-faced over a barbecue pit dug in the ground; a woman stood a few feet behind him and watched as he turned the big fragrant chunks of grilling pork and beef with a pitchfork.

"Ida and Rufus Finch," McLeod said. "That is their house. Kind of an inn and trading post and post office combined. Rufus was one of the first of this breed of pioneer. Don't mind Ida. She's . . . well, you'll see."

McLeod waved to them and the man waved back, set down the pitchfork, then took the woman by the arm and strode over to meet Clara and Harry.

"Welcome to the bay!" Rufus said and held out a work-roughened hand to shake. His face was long and horse-jawed, his eyes so small and deep set his look was a perpetual squint; it gave him the reputation of a skeptic, though he was really an optimist. "We was waiting for you to get settled in and come over." Some of his teeth were missing, and when he laughed—which was often, Clara was to find out—he was conscious enough to cover his mouth. Ida stood next to him, his hand gripping her arm, and Clara thought she looked as if she might bolt if released. She'd been pretty once, anyone could see that, maybe even a beauty, Clara mused, with those big blue eyes and heart-shaped face. But now her chin was held back and her eyes and mouth had hard, tight lines around them. Clara wondered if she cried a lot; even now she looked on the verge of some strong emotion, anger or tears or maybe even a big belly laugh.

"Rufus been at it all night, Ida?" McLeod asked.

"Can't keep that fire going no other way," Rufus said with hardly a glance back at his wife. " 'Course I did manage to fortify myself with a nip every now and again." He laughed and turned to Ida. "Ida, why don't you show Mrs. Reade your kitchen." He smiled at Clara. "Got a new coat of whitewash and she's dying to show it off. Go on, Ida." Ida hesitated—would she actually run off now? Clara wondered—then tugged her arm away from Rufus's grip, and rubbed it as if he'd hurt her. She bowed her head to Clara and gestured for her to follow. Clara smiled at Rufus—he seemed to think nothing of his wife's reproach—and walked quickly to catch up with her hostess.

On the way they passed a table—long enough to seat the whole group—set up in the shade of the roofed breezeway. Off to one side of it was a low shelf that held a washbasin, waterbucket, and towels. Clara followed Ida up the side steps to the kitchen and stopped at the screen door to watch Harry join the line of men and children at the water basin.

The line snaked back a few yards, as everyone was expected to wash before eating no matter how spruced up they'd been when they arrived. Seventeen-year-old Ned Sparks, all pointy elbows and scrawny neck and red ears, with hands and feet he had yet to grow into, was in charge of the basin. His younger brother Fess, as wiry and fast on his feet as Ned was slow and lumbering, tossed the dirty water on the ground and stood by the refill bucket. It was their older sister, Maria, in charge of keeping clean towels at the ready and prepared to swat either of her brothers if they got unruly, who caught Harry's attention.

He'd already noticed her while he was slicing open his lemon, even thought she was someone from Middleton, but that was impossible. Then he thought maybe it was the closeness of their ages or maybe because they both had green eyes or... Well, Harry couldn't quite figure out what it was exactly that made her so familiar, but she did seem to him like the one person here he already knew. Now that's a crazy thing, he thought, and was excited to meet her face to face on the washup line.

The view of her now was blocked by Ned's wide shoulders as he poured fresh water in the basin. Harry pulled up his sleeves, heart pounding, rinsed his hands, and flicked the water off them. He swallowed hard.

"Careful you don't get water spots on your nice suit."

He looked up; she held the towel out to him. She was not much younger than Harry, eighteen or nineteen at the most, tall and just the other side of skinny, with a nice swell at the hip that Harry found attractive. It had never occurred to him until that moment that he had preferences in the way a woman appeared, and it made him smile to himself to think she suited him. She wore a full calico apron over a lacy Sunday dress, and Harry had a passing vision of her untying it at the neck and letting it slip down to the ground. He stared at her fingers toying with a sprig of silk pansies at her throat and spotted a throbbing blue vein.

She was looking away from him now, and Harry noticed how the flare of her nostrils gave her profile a fierce, almost angry look, as if something was holding her at bay. She turned to him suddenly and met his eyes, and her expression changed swiftly to sweetness: head bent, wide green eyes peering up from beneath long lashes, lips pressed modestly together. Harry could not tell whether a mask had been put on or taken off.

"Come on, son." He was being jostled from behind. "We're starving back here."

Harry blinked himself awake and took the towel from her. "Thank you." He wiped his hands and gave it back.

"It's all soppy now," she said, then folded the wet towel neatly in half and ran to take it inside.

Clara was marveling at the bright coolness of the kitchen. A screened corner cupboard held Ida Finch's best dishes; on the opposite wall was an incised pie safe. All her dry goods—cans and sacks of flour and sugar—were set on table tops, the table legs standing in cans of kerosene.

"Ida hates snakes," Flora explained.

Clara glanced at Ida and saw her staring at her tables and nodding.

"Taking 'nother towel, Miz Finch!" Maria cried as she hung the wet one to dry by the cook stove. She pulled a dry one from the pile, curtsied her thanks, smiled pleasantly at Clara, and ran back out to the wash line.

"Poor motherless child," Flora said and turned to see Clara hefting a tureen of squash soup. "Now listen, Mrs. Reade. You put that down and get out of this kitchen and take your place at the table."

"But I want to help," Clara protested as Flora wrested the tureen from her.

"Your first time, you're a guest. I'd take advantage of it if I was you," she added with a husky laugh that was a surprise coming from so small and delicate a woman. "Things is gonna be hard enough soon enough."

Clara let her have the soup. "Next time I'll bring some elderberry pies. I promise."

"I'll hold you to it, too!"

Each of the women had supplied her specialities, and there was food enough even for this hungry group: venison steak and liver and home-cured bacon, sweet corn bread and Johnsie cake, sweet potato pie and Indian pumpkin pudding with guava jelly for dessert and enough cut limes to squeeze on just about anything including the coffee. Ida and Flora and Maria were up and down the whole time, bringing out steaming platters and hot pots of chickory-flavored coffee.

The men paid little attention to the food being set out before them— with the exception of Harry, who could not help but catch Maria's eye whenever she put something down in front of him, but he just leaned in and took and ate and drank without interrupting the flow of conversation.

"What's wrong with wrecking? It's a good honest living." The gravelly voice of Calvin Sparks was tinged with petulance today; his monthly haul was pathetically low on account of calm seas. The one thing he hated about his business—though he'd never admit it, especially to his boys Ned and Jim, whom he relied on to take over for him one of these days when his gout made it too hard to crawl in and out of reefed boats—was hoping for bad weather. Like hoping for death, his wife used to say. Cal sucked on his pipe between mouthfuls of turtle stew. "Once the hurricanes start up again—"

"I don't care how many ships're wrecked on these reefs," McLeod said. "There still ain't hardly any way to make a decent living." He took a fierce bite out of a biscuit and talked as he chewed. "Living off wrecks, making starch out of arrowroot,"—here he pointed his biscuit at Farley Goram, who just shook his head as he cut his meat—"raising skinny chickens, peddling cartloads of vegetables . . . Why, I bet one little clerk up north makes as much as the labor force at this whole table. Isn't that right, Mr. Reade?"

Harry was startled to be asked a question. "Why, I don't know. I guess . . ." Clara took her seat beside him.

"I can't even hardly recall what real cash money looks like," Rufus Finch said dreamily, still red in the face from exertions over the barbecue pit. "I thought this country was on the way to bypassing the barter system, but try telling that to the Indians coming to my store."

"The crime and the pity of it is that we got so much that's wonderful here," McLeod said. "But we can't seem to make the most out of it."

Harry thought of what his father's ironworks had made of the city of Middleton and couldn't help speaking up. "Why make anything out of it?" he asked. "Why not just leave everything as it is?"

McLeod swallowed hard. "What do you mean, son?"

"It seems to me that no place on earth could be as pretty or as nice as this, and wouldn't it be ruining it all to do something to it?"

"Now there's a sensible boy!" Goram said. "These folks just won't be satisfied. It's like what Wordsworth wrote: 'Late and soon, getting and spending, we lay waste our powers.'"

"I'm talkin' about *increasing* our powers, Farley," McLeod said. "Not laying 'em to waste."

"But surely you don't want to alter God's landscape," Harry said, glancing at Clara and remembering their day at the orange groves. "Where my mother and I come from, we've seen the results of that kind of meddling."

Clara put a restraining hand on his arm. "Harry, you're offending Mr. McLeod."

"Not at all," McLeod said. "But I'm curious, Mr. Reade. What would you do if you had, say, a crop of, oh, I don't know . . ."

"Oranges?" Harry said. "But we do! My mother and I are going to bring back my grandfather's old groves!"

McLeod nodded. "When were you planning on doing that?"

Harry smiled. "I've already sent for the boxes."

McLeod looked around the table as if to ask the others to bear witness. "I wouldn't go getting my hopes up for a harvest just yet."

"Why not?"

"It's too late for a crop this year," McLeod said.

"Oh. Then we'll start earlier next year."

"The natural order of things is what I'm trying to explain, Mr. Reade," McLeod said. "Things grow, ripen, and then they're either picked or they fall. It's a mistake to try and turn it into a harvest."

"But that doesn't make any sense," Harry said.

Clara nodded her head in agreement. "Surely everyone would want our Reade Beauties," she said. "I've never tasted anything so delicious."

"Oh, there's a demand," McLeod admitted. "No question of that. The citrus industry's booming in most of Florida. But way down here we've got a problem most of 'em upstate don't have."

"Where there's a problem," Harry said, "there's a . . ." Maria passed behind her father and smiled over his head at Harry. Harry sat up straighter and missed the first part of McLeod's response.

"The problem is, there's no way to get the crop out. First of all, you've got to get it to the river, and there's no roads except for some old Seminole trails."

"It didn't seem to us like it would be so difficult to carve a road alongside the grove," Clara said. "Harry?"

"Maybe, maybe not," McLeod said. "And let's say you do get the harvest to the river. Somehow. Then you take it by schooner down to Key West, and from there you transfer it to a steamer like the one you came down on, only going north."

"That's what we were planning on doing," Clara said eagerly. "So it's just a matter of—" McLeod was shaking his head.

"Let him finish, Mother."

"Except by that time it's already five days since you picked it; already your crop is just this side of going bad, and it's nowhere near a market."

"Then all you'd need to fix the situation would be some sort of transportation that would get the crops out faster," Clara said.

"For example?"

"Steamboats?" Harry suggested.

"Or ocean liners," Clara said. "They could dock right at the river."

McLeod shook his head again. "Biscayne Bay's too shallow to accommodate big ships. Their bottoms'd scrape right off on the reefs. Play right into Mr. Sparks's hands here."

"Something else then," Harry said impatiently. "A paved road."

"We wanted a paved road," McLeod said, "so we wouldn't always have to rely on the bay to get from here to there. I guess that's everyone's goal but Mr. Goram's. An isolationist, pure and simple."

"I resent that," Goram said. "I may be an idealist, but that's about the worst you can say for me."

McLeod ignored his protest. "So Dade County built us a mule stage line from Lake Worth on down. Twenty-five bucks a mile just to clear the trees and palmetto and that's not counting bridges and wooden corduroys over the swampland north of Pineland City. Poor old Johnny Briggs was the first driver, let his soul rest in peace, and he'd ruther have walked, he said, 'cause that road wasn't nothing but ruts and rocks and sand. Sixty-five miles took three days. Johnny led the mules on foot, playing his fiddle all the way." He turned to Calvin Sparks beside him. "Isn't that how you and yours come down, Cal?"

Sparks nodded. "And I still got the sore butt to prove it!"

Farley Goram turned to Clara as if she were the arbiter of the dispute. "And you know what people say about the road now that we have it? 'It starts nowhere and it ends nowhere.'" He sat back and grinned at McLeod as if his point was incontestable. "That's what I mean about not being satisfied. It's a bottomless well of wanting, that's what it is."

Flora leaned over her husband's shoulder to pour coffee. "Still," she said, "it would be nice to be able to ride up to Palm Beach in a carriage and buy some store-boughts." She turned quickly to Ida Finch, who was carrying a tray of empty plates to the water pump at the side of the house. "Not that I'm complaining about the stock in your store, Ida!" Ida shrugged and kept walking.

Harry felt Maria pass behind him then to set a plate of steaming pudding in front of him; her apron dipped and slid back across his arm. He didn't dare turn his head to her, but he'd lost part of the conversation again.

"Here we are," McLeod was saying, "sandwiched between the Atlantic Ocean and the Gulf of Mexico, with natural harbors and navigable rivers flowing to both coasts—"

"Uh oh," Cal Sparks said. "I hear a familiar tune being played."

McLeod glanced at Sparks and set his fork down. "So what if I've said it before?" He turned to Clara now. "The thing that's gonna take Florida into the future, Mrs. Reade, is canals."

"I knew it!" Sparks said. "Him and those damn canals."

"They're already raising money for 'em in the northern part of the state," McLeod insisted. "You just don't want 'em because boats won't get wrecked in canals. You'd be all for 'em if you could plant reefs all along 'em."

Sparks let out a whoop of laughter. "Maybe I should!" he said. "Long's I don't get caught at it."

His boys Ned and Jim laughed and slapped each other. Harry saw Maria's face tighten in anger at her father and brothers. Farley Goram was banging his pipe on the table to get everyone's attention.

"That's the trouble with the American people," he said. "As soon as a group of them come together, they want to start civilizing the place and making a town. Next thing you know, they're framing a constitution and half of 'em are running for U.S. senator."

"Farley likes to think of himself as representing the educated classes," Cal Sparks said.

Harry saw the sense in what Goram said and was surprised to hear the others laughing at Goram for saying it.

"But it's natural for people to want to better their situation," Clara insisted.

Goram turned to look at his wife. "What do you need that you haven't got?" he asked her. "Last time you had any cash you splurged and bought a box of sugar candies for the kiddies."

"Are you saying things couldn't get any better?" McLeod asked.

"Of course they could," Harry said. "But what man in what place since history started hasn't said the same thing? And look what happens!"

"Let me tell you something, Mrs. Reade," Goram went on, emboldened by this new ally in Harry. "You got a yen for eating venison? You don't have to have a store or cash, and you don't have to kill a deer neither. You just pick fifty blood oranges from that grove of yours, and any of those Seminoles'll kill one for you. Twenty-five if you want a ham. Any of us here catch a mess of catfish, let's say, we share 'em, expect you to do the same. Just blow on a conch shell, that's signal enough for folks's ears to perk up."

"Hey, 'member how them shells blowed at the wine wreck?" Cal Sparks said. "I got so drunk..." And here he set off choking and laughing too hard to finish the story.

"He's talking about a ship out of Bordeaux, France, got wrecked on its way to Havana," McLeod explained with a wink at the wheezing old man. "The shore up and down the bay was littered with casks and kegs and barrels of wine for a week. This old fool hauled in so much French champagne he started taking baths in it. Says it cured his gout."

"It did! It did!" Sparks managed to say before erupting into laughter again.

Maria bent over Harry to pick up an empty platter. "His gout's bad as ever," she said under her breath, and Harry knew she'd said it only for his ears.

"And what would have been the advantage if there'd been a canal?"

Goram demanded. "The ship would still have gone down on the reef. I say we stay as we are."

"If we'd wanted so-called civilization we would've gone to Chicago," Harry said.

McLeod shook his head in consternation. "You yokels haven't got the vision of an owl at high noon. Just dig a ditch linking this river to that lake and to the next creek over, and before you know it the Atlantic's connected to the gulf. People'll be steaming down the Miami River and out into the bay—why, the whole place'll come alive!"

"Oh, it's nothing but a fad," Goram said. "We're in the age of canals. Ever since the Erie in New York, every cracker barrel in every town in America's got its schemers and dreamers coming up with plans on how life'd improve if only they had a canal."

"It's true," McLeod insisted. "A thousand miles could be cut from the sea route if the ocean and the gulf were linked by a canal. The reefs are a graveyard. The damage done in one year would be enough to make a canal worthwhile."

"They tried it twenty years ago," Rufus Finch said sadly. "That's what encouraged me and Ida to come down and buy in here. Then they discovered there wasn't any port on the gulf side that'd be deep enough for a real harbor and they let the whole plan die. Too bad, though. Too bad."

"I have an idea." Clara hesitated as all faces turned to her. She put her hand on Harry's as if to reassure herself with his presence. Harry squeezed hers in return and Clara continued. "I mean, I'm new here, of course, and I'm sure you've all thought of every possibility, but . . . wouldn't a railroad be more efficient than a canal?" The laughter that greeted this suggestion told Clara more than she needed to know about its feasibility. She glanced at Harry and saw his eyes were wide with hurt for her.

"Nobody loves this place more'n me, Mrs. Reade," McLeod said. "But even I got to admit it: canals or no canals, the only people likely to come here"—he looked around the table with a sly smile—"is other fools like us."

"I hardly consider—," Harry began, but Clara interrupted.

"Why, though?" she demanded. "You said we had so much to offer."

"The whole state's got what we've got," McLeod explained. "There's orange groves all over the place. Why would the railroad need to lay tracks through fifty miles of hammock land just to get our oranges? Reade Beauties may be sweet, but they ain't that sweet."

Clara nodded and looked at Harry. "I believe Mr. McLeod has given it a lot more thought than we have."

McLeod shrugged. "I'm not much of a businessman—wouldn't be here if I was—but I do know a bad deal when I see one. And if I can see it, the railroad can certainly see it."

"It seems, though, that the expense of the canals would make them even less practical than the trains," Clara said. "And you'd still need to take everything to Key West," she added. "The railroad, though—"

Harry laughed. "My mother is a very stubborn woman, you see?" he said to McLeod.

"Why not just enjoy what's here, Mrs. Reade?" McLeod said. "This place is what it is and that's the way it's going to stay. It's why you came here, isn't it?"

Clara shrugged and looked away, but she thought no, it was not why she had come, not at all. Just a simple thing like the achievement of a wide expanse of tended lawn demonstrated that humanity need not be crushed by the power of the land but rather could work with the land, each bringing out the best in the other. That was the way the whole of America was going, and damn it, Clara knew that they could go the same way here. What was the use of sitting around, exclaiming over their good fortune, smug in the knowledge that so few knew the wonders they knew? What was the point in being complacent when with the effort that distinguished human beings from unthinking beasts—their will to know, to do, to be more, never satisfied, always striving to perfect themselves in God's eyes—they could take this wonderful place, attack it with imagination and plain hard work, and create from the wilderness a magical place? She turned to McLeod, but the sunlight had carved on his face an expression of such peaceful pleasure that Clara swallowed her words. There was time enough to tell him, for she knew that she would be here a good long time.

After dinner the company repaired to the porch of the Finches' house. Harry wanted to be alone to mull over all he'd heard said today and so strolled down to the bay. Cal Sparks drew an audience of some Goram kids and his own sons as he spun stories about pirates and treasure and the legendary galleons come to grief on the reefs. The kids perched on the railings to listen or sprawled on the porch steps, chewing on sugar cane and teasing each other with switch sticks. Ida and Flora served bananas and sapodillas on big woven straw mats. Farley Goram continued the great canal debate with McLeod while Rufus Finch doused the embers in his barbecue pit, then joined the men and lit his pipe so that the late afternoon air was scented with tobacco and eucalyptus.

After sunset there would be a magic lantern show and Rufus promised that Ida would play a few songs, though he apologized in advance to Clara for the condition of the piano. "I think the only right notes is between the keys." Clara and Ida sat together on the swing seat at the opposite end of the porch from the men. Flora Goram sat at their feet on a big pillow with her sewing on her lap, cross-stitching a fancy G on a mail-order kitchen towel. "In winter," Flora was saying, "the fireplace keeps the piano dry, but when it's damp like this and the keys stick, Ida keeps a little kerosene lamp lit under it and dries it out enough to play. Sometimes, though, she just puts in one of them old piano rolls and lets it play itself."

"I can cook a turtle steak in the time it takes a roll to play all the way through 'Afternoon of a Faun'!" It was the first thing Ida had said; Flora smiled up at her and patted her knee. Clara was surprised at the youthfulness of the voice, a girl's voice still, still full of enthusiasm.

The wind was up on the bay as afternoon waned, stirring up whitecaps that peaked and folded over each other in shades of blue and green and deep purple; it'll be a swift sail home, Clara thought. Home. "I have some music back at the house," she said. Ida turned her wide blue eyes to her. "Chopin. Brahms. Debussy. I'll bring them soon, I promise."

"Oh, Mrs. Reade!" she exclaimed and her eyes filled with tears.

"These church services is mostly our way of staying in touch with each other," Flora said as her fingers moved swiftly, piercing the surface of the cloth like a diving bird, "though we don't have 'em near often enough. So hard getting everybody together. Once a month is probably the most regular we are, and even then not everyone shows up. One thing and another conspires against us, it seems. Next month's the fish fry, though, and then the Easter egg hunt. Maybe a baptism soon too," she added and rested a hand on her belly.

Beside her, Clara heard Ida moan deep in her throat. As Clara was to find out, Ida's own firstborn died at birth and her second at two months, and her third never made it to term but ended Ida's chances for any more. Flora was saying, "We're the first settlement down here that really dug its heels in." She shook her head as if this satisfaction in their accomplishment might be misconstrued as pride or boasting. "We got roots here now, is what I mean." She looked at Ida and laughed. "Though when these hurricanes pay a call, we're about as rooted as a dandelion, isn't that right, Ida?"

Ida nodded slowly, uncertainly, hesitating as if deciding whether to speak, then sank back, silent.

"You know, Mrs. Reade," Flora said, "I never truly understood the meaning of saying grace before meals till I come here." She looked at her hands now, embarrassed. "Because I am truly thankful for the Lord's bounty." She raised her hand to shield her eyes from the glare of the sun on the bay. "Oh, it takes getting used to," she said. "The first month I was here I never took my bonnet off. Farley thought I was modest, but I just didn't have the heart to let him see me crying all the time." The other women nodded in silent understanding. "I used to have the most beautiful skin," Flora said. "I don't know when it went to leather, but no matter how you try, you can't stay out of the sun. And wait till spring! The horseflies are so bad we make pants out of fertilizer sacks for our mules!"

Amid the laughter that followed this remark, Rufus Finch joined them, squatting on his heels at Ida's side, his pipe clenched in his mouth, and placed a gentle hand on his wife's. "When I die, Ida," he said, and pointed to the gardens where the late afternoon sun burnished the flowers gold, "bury me right there."

Harry stood at the water's edge, secretly pleased to have been so easily accepted by this group and proud that he'd stated his opinions so firmly. Was this all it took to be a member of society? He was surprised at the ease with which these people simply sat in each other's presences, ate and laughed and argued even and drew strangers like him and his mother to them. His chest filled with air; life seemed so . . . possible here.

He heard his name and was startled out of his reverie; his mother was standing on the porch and calling for him to join her. Harry waved back, but he was content at that moment just to stand by himself. He could see now, moving back and forth across the space between the kitchen and the long table, with plates and platters balanced on her sturdy arms, the girl who'd given him the towel and served him during the meal. Maria Sparks, he thought, then said the name aloud to the bay as she disappeared inside the house. She had certainly been modest in her behavior, but Harry couldn't help noticing that every time he'd stolen a glance at her she was stealing a glance right back at him. He knew what that meant. She'd touched him too, that careless swipe of her apron, and he knew what that meant too. Oh, she was sly, he thought. He'd caught her little smile: she knew how that touch made him shiver. But he felt so on display here with everyone eating and talking and carrying on. He'd have to find a way to see her alone sometime.

There she was again, her hands adjusting her hair as she stood looking out at the bay from the bottom step that led to the kitchen door; she's looking at me, Harry thought, and she doesn't care who sees her. She'd taken off the apron, and with the setting sun at her back, Harry imagined that he could see through her lacy dress, but the illusion was created by its pale amber color that matched the color of her flesh. He shivered and felt a little giddy to think about her flesh.

Clara too was looking out toward the bay, watching her son. Cal Sparks started banging a spoon on a pot bottom and herding the whole group of them back behind the house to stand on the edge of the Finches' flower garden and watch the sky burn up red and orange. Ida ran across the field to the church, and soon they could hear her playing the piano, not a church song but the simple notes from a child's book of music studies, and so filled with feelings of sweetness and longing that Clara wanted to cry for joy. She looked at all the good people around her, hearts to the sun, faces glowing gold. Harry came to stand by her, slipped his hand into hers, and she thought that maybe they hadn't really missed the service after all.

6.

During the months that followed, McLeod began showing up regularly at the little settlement on the river, at first just to deliver special supplies he thought Clara and Harry might need—coffee, garden tools, yellow soap. When he ran out of things to bring he helped Edmund finish off the canoe, and when that was done he volunteered to give Harry pointers and a practiced hand on shoring up the dock and then reroofing the house, and then he took him upriver to find the right logs to turn into short beams to replace the rotting ones under the porch. McLeod and Harry didn't talk much—McLeod never did with men; Harry never did with anyone except Clara, and even then it was usually in response to things she said—but working side by side gave an ease and a focus to their silences, and they got to feel comfortable enough around each other to make unnecessary the exchange of more than the essential words. And if Harry was embarrassed about the way McLeod stared when Clara brought out a pitcher of lemonade, he was sensible enough to grin and shrug it off.

"Your mother's a fine woman, Harry," McLeod said one day in a voice husky with feeling. Harry was relieved that the subject had finally been broached and proud that McLeod had spoken to him as one man to another.

After a while McLeod began to be expected, and if more than a few weeks passed without a visit, it was peculiar and he was noticed as much for his absence. "Oh, Mistah McLeod, he travel," Edmund told Clara and opened his arms wide to indicate the river and the bay beyond and the sea out past the reefs. When he did show up finally, no one made anything special of it, though all were glad to see him. Clara affected nonchalance at his return but smiled to herself, surprised too that she could be so happy to see someone.

"What do you do otherwise, Mr. McLeod?" she asked him one day as he was packing his tools back into the *Newport* after a day on his knees hammering newly cut palm fronds onto the roof of her house. "I mean, besides doing favors for tourists like myself?"

McLeod laughed. "Well, I done a little of a lot of things. Because there's a whole lot of things to do and not a whole lot you can do about any one of 'em. So you start to spread yourself out. Let's see . . . I served in the county legislature and I ran the mail boat along the keys. I was the county treasurer once, only that didn't last 'cause no one's got much in the way of actual cash money. I been superintendent of the houses of refuge along the coast. Met some pretty interesting people that way. Desperate ones too. No money, no boat, no place to live, and nowhere to go back to. Sometimes it seemed to me like half the state's population started out wandering like that and just stopped here on account of being temporarily exhausted. Now, let's see . . . I been a customs inspector in Key West in the hardest of winters here on the bay. 'Course I'm a homesteader too, got some riverfront land and I raise what you could call exotics. I travel quite a lot to get new specimens too. Been to South America, Central America, Mexico, lots of places. I tried growing sponges once and sisal once and made guava jelly too. I'm not saying I ever made much of a success at any of these things, but it's right pure amazing how you don't have to be a success to live a good life down here." He took a deep breath, looked around him, and glanced at Clara as if he would point out each feature of the landscape that gave him pleasure. "Mainly I got the *Newport* and nothing gives me more satisfaction than riding the wind on her." Here

Clara saw him run his hand along the *Newport*'s tiller like a man caressing his beloved old dog. "Oh, we been through hell and high water together, we have," he added with a laugh.

"I was under the impression you were in business selling land for the Biscayne Bay Company."

McLeod nodded. "Yeah, supposed to be developing the area. Least that's what it says in the real estate prospectus of the company. Anybody over twenty-one's got the right to a homestead of a hundred and sixty acres." He shrugged and shook his head. "The tourists hardly ever come this way, 'cept for a fisherman every now and again. And I guess I'm not much of a salesman besides. There's not many sees any sort of a life for themselves in this wilderness."

"Why do you think that is, Mr. McLeod?" Clara asked. "Why are there so few people down here?"

"This is a hard life, Mrs. Reade. Me and the folks at Palm Grove and the people who're eking out the barest kind of living on those god-forsaken keys, we're all plain people. Most of us come from somewhere we'd like to forget maybe. Poor, most of us, come down here with nothing but wanting a chance at life. A chance to live on the land, to be somewhere no one was before. But most people looking for the simple life go west. Oh, a family might come down here if they had a coupla bad winters up north. But making a living off the land here's no picnic neither. Most of 'em take one look at their plantings after a heavy rain and're packed up and gone by morning. The isolation gets to 'em too, makes 'em leave. Especially the women." He essayed a quick look up at her, then turned his eyes back to the bay. "All alone all day, while their husbands or brothers or sons is catching fish on the bay or stalking game in the hammock or tending to coontie starch mills. There are stories of some who lost their senses, so long and far away from civilization. Poor Edwina Sparks—you met her mister and kids—she just up and wandered off one day and drowned herself in a pool of shallow water. Like Ophelia, with fig vines wrapped around her ankles. Another woman shot her brother, then herself, when he refused to take her back up north."

"Are you trying to frighten me, Mr. McLeod?"

He looked at her again. "You don't seem like the type gets frightened easy."

Clara shook her head. "I don't want to give you the wrong impression," she said. "I'm scared, all right. I'm just not going to let that stop me from doing what I want to do."

McLeod nodded. "A handful of determined souls always stays on. They're the ones who take to the heat, who find it's their natural climate somehow. Like they know instinctively that it's right for them, that they'll thrive in it like nowhere else." Clara was nodding as he spoke, thinking that it was she and Harry he was describing. "They don't mind the insects neither, or the snakes or the panthers or the alligators, and they'll cope with the hardships of farming this land for the advantages of blue skies and waters teeming with fish and no dust in the air or soot or mud even after a rain. And a golden yellow sun and groves that drop the Lord's bounty at their feet." He looked at Clara and laughed. "I been going on some, I guess." Clara laughed with him, and when their eyes met they stopped laughing and there was only the sound of the wind filling the sails of the *Newport*. McLeod cleared his throat. "If you're going to stay here, Mrs. Reade, I better teach you how to sail."

Though neither of them acknowledged it, Clara and McLeod were both aware that a shift had occurred in their relationship. Clara could see he no longer thought of her as a tourist out to soak up local color with one of the native characters. McLeod could see she had dropped her view of him as disapproving and overly protective of the area. Both felt that to give voice to these mutual perceptions would add a note of self-consciousness that would only inhibit their growing pleasure in each other. Until now, McLeod had not the courage or the will to open his heart to another woman and the baggage of this reluctance was the sorrow that people perceived in him. As for Clara, she felt on the verge of the transformation she had so longed for in her marriage and had been reconciled, until now, to never achieving.

In the next few weeks of sailing on the bay, McLeod showed Clara how to hold the tiller and how to come about, how to tack into the wind and what to do when there was no wind at all. He showed her the place in the bay where you could dip a tin pail and come up with fresh water from an underground spring.

"Rufus and Ida Finch think it's what Ponce de León never found when he was looking for the Fountain of Youth," McLeod said.

He taught her how to hang a fish line over the side and how to use a long-handled scoop to catch green turtles and loggerheads and crawfish and how to use a few native spices to cook up a meaty stew. He took her to the freshwater mollusk beds and the hidden coral reefs and the most fertile fields of turtle eggs.

The *Newport,* which McLeod had designed and built himself—and which was as much an extension of the man as Clara had ever known any inanimate object to be—was fine for sailing on the bay, but for navigating the river waters, he'd designed and built a bugeye canoe with an almost flat bottom and a hard turn to the bilge that made Clara feel like they were floating above the surface of the water. "Practically no drag at all to her," McLeod said proudly. "A bigger boat'd stir up the bottom and probably get stuck in the shallows."

"Even with someone as experienced as you?" she asked.

McLeod smiled at the flattery. He picked up the paddle, jumped in after Clara, and the boat slid out into the water. As always there was on this outing the unspoken, the ineffable, inevitable sense of drifting toward some end to which neither could attach a name.

The canoe glided in silence but for the rustling of the wind in the high canopy above them. The water was very clear; Clara could see ribbons of rainbow fish darting ahead as if they would lead the boat deeper into the mysteries. The mangroves' twisted roots reached out into the stream like grasping fingers. A sudden coolness descended on her shoulders as the stream narrowed and the banks closed in to let a curtain of shade drop down on them.

McLeod dragged the paddle of the canoe against the direction of their motion and edged them into what looked at first to Clara like an impenetrable wall of mangrove, unrelievedly green except for a distant cluster of trees where large birds rested, one tree overloaded and drooping with brown pelicans as if the birds were some exotic fruit. A narrow opening appeared and the canoe moved easily through the wall of foliage; immediately they crossed from dappled sunlight into deep shade. At first the sensation was like a spectral gloom, quiet, chilly, devoid of life, but Clara, watching closely, saw that the tangled roots and tree trunks rising from the water were actually teeming with activity. Tiny black crabs the size of tarantulas scuttled in small groups up and down the trunks and the branches that shot above the canoe. The sight chilled her under her skin, a feeling she knew had little to

do with being cold and everything to do with a fascination and revulsion that was deeply physical. She stared at McLeod, at the fine lines
of his profile etched against the deep, lush foliage, and smiled uncertainly when he caught her at it. She turned away and cleared her
throat; she wanted to sing with the odd, tactile excitement.

Ahead of them was an area of intense light. McLeod nosed the canoe
toward it, and they moved into a secluded, brackish lake surrounded
completely by mangrove. Alligators slithered by half submerged, in
total, malevolent silence. The water was no longer clear, despite the
clear sky above, but muddy; a film of black silt remained on Clara's
palm when she ran her hand through it. Awed by the silence, she had
to give words to her feelings so as not to succumb, fainting, screaming,
swooning from the headiness of the spell. "I want to . . . to wrap my
arms around it. I want to . . . to be inside it, to . . ." She stopped, laughing. "Oh, Quentin, this place is so . . . so . . ."

"I know," he said simply.

She looked at him shyly, reluctant to meet his gaze now for she felt
naked, her feelings on display. "You do, don't you?"

"I felt the same way my first time out, Clara," he said, and flashed
a grin she had never seen before; she could imagine him at eight years
old grinning the same way. They said nothing more but listened to
the wondrous myriad din of sounds around them.

By the time McLeod got them back to the river and onto the *Newport,*
the sun was setting. The sky was layered in yellow and purple, the air
still and warm. Once darkness set in, a flock of mosquitoes joined on
as passengers; McLeod lit a few smoke pots and placed them in a loose
circle around himself and Clara. Clara could hear the faint buzz and
see the mosquitoes in the smoky flames. Water lapped gently at the
boat; the breeze had all but died. Clara felt warm and contained in
the circle of dusky lights. A gull cried in the distance, a sound of
sadness and longing. McLeod's face came in and out of the light. And
now she felt her own grow hot.

"The smoke bothering your eyes, Clara?" he asked. "I can put 'em
out, but the mosquito netting's full of holes."

She wiped her face with her handkerchief and brushed her hair
away. "I'm fine," she said. She looked from McLeod to the denseness
at the riverbank. "I never had the time or the courage before to think
of all this as real. It was too painful when I was back in Middleton and

knew I couldn't have it. Harry and I would make a game of pretending to be here, pretending . . . I never slept so well in my life as when I came here in my dreams. What peace . . . Oh, and now I just . . ." She wanted to take it all in, to hold the joy to her breast. She had crossed the bridge from one life to another, from one way of being to a new way. She was liberated from the chains of her past; she felt free and strong and alive.

To McLeod she looked inspired, nearly transformed. He'd seen that expression on a few others who'd come here—the Finches had it and Calvin Sparks—people who despite everything never found it in their hearts to leave. He was one of those people himself. No matter what the river had taken from him, he was caught by it.

"No regrets?"

Clara shook her head. "There was no life for me left in Middleton. My husband . . . It was . . . it was his life."

McLeod, sensing the welling up of feeling in both of them, did not trust his own words but dug into the canvas bag he'd tossed on the floor of the boat and pulled out a much-thumbed book of essays by Ralph Waldo Emerson. It fell open to a page; he leaned into the smoky light to read.

"At the gates of the forest, the surprised man of the world is forced to leave his city estimates of great and small, wise and foolish—the knapsack of custom falls off his back with the first step he takes into these precincts . . . the incommunicable trees begin to persuade us to live with them, and quit our solemn trifles. . . . How easily we might walk onward into the opening landscape, absorbed by new pictures and thoughts fast succeeding each other, until by degrees the recollection of home was crowded out of mind, all memory obliterated by the tyranny of the present, and we were led in triumph by Nature."

Clara hardly heard the words he'd said, but the sound of his voice reached her like vapors, penetrating her, spreading out inside her until she tingled with the sense of him. She watched his fingers fiddling with the book, touching the letters of the page as if there was a talismanic power to them. His fingers were long and bony, freckled, with large, wide, squared-off nails. There was a scar on the back of his left hand that gleamed white in the light; imagining the wound and the blood gave her a chilled sensation in the small of her back. She reached out and ran her fingers across the scar. He put the book down in his lap; she looked up into his face just as he turned to her.

Her breath caught in her throat when his fingers closed over hers. Their eyes met and each saw in the other's a frankness, an openness that Clara had longed for all her life, that McLeod had despaired of ever finding again.

He stood and leaned forward slowly, slowly. A lick of his white-blond hair fell over his forehead and touched her first. Clara felt the heat of him before he pressed his lips to hers. She wanted to cry out with the joy of it. So right! So free! It was the first kiss of her life that invited her natural response. His mouth on hers was demanding; she gasped with the sharp touch of teeth, yet the softness of his lips lulled her. A small sound escaped his throat. Her hands, guided by desire to know him, were in his hair, on the thick column of his neck, on his shoulders and the round hardness of his arms.

McLeod drew her in; she fell easily, gladly against him, his body pliant yet strong. His breath was the earth, cinnamon and brine. He knew just what to say, just where to run those bony fingers, and how long to touch her here to make her shiver, there to make her burn; and how much to be silent and how much to whisper her name, as if he had crept unseen into her most secret midnight longings and now lay the bounty of his knowledge at her feet.

His lips were at her ear. "Oh, Clara, your skin," nuzzling her neck, in her hair ... "Clara, your smell ..." His hands, those wonderful fingers were everywhere. Here, she thought, here, and as he moved into her, whispering, she clung to him with a ferocity she had not imagined herself capable of.

She was losing herself, flowing into him, adjusting to the curves and planes of him, sliding against him, his legs holding, hers releasing as she opened to him, thrashing against him, accepting, then demanding, unashamed.

All around them was the dark voice of the river, a whispering rush, a murmuring, welcoming undertone, an accompaniment to their love-making. The first time, she thought in a kind of exaltation. The final transformation she had sought and despaired ever of finding was hers at last.

Later, when the moon had risen and hung above them a creamy gardenia white half-hidden by smoky clouds, she lay in his embrace, drifting, floating, unable to distinguish between the rise and fall of his chest and the shifting of the boat in the current as the river flowed toward the bay. With her eyes closed, there was no difference: man, river, bay, all were the same.

"Clara," he said, his lips at her ear.

Clara shivered and burrowed closer. "What?"

"I like saying your name."

The water around them was suddenly disturbed by tinkling splashes. Clara got to her knees and looked over the side to see a flurry of tiny minnows shattering the moon's reflection. There followed sharp, liquid tearing sounds as several foot-long tarpons leaped from the water in eel-like pursuit. After that there was silence but for the buzz of insects above them and the distant call of a loon. The clouds parted for the moon and the silver shadow of a royal palm fell across the boat.

"I don't know how we did it," McLeod said, "but we've stumbled into Paradise here."

"I know," Clara said and turned to look at the shore. "Somehow it doesn't seem fair. When I think of all those people in Middleton . . . *This* is where a thriving little city ought to be. Can't you see white houses with wide verandas right along the river? And all of them surrounded by grassy lawns and flower gardens and gorgeous shade trees. A main street ending in a park along the bay. A promenade along the river. Sunset Walk, how does that sound?"

"Now you're dreaming, Clara," McLeod said and extended his hand to her. "Come back here and dream with me."

She turned to him and took his hand. "I'm going to sell everything in Middleton," she said, thrilling to the sound of the phrase, at how right and natural it felt, as if it'd been waiting all along to be said by her. "I'm going to buy orange groves and hammock land and bayfront and riverfront. I'm going to buy Fort Dallas too, and start up—"

McLeod laughed. "All right, all right," he said and pulled her down to him, looking at her as if not quite believing that this woman, whom he'd thought he had pegged so accurately when she first arrived, had turned out to be so different and so much to his liking. "It's been a long time since I felt anything like this, Clara."

"It's the same for me, Quentin," she replied.

"I'm so damn proud of it," he said. "If there was a newspaper, I'd run a story." He laughed. "Maybe I'll just put messages in bottles and toss 'em in the bay. I want to tell folks, I want to brag about it!"

Clara was laughing now too. "Don't."

McLeod laughed. "OK. No bragging. I'll be a perfect Southern gentleman."

Clara shook her head. "I mean ..." She hesitated, not realizing until this moment that she felt this way. "I don't want anyone to know at all."

McLeod moved closer. "Secret lovers, hmm?" He bent and put his lips to her hand.

Clara touched his beautiful hair. "Quentin ..."

He didn't look up. "Mmm?"

"My whole life in Middleton, my whole marriage, all I was was Mrs. Cameron Reade. I doubt more than half a dozen women acquaintances ever even called me by my first name. I was my husband's wife and nothing else, and everything I did and said, everywhere I went, everyone I saw and spoke to was defined by what he needed me to do and be. Even what I looked like was ordained by him. You saw me the day I got here. That was Mrs. Cameron Reade. Do I look like the same woman?"

McLeod appraised her with mock seriousness. "Distant cousin, maybe, on the side of the family with the good looks and the stubborn streak."

Clara sat up straight. "I'm not going to be thought of anymore as anyone's anyone. I mean, I won't have people down here think of me as McLeod's woman."

His voice was tight when he replied, "Aren't you?"

"I love you, Quentin," she said simply. "But I'm going to buy land and I'm going to make things happen here. I'm going to build new roads and get the Reade Groves going again. I'm going to start a town, and I'm going to bring in the railroad to help me do it, you see if I don't. But not as anyone's woman. As myself. As Clara Reade."

McLeod drew her to him and quieted her with a kiss. After a moment Clara pulled back.

"Did you hear me?"

"I heard 'I love you, Quentin,' then I went stone deaf." His lips were on hers again, and in a moment she was in his arms and he was breathing in the smell of gardenia in her hair and they were whispering each other's names again and again and again.

Later, in the darkness, each of McLeod's homeward paddle strokes stirred up liquid fire as the moon was reflected and shattered in the still, dark water. Clara was laughing, running her hand in the water and tossing bright sparks of moonlight in the air.

She had begun to make her mark.

Harry and Clara stood in the middle of a long row of orange trees. All around them, in stacks as high as Harry's shoulder, were the boxes he'd ordered from Key West, but the oranges in the Reade Groves had ripened, then overripened and dropped to the ground; there was no need for boxes now. The smell, only a few weeks ago the perfume of heaven, was now an acidic, overpowering stench. Harry shaded his eyes from the sun and turned a slow hundred and eighty degrees; the same sight met him at every angle.

"To say that we miscalculated is an understatement of immense proportions."

What fruit still hung on the trees was a deep, dull, lifeless brown, the skin withered and dry. Harry pierced one with a small penknife, and the juice did not so much squirt out as leak and run down his hands. He licked his fingers of it; the taste was bitter. As they walked along the row to survey the full extent of the disaster, the ground, was so littered with fruit that with each step they crushed another one, the skins splitting open and spewing the spoiled pulp on the ground.

"There must be something to do to get them out before this happens again," Clara said. "I won't believe their fate is just to rot here on the ground."

"Next year," Harry said. "We'll have to learn how to plant and tend and harvest. Dr. Tiger says—"

"Oh, Dr. Tiger, Dr. Tiger! With all his supposed knowledge, he couldn't prevent this from happening, could he?"

Harry shook his head. "He warned me. He said that without a road to get this crop out . . ." He took another sweeping look at the devastation. "We'll be able to sell some in Key West at least, and if that's as far as it gets before . . ." He shook his head. "Of course first we'll have to put in a road to the river from here. That'll save a full day of transporting them. Still . . ."

Clara took his arm. "I hate to see you put so much work into this with so little promise of a return."

Harry shrugged. "Oranges, oranges everywhere . . ." He laughed lightly. "First thing to do is clear these away. Then we start on next year's crop."

Citrus growing in southern Florida, as Harry discovered, was a lost art; all the knowledge acquired by the planters in the early part of the century had died with them and had to be rediscovered by the new arrivals. When he went looking for it over the next few months, Harry found there was certainly no shortage of available advice, but what one man told him another contradicted, and a third took him down a different path altogether.

"Fertilizer and plenty of it," Sparks told him.

"Fertilizer!" Goram exclaimed. "That is certain death to the trees."

A Pensacola grower passing through the area on McLeod's boat showed him how to grub a new field before laying out the grove. When he went home, Dr. Tiger told Harry to burn off the old trees and use them as fertilizer.

Harry tried a bit of each suggested method on different parts of the grove and bought some new root stock from the Van Lieu Groves in Pineland, where an experimental station had been set up. Hundreds of varieties of exotic plants were being tested there, some in a hothouse built on a rise overlooking the bay, others in the grove itself. McLeod had supplied many of the plants and seedlings from his scouting trips across Latin America. He had found pineapples in the Andes, and Van Lieu was growing them in sand. He had also brought back Mexican chayote, Cuban mamey, West Indian malanga, and Guatemalan ate-moya. Van Lieu even had a still for extracting perfume from flowers. "Best protection for young trees is seaweed," Van Lieu told him. "Keeps animals off, puts nutrients in."

Harry reported his findings in detail to Clara. "The thing is, even Van Lieu can't help but admit that no matter how successful his experiments are, he has the same basic problem as every other fruit grower down here. How do we get the stuff out before it all goes bad?"

Dear Mr. Wheeler,
      It is my intention with this letter to entice you to bring your railroad to the Miami River. I can think of no plainer way to say it.
      Of advantages to my proposal there are many. Please allow me to

enumerate: a climate whose range extends from temperate to warm, with rainfall enough to keep the area ablaze with flowers and the crops healthy yet not so much that the human population suffers; a hammock land rich in mahogany and ironwood trees; fruit groves in abundance; a river of beauty that is also a passage into the interior; legendary Biscayne Bay, whose supply of food fish is enormous, and of which they say that Ponce de León did not merely seek the Fountain of Youth here but found it in a freshwater spring bubbling up in its middle. The natural resources of the bay area include orange and lime trees plus many exotic fruits that would do well to be exported. Life here is pleasant, invigorating, and plainly beneficial to one's physical well-being as well as to one's sense of the rightness of nature's balance. But in order for the area to grow and its resources to develop, we need the railroad to bring our crops to market. Boats cannot do this fast enough to prevent spoilage, but the railroad can.

As a businessman I am sure you can see the sense in my proposal. It is a distance of fifty miles from Palm Beach to the Miami River. There are many thousands of acres of land available for purchase and development, which would be offered to you at well below the current rates.

Please take the time to consider well the potential of this situation. In addition, I would recommend a visit to the area, for which I offer myself as your guide. Until I hear your answer, I remain very hopeful and

> Very truly yours,
> Clara Reade

She sent it and she waited. She told no one she had written the letter, not Harry, whose plans for the orange grove had been battered once already, and not McLeod either, who had warned her not to invest either her money, her time, or her hopes in this dream.

But her hopes ran high nevertheless, and the keeping of the secret put an exhilarating edge of expectancy to her days. Until it was proved otherwise, there was the very real possibility that F. Morrison Wheeler of the Florida Eastern Star Railway Line would come through.

The mail was not delivered every morning as it was in Middleton; one round-trip by the barefoot mailman was made twice a month between Jupiter and the bay, and even that was not expected with any real regularity. While she worked in the garden or when she was on the *Newport* on the bay with McLeod, Clara's eye was peeled for Asa

Hamill's arrival with a corn sack of mail and small dry goods items draped across his back.

F. Morrison Wheeler did not respond to her letter immediately, as Clara hoped he would, and as the weeks went by and then the months, she tried to see his lack of response as a good sign. He's considering it, she reasoned. A man in that position can't make a decision like that without giving it a lot of thought. He has advisors too, no doubt, and they've got to approve it. The more Harry worked in the groves, the stronger her hopes grew.

She was alone in the kitchen, rolling pastry dough from the Gorams' arrowroot starch mill, the day the response finally came. Harry was at the grove, Edmund and Geneva gone visiting his folks in Pineland. Wiping her hands on her apron, she ran out to meet Asa Hamill and waited with her usual impatience as he unpacked his sack so Clara could make her purchases from the stock of water biscuits, coffee, matches, and tinware. It was only then that he gave her the letter.

"Important business, Miz Reade?"

Clara saw the initials F. M. W. in the corner of the envelope. "Could be," she said.

Hamill repacked his sack and trudged off upriver, where he would cross the Arch Creek Bridge to the south bank. Clara walked slowly back to the porch and sat down in the wicker rocker, arranged her skirt, and ran a hand over her hair, conscious of making a kind of ceremony of the opening. She weighed the letter in her hand. Good heavy paper, she thought, tore open the envelope, unfolded the letter, and read it.

Then she read it again, refolded it, and replaced it in its envelope. "My dear Mrs. Reade," he had written. "I have no intention of bringing my railroad to nowhere." She stood up and looked around at the yard, the bay, at the lush jungle around her. Something's got to change around here, she thought. She was not about to sit by and watch Harry's heart be broken by another crop ripening on the vine and no means of transporting it out.

What would make Wheeler come here? What would make him think this place was somewhere?

7.

Until he was thirty years old, Frederick Morrison Wheeler used variations on his name that suited his current station in life: he'd been Freddie as a boy, the slangy familiarity hateful and demeaning to his early sense of dignity, especially when spoken by anyone but his revered mother; Frederick M. Wheeler as a junior clerk in his uncle's hardware business; Fred Wheeler as a land speculator during the Gold Rush of '49 and '50; F. M. Wheeler when he parlayed his land holdings into a modest fortune in crude oil; and finally F. Morrison Wheeler for his partnership in the steel manufacturing plant that made him his first millions. It was as F. Morrison Wheeler that he became familiar to newspaper readers across the country and to editors, who learned very quickly what a misplaced initial meant to their advertising pages. And nobody—not even those particular females who might whisper it in his ear—was ever again permitted to call him Freddie.

As a boy he stood beneath the trestle that spanned twin peaks in Stone Ridge, New York, at the end of a long day of chores, the setting sun shooting through the iron fretwork above and illuminating the pinched, suspicious features of a child who had grown up with a heavy dose of fundamentalist religion and a vaunted sense of responsibility to his widowed mother and her sisters; he ever after had a soft spot for women in need. He would wait patiently—"Genius is nothing but a greater aptitude for patience" was a sampler that hung on the parlor wall—for the Ohio, Boston and Allegheny to round the bend out of Cripple Creek chugging, belching smoke, powerful, barreling toward him, the wheat fields on either side bent back by its winds, the smell of oil and tar the headiest of perfumes. Oh, the clattering roar! The boy Freddie stood up tall to it, his thin chest puffed with pride: "It cuts 'cross our very own fields, Ma!" The wind whirled around him as the O, B and A sped by eastward-bound, and for those few moments the narrow face, dour as an old minister's, would be transformed to that of a nine-year-old boy touched by the magic of the future. It was never the land that made him wonder about God's graces; it was the railroad.

But like many timid, hardworking young souls, he did not permit himself to follow his dreams. A case could even be put forth that he had none, but more likely the grind and boredom of his daily life wore down his imagination at a very early age. And as he grew to manhood, ambition and unquestioning allegiance to the work ethic took its place. Added to those qualities were a nose for opportunity and a singular lack of sentimentality, so that the F. Morrison Wheeler that emerged in his final incarnation was the personification of the American business tycoon who made his way to the top without benefit of friend, charm, or love.

The pinched features of his childhood, often a source of mockery by his elders—"born old" was the kindest jibe and the most accurate— metamorphosed by twenty into a scholarly mien, though Wheeler had little use for study of anything not directly applicable to the work at hand. At forty his face had changed but little; never having appeared young, he bridged middle age with little apparent alteration. But the death of his only son and the consequent mental disintegration of the wife whose youthful beauty had produced in him the feelings closest to tenderness he was ever to know made their mark.

He took the once-beloved, once-beautiful wife south to Florida; illness had turned her haggard and shrewish, and he often stared at her, puzzled, as if trying to find in the hag the girl he'd married. He retired from the steel manufacturing business, severing all business relationships save the one with his banker. There was a slight stoop to his posture now; his still-full head of hair had gone white. He grew an elaborate mustache that added heft and expansiveness to his face, so that by his late fifties he had acquired an unexpected physical appeal characterized by gravity and calm.

He built winter homes in St. Augustine and Jacksonville, lastly in Palm Beach, in the late 1880s a burgeoning mecca for the ill and infirm; while his wife alternately languished under the care of doctors and private nurses and socialized with Vanderbilts, Carnegies, and Duveens, who had also made the city their winter quarters, he took long solitary walks along the beaches to ponder the meaning of his life and wonder how he had come to inhabit a world he had had no part in creating. He could find no answer, not in the wonders of sea or sky or stars; once again, God's grace left him empty. He was bored without work; he seethed with resentment and envied younger men their futures.

But salvation was to come in the form of an epiphany. Even years later, when all that he had envisioned that day had come to pass, he was still not sure that it had not all been a figment of a long-dormant imagination come finally to his rescue. He had been walking on the deserted beach near sunset, the blue of the day slowly draining of color, when he came upon a boy he had never seen before, a boy whose narrow, pinched features bore the familiar innocence of a bygone generation. The boy was staring out to sea; the sea was still. From nowhere, it seemed, but the very air itself, a flock of white gulls appeared in the sky, shrieking and flapping in a cloud. The boy lifted his head and the milky, translucent gray of the early evening sky illuminated the small features, and on the face of this boy as he looked at the gulls was an expression of such transcendent hope, of such rapturous joy, that F. Morrison Wheeler was pitched back in time, struck at that moment with an inward glimpse of the boy he had been himself, whose own face had lit up with hope and wonder at the sight and smell and power of the Adirondack and Ohio crossing the Esopus River bearing stones bound for the streets of New York City and a tiny spark was set off in a place deep inside the man that, for want of a better word, he called his heart.

"Buy a railroad?" His wife was swathed in white gauze, soaking in a bath of goat's milk and honey to soothe her nerves. "Buy me my health instead. Hand me my medicine, Fred. Don't look so put upon! Wait! Don't be angry. Don't leave me."

The response from Parker Wadell, president of the First National Bank of Chicago and Wheeler's personal advisor, though less emotional, was no less skeptical. "There's no money in the whole state of Florida," he said. Wadell had made the trip south to Palm Beach at the request of his most important client, and how he hated the heat! Now that the point of his journey had been revealed to him, he could not help but lean back from his host's dining table and laugh at the outrageous impracticality of it. "Don't know how you stand this damn heat besides." He brushed a mosquito from his face. "What is this place anyway but an elephant burial ground for human beings? You plan on transporting corpses up north?"

"The tourist industry is in the bud stage," Wheeler said patiently. "It's the latest craze for Eastern society to come here to escape the winter. It's always warm here in Palm Beach. And where the Astors go the Joneses are sure to follow. Why my wife's canasta cronies alone could keep the tracks vibrating."

Wadell turned his considerable bulk to face the emptiness of the beach stretching outside the long French doors of the dining room. "Just pitch their tents on the sand, I suppose."

Wheeler laughed; it was the first time in their long association that the banker had heard this sound and the startled man described it later to his wife as being as high-pitched as a dog's bark. "This coast will be the American Riviera, mark my words."

"See that in your crystal ball, Mr. Wheeler? Now what do you know about the Riviera, anyway? Why you're the most American man I know."

"I've taken the Grand Tour," Wheeler said in his defense.

Wadell lit a cigar. "Only for what you could buy, pack in crates, and bring back with you."

Wheeler rose and strode to the French windows, hands clasped behind his back, fingers lacing and unlacing. "I don't need your approval to do what I'm going to do," he said and the firmness in his voice reminded Parker Wadell exactly with whom he was dealing.

Cowed, Wadell added hastily, "I simply don't want to see you making a bad investment."

Wheeler nodded. "I appreciate that, but my mind is made up. Start drawing up the papers. I want to incorporate as the Florida Eastern Star." Wadell noticed a strange expression flit across the man's usually dour face when he said this. Wheeler then unfurled a map of the United States on the table. "Florida's the forgotten frontier, don't you see?" The banker stood up dutifully and nodded. "Twenty years ago the golden spike joined east and west by rail, and still the only way to get down the east coast of Florida is by steamer. Look." Wadell observed Wheeler's finger trace along a spidery black line. "This is the route of the Jacksonville, St. Augustine and Halifax River Railway. Write that down. Buy it in the name of the new corporation. And buy these too,"—he ran a finger along two more black lines—"the Florida Coast and Gulf Railway, and the St. Johns and Indian River Line."

The banker nodded, no longer outwardly doubtful. "One other thing," Wheeler said and waited until Wadell stopped making notes. "I want you to move down here permanently."

Wadell stared for a moment and calculated quickly; each moment of hesitation cost him more of Wheeler's confidence. He drew a deep breath and acquiesced. As instructed, he drew up incorporation papers and bought up the lines. Within two years the Florida Eastern Star was endorsing checks to cover material costs and land purchases as Wheeler, unsatisfied with mere acquisition, began laying tracks for his own line south: to Daytona, to Smyrna, to Cocoa and Eau Gallie. In another year eighty miles of Florida Eastern Star Lines were constructed and put into use. People all over the state wrote to him asking that he bring the rail lines to their settlement or their orange grove or their bean farm, but he brought the line no farther south than Palm Beach, where he built a forty-room house on the beach and stocked it with what his critics called "European trash."

The health of his wife noticeably improved when she could exert her identity in the exercise of material consumption. "We must set an example," she told her husband, and though her frequent bouts of despondency kept her from becoming the doyenne of Palm Beach social life, his buying power was often solace enough. With his blessings and a bottomless bank balance, she was able to install in her dining room the carved mahogany doors of the Abbey St. Jauvin, affix to her boudoir wall Empress Josephine's silk moiré panels, add to the library the leatherbound first-edition sets of Thackeray and Fielding and Defoe from Simmons and Sons of Jermyn Street, and improve the quality of light in the portrait gallery—ancestors bought by the yard from a warehouse in Pigalle—with the stained-glass windows from a cathedral in Montreux.

When she was done, Wheeler commissioned society architect Carlisle de Beaupré to design the Embarcadero Hotel, so that the society tourists had the proper accommodations, and to lay out the streets for West Palm Beach, so that their servants had a nice place too.

The town filled up quickly with the American newly rich: copper barons, ironmasters, gold miners, stock brokers, public utilities operators, realty speculators, Civil War profiteers. Many of those who came to winter at the Embarcadero stayed on, and the town soon saw the laying out of avenues and the construction of mansions that were warm-weather equivalents of the ones in Boston, Philadelphia, and New York. The taste of these arrivistes was as raw as their money was new; their aesthetic sense was most accurately defined as lavish excess. Architects were encouraged to mix classical styles in the hope of coming up with something "American," but with no tradition to give focus to their work, bombastic mutations sprang up along Worth Avenue and the beach: Romanesque villas with Elizabethan details, Tudor mansions with Gothic spires, Queen Anne colonials with Italianate stone carvings.

Successful as the tourist industry was—only in the intense heat of mid-summer was a vacant suite to be had at the Embarcadero and Wheeler actually decided to close the hotel for July and August— visitors only could not possibly keep the railroad running at a profit. And though imagination was at the root of the railroad as an idea, finance was at its core in reality.

"The railroad is still the key to financial success here," he told Parker Wadell, who had grown tan and even fatter with southern living.

Wadell slapped a mosquito; he loved Palm Beach, but he'd never get used to these bugs. "You sure it's not insect repellent?"

Wheeler ignored him. "And the future of the state is in the development of crops most suited to shipping. I've hired botanical and horticultural experts to determine exactly which varieties of which fruits and vegetables are best adapted to be grown here." He looked up at Wadell now, his eyes shining with excitement. "Once the results are in, we'll start laying new tracks to suit the crops, start up new towns along the routes."

And in this way a bunch of one-store towns sprang up: Carlisle, St. Mary's River, Halley's Junction, Pineland City, shipping points that barely existed before, now flourishing so that all even the most modest truck farmer had to do was bring his crop to the depot to see his lemons and citrons and scarlet plums turn a handy profit. Wheeler's vision was coming to pass: he was changing the face of the state.

"There's simply no end to it," he told Wadell. "Simply no end in sight."

Much later, he was to recall that the first inkling of the disaster came from his wife. He had been working late in his study that night, observed from on high by busts of a half-dozen anonymous Greeks and Romans, fortified by shots of brandy that kept his ears burning and gave a glow of impending triumph to the latest purchase of a vast orange grove near Lake Okeechobee whose output promised to put the Florida Eastern Star completely in the black. A cold draft whipped across his face; he looked up and saw his wife wafting toward him out of the darkness at the far end of the study, barefoot, wraithlike in her white nightdress. He found himself in a rage at the very sight of her, as he often did when she was distressed and weeping.

"What is it?" he asked as she approached his desk. Tears streamed down her face; her lips were bitten raw. "Isn't the nurse . . . ?"

She shook her head, her hair in disarray, and stumbled toward him. He knocked over his chair as he stood up and backed away. Cold white fingers gripped his arm and she fell against him, pressing her cheek to his chest. "Hold me," she pleaded in a desperate whisper.

"What's the matter with you? Why aren't you in bed?"

"I'm freezing," she said.

"Nonsense."

Yet she was trembling; the cold of her skin came through his shirt. About to deny again her unfounded fears, he noticed the cold himself in his fingertips, his feet, his legs, across his shoulders. He turned to the windows only to see that they were already closed. But this was quite a different cold than a Palm Beach evening chill; this felt . . . northern.

The fire had died in the fireplace. His wife was moaning; it was unbearable. He tried to push her away from him, but . . . No, it was not she who was moaning. The sound was coming from outside. He opened the windows—My God, he thought, it *is* freezing!—and heard, deep in the distance, the lowing sound of conch shells being blown. Something was very wrong.

His wife pressed herself to his back. "I'm freezing," she said again.

He wrapped her in blankets and rang for the nurse, who came with his wife's evening dose of laudanum. The air outside was as crisp and black as December on the banks of the Esopus River. The conch shells were blowing regularly now, their sound as mournful as bells that tolled for death. And the temperature was still dropping. He called for a carriage to take him to his newly purchased orange groves, hoping that his own impression of the cold was exaggerated. This was Palm Beach, after all. It was always warm here.

But bundled in a woolen lap robe, he shivered all through the ride, trying not to think of the cold and what it meant. The plaintive wails of the conch shells set his nerves on edge. His mind leapt ahead: "Disaster," he muttered and recoiled in surprise as his words became mist in front of him.

He shifted position to look out the carriage window; clouds loomed ominously over a moonless landscape. Men moved all along the outer rows of the groves lighting smudge pots against the cold, tossing tarpaulins and gunny sacks over smaller trees and weighting them at their bases with rocks, while women scurried back and forth with steaming pots of coffee. The scene had the silent, frantic atmosphere of a medieval night of plague.

Suddenly the silence was shattered by the sound of gunshots from behind them and from the sides, first scattered and random, then building to a barrage. Wheeler beat on the front of the carriage. "Stop! Stop!" he cried to his driver.

The driver tied the skittish horses to the trunk of an oak tree and came around to peer in Wheeler's window. The great man's scared stiff, he thought.

"What's the gunfire?" Wheeler demanded.

The driver looked around and shrugged. For the first time in a long time he was not envious of men who owned things; he, at least, could not be ruined. "Not gunfire, sir," he replied.

"What then?"

"It's the trees 'emselves," he said. "The rising sap in 'em's freezing, see? Then they swell up and pop open. Explode like."

Wheeler stared as if the driver had spoken a language he did not understand, then fell back inside the carriage, trembling now from more than the cold. "Let's go on," he managed to say.

They continued riding into the groves, the sharp popping sounds coming from all sides. Wheeler stared ahead at the wall of the carriage, unable to wrap his mind around the enormity of what was happening. A few miles on he knocked again for the driver to stop and stepped out of the carriage. It was dark at this outer reach of the grove; the popping sounds continued but with periods of silence between; the conch shells were keening in the background. He forced himself to take step after careful step along a row of trees. The ground cracked like broken glass under his shoes; the lush, waxy green leaves that characterized the orange trees now lay in withered piles at his feet.

He touched a tree trunk and caused a half-dozen oranges to crash to the ground around him. He stooped to pick one up; it had broken neatly in two. He squeezed it and a tiny teardrop of ice fell to his shoe top.

Suddenly the dark clouds parted; in the long, moonlit silence that followed, a macabre beauty was revealed: the trees, endless silvery miles of them against an ink blue sky, were bare of fruit and leaves, the ground a burial mound of what had fallen.

A shadow passed over him as clouds covered the moon; the horror was too much for eyes to contemplate for long. He thought of his wife now, shivering, pale, ghostly; he imagined her drifting through this spectral midnight scene, touching the trees with her cold fingers, the land becoming a dreamscape of death.

The freeze held, and for days afterwards the sickening sound of the trees popping made the whole state of Florida seem like the field of a losing battle. Stories of loss and disaster poured into Wheeler's office: the frost had struck all of the northern part of the state, with Palm Beach the southern tip of its icy reach. And though the weather warmed up after a while, it was too late; the citrus crop was wiped out to the tune of seventy-five million dollars. People dependent on it—truckers, farmers, remittance men, suppliers of fertilizer and seed, realtors—saw their life's work come to nothing in one night of mean weather. Families abandoned their farms with their dinners half-eaten on the table.

That the gift of their wonderful warm weather should be snatched from them so cruelly . . . But what lesson could such bitter irony teach? The head of the weather service's being sacked because he failed to predict the disaster was cold comfort to all.

Wheeler and the Florida Eastern Star did everything possible to support those who lost so much: made personal loans to people, hauled fertilizer free of charge, encouraged farmers statewide to start again with different, hardier crops, and tried in vain to make them see the blessing, dubious at best, in the calamity.

"You're an inspiration to these people, a savior," Wadell told him as the two men oversaw the distribution of free seeds and crates at the railroad depot in St. Mary's River.

Wheeler counted off the last of the boxes and shrugged. "I'm a businessman," he said. "In the long run—and despite my age I am in this railroad operation for a good long time to come—these people're more important to the state of Florida than the Astors and Duveens that fill my hotels and build mansions on Worth Avenue. These are the pioneers. They're the ones who settle my towns and make 'em more'n just dots on a map." The crates and seeds now loaded on a flatbed car, he gave the high sign to the engineer. "Let me put it this way," he said to Wadell as the train moved off. "No crops, no freight; no freight, no income; no income,"—he looked at his train slowly moving out of sight—"no railroad."

When the train was gone he crossed the platform to his waiting carriage—there was a long ride to the next town and his next mission of mercy—and as he raised his foot to step into it, a Negro man, sweating and out of breath, came running up to him.

"Mistah Wheelah?"

Wheeler gave him a brief nod—"See my man in the depot for seed distribution"—and got into the carriage, settling back inside for a bumpy trip to Eau Gallie. The Negro came up to the window and peered in.

"Mistah Wheelah," he said. "I have somethin'." He held up a white box in his hands and thrust it into the carriage.

Wheeler looked at the man for a moment, then took the box. A familiar perfume rose as he opened it. He unfolded tissuey white paper to reveal an exquisitely formed orange blossom nestled in its waxy green leaves. "What the hell kind of joke is this?" he demanded of the Negro.

"There be a note."

Wheeler found the envelope, tore it open, and looked first at the signature: Clara Reade. Hadn't he once before got a letter from someone named Clara Reade?

"My deepest sympathy goes out to all of those who have lost their crops in this terrible freeze. The orange blossom you are holding in your hand was picked this morning from the grove behind my house at the mouth of the Miami River. I hope it will encourage you to reconsider the Miami area as a terminus for your railroad. As you can see, it is no longer 'nowhere.' "

8.

Clara read and reread Wheeler's brief reply, and when she boarded the *Newport* that morning, the first thing she did was recite it to McLeod. McLeod was fitting a handworked feather fly onto a jimmy hook and nodded cursorily as she spoke.

"Just 'cause he's coming to look at the bay don't mean he's bringing his railroad with him."

Hadn't Quentin heard what she'd recited? "Why would he come all this way if that wasn't the reason?"

McLeod shrugged. "Maybe his yacht needs airing."

"Quentin, I'm being serious. Please don't make fun of me."

"I'm not, darlin'," he said with a smile and reached out to run his hand along her bare arm. "I just wouldn't go gettin' my hopes up about this visit, that's all."

Clara shifted in her seat; she could not think very clearly when he had his hands on her, and his quick smile told her he knew it too. "If the world ran on that attitude," she managed to say, "nobody'd ever have ventured past the horizon."

"I'm a fisherman, Clara. I never claimed to be Christopher Columbus."

Clara looked at him curiously, at the deft way his long fingers handled the delicately feathered lure. "Don't you want the railroad to come here?"

McLeod was silent for a moment, his eyes following the flight of a blue heron back to shore. "I'm not so sure," he said finally. "Men like Wheeler—men with money—have a bad habit of throwing their weight around, doing things *their* way..."

"But you yourself talked about building canals across the state."

McLeod sighed. "Maybe you don't know how it is when lonely men get together on a Sunday afternoon. Things get stirred up just for their own sakes." He looked away, embarrassed at this admission. "I guess 'talk' is about all it was." Clara was silent, and when McLeod looked at her he could see her disappointment. He wanted to draw out this rancor between them with an embrace, but something rigid in her posture told him she wouldn't let it happen. "Look, Clara, all I'm saying is that even if the freeze did kill the state's citrus crop, F. Morrison Wheeler's not going to bring his railroad here just to transport Harry's oranges."

"Why not?"

"Simple economics," he explained. "There's just not enough profit in freight rates to make it worth his while." McLeod could tell by her continued silence, by her lips pressed tightly together, that she was not pleased either with him or his answer, but he pursued his point nevertheless. "He's going to want more than you've got to offer him— I don't care how sweet Reade Beauties are—and you're best off facing that now." He paused and smiled as if this was the end of it. "Come on, your line's all baited and the fish're as hungry as they're going to be all day."

Clara's jaw was set tight. She hated him; she wanted to squeeze those opinions right out of him, but she also wanted to fall into his arms and let their bodies put an end to this disagreement. She looked at the letter again: damn it, he was wrong!

Despite the catfish she caught that McLeod swore would set a new bay record, and a blue marlin that he promised to skin and salt and bring to Geneva, their day's outing was spoiled. McLeod knew enough by Clara's silence to keep silent himself, and when he took her home at noon, he didn't try to touch her and was saddened by the expression still on her face.

"Are you still planning to take the *Newport* down to Mexico?" she asked as she stood on the dock, afraid that if he touched her now, much as she wanted him to, much as she hated parting in anger, she might be forced to resist him; she had to make him see this her way.

McLeod had one foot on the dock, one on the boat, his fingers holding the guidelines, hesitating to ease the rope out and let the boat go. "Oh hell, Clara," he said finally. "I'm sorry about all this. Why don't we just—"

"Oh, no no no. I'm sure you're probably right," she replied with a bright, forced laugh. "I'm probably just being stubborn." But still they did not embrace, and both knew they had not really yielded their positions.

After he'd gone, Clara found herself repeating their conversation to try to reassure herself of the flaws in his side of it, only to see that there was some bitter truth there instead, and so spent the night trying to find a way to head off Wheeler's possible objections and also to make peace with McLeod's position. She loved him, his opinions notwithstanding; she only wished they could have been allies in this, because she sensed a long, exhilarating journey ahead of her and if he wouldn't take it with her, she'd have to take it without him. She was tired the next day when she set about calling on the other settlers to try to enlist their cooperation, but she did have a plan.

She went first by canoe up Arch Creek to the Gorams. Farley would be the toughest nut to crack, and if she could convince him of the wisdom of her plan, they'd be a long jump on the way to a united front.

Farley Goram had devised and built a primitive mill by the Arch Creek Bridge—water was essential to the process of making starch—and Clara knew she was near it by the powerful stench. "That's what happens when it decomposes," Goram said as he came through the hammock to the creek bank to greet her. "Sometimes we pick more'n we can grind. I don't hardly notice the smell much myself anymore."

Not far behind him was the house—a ramshackle series of additions tacked on to the original one-room cabin—and the mill itself. A mule was hitched to the grinder in the front yard and walking in slow, plodding circles. Flora, in a sunbonnet and faded gingham apron, was supervising her five young children in digging up and washing the coontie roots—they looked to Clara like giant sweet potatoes—and setting them out to dry in a sunny spot by the porch. Some of the ground-up powder would be used by Flora to cook pudding and pies; Goram sold the bulk of it to the markets in Key West. With the whole family working, two hundred and fifty or so pounds of starch could be ground in a week. But the twelve or thirteen dollars realized was barely enough to keep food on the table and clothes on their backs.

Flora wiped an arm across her forehead and unhooked her bonnet when she saw Clara coming through the hammock with her husband. She gave her oldest girl charge of the mule and took Clara inside for a sit-down while she made lemonade.

They lived right at the edge of poverty, Clara saw as she entered the main room: a couple of chairs made from barrels, a few sleeping hammocks of sailcloth, a table of mismatched boards, and a mattress stuffed with palmetto leaves were the main furnishings. The cooking was done on an open fire out back. There was a pretty hand-braided rag rug, though, a knot of rust and blue thistle was tacked to the wall, the plain muslin window curtains were trimmed in scalloped rickrack, and over in the corner was their proudest possession, a gramophone with a red morning-glory horn.

"Are you going to be all right with the baby coming?" Clara asked as Flora hunched over the dry sink and squeezed lemons into a bowl. Flora paused, then nodded slowly and kept her back to Clara. Clara said no more about it.

When the lemonade was ready, they joined Farley on the porch, and the talk was all of the freeze and who they knew who'd been forced out and who'd been ruined and how much was lost and other hair-raising details of the disaster. The initial news of it had taken a day to reach them. Edmund got it from Geneva's cousin who worked for a white family in Pineland City ten miles north of the Miami River, who heard it from a cousin in Jumel, eight miles south of Palm Beach, who got it straight from Asa Hamill, the barefoot mailman, who'd been a firsthand witness. It was the worst anyone had ever heard of, worse than the worst reef wreck, which only took a few lives and some property, and as various stories of disaster were exchanged and compared, Farley Goram loudly predicted the end of the notion of Florida as a land for development.

"Might just as well hope for a miracle as for a bright future of Florida. Because if the state can't guarantee the very things it's supposed to guarantee—sunshine and balmy weather—then what's the use of it? According to the lights of progress, I mean."

"Not if the railroad comes to the Miami River," Clara said and the Gorams both laughed.

"Railroads come here? No offense intended, but that's crazy talk."

"Farley, hush!"

"Palm Grove didn't freeze, did it?" Clara said.

"I don't think that rightly makes us God's chosen terminus, Mrs. Reade," Goram replied.

"Look around you," Clara said. "The river's warm as a bath; the bay's jumping with catfish. Just this morning Harry brought in a bushel basket of the sweetest oranges you're ever likely to taste. If we're not chosen, we're darn lucky."

"I agree," Goram said.

"But is that enough?" Clara said. "Why not use our luck to make our part of the state prosper? Wouldn't you like to do that, Flora?"

"We'd be fools to say no to prosperity," Flora replied quietly.

"Harry is working so hard to get the groves ready," Clara said. "And if they fail again it'll only be because of transportation. But we've—"

Goram looked at her with sympathy. "No reason to raise his hopes when there's no local market and no means of shipment," Goram said. "We grow oranges too, you know. And lemons and limes and tamarinds, some figs and bananas too. But only what we and our family can eat. No use overgrowing."

"But that's the whole point," Clara said. "The opportunity to expand is staring us in the face."

"Expand?" Goram echoed the word as if it had a bad taste.

"I think we can all agree," Clara said, "that to get our land to prosper, we need the railroad." She looked at Goram, who shrugged and shook his head. "Until now there hasn't been much of a reason for the railroad to come here, because what we have to offer, the whole state has had to offer too. But now we have something the railroad wants."

Clara leaned forward in her chair and proceeded to tell them about sending the orange blossom to Wheeler and the note that accompanied it. "And he's interested," she said in conclusion. "He's coming to see me next week. He's coming here!" She waited to let the import of her news really sink in. Flora pressed her husband's arm excitedly, but Goram continued to shake his head. "I have a plan that I hope I can get you and the others to come in on," Clara continued. "It's something that'll do more than make the railroad just sit up and take notice of us. The way I see it, in order for the railroad to go through all the trouble and expense of plowing through sixty-five miles of hammock land to lay their tracks from Palm Beach, they've got to have some real incentive."

"Isn't the fact that the freeze didn't touch us incentive?" Flora asked.

Clara shook her head. "F. Morrison Wheeler isn't going to build his railroad here just to collect the freight charges for transporting our crops. He's got to have some land of his own."

"There's plenty of that available," Farley Goram remarked drily. "Nothing but."

"You're right," Clara said. "But the best of it's already been taken. I've bought all the acreage at the mouth of the river on up to the groves and all along the north shore of the bay. The Finches have the same on the south bank. You folks have this and the creek, and I've got some prime upriver acreage."

"The Biscayne Bay Company's got plenty of Everglade swampland available," Goram said. "Ask Quentin McLeod."

Clara waited patiently until he stopped laughing. "What I'm suggesting," she said, "is that each of us offers F. Morrison Wheeler some of our own land as a donation in return for him bringing the railroad here."

"A donation?" Goram said.

Clara rushed on. "You see, if we give Wheeler some land and he brings the railroad here, what we've got left will be ten times as valuable as what we've got now."

Farley Goram stood up. "Wait a minute," he said and went inside the house.

"It sounds wonderful," Flora said, "but will it work? I see the sense in it, but—"

Farley reemerged, leafing through a book. They were all silent as he searched for a page, found it, and looked up at them. "Jean-Jacques Rousseau," he said angrily. "You ever heard of him? Frenchman. Never mind. Here's what he says. 'The first man who, having fenced in a piece of land, said, "This is mine," and found people naive enough to believe him, that man was the true founder of civil society.'" He slammed the book shut. "Pity poor society if that's what you got in mind for down here." Clara was not really surprised at his response, only at the virulence of it. Goram pulled his wife to stand up next to him and she did so, but Clara could see the reluctance in her eyes. "Anyone who says he loves this place, then gives it to the man who'll destroy it by making a 'civil society' out of it ... unspeakable. Unspeakable."

When he heard the story a few days later, Rufus Finch listened in silence, then rose to his feet and banged his fist on the porch railing. "Farley Goram's a fool!" he said. "This land he's so crazy about— what's it worth if no one can get to it and do anything with it?" He looked down at his wife sitting in a rocker and staring out at the bay. "If it leaves people stranded and lost? You're right, Mrs. Reade. Goram just can't see it. Can't see no further into the future than day after Tuesday. When me and Ida come down here, this was just the kind of thing we hoped would come to be. Maybe if it'd come sooner, Ida'd be ... not so lonely." He turned to Clara and extended his hand to shake hers. "Wheeler can have our land and we'll be better off'n he's ever gonna be. Let him be the one to put money into it and build it up. Me and Ida ain't got nothing *but* land, and we can't do nothing with it. He wants it, let him have it. Long as we benefit in the long run. The long run's the key here."

"You're doing the right thing," Clara said and shook his hand.

While he waited for this Clara Reade woman in his padded leather viewing perch on his boat's highest deck, F. Morrison Wheeler surveyed Biscayne Bay: a gleaming expanse under an impeccable, cloudless sky, its water clear enough to make visible schools of rainbow fish, gentle enough for bathing, brisk enough for sailing, its shores luxurious with vegetation, teeming with wildlife and game. He was impressed by its lushness and especially by its royal palms; he appreciated things that towered above other things. Yes, the place definitely had possibilities, and he could see the irony in its inaccessibility. No wonder Mrs. Reade wanted the railroad.

The bay was shallow enough in the most reef-filled places to rip the hull from a boat as big as Wheeler's seventy-five-foot yacht, the *Esopus*. That discovery made, its captain would take it no further than the Carysfort Reef lighthouse, where he dropped anchor. Through his spyglass Wheeler spotted a small sailboat making its way from the north, and there appeared to be a woman at the tiller. He rested the glass in his lap and leaned back, smiling to himself. This is going to be too easy, he thought, a little disappointed. When it came to business dealings, he usually liked a good fight.

Clara hadn't wanted to go alone. Just the memory of Wheeler's first response to her original request—"I have no intention of bringing my railroad to nowhere"—made her imagine him as a tyrant. But McLeod had left the week before on a long scouting expedition to find new seedling variations for Harry's groves, and Harry had his hands full now, preparing for the next year's crop. But her experiences as Mrs. Cameron Reade of Middleton, Ohio, would stand her in good stead with F. Morrison Wheeler. The Clara Reade he would be dealing with was not a simple country girl who owned a strategic piece of property but a city-bred woman used to the ways of business. She wore her best Middleton Sunday suit of powder blue with embroidery work on the jacket and cuffs. She had coiled her hair and set a small straw hat on the back of her head. When Wheeler's yacht loomed into view, she checked her appearance and reminded herself of what she had to offer and what she had to gain: with the Finches' acreage on the south bank of the Miami River and her own on the north bank, there was at least a decent chance of enticing F. Morrison Wheeler to do exactly what she wanted him to do.

He'd expected someone drawn and plain-faced, with skin the color and texture of tobacco leaves and a body lumpy and hunched in calico, like a wife of one of those citrus farmers, but the woman his steward helped up the gangway was one who'd make men's heads turn on her entrance into the dining room of the Embarcadero Hotel in Palm Beach. The sight of a beautiful woman always humbled him and reminded him that he was once a poor boy who stood beneath a train trestle, and even as he took her hand, he knew with a certain sadness that he would have to steel himself all the harder against her.

"It's a pleasure and a surprise, Mrs. Reade."

Clara was relieved to see that F. Morrison Wheeler, Panama hat and white suit aside, could have been any man on the board of directors of Reade Ironworks; he was familiar, even homey, right down to his round belly and his slightly condescending bow. She also saw his look appraising her and determined to make whatever use of it she could. "You are exactly as I pictured you, Mr. Wheeler," she said, allowing her hand to be pressed in his. His air of confidence, the stature that this impressive-looking yacht lent him, intrigued her; she was reminded of the time she'd first seen her husband surrounded by his factory and how excited she'd been at the sheer enormity of his accomplishment.

"Let me show you around my little boat."

Clara laughed. "A modest description," she said as she followed him along the main deck.

"Seventy-five feet of floating furniture," he said drily, and indeed its interiors of teak and mahogany, silk and velvet, reminded Clara of nothing so much as the house on E Street in Middleton where she had reigned as Mrs. Cameron Reade. There were four bedrooms, each done in a different period—"The wife's homage to history," he explained—plus a bath for each bedroom complete with copper-plated showers, a formal dining room that sat sixteen, a music room with a spinet and a bust of Beethoven, and a library with footstools and a fireplace.

The tour concluded on the upper deck, commanding a sweeping view of the bay, where Wheeler's steward had a table set for late lunch. He's picked a perfect day to judge, Clara thought proudly. While they ate lobster and drank cold champagne under the striped canvas awning, she looked out at the shore, where the tall royal palms swayed in the breeze like old friends wishing her well. She indicated the lush growth on the shoreline, the cloudless azure sky. "How do you like my backyard, Mr. Wheeler?"

"Doesn't seem quite real to me," he replied without looking up. "Not to a man raised in Stone Ridge, New York. Rocks are real. Hard labor and true seasons are real. This place, this sun, this bay and all those damned pretty flowers—it's too good to be true."

"But you're here."

"As an observer."

"And you're interested in my proposal."

The bottle of champagne was empty; he opened a second and refilled his glass. "Mrs. Reade, have you seen the Parthenon?" Before

Clara could reply, he went on. "I was just wondering how long it would take for Florida to have her own ruins."

The steward reappeared bearing glasses and a crystal decanter on a tray; they waited while he cleared the table of their plates and poured the amber-colored liqueur. Clara raised her glass. "To the next three hundred and sixty days of warm weather and sun," she said.

Wheeler hesitated, looking at her in a way that made her drink more quickly than she'd intended, then threw back his head and downed the liqueur in one gulp. When he came up he was red in the face. "All that sun goes against something in me," he said hoarsely. "It's like this drink. Feels good and warm going down, but too much of it can rot you, make you lazy."

"But here, the land is so lush even the lazy can prosper," Clara replied. "Oranges and lemons just drop at your feet on an evening stroll. All a person has to do to harvest the crop is bend over."

Wheeler's sharp, barking laugh startled her. He poured another glass of liqueur for himself, and downed it as quickly as the first. "I am the railroad," he declared and dropped the decanter noisily on the tray. "I am the Florida Eastern Star. I've run tracks east and west all over this state and as far south as Palm Beach, and that's as far as ever I intend to go."

Clara drew back in her chair as if he had pinned her there with the point of a dueling sword. "Until the freeze," she said, relaxing as she saw her own thrust reach its mark. She felt exhilarated because the conversation was going exactly as she had hoped it would; Wheeler understood something about a challenge that McLeod did not. "Can you smell the oranges, or is it my imagination?" she said. A blue heron dipped and dove above their heads. She turned to Wheeler. "Let's say, for the moment, that all I've got to offer is the weather. I should think that'd be enough."

"It is and it isn't," he replied. "It is, because it's freezing everywhere else and the crops are ruined, that's no secret. It isn't, because this whole meeting between us is about each of us having something the other wants badly, and I for one am gambler enough to be willing to lose unless I get it my way. So tell me what you want, Mrs. Reade."

Clara did not hesitate. "For you to bring the railroad here."

Wheeler shook his head. "Give me the details of what you see happening to this place. You don't want to be an orange grower, Mrs. Reade. I can tell you have bigger plans."

Clara heard the hard challenge in his tone and was charged by it. She met his probing stare, refusing to be cowed into thinking that she wanted this more than he did. All she had done was send a flower, after all; he had lost millions and he had come to her in person on his yacht, served champagne. Indicating that he follow her gaze, she looked out toward the shoreline where the water around the mangroves eddied in darkening purple whorls as the day waned; the only sign visible of man's hand on all this expanse was the shadow of the lighthouse on the reef behind them. "I want to build a city," she said and looked at him, daring him to laugh.

"You want a lot," he said, smiling now that he'd drawn this from her.

"I'm prepared to give a lot to get it."

"Details, Mrs. Reade. Entice me. Now's no time to be shy."

"I thought a donation of a certain amount of acreage—"

"Underwater acreage? Mangrove swamps? Or the acreage that's overgrown with scrub and pine?" The game was over and he wanted the victory to be clean and swift. "No, no, no. That kind of thing won't do at all. I'll tell you what, Mrs. Reade. I'll take half your land."

The last of Clara's smile faded. "Half?"

"For sixty-five miles of railroad tracks," he said. While Clara gaped at him, he took a cigar from his inside pocket. "Come, come. Did you think I was going to do this as a charitable gesture?"

"Of course not. But—"

He lit the cigar and spoke through a cloud of blue smoke. "Half your land, and as a concession to your being new at this, I'll take it in alternating plots."

"I won't accept special favors because I'm new at this."

Wheeler laughed. "Take advantage of my good nature, Mrs. Reade. This is the last time you're likely to meet it face to face." He stood up and walked to the railing, leaving her alone with her decision.

Clara was silent, thinking of what she would be giving away and what she might be getting; it was not only her land she was bargaining with but the Finches' too. She contemplated Wheeler's back, thinking how naive she had been to underestimate his power. He was a man who yielded to no one, and it was this very implacability, this very assuredness in his own counsel, that would help her decide to trust him or not. The very fact that he wanted to bring the railroad was sign enough that his assessment of the situation paralleled hers: they wanted the same thing. And he had not laughed at her ambitions, had not treated her as a woman; there was something in his very coolness that interested, even flattered her. Oh, he notices me, all right, she thought, but he won't budge an inch on account of it. Good for him; she admired him for his restraint.

But finally it was in their mutual desire to attain the same end—the railroad's trek through the jungle—that she saw how they might strike a bargain of mutual trust as well. Her mind leaped ahead a year into the future, and instead of impenetrable mangrove swamps and hammock land and wasted orange groves, she saw a beautiful street and stores and homes and Harry's thriving crops and a shipping depot. There was a risk, there was always that, but . . .

"All right," she said, and he turned to her. "Half."

Wheeler nodded, and though his posture remained unchanged, his body ached with the effort. He poured himself another glass of liqueur and drank it quickly. "You've got the best part of the deal, you know."

"I don't see that I had much choice in the bargain." Her heart pounded; she gripped the arms of her chair to hide her trembling.

"Bargaining's what I do best," he said with a little shrug. "A rich man's got to have some fun in life, don't you think?" He dared to look at her now, hoping she would make it easier by a quick departure.

Clara stood up, looking at the bay. The sun was going down; she would be sailing back at sunset and was glad McLeod had instructed her so well in navigating the treacherous waters. She hoped Harry would be at the house when she returned. Oh, Harry, wait until you hear! "When would you want to start?"

"I'll have my lawyers draw up the papers right away. Oh, and I'll want rights of prescriptive easement too. That means fifty feet on either side of the tracks is mine no matter what." He made a few notes on his napkin and capped his pen, then stood and extended his hand to her. "I'll even put in a waterworks, how'd that be? I don't want you thinking too badly of me."

Clara watched him take her hand, conscious of holding her breath. She could hardly contain the exultant feelings of wanting to burst into tears or wild laughter: I have got what I came to get! The touch of his lips on the back of her wrist was hot and dry and brought her suddenly back to herself.

"I guess we've got ourselves a partnership, Mrs. Reade."

Clara smiled at him; he dropped her hand and bowed. And she was surprised to see a look of sorrow and regret when he said good-bye. All the way home, this parting look of sadness on his face haunted her and threw into a different light everything that had come before. Had she made a good deal, she wondered, or had she just given her land away in a fool's bargain and he pitied her for it?

From inside his cabin, excited and stimulated, Wheeler watched her push off in her sailboat. The sun was setting, the sky lavender and smoke, the horizon soft as fur. Only the delicate splash of the waves on the hull of her boat intruded on his silence; an oil lamp burned in its prow, throwing a cone of illumination on the rippling dark blue water. He watched the light recede until it was swallowed in the open expanse of night sky. Her hand had smelled of gardenia. Clara Reade. Now where'd she learn to smell like that? He knew he could never allow himself to come as close to her again as he had today; if he did he would be forced to ruin her.

Aaron Fine was the first to appear, and though he was certainly not typical of the kind of people who were drawn to the area after the announcement of the Florida Eastern Star's plans to extend their line south—not a citrus grower or a farmer at all, not a land speculator or a real estate booster—he stayed long enough and was influential enough finally to become himself a kind of prototype, so that years afterwards, people who were scrupulously loyal to the Reade faction of the growing city and smart as a whip in business to boot would be described as "just like Aaron Fine." It was not always a compliment.

Clara spotted him from the house, a huddled figure asleep in her canoe tied to the pier. Initially affronted by his trespassing, she climbed down, ran to the dock, and rocked the canoe with her foot. "Hey!" Fine awoke with a sharp, nasal yelp of fear. "Was just going, was just going," he muttered, stealing glances at her and opening his hands as if to demonstrate that he meant no harm.

When he scrambled out of the canoe, Clara saw that he wore no shoes and that his feet were scratched and bleeding. His clothes hung on him in tatters that seemed held together by long, random strands of dried tar; his belongings were contained in a small sack strapped to his back. He edged away from her, turning his head quickly, nose to the air, as if to determine by smell the direction he must take. Ahead was the bay, to one side the river, to the other the hammock, and behind . . . He could not go back there.

Clara saw the terror on his face and regretted her part in putting it there. "My cook's made some coffee," she said with a placating gesture toward her house. The man stole a glance at her and hesitated. "It's not real coffee, actually. It's made from chickory and malt, but it's not bad. And our prize chicken laid two eggs this morning just after we'd all finished eating; you're welcome to those."

The man's posture changed as she spoke; the shoulders hunched to his ears came down, his head came up, his back straightened. When he essayed a tentative smile, Clara was amazed to see that he had bright, beautiful teeth. He looked down at himself and shrugged. "I am not always in such disarray," he said; his voice was thick with an accent Clara could not place.

"The river's warm as bathwater," she said. "Why don't you clean yourself up and I'll have some of my son's clothes brought to you."

He stared at her as if in disbelief; Clara was held in the intensity of his gaze as his eyes filled with tears that ran slowly down his cheeks. She had the urge to go toward him but sensed from his posture that his pride would not permit it. She turned to go. "I'll see to that coffee."

Bathed, shaved, and dressed in a pair of Harry's doeskin trousers and a homespun shirt, he was not the same man, his face no longer feral with anxiety but lean and angular and almost handsome; he looked younger too, though his dark, deep-set eyes had seen more than his youth suggested. His story was one with which Clara was unfamiliar, though he related it with a matter-of-factness that defined it as typical.

"When I came to America from Germany, I spoke no English. There were no jobs for a boy like me. So I make my own job, peddling. Money lending and selling door to door, that is a Jew's commercial legacy. It is rare in history that a Jew be allowed to own land or join a crafts guild and learn a trade. I don't complain. The open road has many advantages, especially in the South, where the weather is so friendly. People like to see a Jew. 'The living witness to the truth of the Bible.' Like a good luck charm, eh?" He said this with wry acceptance.

He ate with the speed of a man unused to lingering over a meal. Coffee and eggs were followed by Geneva's elderberry muffins, and she and Edmund made many unnecessary trips from kitchen to porch, fussing over the food and the silverware and dishes; until now they had only heard about the fabled race of Jews and to come face to face with one was quite an event.

"But some people . . . some people are not always so friendly. In the last town someone did not like me talking to the pretty young daughter of the minister. I was merely selling ivory buttons for her Sunday school dress. Someone thought I looked at her . . . in the wrong way, so they took mostly everything and ran me out." He wiped his mouth with a cloth napkin Clara had set out for him and leaned back, satisfied, relaxed. He looked at Clara frankly now; her generosity had made her a friend. "But you know, missus, I have to admit, a man gets lonely. It is rare to find a Jewish woman in the countryside. And the few in the cities that are eligible are not looking for a peddler. I would never cross the boundary that so many of my fellow Jews have done. To marry a gentile—I couldn't, not possible. But I ask you, certainly a lonely man's thoughts are no harm to anyone?"

Clara refilled his coffee cup. "This will not be a town like that."

"Oh no?"

"I promise," she said.

Fine looked at her over the rim of his cup and smiled. He downed the coffee in one long gulp.

As Geneva cleared his empty plates, Fine rifled through his sack and began piling its contents on the table: a length of gold ribbon that shimmered in the sun, a few silver-plated rings, a stack of thimbles, a small packet of needles and threads, a bolt of bright blue calico, pairs of lisle stockings, a painted tin of tobacco, another of snuff, two razor blades, a pair of spectacles, a hairbrush, a tortoiseshell comb, suspenders patterned with tiny roosters, buttons of various sizes and shapes strung together like beads. "I had a wagon," he said when the sack was empty. "I carried pots and pans and chairs, shoes and brooms, yard goods. This is all they left me with in that town." He looked sadly at the pile in front of him. "My dream is to open a store with a roof and floor and walls and a sign and to lay the merchandise on table tops. I'm thirty-two years old and been a peddler seventeen of them. I've got feet like an old man." As he spoke he touched the objects on the table with absentminded fondness. "This railroad I heard about. It comes here? It makes a town?" He looked up at Clara, who was nodding. "I would work for you. I would do anything. Just so I don't have to walk no more."

Clara had Geneva make up a place for him to sleep in the storage building. For her trouble Fine gave Geneva the length of gold ribbon and Edmund the rooster suspenders. The next morning Clara put him to work alongside the Negro, hacking away at tree trunks, pulling up roots, clearing away coral and rocks to make a smooth open place for what would become the first street of the town. Later that same day the Starger family arrived on the mule trail from Lake Worth, where their once-thriving orange grove had been destroyed in the freeze.

"Heard there was gonna be a town here," Mr. Starger said to Clara. His eyes were the cornflower blue of the sky, and they had a powerful hurt in them that Clara was to see in the eyes of many of those displaced and disenfranchised by the freeze. Their buckboard contained all they could take with them: feather beds and quilts, pots and pans and a washboard, a copper bathing tub, two caged chickens, a rooster, and a terrier mutt.

Clara showed Mrs. Starger and her daughter where to pitch the family tent in a hammock clearing near the river and the best place to gather firewood and get water, and she set Mr. Starger and the three grown sons to work alongside Fine and Edmund.

During the night a dozen single men straggled in on foot, some with no more than a canteen and a change of shirt. Clara found them asleep in the hammock; clutched in one's hand was the flier announcing that the railroad was coming to the Miami River. Geneva's sister in Pineland City was sent for to help feed the growing work crew.

The work was hard, the workday long. Progress was slow. The men waged a constant battle with the natural terrain, which didn't seem to want to cooperate in its own transformation: horseflies and mosquitoes were always on the attack; palmetto stumps resisted even the hardest swings of the axe; yucca plants were forever stabbing razor-pointed leaves into bare flesh, and puncture wounds were common; the heat was heavy as a weight. Men collapsed, men were sick to the stomach, men had muscle cramps and back spasms. But when one man dropped there were new arrivals to take his place.

Aaron Fine, strong and willing though unused to the physical labor required to chop trees and plow up roots and rocks, had a good eye and a quick mind, and he soon was suggesting improvements to Clara. It was his application of Dr. Tiger's method of shooting kerosene into recalcitrant root systems that got rid of the palmetto stumps; it was his soap mixture of common lye, quicklime, and the sediment from refined whale oil that kept the mosquitoes off. The crew viewed him with suspicion nevertheless, because of his Jewishness, but they admitted that when it came to bright ideas, he had more than his share.

Fine was often exhausted playing both overseer and assimilator; though he appreciated his accommodations in Clara's storage house, he wanted to avoid all appearances of privileged status, of difference, and so pitched his tent in the hammock alongside the others. He saved the few cents in wages Clara paid, pored over catalogues by the last rays of sunlight, and spent his final moments before sleep each night planning for the store he would have.

More and more people arrived, on foot and on muleback, on horseback, by raft and canoe; Clara could have sworn some of them dropped out of the trees, because one day there'd be fifty new arrivals and by next morning the number would've grown to seventy-five. Much to Clara's dismay and Harry's delight, Dr. Tiger's family came from far upriver, beyond the rapids, from the Everglades themselves, pitched their camp in the hammock and traded pelts and coon meat for tobacco and beads and tin.

McLeod had been gone nearly two months, and the secrecy of their relationship made it impossible for Clara to show her concern. Though she had been assured by Rufus Finch that such absence was typical of the man, she could not help but worry about him and realized that she worried because she missed him. And things were going so beautifully now, she longed for him to come back and take his part in it, next to her, in her arms.

Some of the new arrivals slept out in the open, their bags of belongings their pillows, or under the oak trees in the dense hammock; some pitched the tents they carried, and a small city of tent dwellers grew up. The more resourceful—and these were usually the ones with families who had lost the most in the freeze and meant to stay—built palmetto-thatched houses that a strong wind would probably flick over, but they were patient, these folks, and sometimes a treasured rocking chair would make its appearance from the back of a buckboard and a woman would be sitting in it, rocking, sewing, stirring up a pot of stew while she watched her men working to make the first street, and she'd nod as Clara passed, and it struck Clara that this felt right, this neighborliness, and that this wilderness was going to be a town after all.

Clara and Harry had never seen the Sparks house, for though it was on the bay only a few miles south of the Finches' store, it was hidden from view behind the mangroves. The only sign of a human presence was a small dock supported by rotting pier pilings swathed in slimy moss. The dock was empty when Clara and Harry pulled their boat in, and they hoped they hadn't made their trip in vain. There was no sign of a dwelling either, and they clambered over the mangrove roots, looking around for the house in confusion, when Sparks appeared from the middle of an enormous pile of salvage.

"You're staring at it! Never found something I didn't have some use for." He was standing at what was apparently the front door, unlit pipe clenched between his teeth, and he beckoned them forward. The house looked like something washed ashore in the storm: crude siding was thrown together with uneven boards and rusty nails; a ship's prow carved in the form of a Medusa loomed over the front door above Sparks's head; the roof was thatched with randomly sized pieces of tar paper; sheets of isinglass were tacked helter-skelter to the windows. "No storm ever did or will knock this down. I see you doubt me, young fella." He pointed his pipe at Harry and narrowed his eyes. "This door's solid mahogany, got the crest of the Royal Spanish Navy carved in it, see?"

Harry and Clara came up onto the porch and peered inside. Hazy yellowish light came through the isinglass, dim but bright enough to illuminate a room with tar-paper walls. The floor, however, was laid with hand-painted Spanish tiles, and there was an ornately carved crystal chandelier above a French chaise longue upholstered in water-stained silk moiré. In front of a bent-willow rocker was a petit-point footstool.

"My daughter complained I didn't get nothing nice off the wrecks, so I got her this stuff. Now what can I get for you folks?"

"Lumber," Clara said without hesitation.

Sparks nodded as if that request was assumed. "What else?"

"Lumber first of all and last of all," Clara said. "We've got a town that needs to be built."

"Lumber's maybe the most precious thing there is down here, after fresh water," Sparks said.

Harry looked out at the woods that surrounded the house. "With all this? How is it possible for wood to be hard to get?"

"Not wood, son. Lumber." He shrugged. "Ain't no workin' lumber mill is why."

"But—"

"And if there was one, there still wouldn't be no way to get a tree to it." Sparks drew on his pipe and spit into the yard. "Easier to move the mill to the trees than the trees to the mill." He looked at Clara and laughed. "Don't look so down in the mouth, missus. My boys is out now down by the Florida Reef. Nasty little storm last week, but good for business. Two wrecks that we know of so far. I'll get you your lumber. Only it ain't gonna be today, and it ain't gonna be pretty, and it ain't gonna match one board to the next neither."

While Clara detailed for Sparks the extent of their needs, Harry kept an eye peeled for Maria and when she didn't appear, left his mother with Sparks and walked back along the bay on the pretext of bailing water out of their canoe. Where was she? He couldn't ask. But had he come all this way only to have her be gone? He tried to stay away from any trees that might hide him from sight, so that if there was a chance she was anywhere near, she'd see him and come down to talk with him again. He thought of her smile—half shy, half sly—and it made him smile to himself. That smile seemed so full of promise, but of what, Harry was not quite sure.

His sexual impulses, stirred by chivalric literature and nudged by dancing classes, had been fired in the flesh that night at Mrs. Poole's and stanched that same night too by the raw reality of his father's death. Whenever his appetites let his mind wander back to the candlelit room and the girl undressing behind the screen, he would inevitably be confronted with the image of his father's body sprawled and bleeding on that bed. He needed to erase that sequence from his mind so that death was not the climax of pleasure.

Since the settlers' dinner, he had thought often of Maria Sparks: the easy sway of her hips as she moved back and forth between the house and the dinner table, her sly, tentative smile, the sweet smell when she leaned over him, that lacy dress under the calico apron, the sliding caress of it across his arm. These images rose up in his mind with such startling vivacity—in the jungle, in the groves, on the river, at dinner with his mother—that he imagined they were emblazoned across his face, and he would blush, sure that the tingling in his body had taken on a distinct color and sound.

When he looked up from the boat, Maria was on the shore, pretending to search for something in the mangrove roots. She wore the same dress she'd worn that Sunday, and Harry smiled, knowing she'd put it on for him. As he walked back along the dock, he counted twenty-two pearl buttons up the front of her dress, topped by a tiny sprig of silk pansies.

"It's a fine afternoon, isn't it?" Harry said.

"We have one every day, you know." Her voice was deep and reedy; the vibrating hum sang in Harry's ears.

"In Middleton a day like this would be cause for a parade down Main Street."

"Didn't you like Middleton? I thought everybody liked his hometown."

"In a way I feel more like this is my hometown. My mother was born here and—"

"Oh, I know your whole story," Maria said.

"Really?" Harry said. "How?"

"I have spies in all the right places." She laughed, showing very white teeth with a space between the front two. "I'm teasing you. Do you mind?"

Harry shook his head. "You do it very nicely," he said in a low voice and felt an intimacy had suddenly occurred between them, though he wasn't sure how it had happened.

She looked at him again. "So you've come south to be a pioneer."

Harry laughed and shrugged. "I don't know about that," he said, though he was pleased and flattered to be perceived this way. "The orange groves are what really interest me, so I can't say I care that I'm a little late for the great movement west. That's where the real pioneers go. Though some of the men here do seem to think this area's the next frontier."

"I don't care about them," she said. "I want to know what *you* think."

Harry blushed and looked out at the bay; a light breeze ruffled the surface, creating ripples of deep, shimmering green. The sky was very pale, as if last week's storm had exhausted its capacity for color. "It certainly is the most beautiful place I've ever seen. Isolated and kind of . . . raw. A storm here is really something to see." Harry stopped, surprised at how much he had talked.

"I hate them," Maria said. "They just mean more wrecks, and more wrecks mean more junk." She looked out at the bay and shrugged impatiently. "Did you know that the whole treasury of Spain was lost not far from here in 1702? It changed the entire course of European history. Just that one wreck. Isn't it a shame—all those jewels down at the bottom of the bay where only the fish can wear 'em. Can't you just see a hermit crab in a diamond tiara? My father and brothers aren't interested. Lumber and furniture and kegs of nails is what they dive for. Nothing but junk, if you ask me, only nobody ever does. Why, I've found nicer things just walking on the beaches than they've ever found picking apart those boats that go aground on the reefs. Found an old coin once. And a chipped piece of a porcelain cup after a storm."

Harry was staring at the delicate curve of her ear, just barely visible through the curtain of her dark hair, and it led his eye down to her throat, where he could make out the faint throb of a pale lavender vein. Maria turned full-face to him and smiled.

"Just washed up, just laying in the sand, Mr. Reade," she said. "Just laying there waiting for the right hands to come along." She held out her hands to him. "Think these are the right ones, Mr. Reade?"

Harry stared at her hands: long-fingered and tapered to pearly nails like the palest pink hibiscus cupped in prayer; the palms were callused with work, though, and his heart went out to her. To put her hands between his own and press them to his face for their fragrance . . . He reached for her, and Maria hid her hands behind her back.

"I'd love to see your orange groves someday."

"You would?"

Maria nodded. "I was hoping we might become friends, Mr. Reade."

"I was hoping the same thing!" Harry said and laughed a little wildly.

Maria spun away and took a step toward the house, then stopped and turned her head to him so that Harry once again felt he was peeking at her through the shield of her beautiful hair. She held out a hand to him. Harry took a long step toward her and fit her hand into his, and she led him back across the mangroves to her house.

9.

Once back in Palm Beach, Wheeler lost no time in ordering a survey team to begin chopping through the wilderness. After the frozen wasteland of the northern part of the state, the primitive charm of the Biscayne Bay area, its green landscape and flowery coastline, was like an oasis; its frostless crops would bring thousands of people to the area, and he was going to be prepared. In addition to the waterworks he'd agreed to, he was already laying out on paper the streets of a city and had talked to an Atlanta reporter about becoming the editor of the town's first newspaper.

To design and execute a new hotel, he called in the reigning Palm Beach architect of the day, a pompous, portly young dandy named Carlisle de Beaupré, who sneeringly informed him that an artist did not submit sketches for a businessman's approval no matter who was footing the bill. "Don't go grand on me, you," Wheeler said. "I have had you investigated and know that you are really the son of a Maine potato farmer named Carl Bumpers." The man blanched; Wheeler waved his hand to dismiss his embarrassment. "But that's no matter.

You've got the eye for just the kind of excess these new rich are so nuts about. Least my wife says you do. What is it—Spanish Moorish something? Anyway, do what you like with it, only don't make it too ridiculous. I don't want everything crawling with that damn magenta bougainvillea. Can't take that kind of vegetation seriously. It's gotta have eight hundred rooms, a dozen suites at least, hot water in every one of 'em, a swimming pool, a grand ballroom, and an exhibition room—show off all that native stuff, Seminole beads and pipes and what have you, good for tourist interest—an outdoor pavilion too, and a promenade and a boat dock on the bay. The sport fishing's got *tre*mendous potential as an enticement for tourists, and these lordly fishermen need a place to hang their reels. And an arcade for little shops; use your New York connections to get a jeweler and a stationer and some mug selling furs and evenings clothes. The wives need a place to shop, isn't that right?" He called this last to his wife, who was fitting pieces of a picture puzzle together at the far end of the long dining table; she neither looked up nor answered. Ever since the night of the freeze there had been a change in their relationship. Her physical demands upon him ended; she no longer sought him as a refuge against her misery.

Wheeler turned away from her, back to the architect. "Go down there and take a look at the place, Mr. Bumpers. Get what you need for money from Mr. Wadell here."

While his banker wrote out a check to the ruffled but mollified de Beaupré, Wheeler smoothed the large sheets of paper on which he was sketching rough plans for the town. "The trains'll bring tourists as well as cargo for my boats going to the Bahamas, Key West, and Havana," he told Wadell after the architect had gone. "The same trains'll haul back oranges and lemons and limes and truck crops. The depot ought to be by the water, with extension tracks going right to the dock. I'll put a market in back of the depot for specialty crops. Eventually I'm going to dredge the bay and make it deep enough to take my damn yacht right up to my damn hotel. And I'm going to call the place Wheeler, Florida," he said, "and to hell with anyone who objects."

"No one will object," his wife called out.

"Not to my face anyway," Wheeler said and winked at Wadell.

"And where are we to live in Wheeler, Florida?" his wife asked. "A tent?"

He looked up, glanced without shame at Wadell, relieved that the subject had at last been broached. "You are not going to Wheeler at all," he said.

His wife added another piece to her puzzle and looked up in triumph. "Thank God," she said and locked the last piece in place.

        McLeod had been gone for over a month and Clara still had not heard from him, though word of his whereabouts trickled into town from sailors and boat captains who'd recently crossed his sea path. Clara missed him and was frank in admitting that to herself. Their parting had been acrimonious and she regretted it, wondering if that had anything to do with how long he'd stayed away. She thought that a letter perhaps would begin to repair the damage and hasten his return.

Dear Quentin,

I hope this letter finds you well. Indeed, I hope it finds you at all! I thought I might have to put it in a bottle, pitch it out to float in the Caribbean, and hope for the best. But Rufus Finch said he knew of a fishing boat that was bound to meet up with you at some point in your travels, so I've placed my trust in that dubious piece of information.

How I wish you were here to see what is happening to our little backwater paradise! It is becoming a town before my very eyes. I try to keep a count of the new arrivals and estimate that there are three hundred of them at least! And that includes small groups of Seminoles coming in from the Everglades.

Poor Rufus Finch. Or should I say rich Rufus Finch? No sooner did he move his trading post across the river to the south bank, than all his stock got bought out. I never saw so many empty shelves before and neither did he, I am sure. I suppose this is a merchant's dream come true, but now that demand exceeds supply, all he does all day long is turn people away and keep his eye peeled on the bay for his next shipment from Key West. At least I can say that Rufus and Ida share our enthusiasm for the future. F. Morrison Wheeler made Rufus an offer for his share of the south bank—quite a substantial sum too. Rufus, gentleman that he is, refused politely, but Farley Goram was another matter. When Wheeler asked Farley to sell him some of his trees— lumber he needs for the tracks—Farley asked if Wheeler had considered the bottom of the bay as the terminus for his railroad. The attitude of the Gorams and the Sparkses continues to disappoint me. Can't they see the wonders of what this place will be? There's still a feeling among them that all of it will come to naught.

I saw Flora Goram last week when she came to the trading post to pick up some parcels her family in Illinois sent her. She stood for the longest time on the south bank of the river, just staring across at the activity over here. I feel badly for her. I know she disagrees with her husband and would like to join us and be part of things.

Speaking of the Sparks family, one of them had quite a narrow escape the other day. Young Fess was swimming in the river with his brothers when an alligator they say was fifteen feet long—though boys do tend to exaggerate, I know—clamped his jaws clear around the boy's waist and began swimming away. Lucky for Fess he had the presence of mind to dig his fingers in the beast's eyes. The jaws popped open and the boy swam away. He is OK, though he will carry some nasty scars with him. This is just the kind of news we don't want getting around, not while we're trying our best to make this place civilized.

And to that end, Harry and I have started building the hotel we talked about before you left! Nothing fancy, of course—more like a barn with doors and windows and rooms—though that doesn't mean it won't cost a bundle, the price of lumber and nails being what it is and all of it having to be brought up from Key West. We've already come up against thievery—piracy is maybe what you call it, since they came upon our boat at night and at sea—and a whole lumber shipment is gone. From now on we have to meet the supply boat at Cape Florida with an armed man on board! How we all long for the day when Key West will no longer be our lifeline to the world! The hotel is a simple sort of building, as I said, three stories—eventually!—with porches all around, two dining rooms—one for guests, one for workers—and about a hundred or so rooms. We've got the first story done already, and some men have moved in, sleeping on the floor as the place goes up around them. All we've got for furniture is a dozen cots, and the only way to get upstairs is by ladder, but no one can wait till we're done.

Harry threw a party the night the floor got put down, and the clog dancing went on past midnight. Mrs. Starger and her daughter are doing the cooking for the guests and the work crew, with the assistance of Geneva's cousin Missy from Pineland City. Not much of a menu to start with, mainly turtle steak, bacon, and grits. Harry has named it the Miami Hotel—his other choice was the Hotel Miami—and figured out how to give every room a river or a bay view.

Daily reports come in as to the progress of the track laying. Men are taking bets as to when they'll reach us. The latest news is that Wheeler's construction engineers are using dynamite to get through the hammock. What a waste of trees!

Harry also takes care of tending the groves. I rely on him completely and am mighty grateful I can. Town work seems to take all the rest of my time and each day, each new arrival, brings more work and makes more demands on me. I am not complaining, but it does not leave me any time to attend to anything other than the work of the moment.

I hope you will be proud of me, Quentin, and pleased at the way things are going here. You have been away far too long, and not a day goes by when I do not regret that we parted as we did. Our disagreement seems so small and petty in the face of my feelings for you and the future we might have together. Though I am proving myself capable in ways I had never even dreamed, there is no one but you to tend to the ache in my heart.

Your Clara

A reply came a few weeks later, a letter hand-delivered by the first mate of a Cuban fishing boat who'd met up with McLeod in Havana. Clara's heart pounded at the sight of the familiar handwriting. She tore open the envelope and saw that the first sentence was exactly the response she had hoped to get.

Dear Clara,

Everything you say in your letter makes me itchy to get home. From the way things are moving, I'd better get there fast, before the town's got a bank and a mayor and traffic jams.

I've docked this old rig up and down the coast of Mexico and Central America, all the way over to Maracaibo and Caracas in Venezuela and back up through the West Indies. Some of the fruit specimens I've found in these places would not survive either the trip back to the bay or our particular growing conditions once they were there. But I have stored and cultivated two dozen or so kinds of oranges and limes, something called passion fruit, something else called atemoya that's got a taste like custard. All these I think will do nicely in our soil, and I have some ideas about what to do with those grapefruits we usually leave to rot on the ground. Somebody somewhere's got to love that sour taste. It is just a matter of finding that person and getting that fruit to them.

I am on board the *Newport* as I write this, docked in a small fishing village down the coast from Havana. It is my final stop on this long and tiring scouting trip. I am getting anxious to leave too as the political situation in these parts is excitable, to say the least. The hills are crawling with revolutionaries who want out from under the rule of Spain, and more and more the townspeople are agreeing. But royalist soldiers make it pretty tough. There are shootings every night—I can hear the rifle fire in the hills all the way down on the boat—and lynchings in the trees alongside the roads are supposed to set examples so people stay in line. I am not in any danger, but I am not having a high old time of it either.

Tell Harry to save a room for me in the Miami Hotel and run a hot bath as soon as you see my flag on the horizon. Tell Geneva she had better start beating up the batter for her elderberry muffins.

I'll admit to you that I have stayed away as long as I have this time in the hope that I'd reach the point of not caring that we said good-bye in such a cold and empty way. But I was only fooling myself, hoping distance and time would do the work of making me stop caring for you. Your letter only made me feel the folly in that plan. I have missed you more than I thought I would, more than I have missed anyone in a long, long time. And I agree that any differences of opinion as small as ours are not worth the pain and fuss. I hope that I will beat this letter to your side.

My love,
Quentin

The mule path that led Clara and Harry through the hammock out to the Reade Groves was so overgrown it was nearly impenetrable. The pathway itself was one cart wide, the cart wheels dragging over a surface of sand and dead brown leaves and brittle twigs. Brain coral poked up from the jungle floor; lizards darted from leaf to leaf so quickly they were seen only as a flurry of movement. From tree branches, vines hung as thin and abundant as hair, reaching down to root in the sandy soil or twisting across the open space of the path to join two trees in a graceful loop.

Until recently the path had been all but invisible; once the Seminoles had been forced away from the bay and into the Everglades, the jungle had proceeded to erase it. When Harry had first taken over the groves with plans to bring it back to life, Dr. Tiger appeared and took him along the remnants of the original path. Since then, Harry had hired a crew to machete it back into a usable state, but he still kept a machete under the driver's seat of the mule cart so that when he and Clara drove through, he could continue to hack away at the leaves; the jungle would reclaim the path once more if he was lax.

Harry had worked miracles in the groves. Heading up a work crew handpicked from the most sparsely populated keys, he had pruned the trees and cut them back, uprooted some old ones that bore only bitter fruit, fertilized, reseeded, constructed watering troughs, plowed mule paths, and built ladders for the coming harvest. His main fascination, though—and one he could not yet give enough attention to— was experimentation with new varieties, and he set aside a certain amount of acreage in each grove for grafting and hybridization, trying out different paths to different strains of fruit: ones with fewer seeds or thinner skins or richer color or sweeter taste.

The mule moved with a slow steadiness, ignoring the irregularity of the terrain. The heat was mitigated by the shade; what sudden breezes came set the jungle into a frenzy of whispering. Harry and Clara swayed with the movements of the cart, bumping shoulders and knees, and occasionally she had to grab his leg for support as the cart pitched precipitously to one side or the other.

Sunlight penetrated the dense overhang and dappled their faces and hands; Clara watched an errant shaft of sun suddenly light up the gold deep in Harry's eyes. What a wonder he was to her! No matter how old he got—and Clara could not help but remember that he would be twenty-one years old soon—he did not seem to age in her eyes. The fresh coloring he'd taken on only emphasized his youth. The closely shaved skin gave no hint of shadow. Only when he smiled and lines appeared at his eyes did she have even the vaguest sense that he might someday grow up all the way into adulthood. She smiled to herself; words were inadequate to express what she felt for him.

Finally, they emerged from the long, covered aisle that was the mule path into the outer edges of the grove. Clara squinted and shaded her eyes with her hand as she looked up at the sky. The black figures she saw wheeling above the trees made her shiver and grip Harry's arm.

Harry laughed. "Don't tell me you're afraid of a friendly old buzzard?"

"There's no such thing as a friendly buzzard." Clara looked up and shivered again. "I'm remembering that story about the man who got lost in the hammock."

Harry was still laughing as he jumped from the cart. "First thing Dr. Tiger told me—'If buzzards don't circle fertilizer, the smell's not high enough!' " He scrambled up a short ladder leaning into the branches of an orange tree, reached inside, then jumped down and came back to the cart. He bowed slightly to Clara and presented her an orange on his open palm. "Reade Beauties!" he proclaimed. "First of the new crop."

"Oh, Harry!"

Harry turned the orange in his hand, snapped open a long, thin-bladed knife and peeled the skin down halfway. "The blossom end is always sweeter than the stem end." Juice poured down his wrist as he peeled. The shards of skin fell in Clara's lap. He handed her the fruit; she bit into a section and the sweet juice filled her mouth.

"Mmm! Have to change the name to Nectar of the Gods!" she cried. "They're so much better than the ones we first found out here."

"Picked from the south side of the tree," Harry explained. "Sweetest of the lot. We've got Dr. Tiger to thank for that piece of information too. He sure knows his way around an orange grove." He climbed back up into the cart next to Clara and looked out proudly at his grove. "When the crop's ready for picking, Mother, we won't see it going to rot on the ground again. Trust me on that. Harvest it, box it, crate it down to the railroad depot, and we're set." Harry shielded his eyes from the sun as he scanned across the even rows of trees. "Look at 'em! Reade Beauties one and all."

Clara did not follow his gaze but looked at him instead, at the crystal glinting in eyes brighter than the sky. She took his arm and pressed herself to his side, her face against his shoulder. The scent of orange blossoms sweetening the air, the dark green leaves sharply etched against the pale blue sky filled her with tenderness, and the sweet, sour taste of sadness rose in her throat.

"Hey." Harry squeezed her shoulder. "I have another surprise." He left her side and ran to where he'd tethered the mule; he came back swinging an orange crate and presented it with a little bow. Clara took it and curtsied. "Oh, you want me to start packing oranges, sir?"

Harry scratched his head and grinned at her. "Never mind the sarcasm, Mrs. Reade." Clara laughed. "Go on," he urged. "Look at your surprise."

Clara turned the plain box over until she came to the side that was plastered with a wide blue label. In the center of it was a brightly colored, perfectly drawn orange emitting golden rays as if it were the sun itself, and arcing over it all was the legend: Reade Beauties of Florida. Her hand touched her heart; she looked up at him quickly.

"Oh, Mother, now don't cry, darling." She clutched the box to her chest. "I drew it myself and sent it to a printer in Philadelphia." He put his hands on her shoulders and kissed her forehead, bringing her closer to him.

They walked aimlessly about the grove while she spoke of her responsibilities in town, her plans and ideas for the future, the land deals, the street work, the store construction, the lumber contracts and negotiations with Wheeler over the various land and title divisions. Her voice flowed on and on; Harry heard it blend with the drone of bees and the whisper of the leaves in the wind off the bay. He was not listening to her words; the particulars of what she said didn't matter to him. What did matter was the fact of their being together in this charmed and glorious place. And he made a silent vow that for as long as he lived, nothing would change that. He would preserve and nurture the love between them as carefully as he would tend the orange groves. He had no doubts that this was in his power to effect. In this most Edenic of places, the simple truths of life were what mattered.

Harry took his mother's hand as he looked down the row of orange trees. This, he thought, this is home.

10.

Three months after his departure, six weeks after he'd received Clara's letter, a month since she'd received his, two weeks since a storm off the coast of Cuba bent the tiller of the *Newport,* and three days since he'd had it fixed in Key West, McLeod returned in the dusky, fading light of a damp August day. His white hair had grown nearly to his shoulders. Harry kept calling him Buffalo Bill as he and Clara escorted McLeod to the house to celebrate his homecoming with Geneva's crawfish soup, turtle steaks with onion rhubarb relish, a specially baked elderberry pie, and real brewed coffee.

Clara watched him eat, his rough, suntanned hands never still; reaching for a biscuit, spooning out some guava jelly, swizzling lime in his coffee, slapping at Geneva's flank and having his wrists slapped back, and even getting a snorting sort of laugh out of that serious girl. Clara was too restless and happy just having him opposite her at the table to do more than pick at the food before her, too full of feeling to say

150

much, itchy to touch him, to be in his arms, to meet his look straight out without having to avert her eyes for Harry's sake.

Tomorrow, she thought, shivering at the sudden touch of his bare foot on her ankle under the table, almost laughing out loud at the tickle; tomorrow they'd go out on the *Newport,* away from everything and everyone, and they'd pick up where they'd started before temper and stubbornness had made each withdraw from the other. McLeod's quick grin told her he felt the same way. Desire blurred every moment so that Clara would have been unable to say what McLeod had recounted of his travels—even if he'd spoken about them at all, or if Harry had hogged the conversation with nothing but talk of his orange groves. She only knew, as she lay in bed that night, that McLeod was back, asleep on the horsehair sofa in the next room, and if it was not the same as being next to him, there was something delicious, even satisfying, in the anticipation.

She watched the moon rise in a slow diagonal across the frame of her window, knowing she would not sleep, knowing she would never find a cool spot on the sheet or a soft place for her head on the pillow. She had barely touched him since he'd arrived, just a dry kiss on his cheek, a neighborly squeeze of his hand. She would think of him all night; he would be there in the breeze that caressed her shoulder, in the smell of hay and sea. And tomorrow . . .

Had she slept? Was it a moment later? Or had she lain there for hours when she heard him whisper, "Not a word," and the faint light from the rising moon lit the shock of silvery hair beside her.

Next day, when Clara guided McLeod through the progress made, he joked at first that she had taken him to a different place altogether, a settlement not on the Miami River at all, because the changes were so extreme it seemed impossible they'd all been accomplished in such a short time.

"The railroad's the incentive" was the only explanation Clara could give. News of its imminent arrival had spread across the state in everwidening circles. To many once hurt by their unquestioning belief in Florida's balmy weather, the prospects had seemed too good to be true at first, and a "let's see" attitude kept them watchful but unmoving. But as the tracks made their slow, torturous progress through the dense wilderness, hundreds of new people had taken the challenge and made their way to the Miami River.

The town's prospects became more real with each new immigrant. Faith drove people on: the town already existed in their minds, and all they had to do was build it. They were no longer only citrus farmers and manual laborers but lawyers and doctors, butchers and bricklayers, bakers, smiths, builders, retired seamen, and an occasional escaped convict. They passed each other in the hammock, on the riverbank, by the bay, working, eating, doing the wash, laughing, and before long they started thinking of themselves not as a group of homeless wanderers looking to settle in somewhere, but as a group with a common purpose, a population.

They built the first street forty feet wide and banked by wooden walks in the hope that one day horse and carriage traffic would justify the expanse and, by a majority vote taken at the big meeting tent at the north end of the street, named it Miami Avenue. A few dissenters led by Aaron Fine pushed for Reade Street after Clara, who was considered by some the mother of the town. Clara squelched the praise and was admired all the more for it.

Not every arrival saw it as the Eden rumor promised. Swatting horseflies was surely no way to spend the day, though Aaron Fine hardly minded making a tidy bundle selling his whale-oil soap. Worse, Finch's trading post couldn't be relied on for supplies, and food was scarce, especially if you didn't know how to trap a turkey in the hammock or handle a reel in the river or catch a bay turtle with your bare hands. Even once the stores went up along Miami Avenue, the newer arrivals got queasy with the bay so close by, as if it might rise up and swallow the whole thing some dark night to prove the skeptics right. They objected to the Seminoles too, thought them savage interlopers, even though the Indians had earned an honorable place in the area's history, a fact which was explained often enough. And while building was going on, the noise was fierce enough to drive away those who had, admittedly, come too soon. "We wanted a town," they said as they turned their backs on the tumult of Miami Avenue, "not an idea for one."

The stake pounding and sawing and shouting and hammering only increased as results were seen and enthusiasm grew. Clara became so used to these sounds that when work broke with the sunset, the quiet startled her. She even came to like the noise because of what it meant: the wilderness was becoming a civilization.

New homesteaders in the Piney Woods wielded axes and grub hoes to make little clearings for themselves, but log houses were nearly impossible to build because of the density and hardness of the trees. "We want our womenfolk living in the comfort of walls and a roof," the men told Clara, complaining over the lack of usable lumber. "Not under canvas sheets that flap in the breeze."

Clara made a deal with Calvin Sparks to supply her exclusively with lumber so she could fulfill these latest demands. She sold or leased small plots of land to homesteaders and had them all sign an agreement not to make, sell, or consume alcohol on the premises; if they did, the land would revert to her. The last thing she wanted was for her town to stumble into the trap of so many Western towns and fall into disrepute and lawlessness.

To deal with land sales and leases to new arrivals, with store and house construction, with answering questions and giving advice on a hundred details that people brought her daily, she had herself built a one-story office smack in the middle of Miami Avenue. To accommodate newcomers and encourage the growth of small businesses, she built a series of plain, unpainted stores flanking hers and rented them out for twenty-five dollars a month. She made sure her first customer was Aaron Fine, whose General Merchandise sign could be seen directly across the street from her office.

She had the town's first piece of plate glass shipped all the way from Pittsburgh and had it installed so she could see the street grow without sticking her head out the door. Her own house was set just far enough back from the bay and the growing town to feel part of things but still be on the outskirts where the hustle and movement didn't reach. Alleys ran between some of the stores and cross streets were planned to run east and west. There were a few houses, of the same unpainted wood as the stores, that had a catch-as-catch-can look to them since lumber continued to be as scarce as snow. The standard cuts were supplemented with wood salvaged from the wrecks that stayed snagged on the reefs or that washed up onto the beaches. Some of the poorer people rustled up wood in the tangle of mangrove roots; sooner or later every bit of flotsam on the bay found its way to the town. Native hammock trees—mahogany and ironwood—were simply too hard to cut down. By controlling the lumber supply, Clara kept waste to a minimum and saw to it that no one with a lot of loose Northern cash could grab up and monopolize the street.

Each store had a hitching post outside, usually made of a palm trunk, since no one was fool enough to waste a real tree, palms being considered a strange hybrid of tree and house plant. All kinds of things were tied to these posts: buckboards and wagons, pack horses and Indian ponies, mules and even pigs. Much to everyone's amusement, Tommy Schell, the blacksmith, spent a good deal of money having an elaborately carved and gilded buggy shipped in pieces by steamer and reassembled in front of his forge. He'd had his name painted in gold letters on the door too; "advertising," he called it, since he only rode the thing on Sunday to the meeting tent that now doubled as the First Methodist Church. (The day the railroad came in, he took orders for a half dozen of them and nobody laughed anymore.) A grand piano was brought up from Key West on a barge by Madame Carney, who promised lessons for ten cents and who supplemented her income making pies for Clara's hotel guests; her first pupil was Ida Finch, who came to her with a book of Chopin in her arms.

Clara let out spaces in the back of the hotel, the ones with no water view, to Smiley's Shoe Store and Sinclair's Hardware. Next door to her on Miami Avenue was young Dr. Charles MacKenzie, come down from Kissimmee when all his patients left after the freeze; his wife, Linda, wept the day she arrived. "I feel hope again," she said, and everyone knew exactly what she meant.

Except McLeod.

By the time she'd finished conducting the tour, shouting over the construction noises or filling the silences between them with a narration of what he was seeing and what he would see in the future, rattling off comical anecdotes about people who were still just names to McLeod and nodding howdy do's to just about everyone in sight, McLeod was visibly bored, though Clara, intent on showing off her accomplishments, hadn't noticed. "My next plan is to pave the streets. One good day of rain and we're up to our knees in muck."

At the end of the street, McLeod took a quick glance back. "You've done a hell of a job."

"And this is just the beginning," she said. "Once the railroad actually—"

154

"That's enough about the railroad." McLeod took her arm and pulled her toward him. Clara squirmed away, eyes darting to the two men loading a buckboard in front of Fine's and the lady in the straw hat waiting, still self-conscious of exhibiting their relationship in public. McLeod continued pulling, smiling at her, until they were well hidden from view behind a tall stack of felled pine trees. "You sprouted a couple silver hairs since I been gone," he said softly.

"Oh, that's a fine compliment," Clara said, but she moved into his embrace, pressing her cheek against his chest, into that familiar smell of hay and the sea.

McLeod caressed her hair. "Never thought I'd meet up with anyone fit me like you do," he said, "and I think you know what I mean." Clara laughed and nodded against him. He held her at arm's length and looked at her face. "And I don't think I need correcting for thinking you feel likewise about me. Now that I—"

"You know I do, Quentin. I've never—"

"Wait a minute, I got a little speech. Lord, I never did meet a woman so itchy to holler her opinions." Clara laughed and he went on. "I love you, Clara, and . . ." He shrugged. "Hmm, I guess that's the end of my speech."

"It was a very pretty speech. And you already know that I—"

"Oops. One more thing. Now, I know the *Newport*'s a mite on the cramped side for actual permanent living, but I also got me a little cabin upriver that's—"

"The *Newport?*"

"Sure. You *are* going to come with me, aren't you? It's customary."

"Customary?"

McLeod smiled and shook his head. "Darlin', we're not gonna get very far if you just keep repeating after me."

"But what—"

"I want to marry you." He laughed at the expression on her face: open-mouthed and speechless. "Now don't go looking so shocked," he said. "Hey, you're not gonna laugh, are you?" She shook her head and turned toward the street. The sounds of hammering and sawing stopped, and the sky seemed bigger in the quiet. McLeod stood behind her, his hands on her shoulders, and spoke into her ear. "Sail down to Caracas on a honeymoon. How'd that be? I found me some fishin' ground where you use the rod and reel to fight the fish off from jumping into the boat."

"Quentin . . ."

"Then we cruise our way into the Amazon. Never been there, have you? They say the island at the mouth's big as Switzerland."

"It sounds wonderful, but . . ." She turned from the street. His face was open, expectant. She turned back to the street. "Look what I've done here, Quentin. All the work I've put into this town. You've been gone, you haven't seen, you have no idea. I'm the one who started this whole thing. People rely on me. I've got to make sure it works. I couldn't just go off and leave it."

"You could if there was something you wanted to do more."

"Oh, Quentin, don't put it like that! It's not a case of one or the other. You know I love you. How could you even doubt it? But . . . don't you see? I can't leave. Everything's changing."

McLeod took a step back and looked at her for a long moment, slowly shaking his head. "From where I'm looking, it seems like nothing's changed at all."

When the tracks had edged but five miles short of the Miami River, F. Morrison Wheeler did as he had done in several other towns where his railroad had touched down: he founded a newspaper. *The Metropolis* opened its offices in March of 1896 and this, even more than the imminent arrival of the Florida Eastern Star, even more than the three hundred citizens who'd come to settle and the tourists in and out and the gridwork streets that crisscrossed Miami Avenue now, was the ultimate symbol of the town's emergence. It proclaimed to the citizens that what went on where they lived was significant enough to warrant being observed and thought about and argued over and written down for the nation at large to consider. And if ever a man was born to do the observing and thinking and debating and writing, that man was Elliot Iverson, former ace of the Atlanta *Star Ledger* and the New York *Legion.*

"The purposes of *The Metropolis* are several," Wheeler told his new editor. "To herald the arrival of the first train. To escort into history the development of the town. And"—he paused here to make sure Iverson appreciated the significance of what he was about to say—"to chronicle and celebrate the extension of my empire southward."

Iverson took the job because of the possibilities for drama and excitement, for the sheer American pageantry the town offered: pioneers and visionaries, promoters and speculators, fast-buck artists and victims, the whole mythic cast of characters of any boomtown.

"Don't expect too much," Wheeler added. "We're not even incorporated yet."

Iverson looked up and down Miami Avenue and shrugged. "Raw material's all I need."

In a rare display of bonhomie, Wheeler slapped him on the back. "There's plenty of that!"

As a writer Iverson had a facility for extrapolating the larger significance from the ordinary act that most reporters of the day couldn't match, and he was accused by many of them of having an unfair advantage. "A damn novelist!" was the most stinging epithet. His accounts of the Johnstown flood, the laying of the golden spike at Promontory Point, and the great Chicago fire were more colorful, more exciting, more sentimental, and in the end more believable than the truth, whose ultimate emergence in rival reports was often overshadowed and overlooked. His personal belief was that a good story had to transcend its own facts.

The first editorial of *The Metropolis* appeared on May 30, 1896:

This is the first paper ever published where Biscayne Bay meets the Miami River, two bodies of water as beautiful as any ever seen in these United States. It is the most southern newspaper on the mainland, published at the most southern telegraph terminal and express office on the mainland, in a town with already three hundred souls and the survey of the place not even complete. And isn't it high time—isn't it past the time in fact—to make this city-in-the-making a city-in-fact? Isn't it time to draft a charter? To pave the streets? To incorporate? To give ourselves a name, for Lord's sake? How long until we pray in a real church building instead of a makeshift tent? We are sitting on ancient land here. Hernando d'Escalante Fontenada was shipwrecked hereabouts three hundred years ago and called the place the Lake of Mayaimi. He got the name from an old Seminole Indian word that means "sweet water." But all that past is behind us. Everything here is potential. All is about to be. The past is shucked off with each uprooted tree, with each chunk of coral taken out of the sand. The future, like the land itself, will be smooth and free. The future is a place to build on where the past once was. So come one, come all, to this Baghdad by the bay, this ocean Paradise, this place of eternal sunshine and youth, this new metropolis of Florida!

Iverson applied for residence at the Miami Hotel and gave Clara very specific instructions as to his preferred accommodations. "I want a corner room with no neighbors and one that doesn't get any light."

"They all get light," Clara told him. "My son designed it that way."

"Shutters," he suggested. "I don't want to be distracted by sunrises or sunsets. I don't want your famous balmy breezes bringing the stench of flowers either. I don't want a view. And I don't want to come down to the dining room for my meals. You think you can arrange things to suit me, Mrs. Reade? I'm willing to pay a little extra, of course."

Clara had a set of slatted shutters fitted for two rooms on the third floor in back and arranged for Geneva to place meals twice a day at his door with only the softest knock to announce their arrival.

"But I'm curious," she said to him. "Why would you come to an area like this to work and then shut out all its amenities?"

"I don't want to be unduly influenced by pleasure, Mrs. Reade," he replied in earnest.

In a series of interviews with Clara conducted in the darkness of his room, Iverson began to put together the pieces that would become the official story of the town's beginnings.

"And so you leveled all the ground around the house with your bare hands . . ."

"It was I and my son to begin with," Clara said. "And not with our bare hands! With a hoe and an axe. And certainly not alone. Dr. Tiger showed us how to do it; he even supplied the seeds! And then Edmund joined in to—"

"Negroes and Indians, Mrs. Reade?" He shook his head. "Go on. After that. Tell me about that orange blossom you brought to Wheeler. I want to hear all there is to tell about that one. I know that you walked through the jungle up to Palm Beach with the blossom." He looked up suddenly and smiled. "Let's get some details. What kind of shoes did you wear on such a long walk?"

"Oh no," Clara said. "I didn't do the actual walking myself."

Iverson's smile faded. "No? Not yourself?"

"I sent the orange blossom with Edmund," Clara said.

"The Negro again?"

"Nobody's got a stride like that man. I think his legs must be—"

"But it was your idea, at least, wasn't it?"

"Oh, yes . . ."

Iverson nodded and resumed his note taking. "Your idea, the whole town . . ." He took notes for a moment and spoke without looking up at her. "So, Wheeler just came along at the right time, just part of your master plan."

Clara laughed. "That sounds a little grand for what I had in mind," she said.

"And that was—?"

Clara shrugged. "I was just looking for a way to get Reade oranges transported north without their going rotten on me."

Iverson replied with barely concealed impatience. "But you must have had a dream, Mrs. Reade."

"A dream?"

"Something that made you leave Middleton—I love that name, by the way, I couldn't have invented a better one. So? Your dream was—?"

"Well, when I think back to the time of my decision to come here, it seems to me that it was made more out of an instinct to survive than anything else."

Iverson sighed again; was this woman ever going to give him what he wanted? "OK. OK. You wanted to survive. I can do something with that. And then what? You survived and then . . . ?"

Clara shrugged, but her eyes were bright. "I wanted to build a city."

Iverson clapped his hand. "At last! Thanks, Mrs. Reade."

The story, "Founding Mother," was written in the dim light that came through the slats of the half-open shutters in Iverson's third-floor room and set in pica elite on the Fairhaven press brought in from the Massachusetts Ironworks. The press was driven by steam and could print a thousand sheets an hour and stack them as neat as though by hand.

She was just a woman with a dream to create a city where there was only a wilderness. Clara Reade—five feet five inches tall, with the kind of proud, visionary beauty you see on the hand-carved prows of seagoing ships or beneath sunbonnets in Conestoga wagons going west, an American face, full of passion and the strength that comes from purpose.

Clara Reade came to the Miami River, this true American pioneer, and single-handedly cleared her land, pulled coral from the sand, chopped down trees, planted a garden. The going was rough; the land fought her at every turn; the sun beat down on her head; the insects were merciless on her flesh. She worked without rest, with only her young son to help her and only her dream to be her guide. At night she would pray for strength, and in the morning she would be on her hands and knees. She had the vision of a believer and the hands of an artist, a sculptor, wresting a city from the jungle that surrounded her. And isn't all America built on just such dreams as hers? Dreams that fuel our ambition to be the best, the richest, the most famous—even the most notorious!

Clara Reade's dream is being realized even at this writing. She has been able, as no man or woman before her had been, to bring to the wilderness the instrument of modern, nineteenth-century civilization: the railroad. F. Morrison Wheeler has crisscrossed our great state with the tracks of his Florida Eastern Star, because Clara Reade appeared one day before him, her clothes torn, her feet raw and bleeding from her two-day trek through the jungle. The citrus crop in all of Florida had frozen. But in her hands was cupped an offering: a fragrant orange blossom from her garden on the Miami River. I have a dream, she said through parched lips, and told him about the city that would one day come to be. And F. Morrison Wheeler listened. He believed in her dream as only a true visionary would have. He saw in this wilderness what Clara Reade made him see and said to her, I will build your city.

Together they are giving birth to what you see around you. They are the mother and father of our city by the bay.

Flattered by the attention, embarrassed by the aggrandizing misinformation, Clara denied it to anyone who would listen, but she found that people liked the story even if it didn't stick to the facts one hundred percent.

"Striking images, Mrs. Reade," Iverson replied when Clara demanded he print the truth. "We all want this town to take its place in the national scheme of things. And loosely speaking, it *is* what happened. I just put it in a way that won't be forgotten. A way that'll get told and retold. You do want to be remembered, don't you?"

"Not for something I didn't do," Clara replied.

"I never make anything up," he said, adding with a wink, "Not completely."

Wheeler read the account by Elliot Iverson and recognized the power of invention at hand. He had little experience with imaginative literature, having neither the time nor the patience with another man's version of reality, and considered any writing not factual, feminine. But he saw that the public was inspired and cheered when they read Iverson's "Founding Mother" story and that they appreciated the way he made things that simply happened in the daily life of their town seem like true and stellar moments in the long pageant of American history. He did not mind the inaccuracies, for he knew what had really happened and so did Clara Reade. He thought perhaps, though, he ought to remind her more precisely of who really controlled things around the mouth of the Miami River. It didn't pay to let things go too long without making them absolutely clear.

11.

He had to oversee the final miles of track laying anyway, Wheeler reasoned, and so there was more than just Clara Reade to travel south for. He had de Beaupré refurnish his private Pullman car, stocked it with food and wine, and had it transported to the end of the tracks. His private barber, installed in a separate car along with a valet and cook, trimmed, shaved, and massaged him. He checked his appearance now as his valet brushed him down. He still had his posture—straight as a ramrod, his mother would be proud— and all his hair. The starched white shirt and red silk cravat gave his pale face color, and the black cutaway jacket slimmed him down.

His valet backed out of the room. Wheeler tried a smile in the pier glass and thought better of it; he was so used to a stern appearance that when his face relaxed he looked to himself like the poor boy he once was. He took a tiny comb from his pocket and ran it down his sidewhiskers, shaking his head at himself to be discovering this kind of personal vanity at his age. His face and body tingled. He was ready to meet her again.

His good humor was sullied at this moment only with the knowledge that once again his wife had had to be confined to a sanitarium; his patience for this situation was fast wearing out. Their marriage was a bitter charade of what it once had been; it had been reduced to an endless, irritating series of obligations—social, medical, emotional, and financial. So gradual had been the descent, so slowly had he been enmired, that he had not taken full notice until it was far too late to alter the course. He built bigger and bigger houses, yet as long as his wife was in the room, there was barely air to breathe.

And now he waited for Clara Reade, a man in the prime of his maturity, healthy, glowing with anticipation. He poured a glass of rum and lifted it to the light to admire its clarity. "To the future," he whispered in the quiet opulence of his private railroad car.

The door opened and she was silhouetted by the glaring sunlight. Wheeler rose to welcome her. The heat seemed to have wilted her a bit, and a fine sheen of perspiration made her face glow. "Come sit in the breeze," he said sympathetically.

Inside all was dark red, mahogany and brass. A ceiling fan moved the warm air around, heavy damask curtains kept out the sun and the ash-laden air. Clara sat on a small velvet settee, her hand on a carved lion's-head armrest. Wheeler sat opposite at a leather-topped desk, his feet propped on a footstool of elephant tusks bound with hide. He crossed his legs and folded his hands in his lap. His lips were dry; he licked them. With the door closed, the light was dim. Wheeler took pleasure now in how calmly he could look at her and maintain his composure. A marvel of self-containment! He cleared his throat. "May I extend my compliments as to your very charming dress?" He had not paid a compliment to a woman in so long he feared he might have been clumsy, but he could not resist just this little one.

Clara stared at him as if not sure he had said what she had heard. "Thank you," she replied uncertainly.

Wheeler nodded. "Perhaps you might advise me on the kinds of fashionable shops that might appeal to the women guests of my hotel."

Clara shrugged. "I don't follow the fashions much myself," she said.

Wheeler murmured as if this made good sense. "My wife used to advise me on these matters, you see. But . . . she is no longer able."

"Oh. I'm sorry," Clara said. "I didn't know."

"No, no, no. She's not dead," he said. "She is . . . unwell in her mind. Has been for many years. Very sad . . ."

"Poor thing."

"Yes. Yes, she is."

"It must be very lonely for you."

"We each have our cross to bear, Mrs. Reade."

Clara hesitated to say more, sympathetic to his situation yet wondering if this softening of his demeanor was yet another tactic of negotiation.

"Can my man get you anything? I've got a generator-powered freezer back there somewhere. Anything with ice? Anything at all?"

Clara shook her head, eager to start business. "I'd like to get right to the point, if I may."

Wheeler smiled. "If you must, you may."

"There is a water problem, Mr. Wheeler."

Wheeler stared at her. "I don't understand. We are surrounded by water. Unless that is the problem. 'Water, water everywhere!'" He smiled.

Clara shook her head. "But it's hard water," she explained. "Full of lime. Fine for fish and coral and mangrove, but bad for people. You can't do your laundry in it, you—"

Wheeler laughed. "My laundry?"

"We're not all rich enough to throw our clothes away once we've worn them, Mr. Wheeler."

"You hurt my feelings, Mrs. Reade. I was once a poor man. My mother washed clothes to earn enough to put food on our table."

"I apologize," she said. "I don't mean to be flippant, because the problem is extremely serious." She leaned toward him. "I've tried to keep this from becoming general knowledge. A family of tourists from Ohio staying at the uncompleted Miami Hotel had to be treated by Dr. MacKenzie for convulsions after drinking the water."

Wheeler stiffened and moved some papers back and forth on the desk. "Tourists? Hmm . . . well, that could be serious. I thought you meant workers were . . . Convulsions, you say?" He looked up as if he'd thought of another way out. "Of course, that happened at your hotel and—"

"If tourists get sick at my hotel, tourists will get sick at yours."

164   · *BISCAYNE* ·

Wheeler stared at her, a half-smile playing on his lips. "It sounds like you've given this a great deal of thought."

Clara nodded as she rummaged through her purse; she liked that he noticed her thoroughness. "What I'd like you to do is construct a pump upriver near the rapids. There's a site there about four miles outside of town where a natural spring can furnish fresh water. A small gasoline powerhouse could run it with no trouble at all." She found the papers she was looking for. "The gasoline can be carried upriver on light barges." She held the papers out to him. "I've worked out the financing and drawn these rough sketches."

Wheeler looked at them cursorily. "This is going to cost me."

"I'm sure you don't want tourists being poisoned. If Mr. Iverson of *The Metropolis* heard, he could make quite a little story out of that, don't you think?"

He looked up at her, disappointed that she trusted him so little, yet admiring her caution. "I don't need that sort of pressure to do my duty, Mrs. Reade."

"I apologize again," she said and stood up to go. "If you would finance one more thing, though . . ."

"Only one more?"

"I was thinking of a census," Clara said. "With people living in tents and on boats and in the jungle, a census'd be the only way to tote up the population. And if we qualify for incorporation, that means we'd be eligible for federal grants, and that'd go a long way toward taking the whole burden off you."

Wheeler hesitated a moment, then nodded. "I bow to the wisdom of your suggestion," he said.

"Thank you."

"Perhaps there'll be something you can do for me someday."

"If I can, I will."

"I sense a touch of apprehension on your part. Some wariness of me. It would make me very unhappy if I thought you didn't trust me. In addition to being bad for business."

"Of course I trust you," Clara said. "I wouldn't have given you half my land if I didn't."

Wheeler smiled. "I admire you tremendously, Mrs. Reade. Not least of all for your frankness. Here we are, on the train that will bring both of us to triumph. Both of us, Mrs. Reade. I admit that I can't do this without you."

"I'm glad you see it as mutual."

"I'd be a fool not to recognize your contributions," he said as he took her hand and bowed from the waist. "They are calling us the founding mother and father of the town, you know."

"I've heard that."

"I think we make a pretty fine pair," he said, and flushed as he stood up slightly out of breath. "And I hope that when the railroad comes in, Mrs. Reade, we may toast our mutual victory."

Clara studied him for a moment: the bony, serious face softened with white sidewhiskers, the narrow eyes, the generous lower lip that belied the dourness of the pinched features, the expensive clothes. There was something about his presence that excited and frightened her, the way high speeds and high places had in the past. These were not the kind of emotions that would make her fall into his arms—her spine was always stiff around him, her shoulders straight, as if she might at any moment be required to jump to attention—but she could not help but look forward to the continued stimulation of their business dealings. That he might not feel as impersonally toward her was a thought that crossed Clara's mind, but she shook it off. Here was a man around whom she could be clear-headed, and what a relief it was!

        Itinerants were hired by the day to peer into overpopulated tents and rooming houses, the hotels on land and sea, even the shacks of Colored Town and deep into the hammock two or three miles upriver. The grand total was published in the June 30 issue of *The Metropolis:* a population of five hundred and two! Since the state requirement for a city was a measly three hundred or more qualified voters, and even discounting the coloreds—because depending on who wanted to invoke the law, they might be eliminated by the grandfather clause requiring voter qualification a generation back—they were home free. Though the new status brought no immediate change and was, in fact, a bit abstract to most folks, they were proud nevertheless to be chartered as the most southerly city on the mainland of the United States.

At the Sunday service at the Finches' a few weeks before the election for mayor, Quentin McLeod's name was put up as the settlers' choice. Clara sat apart from McLeod at this meeting, insisting on keeping their personal relationship a secret from the inquisitiveness of the settlers. That she had refused his offer of marriage had not dampened their ardor, but Clara knew that patience on both their parts was required; she had hurt him and needed to be gentle with his feelings. McLeod sat in silence in a willow rocker on the porch and glanced sideways at her, gauging her reaction as those around them discussed his candidacy.

"He's the best man for the job," Cal Sparks declared with a fond pat on McLeod's shoulder, and for once there was agreement among the Gorams, Finches, Reades, and Sparkses.

"Quentin's a square dealer," Rufus Finch said. "He's got a head for figures and is a crack shot with a rifle, come to think of it."

Farley Goram said, "Not that I have any interest in this town you're all so het up over. But I do think a man ought to live a good long time in a place before he tries managing it. I guess McLeod qualifies on that score."

Clara laughed. "The railroad candidate has yet to be seen on the streets of town two days running."

Calvin Sparks poked the silent McLeod with the stem of his pipe. "No one knows this area better'n you do, Quent. 'Cept me, and I'm too ugly to run."

McLeod roused himself as if from sleep. "Me? Mayor?" He shook his head. "Not with my work being on the *Newport.* Why, I'm in town just long enough to collect my freight, stock my galley, and pay the dockmaster before I got to get back on the water and head down to the keys or the West Indies or on some charter somewhere." He looked once at Clara, and though his words apparently made his position clear to everyone else, it seemed to Clara that they were meant to convey something very particular to her alone. "I'm not on dry land long enough to qualify for voting rights," he concluded, "let alone holding public office."

Clara visited him on the *Newport* that night as she had done several nights each month, all the while persisting in her belief that no one knew of these visits. McLeod, if not resigned to the clandestine nature of their relations, had assumed a patience learned from years of waiting for fish to bite. By unspoken mutual consent they never discussed the town or the railroad when they were alone on the boat, were neither fisherman nor civic leader, but that night, when they sat on the deck in the humid, starless night, Clara urged the job on him. "Your friends meant what they said, Quentin."

McLeod lit a match to his pipe, and the furrows in his brow were cleft into deep shadow. "Too much corn whiskey's what meant it."

"You shouldn't joke about this. It's too important."

"I already told you, Clara, I'm not interested in the town."

"I can't help thinking that your stubbornness is because of me, because I won't—"

"Look, it's your town and I wish you the best of luck with it. You ought to run for the office yourself."

"I would if I thought a woman could win. But I'd just be spoiling our chances to keep the control of the town out of the hands of the railroad. Don't you see? You're our best hope."

A shower of sparks rose in a column of smoke from his pipe and disintegrated in the air. "Your best hope's getting to be pretty much of a stranger around here," he said and brushed pipe ash from his bare chest.

His refusal to run left a gap that Aaron Fine rushed to fill, but he was discouraged from pursuing his candidacy any further when a fire broke out in the back of his store. The incident, which damaged beyond repair a new shipment of women's petticoats, was listed in the town's official records as being "of unknown origin and unrelated"—as far anyway as Sheriff McCordle's halfhearted investigation could determine—"to the victim's political intentions or his religious persuasion."

The election saw Josiah Wells, former director of the Florida Eastern Star's office in St. Augustine, installed as mayor. The early settlers abstained from voting, and in fact the turnout was meager and desultory, composed mainly of railroad workers who never even heard of the man for whom they made their mark.

"Being a company town ain't so bad," Tommy Schell, the blacksmith, said. "Least they ain't never gonna let it go down."

Fritz Starger, the baker, agreed. "The Florida Eastern Star's got as much at stake in the town's success as anyone."

Clara Reade would hear none of this, and though she was determined to leave bitter feelings behind, she wanted to make sure that the railroad did not have its way when it came to what the town would name itself. The next day a large, crudely drawn chart was hung in front of Clara's office on Miami Avenue listing the possibilities: Dade (for the county), Dallas (for the fort), Wheeler (for the man who brought in the railroad), Reade (for the woman who brought in Wheeler), Miami (for the river).

Just after dawn the day of the voting, Clara dispatched Edmund and Geneva to rouse their kin in Colored Town to come and cast their lots with the settlers. Harry took a mule cart out to the groves to round up as many truck farmers and citrus workers as he could. Clara sailed down the bay early that morning and after much cajoling and hectoring, managed to bring back Calvin Sparks and his sons, though Farley Goram was adamant in his refusal to participate and clamped his hand tight on Flora's arm too. Clara got the Stargers to close the bakery and the Finches to row over from the south bank so that they could cast their ballots too. Harry returned at noon with a dozen men and stood by the corrugated box Aaron Fine had rigged up out of an empty case of Dr. Perrine's Alkali Soap to watch that no one made their mark more than once.

The voting was staggered throughout that long, hot July afternoon. Individuals dragged themselves into town, voted, and stayed to cluster in groups and discuss possible outcomes. It was a lot more interesting than the uncontested race for mayor, they agreed. Elliot Iverson, assuming Wheeler would win, set the type for the newspaper headline the night before, had his assistant ink it, and now waited for the formality of the count at day's end to start the press rolling.

The sun was pale in a hazy sky but punishingly hot; the shade was steamy and oppressive. Women set their bonnets back off their heads and dabbed their necks with hankies drenched in lilac water. Men rolled up their sleeves and let their suspenders hang down around their hips. Horses and mules were kept tethered to the watering troughs. The light along the street took on an anxious blue tinge, and at three the sky turned bright white, there was a violent clap of thunder, and the rain began. In minutes Miami Avenue developed a fine sheen of glistening muck. Thinking that the rain might keep people away, Clara dashed across to Fine's General Merchandise and emerged with a half-dozen umbrellas, then ran up and down the clattering wooden sidewalks, first to Dr. MacKenzie's office, then to Tommy Schell's livery stable. "Vote," she told them as she thrust an umbrella in their hands and prodded them out their doors, "or Wheeler's the name."

Wheeler spent the afternoon in his private railroad car at the end of the tracks—less than a mile out of town now—sipping from a pitcher of ice-cold gin and branch water, his face raised slightly to the slowly moving ceiling fan. He was idly writing "Wheeler, Florida" over and over down a long ledger sheet. Too bad for Clara Reade, he thought, and though he felt this sympathy for her, he could not help but relish the thought of his own imminent triumph. Much as he admired her strength and tenacity, he preferred, above all else, to win.

By six in the evening the rain had stopped and the sky was revealed a hazy dampish blue. Wheeler took himself to the observation platform at the back of the car, though the air outside, despite all the rain, was as still and heavy as a hot compress. He breathed deeply and was assailed by jungle smells that made him feel moss might be growing on his flesh. The combined scent of flowers and ordure turned his stomach. Fix that soon enough, he thought; clear the jungle of trees once and for all.

He looked the last mile down the right-of-way to the town, to his city, to Wheeler, Florida, and there was Sheriff McCordle lumbering toward him. Wheeler smiled at the fat man's obvious discomfort in the heat: hat off, limp kerchief knotted around his neck, red-faced, huffing and puffing, his stride as spread-legged as if he had a horse under him. No wonder he wasn't smiling.

"Speed it up, sir!" Wheeler called out to him with a laugh. "I been waiting all day for you!"

McCordle hesitated for a moment, pulled at the soaked kerchief as if it choked him, and advanced the last yards until he was looking straight up into the chin of his boss. He reached in his pocket and drew out a damp, folded piece of paper with the results of the vote. Lips set tight, he handed it up. It ain't *my* doing, he thought.

Wheeler was vaguely repelled by the warm, sweat-dampened piece of paper. He unfolded it with a satirical show of ceremony, glanced down perfunctorily, merely for confirmation. Oh, for Lord's sake, they'd misspelled his name! He blinked and glanced at McCordle, smiling, about to reprimand him half jokingly for his clumsy penmanship, then looked at the paper again.

But the writing had changed since his first look and now another word, the wrong word, a ridiculous word, nonsense, an obscenity! was clearly printed in place of the one that was supposed to be there.

His smile faded as he read that one word over and over and over.

12.

It was a hundred and two degrees at high noon on August 22, 1896 when the Florida Eastern Star began its maiden run from the depot at Palm Beach to the one at Miami, Florida. Trailing behind the engine car were passenger cars—coaches, sleepers, and private cars—freight cars loaded with steamer trunks full of resort wear and others loaded with stock and produce, a mail car, a dining car stocked with champagne and truffles, a caboose, and a Pullman Excelsior for the use of F. Morrison Wheeler and his selected guests: a few officers of the railroad corporation and their wives, recruited for this particular run so that Wheeler could test their mettle in the field. He had political goals for a few of them, and this event was as good as any to get them started. The president of the Bank of Biscayne, Parker Wadell, and his wife rode in the Excelsior along with representatives of the lesser branches of the Astor, Carnegie, and Biltmore clans, who would brave the hinterlands for the thrill of being first.

Inside the lavishly furnished private cars, equipped with porters, cooks, and waiters, gun racks, fireproof safes, stationary bathtubs, electric bells, and even a pipe organ beneath a glittering chandelier, there was an atmosphere of quiet excitement. These privileged passengers, used to luxury, rich, pampered, padded, and insulated as they were from all forms of discomfort, saw themselves on this day as hardy adventurers into virgin territory, for even when protected within lavish accommodations, one could never be quite sure of the unknown, could one? The heat, to pick one liability not quite at random, really was a hardship in the unventilated cars, and who knew, promises of the proprietor aside, what the quality of the air would be in the town itself? They'd face it bravely to be sure, but they would insist that their fortitude be remarked upon.

Sixty-five miles south of Palm Beach as the rail ran, near the mouth of the Miami River, a different sort of excitement was in the air. At just after dawn that day, sailboats filled with families from the keys began rounding Finch Point on the south bank, and other people from as far north as Pineland City and Kissimmee skimmed into the bay, moored their crafts, and came ashore to be witness to the spectacle of an honest-to-God steam-powered locomotive plowing through the wilderness. The track bed had made as clean a sweep through the jungle as a man with a razor on an unshaven face.

The rickety old two-berth dock where McLeod had deposited Harry and Clara Reade their first day was long gone. Wheeler's supervising construction engineer had first shored up the old dock and lengthened it, but water traffic increased so much when building supplies started coming in that in exasperation he cleared two blocks of shoreline of mangroves and had the old dock torn down. The longer, wider docks spawned a dozen extensions that fanned out along the bay with the same kind of interlocking complications as the mangrove roots they had replaced.

Now sloops, skiffs, barges, yachts, short-draft steamers, and barkentines bobbed in the waters, some even sporting flags from England and France. Captain Angelus's floating hotel was there too; during a peak in town building it had accommodated nearly four hundred workers in hammocks strung between poles on its three decks.

There wasn't a real railroad depot yet, just a three-sided shack standing opposite Colored Town to serve as a waiting room. Inside was bare but for a grain scale and a desk for the ticket clerk, a rheumy old retiree named Rainer Ellsroth sent down from St. Augustine to write out the tickets by hand. Real printed tickets were promised by the end of the month, and that was fine and fervently hoped for by Ellsroth, whose gnarled fingers made writing each ticket entry an agony not to be borne long, pension or not.

Aaron Fine, a man with an eye on the future if ever there was one— his General Merchandise now included a pickle barrel, a glass counter of boxed sugar-candy treats, ladies' private garments, and Various and Other Sundries, as his hand-painted sign declared—stood at the center of a little crowd and predicted that the railroad shack soon would be superseded by something grander and more appropriate to the status of the growing town.

"Something with cupolas," he said. "Something with towers and gimcracks. Those kind of things make it look important, see? Railway Gothic style, they call it. I seen it all over."

Carlisle de Beaupré, the architect Wheeler had sent down to design and survey the land for the Royal Palm Hotel, stood on the edge of the group listening to Fine, stoic in his silence until he could bear it no longer. "Maybe the Hebrews require such ostentatious display," he called out in an ersatz Boston accent. "I decry it! I won't design it. I won't approve it, and if I have anything to say, such a monstrosity as you describe will not darken our landscape!"

Much as people were suspicious of de Beaupré's supercilious city ways, they were not as suspicious of him as they were of the only Jew in town, no matter how many civic functions he performed.

In front of the shack was a wooden platform knocked together from scraps of timber left over from the dismantling of Clara's old dock. Out back was a long hitching post where a dozen horse-drawn wagons waited for hotel guests to arrive. Above the weight scale that stood to one side of the clerk's desk was a sign that said, "Personal luggage not to exceed 40 pounds." A zero had been added by hand to bring the number to four hundred because the female guests of the proposed luxury hotel who might be staying for the entire three-month season could hardly be expected to make do with less; their draped, padded, and sashed skirts, their brimmed hats trimmed with feathers and bows came in trunks that weighed by themselves ten pounds or more.

Clara and Harry, arm in arm on this great day, joined the crowd on Miami Avenue. As they walked toward the depot, people were emerging from the sandy alleys between stores, from Tent City, from houses deep in the hammock. At the depot the whole platform was astir with people jostling and gossiping and shouting "Good morning" and "Howdy do?" and "Great day for a celebration!" Harry and Clara were nudged toward a favored place at the north end of the platform, where the view of the tracks was unobstructed.

"Looks like the whole town's turned out!" Clara said and squeezed Harry's arm.

Harry smiled at his mother—she was so proud, so happy today; it was good to see her face so lit with joy—and scanned the platform for other familiar faces. Aaron Fine was there, wearing the funny yellow suit he always wore; and that city architect all in silks, looking over the crowd like he smelled dead fish; and Tommy Schell, hair slicked down for the occasion and bright red suspenders on too; the Stargers with one of the little ones on his daddy's shoulders; and there she was! as if he'd conjured her out of his own desire.

"Maria!"

He waved his Panama hat over his head until she saw him, then turned, flushed, to his mother. "Some of our old friends," he said, embarrassed that she'd seen such enthusiasm.

"I see," Clara replied and squeezed his arm again. "We've got so much to be happy for, darling."

Maria struggled her way through the crowd, her father trailing behind her, until she appeared at Harry's side, breathless, flushed, laughing. "I told you I'd be here!"

"I know," Harry said and smiled at her; he couldn't stop smiling.

"I told Daddy that if he didn't bring me today there'd be no meals cooked for a month."

"Try living on raw possum steak!" Cal Sparks said.

Maria laughed but didn't take her eyes from Harry. "Oh, he stormed around and I fretted and fussed, but I held on tight and here we are!"

"We're leaving soon as that iron beast roars in, Maria."

"What've you got against the railroad, Cal?"

"Nothing personal, Clara," he said. "Business pure and simple. Soon as that thing starts carrying freight, no one's gonna have much use for an old scavenger like me."

"Oh, that's not true," Clara said.

"Well, it is too," Cal replied. "I can see it if you can't."

Maria tugged her father's arm. "Oh, Daddy. You promised. Just for today."

Cal Sparks shrugged and gestured to his daughter. "I know better'n to court eating raw possum."

"Curiosity got the better of you, Cal," Clara said. "Admit it."

Sparks shrugged again and looked out across the crowd. "I don't see Quentin McLeod nowheres."

Clara affected an air of mild surprise. "Oh, I'm sure he's here," she said with a quick, unseeing glance at the crowd.

"He sailed down to the West Indies last week," Harry said. "Some kind of expedition to scout up new seeds."

Sparks nodded. "Yeah, he likes being out on that boat more'n anything."

Clara's smile froze on her face, the disappointment a sudden dark cloud in the otherwise perfect clarity of this momentous day. Somehow, despite everything she knew he felt about the railroad and the town, she'd thought he'd show up today, if for no other reason than because it meant so much to her. She wiped the sweat from her upper lip and fanned herself with her handkerchief, hoping her disappointment didn't show. To Clara's embarrassment, Sparks stroked her arm the way he'd soothe a nervous cat and clucked his tongue in sympathy.

As the hour of arrival neared, excitement grew, and despite the heat, people started pressing closer together; everyone wanted to be standing on the platform for the actual arrival, as if they wouldn't really be part of the experience unless they could be attached to it in a physical way.

So close were people, an orange eaten by one was apt to squirt into the mouth of his neighbor. Babies wailed; pickpockets snaked through the crowd, making the most of the opportunity. A woman fainted and with no room to fall revived finally, standing all the while. Boys stood on their father's shoulders to call out the first sighting of the train, and heads of families read out loud Iverson's editorial in that day's edition of *The Metropolis.*

A locomotive is a simple mechanism—a boilerful of water, a fire to heat that water, and some cylinders and pistons to apply the steam thus generated to the wheels. An American Prairie type of locomotive has a four-wheeled truck immediately in back of its cowcatcher, followed by three pairs of driving wheels and a two-wheeled truck at the back under the firebox. It is this American Prairie type that is coming into town today. It was built in the Lehigh Valley in Weatherly, Pennsylvania, and is expected to arrive at the depot on the corner of Twelfth and Avenue T at two o'clock. This one is going to have a dining car and sleepers with upper and lower berths, private cars with the famous Hitchcock Reclining Chairs, parlor cars with footstools and seats that swivel and curtains on the windows and carved ceilings, and of course freight cars to carry the produce of the area. A simple mechanism . . . but a town like this without that simple mechanism is a town that would never, could never, prosper. So mark the day in your calendar. Save this copy of *The Metropolis* as a historical artifact. This day will long live in the memory of man as the day our town joined the rest of America.

"I see it!" Kevin Starger bolted upright on his daddy's shoulders and dug in his heels for a better look. The stammer he'd had since he started talking was nowhere in evidence; instead his words were clearly pronounced and loud enough for all to hear. "I see it!" he repeated. "It's like a little speck off in the trees!"

His high-pitched, frantic shout would be remembered by those present for years to come. It would blend into the crisp azure of the sky, and the two wisps of clouds flanking the white glare of the sun would seem to be his voice taken shape; it would become part of the memory of close-packed bodies, of the smell of store-bought perfume and real gardenias, the taste of sweet rolls and oranges and the shuffling sounds of feet on the sandy platform.

Time stopped for just a moment after the boy's shout, as if those present were conscious all at once of the significance of the first sighting and honored it with their awe. There was a long moment of silence, and out of it came the sweet familiar toot of a steam whistle, and the crowd erupted in cheers.

They could feel the vibrations just about the time the train came into view. It was like the boy had said, a speck on the face of the jungle, growing, enlarging, barreling toward them. The sun's reflection off the steel rails made it seem the train was riding in on bolts of pure white light. Thick black smoke poured out of its flared stack in a trail that lingered in the air. The train was longer than they thought it'd be, freight cars and passenger cars stretching back in the distance till the train looked like it would have no end but would come on and on for days, a tapeworm discharged by the jungle itself.

An arm was waving out of the engineer's cab and now the crowd started waving too. The vibrations were getting stronger; they could feel the train's power traveling up their legs to their chests and their heads as though the train wasn't just coming into town but moving right inside them.

"Never thought I'd ever see anything like this!" Cal Sparks shouted in Clara's ear, but the train was on them now, puffing, shimmying, chugging over the wobbly tracks, its big bell clanging, its steam whistle blowing, its smokestack sending ash and cinders over the heads of the crowd like a benediction from the world of tomorrow.

Clara was unconscious of holding her breath, conscious only of the enormity of what she had done, that an idea she had had in silence and solitude had produced this great clattering roar.

The people in the crowd used their fans and newspapers to brush away the ashes and smoke while Negro porters in blue uniforms jumped off the train and onto the platform.

Inside, Wheeler steadied himself against the damask-covered wall of his private car as the train screeched and jerked to a shuddering stop. His guests parted the velvet curtains and peered out.

"Are these the settlers? This ragtag bunch?"

"What'd you expect? Peers of the realm?"

"In New York they'd be chimney sweeps and parlor maids."

"Here they're the town leaders."

"Ask the porter to lay something on the ground. His jacket or something. I'll ruin my soles."

Steam billowed from beneath the car as Wheeler emerged, squinting in the glare of the sun, scanning the sea of faces for Clara Reade's. He'd been angered that she'd refused his invitation to accompany him on this ride, but anger filled him with a sure sense of his power as no other emotion ever did. He had never found a woman who would stand up to him in the maintenance of her own principles. But he admired her and her attitude of proprietariness about the town and would have thought less of her if she'd agreed to join him.

A group of men hired for the occasion filtered through the crowd, whispering Wheeler's name, and a circle of them formed around the Pullman car platform where he stood, looking up at him. If not for this, few of the settlers at the depot would have had any idea that this tall man in the white suit and Panama hat was anyone in particular but the first one off the train. He remained standing there, higher up than the rest, in a pose—head high, eyes looking over their heads to some point in the distance—calculated to inspire awe. The name Wheeler had by now been whispered in so many ears it seemed everyone was born knowing who he was, and when a round of applause began, it had all the signs of spontaneity. Wheeler nodded and bowed from the waist as if it were all no less than his due.

Clara had watched with interest as these machinations took place. Aaron Fine came through the crowd to stand by her. "At least," she said to him, "he had the grace not to seem surprised."

"You should be the one being cheered," Fine replied.

"It's true, Mother," Harry said.

"I agree," Maria said.

Clara shrugged. "Everyone knows what I've done," she said with more confidence than she felt. "I don't need a display."

"You deserve one anyway," Fine said and shouted out her name.

Clara clutched his arm, but Fine shouted her name again, and soon it was taken up by Harry and Maria and Cal Sparks and rippled outward until the whole platform cried for Clara Reade.

Wheeler raised his hands to acknowledge the crowd and to quiet them. He took off his Panama hat; a soft breeze blew his hair. He scanned the crowd again until he saw her, then smiled and nodded; the crowd recognized her, as did he, for the leader she was. Her face was flushed with pride, her chin held high. The wind from the train had blown off her hat, and her hair fell loose to her shoulders so that for a moment he saw what she had looked like as a schoolgirl.

Clara gripped Harry's arm. "Come with me, darling."

"No, Mother," he said. "This is all for you." He kissed her cheek, then nudged her forward.

Clara made her way through the cheering crowd. She thought with pleasure that no one had to be hired to tell these people who she was. When she reached the train, Wheeler extended his hand to her and she mounted the two steps to stand next to him. She raised her hand and the crowd quieted.

"It is a proud moment for a little town when a great railroad makes its appearance." She turned to Wheeler and extended her hand to be shaken. "On behalf of all the settlers you see gathered here before you, I'd like to welcome you to our home." A cheer rose from the crowd; Wheeler's smile stiffened on his face as she neatly maneuvered him into this subordinate position. The cheering ebbed only when Clara raised her hands and began to speak again. "This is a great moment. A moment that will go down in history. A moment to describe to your children and your children's children. But this is only the beginning of the great union of the railroad and the land. We've seen it happen all over America. The rails have connected East to West, and all along the way there has been prosperity. The railroad comes, a town grows, farming increases, industry begins. In the great westward movement we were pretty much forgotten, but now the railroad's come. The Florida Eastern Star has connected the deepest South with the North and the East and the West and the Caribbean and South America. And I predict even greater things to come. More people, new businesses, the creation of a city with streets and boulevards and homes as grand as any city in America."

Another cheer rose from the crowd; Clara raised her hand again, a huge smile of victory and pride on her face. "The eyes of the nation are on Miami today. And as for tomorrow, we should think not of limits but of boundless possibilities."

While the crowd cheered her speech, Wheeler leaned toward her, flushed at the way she had taken over. The strain of maintaining a smile hurt the muscles of his cheeks.

"We ought to run you for President," he said.

Clara laughed and took his arm. "Come on, Mr. Wheeler," she said as she looked out over the sea of happy faces. "Let's you and me just run this town."

In the rear of the cheering crowd Elliot Iverson scribbled with haste the words of Clara Reade's speech. She's learning fast, he thought, and the next day printed her speech verbatim.

Part Two

13.

The ground-breaking ceremony for the Royal Palm Hotel took place several months later and involved the cutting of a ribbon by Maria Sparks. The choice of Maria was symbolic—Wheeler said he wanted a representative of the original pioneer families and a pretty one too, if that could be arranged—a metaphorical bridge from the past to the future. All Miami could talk about these days was all the things Miami was going to be, and here was a day of celebration, a new railroad and the start of a new hotel, the promise of rich guests, tourists, more business, a city, a real city built in a wilderness, the demonstration of the undeniable power of modern man to make his dreams a reality.

A crowd made up of a couple of hundred citizens, out-of-town laborers, and Wheeler's guests stood in a loose semicircle watching Maria Sparks take her place at the ribbon. Wheeler had supplied her with a new dress for the occasion and Maria was giddy with the attention, never having been seen by so many people all at the same time in her life. The architect, Carlisle de Beaupré, straightened the sky blue ribbon and whispered in Maria's ear exactly what he wanted her to do.

De Beaupré had cut a curious figure in the town during the months of the survey and planning: short and portly, encased in silk waistcoats hung with gold chains, adorned with brightly colored cravats spilling from ruffled linen shirts. He could be seen at any hour walking purposefully along Miami Avenue, scanning the horizon, measuring the breadth and width of things with one eye closed and a thumb in the air. He seemed not to notice people at all or the stores and buildings along the street but instead peered through them, as if he was trying to see the space cleared of everything. When people spoke to him and he was brought out of his reverie, he looked surprised to see them. His presence made a few people nervous. "If he's an example of the kind of folks coming in," Calvin Sparks said, "let's shore up Fort Dallas and keep our muskets full!" But most people, especially shopkeepers, anticipated the money soon to pour into their coffers, and if all the new people looked like that and had cash at the ready, that was fine with them.

For his part, when de Beaupré first saw Miami he was shocked to find just a bunch of rough wooden shacks on a street that was no more than a wide swath cut out of the jungle. The largest building in town—if you could even call it a town—was the Miami Hotel, built by the good-looking son of the so-called "charming" Mrs. Reade, and he viewed it with contempt. He had to move fast; he'd made promises to Wheeler about the speed with which he could get the land cleared and the Royal Palm built and he would not be put in the position of having to make excuses.

Once he took a closer look, though, de Beaupré relaxed. "The place has possibilities," he had admitted as he and Clara and Wheeler made their way along Miami Avenue. He regarded Clara—with her wide straw hat, sun-reddened hands and face, and plain linen dress—as not very stylish and a little too bossy for his particular taste in women.

"What we need is a city planner," Wheeler said.

De Beaupré nodded. "Someone with an aesthetic vision," he said. "Well, that's obvious."

They passed the corner of Miami and Twelfth Street, where a construction crew was unloading timber salvaged by Cal Sparks and Sons from a Cuban freighter that ran a reef near Passion Key. De Beaupré stopped and leaned against a barrel of nails and took off his Panama hat to fan himself; mosquitoes and gnats apparently loved the taste of his liberally applied eau de cologne, as his face and neck were covered with tiny welts.

"I'm only sorry that I couldn't have got here sooner." He gestured to the shacks and tents that stretched out toward the river and to the Miami Hotel, silhouetted against a palm grove. "Before all of that was built, I mean. My God, Mrs. Reade!"

Clara followed his gaze to the Miami Hotel. "Function and simplicity are my aesthetic vision," she said.

"Exactly," Wheeler said, and Clara at least had the satisfaction of watching de Beaupré flush.

The trio moved toward the bay and stood on a natural mound of dirt and sand twenty feet square, beholding a flat plain of palms, oaks, manchineels and scrub brush on a bed of sand and coral. "Let's make a ceremony out of the ground breaking," Clara said.

Wheeler nodded; his arm described an arc that encompassed a three-acre piece of his land between two borders of Clara's land. "Clear all of it," he said and kicked happily at the mound of dirt with the toe of his shoe. He smiled at Clara Reade and touched her arm. "We'll give birth to a city yet," he said and thought, *My* city and I don't care what the hell you call it.

A few months later, Maria Sparks, shy and nervous to be the focus of such attention, stood on the mound as her brothers held up a wide satin ribbon donated free of charge by Aaron Fine. She knew Harry was in the crowd somewhere, but she kept losing sight of him; he can see me, she thought, and fiddled uselessly with the stiff bow of her new dress.

De Beaupré handed her a scissors; she nearly swooned at the overpowering scent of his perfume. The townspeople held their breath; shouldn't there be a drum roll or a clap of thunder? She snipped; the ribbon dropped and swept her shoes; applause and cheers greeted her act. It was done.

A hundred laborers recruited from Negro communities in Georgia and Alabama began their work advancing into the jungle to smooth out a perfect green lawn for the Astors, Vanderbilts, and Duveens to come. The Negroes were young and strong and armed against the jungle with bush hooks, axes, and grubbing hoes. But over the next weeks it became apparent that their youth and strength were no match for this particular terrain. Fumes released by an axe blow to the manchineel trees brought them to their knees, dizzy, choking, their flesh swollen and raw; de Beaupré ordered the trees burned instead. The aptly named ironwood trees destroyed every axe that tried to fell them; de Beaupré sent for dynamite to do the job. The noise of the explosions, though physically unsettling, thrilled most people because of how efficiently it all worked and how modern it all seemed.

The Miami Hotel had been finished long before the construction on the Royal Palm even began, though Harry wondered if it would ever be actually completed; his mother insisted on addition after addition even before the original plan had been worked out. Yes, there were more guests than they'd ever thought there'd be, but it was as if Clara sensed Harry straining to get away and arranged it so that the job was always not quite done. Though Harry would not admit it, she was right, but the Miami Hotel was not the only thing he wanted to get away from.

He hated the way acres of the hammock were being destroyed to make room for the Royal Palm and its elaborate grounds. If he had learned only one lesson from Dr. Tiger, it was that the hammock must be considered as an equal and treated with respect.

As the town progressed, Harry began spending more and more time away from it. At the beginning he had simply wandered, following the mangroves along the shoreline, just as his mother had done as a child, to learn about the twisted, grasping roots that sapped up the filth and muck of the river and built up soil out of the detritus of the sea. Then gradually his walks took on purpose and he moved inland, deep into the hammock. And where once Dr. Tiger had been his guide, now he had to see the land with his own eyes, and he was determined to learn every inch of it that he could. He liked to think he was developing his natural instinct for the signals the land gave off, though he suspected that this "instinct" could be more accurately defined as a willingness to go where the paths led him and a basic trust that the jungle would not let him come to harm. He had observed this bond between man and nature in the person of Dr. Tiger and used him now as his model.

He would stride confidently forward, the way clear for a few yards or longer, the sun streaming through the overhang and dappling the leaf-covered ground. Frogs hopped out of his way, snakes, slim as vines or thick as roots, slithered through the underbrush, and inevitably he found he was no longer walking a straight path but a winding, curving one, parting thickly clustered grapevines and bamboo shoots, climbing over sudden outcroppings of coral and sidestepping huge root braids. At some point, invariably, his path was blocked by the thickness of the growth, and then he took out the knife to hack away at the vines and leaves, trying to disturb the natural design only enough to clear a pathway for himself.

In his dreams, nothing impeded his forward motion; in reality, machete in hand, he made slow and torturous progress through the dense hammock. As often as he advanced, he also stumbled and set himself off course. The vines wound their way endlessly among the trees, seeming to tie up the hammock in their twisting grasp. They climbed up trunks of oaks and mahogany and sprouted enormous leaves, flung themselves over branches and hung down as casually as if momentarily forgotten by their soon-to-return owner, leapt from one tree to another and formed canopies from which hung spirals of cimbidium orchids, wound around trunks so tightly they broke through the silvery brown bark and grew into the trees themselves, formed doorways and tunnels and animal traps.

Harry thought that, if resisted, the hammock might easily drive a man mad, but once he yielded to its mastery, he felt calmed by the dizzying profusions, and its eccentric density took on for him a sort of sense of its own. It was a place that reigned supreme in its own right; it would not bow to man's greed as the plains of Middleton had done. Man and civilization were mocked here; they were as flies to the sylvan deities, and Harry remembered again something Thoreau had written: "for I knew all the while that it would yield the most abundant crop . . . if I could only afford to let it alone."

One aspect of these forays that Dr. Tiger had warned him of but whose impact only gradually made itself felt was the solitude. Being alone was something Harry was used to. When he was ten years old and suffering through a bout of rheumatic fever, he had been confined to his third-floor room in the house on E Street for the better part of a school year. During that time of meals in bed, lessons with Kurt Gutman, doctors' visits, and daytime fever dreams, he had spent hours poring over Audubon's first sketchbooks, had read Thoreau's *Walden* for the first time with a chill of recognition that to this day had not left him: "I have my own sun and moon and stars and a little world all to myself." He had imagined what a life in nature would be and made plans accordingly, then changed them, remade them and remade them again and again. From the vantage point of his youth, time seemed an endless wheel on which to spin out variation upon variation of the future.

Long after he had recovered and returned to school and society, he was forced to hold at bay this sense of his future. He was sent to dancing school, played soccer, learned to box, and the longing for another kind of life became a need within him that did not abate. He acquired among his peers a reputation for taciturnity and moodiness, tempered by his own sense—given the facts and circumstances—of the inappropriateness of his secret desires.

When he neared eighteen his father had taken him to the ironworks and laid out for him a future of cogs and wheels; the factory seemed to Harry, in its noise and odor and filth, an obscenity, the antithesis of nature. Upon his majority, his presence would be required at business and social dinners; groomed to be a stalwart member of society, he nevertheless kept alive in his heart through all the years of his adolescence this secret desire to be away from all of it.

These feelings were inchoate, inexpressible but for the unacceptable "I want to be left alone." Yet his mother had always sensed this aspect of his true desires. But what could be done? Vacations in the Adirondack Mountains, where the Reade family had a lodge, only whetted Harry's appetite for a life away from ironworks and dinner parties. Clara herself never insisted he visit or entertain, and in fact Harry often thought he detected a like nature, equally hidden, inside this woman who moved through society as if she dwelt elsewhere. In their long afternoons alone together—his recovery from illness did not preclude the continuation of these cherished times—when they imagined tropical jungles and a shimmering bay, was she not implicitly promising him a future of which these stolen moments were but a paltry hint? And so, though he had learned to impersonate successfully if not brilliantly a young man who dwelt in the city in the company of others, he had, in his most essential self, little patience or desire for the bland hypocrisy of other people or the harshness of city life.

But now that he had found his true home, other desires nagged at him that seemed to have nothing to do with cities or jungles but with his own physical need for a sympathetic companion. He had lost an essential connection to his mother, and not so much because she had found a companion for herself in the person of Quentin McLeod; he liked McLeod, who seemed less desirous of supplanting Harry in his mother's affections than of sharing in them. No, the fraying of their connection had begun the night his father died, and Harry was adult enough now to admit to himself that his guilt and secrecy itself had come between them. That he had kept things from her made him unable to challenge the fact that she had a life apart from him, that, in fact, she kept things from him too. Her entire relationship with McLeod was cloaked in secrecy; she had yet to confide in him any of what she felt for the man, though Harry was able to glean much of it simply from observation. He felt now that he spoke to her as if trying to reweave the fabric of their love without the necessary guiding needle of truth and so wavered, faltering and losing the thread.

This division left him with a sadness he had never known. He cherished what he and his mother had been for each other, almost as if she were dead, but her presence was often a painful reminder of what they no longer had. He yearned for another soul to join with his.

When Maria Sparks had come into his life, he had not wanted to appear desperate and lonely, but neither could he manage even an impersonation of the cool insouciance he'd been taught in Middleton society. One day Maria appeared with her father and brothers and their delivery of a supply of lumber for additional rear balconies for the Miami Hotel. She wore the same dress, he noticed, as she'd worn at the settlers' dinner, only the sprig of pansies had been replaced by a red bow and there was a red ribbon tied around her waist, a bit frayed at the edges, and another in her hair. Harry was moved to pity at its simplicity and flattered too that she dressed so for him. That she had come to see him demonstrated her willingness in a way that a girl up North never would have, and he appreciated her forthrightness and lack of guile.

He watched her while her brothers unloaded the lumber. Speculation was that the squall responsible for wrecking the French ship *Bonaire,* which had supplied the weathered timber pile in the Sparkses' schooner, was the last one of the season, although the oldest Sparks son referred darkly to surprise storms as late as late October. Today, though, the sky was clear and cloudless, the bay smooth, the river clear and green. After all the lumber had been hauled from the boat up to the site, and they'd all eaten their fill of Geneva's lunch of cold meats and elderberry pie, Maria walked to the end of the porch and, when Harry followed, asked how his groves were coming along. Harry took this as his cue to say that she could see for herself if she really did want to know.

"Now?"

"The path's pretty rough," he warned her, "just what's left of an old Seminole trail."

Maria made an elaborate shrug. "I was born and raised in the hammock, and I am certainly no stranger to the roughest kind of roads, Mr. Reade."

With a promise made to Cal Sparks that Harry would bring her home before dark, they set out; true to her word, Maria made no complaints, though Harry was aware that she'd snagged her good dress more than once en route.

They hardly spoke as they walked, though Harry was acutely aware of her measured breathing beside him and the faint panting that replaced it by the time they reached the groves. The trees were especially lush and fragrant, Harry thought, the result of the recent rain. "Smell the perfume!" He was flushed with pride in them. He hefted a wheelbarrow full of seaweed and pushed it down a row of young trees with Maria close behind him.

"You see, first I have to wade around the mangrove swamps and pick out pieces of seaweed," he told her. "Or dive down into the bay to get it. That's why my arms are so scratched up." He set the barrow down and rolled back his sleeves to show her. "The reefs're sharp as razors."

"Oh, you poor dear," Maria murmured and reached out to lay a gentle hand on Harry's arm, then hesitated and looked up into his eyes. "Will it hurt if I touch?"

"Mostly they're healed up by now," he said and watched her fingers hover over the scratches.

"Seems a steep price to pay for some seaweed."

"It's the best thing to protect young trees," Harry explained. "Just pack it around, see?" He knelt down and hauled out dripping handfuls of it to pile loosely at the tree base.

Maria looked around at the rows that stretched in every direction to the horizon line. "And you have to do that to all these?"

Harry laughed as he rose, brushing sand from his trousers. "Not to all of them," he said. "Only the young ones so they don't get blown down or get eaten up by possums and coons and rabbits. Nothing a rabbit likes more than tasty roots from a young orange tree. And of course I hired people from Key West to help me," he added.

"That must have cost a lot of money," Maria said.

Harry shrugged. "My mother says you have to know how to spend money to make money," he replied.

"My father says the same thing," Maria said. "Only he's just got to the knowing-how-to-spend-it part," she added with a harsh little laugh. "Junk picker's what he is. Oranges all around him and he never thought they was the way to get rich."

Harry laughed too. "I don't know about getting rich on them. I just work awfully hard." He shielded his eyes with his hand and scanned the rows fanned out before him. "That smell ... Did you know that we're on the same latitude line here as Bethlehem?"

"No, I did not."

"Not that I'm a religious person, but it does make you think, doesn't it?"

Maria shrugged and turned away. "I think I'm gonna sneeze," she said and buried her face in her hands. Harry proffered a handkerchief and she was glad at least to get his attention off oranges and back on her.

Her visit lasted the afternoon, and the next time her father and brothers made a delivery of lumber, she came again, and once she came on her own. On their third outing together, Maria was uncharacteristically silent, even downcast, no chattering about sunken treasures or the jewels of the King of Spain, but as Harry had plenty of chores to see to in the groves, he couldn't pay much mind to her mood. He sort of liked it when she rambled on and on the way she did, though sometimes he found himself wishing she'd talk about something else—he had the privileged young man's aversion to conversation solely about money—and sometimes he just stopped listening to her words altogether and heard the sound of her voice as simply another sound in the grove, a sonorous, not unpleasant drone with an occasional dive or swoop or trill of laughter that easily fit into the chorus of birds and insects.

Maria sat on an upended orange crate as Harry worked, staring sightlessly down one of the seemingly endless rows of orange trees. There was something about their perfume that made her dizzy; she did not think she could spend too much time here—not in this heat anyway and not with her woman's problem having come on her just last night, and though of course it might be interesting to faint at his feet right this minute just to see what Mr. Harry Reade would do, she knew she must not risk spoiling things with the wrong kind of behavior. She was breathing deeply through her mouth, only now she felt a sour sweetness rising on the back of her tongue and she was nearly overcome with the flushed anxiety that always came along with these monthly spells. She started stroking the palms of her hands down the front of her skirt.

"Oh, Mr. Reade, half the time I don't know what to do!"

Harry turned, surprised at the sudden alarm in her voice. "What's the matter?"

"I feel so . . . so in between things. Not quite here and not quite there. No land, no house I can be proud to call my own. I'll be an old maid before you know it, living out in the woods, crazy as a loon, keeping chickens and making quilts for my nephews and nieces."

Harry rose from his knees and stood beside her. "You're too pretty to be an old maid," he said.

"You think I'm pretty?" She laughed sourly. "That's 'cause you don't look at nothing but oranges all day."

"No, I mean it!"

Maria turned away from him and spoke in a low voice that made Harry lean toward her to hear. "Ever since my mama died, it's been so hard for me. My daddy and brothers need for me to take care of 'em. Those men and their big appetites." She was wringing her hands now and gave him a quick, brave smile. "My mama . . . killed herself, maybe you heard. I was only twelve, but I had to take up the slack. Sometimes I feel so sad when I think about her, and then sometimes it just makes me mad. Her leaving us like that, leaving me all her work." Her eyes filled with tears and she blinked them back as if to show Harry that they would not get the better of her.

Harry felt hot and restless; he wanted to regain the cool calm he always felt in the groves, but the image of her distress made it impossible. How could she be so unhappy here of all places?

He reached for her hand; it lay in his, light as a baby bird. Harry covered it gently with his other hand and felt her fingers flutter with nervous strength, as if she might grip him hard or pull away.

"I wish . . . ," she said softly.

Harry saw a lone tear slide slowly down her cheek and a sympathetic fullness rose in his chest. He did not quite understand this feeling, but wanting to stifle it somehow, he pulled her toward him. She didn't resist, nor did she resist when he pressed his lips to her cheek and stopped the track of her tear. A sob caught in her throat and she leaned her head against his chest. He drew her close. Her hair was silky under his chin; their hearts beat against each other.

"I want things of my own," she said, her breath hot against his chest. "Not my daddy's, not my brothers'." She turned her face up to look at him. "Everyone's got nice things but me," she whispered desperately. "Everyone. Everyone. Everyone but me." She fell against him again, crying softly.

Harry thought that yes, he did have things that were his very own, but the revelation that the source of her distress was material seemed coarse and a bit repellent, and it made him pull back for a moment. Maria sensed him drifting and clung to him anew, sobbing, and Harry found that he could not help but smooth his hand over the back of her head. Yet something of him remained apart as a voice in him alerted him to be wary, but so muted was this voice, so evanescent its message, that its import eluded him; as it was very like the voice of fear, he felt he must silence it, that it meant only to interfere with the expression of love, that he would be a coward and a fool, a betrayer of his manly impulses, to heed its warning.

He breathed deeply and the voice quieted, the tension in his chest and neck slowly loosened, and Maria slid deeper into his arms. He looked down the rows of his wonderful orange trees: there was so much tending still to do, and this new love was tinged with such sadness. A woman was weeping in his arms. "You have me," he told her.

14.

Every train brought new settlers; the railroad cars themselves seemed to bulge with people, and baggage was often hanging out windows and strapped to the roofs. Tent cities sprouted up on the edges of the jungle like a new form of plant life, with so many people in each tent they had to sleep in alternating shifts. Flophouses appeared along the bay, thrown together out of lumber scraps and sorghum paste with palm frond roofs. Once-grand floating hotels steamed up from retirement in Key West. Clara began yet another project to expand the Miami Hotel to four stories, and families were camping out on straw pallets before the roof was even put up.

To encourage migration south, Wheeler offered to refund the cost of the railroad ticket to anyone who bought land. Clara found that even the inexpensive lots she owned on the outskirts went fast, especially to the newcomers who didn't know just how far away they'd be from the town, the roads, and the railroad tracks. Some, counting out the payments from sacks of pennies, even bought land west of the tracks in what was called "back country." Of course there was free homesteading land available from the government too, a good deal if you didn't mind ninety percent of it being underwater.

Each train also brought carloads of building materials, and the sounds Clara thought she'd heard the last of—hammering and sawing—once again filled the air like an orchestral score entitled *Town Being Built*. Men worked for a dollar a sunup-to-sundown day, chopping away pine trees and palmetto to clear more acreage to the town's projected limits. If the sky clouded up they set down their axes, insisting they'd only agreed to work when the sun shone; while they sat and waited they burned piles of rags to keep mosquitoes away and passed around a good Cuban cigar and spun tales of how rich Miami was going to make them.

The Stargers expanded their restaurant with a loan from Clara when the Bank of Biscayne turned them down because they did not own land. Mrs. Starger specialized in dishes from her native Germany, and the smell of beer and bratwurst and sauerkraut joined the smells of sawdust and sunshine and brine. There was no public transportation within the city—the official limits of which had yet to be defined—but Tommy Schell, recognizing there was a need, since many had come on the train and hadn't the money yet for a horse and buggy, rented out teams. One of Cal Sparks's boys was the first victim of a traffic accident—he broke his wrist when he backed into the street with a load of arrowroot starch and collided with the mortician's hack.

Clara, as self-appointed watchdog of the city's cleanliness—"Growing lack of it's a more apt description," she noted grimly—composed a warning to be printed in *The Metropolis* and badgered Sheriff McCordle to agree to enforce it and Elliot Iverson to run it in every issue until the situation improved: "Filth, the contents of cesspools, offal, garbage, foul water, urine, stable manure, decay of animal or vegetable matter thrown or placed or allowed in or upon any private premises, street, avenue, alley, sidewalk, gutter, or private reservation is punishable by a fine of from five to twenty-five dollars." Wheeler finally took the hint, and a new sewer pipe was laid that dumped the sewage in the bay. Though Clara objected—"Now the pipe pollutes the water instead of the land"—McCordle was satisfied. "This will do away with any grounds for complaints," he was quoted as saying. Iverson, who published the sheriff's remark, privately told Clara that the man simply wanted her to stop bothering him.

The first wave of land speculators to arrive were full of bright ideas on how to make a buck out of other people's labors. They came in dressed for the city and found instead a wilderness that called itself a city when the city had yet to be built; they were full of sneering contempt for the early arrivals, who still had sand under their finger-nails. Most of them tried to buy the best downtown land from Clara, who refused to sell unless she knew what use the land would be put to. "I don't want slaughterhouses or ice-making plants in the downtown section," she told them. "And no saloons anywhere." Some of Clara's early land buyers, eager to turn a quick profit, let some of their ham-mock acreage go, and the speculators bought fast and for cash, quickly built crude shacks and rough roads and called them homesteads with names like Pinetree Haven, Key Naranja, Sapodilla Springs. Clara turned them away from her office door. "Why won't you sell to me?" each demanded. "Ain't my dollars green as anyone's?"

She and Wheeler had agreed to push vigorously for the sale of lots in what had been plotted as the downtown section. She spent mornings in her office interviewing prospective buyers and arranging financing for those who could afford the down payments: Miami Avenue corner lots of seventy-five hundred square feet went for nine hundred dollars, inside lots for eight. Lots on the bay, cheap at two hundred, still went begging; no one wanted to be that far out of town. On the south bank, where access was strictly by boat, Rufus Finch sold no land at all.

One of those prospective buyers, Emmett Flye, stood at the picture window of Clara's office and looked out at the street. "What this place needs now is a good sketch artist from Harper's Illustrated Weekly," he said to Clara. "Someone to document all that's going on. Because pretty soon, mark my words, it's gonna be very different." He nodded slowly at a woman with bundles of supplies emerging from Fine's General Merchandise. "Progressive too, I see," Flye added. "You're even getting Jews."

Flye wore a yellow checkered suit, tight at the chest, a brown bowler hat, and spats. He lit a thin Cuban cigar bought off a street peddler fresh from Havana and puffed it with great satisfaction. He had just come from Southern California, where he had almost made his fortune selling "Ocean Vista" lots that faced the Mohave Desert to Easterners with little knowledge of the terrain except for what they read in Flye's fantastically worded brochures. The sheriff of Santa Monica county, whose palm Flye failed to cross with silver, blew the whistle. Flye got out of town without serving a jail sentence but also without the fortune promised by that Promised Land.

"Once land starts getting settled like this," he was saying to Clara now, "the whole thing takes on a kind of momentum that's stronger than any one of its individual elements. It's a simple law of science, Mrs. Reade. But I know how you feel and I can help." Flye turned to her from the window. He had white skin that would go pink as a baby girl's after a day in the sun; his smile showed very small, sharp teeth. "The value of your holdings can go up a hundred, make that two hundred, percent. I can put this place on the map."

Impatient with his attitude of having "discovered" the town, Clara shuffled papers on her desk. "It's already on the map."

Flye laughed and waved his cigar at the street, drawing a trail of smoke across the room. "This? A pokey little nothing teetering on the edge of nowhere." He inhaled the cigar smoke deeply, pleased at the aptness of the image, then coughed, tears forming in his eyes; he sat down and caught his breath, burying the cigar in a tin cup of sand filled expressly for that purpose.

"Let me give you a little sample of what I have in mind," he said when he recovered. "Free of charge, natch." He withdrew from his inside pocket a much-folded sheet of paper, smoothed it out on his thigh, and read aloud in a voice gone suddenly stentorian. " 'I will say without fear of contradiction that for those wishing a tropical climate there is nothing finer in the United States and—I believe I am safe in saying—the entire world than Southern California—' " He looked up at Clara from beneath his brows and shrugged. "I've used this pitch before, as a sample. Got State Senator Buddinger to put his name to it. For a nominal fee, of course. You'd be amazed at who you can get for an endorsement, Mrs. Reade. Names are real useful in attracting your higher type of clientele." He cleared his throat and continued reading. " 'Some say that climate is all we have here in . . . ' Here's where we substitute 'Florida' for 'Southern California,' and then we get somebody big, somebody in politics or maybe a famous author. Why, when I was selling land in Southern California, the famous authoress Helen Hunt Jackson was making speeches on behalf of Sea View Acres in Ventura County. Sold 'em out in no time flat for a hefty profit on practically no cash outlay at all."

Clara stood and indicated the door. "I'm not interested."

"Not interested? Or not willing?"

Clara saw him wipe the fine beads of sweat from his upper lip; for a moment she pitied him. "Not willing to throw my land to the dogs and not interested in hearing any more about it."

Flye sat up straighter. "What makes you so tough, Mrs. Reade?" His voice had gone harsh, as if, having ruined his chances, he could lose nothing with a ruder approach. "Or are you just reluctant to see this town get a little help in progressing on its natural course? Does that sort of thing threaten you? Do you enjoy keeping other people down?"

"The town is already well on its way, and I'm tired of people like you coming in here now and wanting to suck money from it."

"I'm talking about the town making money!" Flye insisted, red-faced. "You making money."

"I suppose you would be donating your service, Mr. Flye?"

"Would you begrudge a man a living?" He stared at her for a moment, then laughed unpleasantly. "I just thought you'd want to have some say in what kind of people come down and settle here." By Clara's hesitation he knew he'd finally made a point. "Look," he said and leaned toward her. "We all agree that it's the sun and the soil that's going to make this place if it's going to be made at all. You do agree with me on that?"

Clara nodded reluctantly. "That still doesn't mean I want to have anything to do with you."

Flye shrugged as if to say he was beyond having personal feelings. "See, around the rest of the country no one knows about this place. Everyone went west and forgot all about coming this far south. They think you maybe got alligators waiting for 'em. Malaria and bugs and snakes and who knows what all. But I could make this place sound like South America and the Mediterranean all rolled into one. That's what I'd say in my brochures, Mrs. Reade. Why I bet you could grow Greek olives here and coffee beans too. Maybe silk, with all them mulberry trees. Think what could happen if real cultivation of the land was to happen. The possibilities, Mrs. Reade. Think of the possibilities." He paused for a moment and wiped his mouth. "Or do you want this place to become another St. Augustine or Palm Beach? Full of rich northerners with bronchial congestion. Oh, a lot of doctors'll get rich, but when you walk alongside the river, it won't be the birds you'll hear singing, it'll be some old geezer wheezing his lungs away." One eye on Clara, he refolded his brochure and replaced it carefully inside his jacket, then put his hand on the doorknob and prepared to leave. "Let me just say one more thing."

"Let me save you the trouble, Mr. Flye," Clara said. "I don't need you or anyone else to tell me what has happened or is happening or will happen to my city." She sat behind her desk and began going through a pile of land deeds.

Flye smiled and tipped his hat. "I bow to your superior wisdom, Mrs. Reade," he said. "But don't kid yourself."

Clara looked up from her papers. "I beg your pardon?"

"Take a good long look, Mrs. Reade," he said and bowed from the waist. "The wave of the future is walking out your door."

The official tourist season was determined by the Northerners who constituted it—Northerners who knew well that the crystalline joy of Christmas and New Year's in New York, Boston, and Chicago, as depicted in the charming etchings of Currier and Ives, bore little actual resemblance to the slush-bound streets, punishingly bitter cold, and stuffy, overheated rooms of those cities. So sheets were thrown over heavy furniture, winter clothes dusted with camphor, summer clothes cleaned and ironed, and by the middle of January luggage and passengers—including maids, valets, and pet Pekinese—were headed south.

Though Clara and Wheeler and other businessmen investors had long-range plans to the contrary, for the time being, tourism was the town's most lucrative industry and time was calculated by the season. In between the end of one season and the beginning of another everyone rushed to improve the city and to get it ready for the tourists to pour back into town. Thankfully, tourism was on the rise, due in equal parts to the sheer glories of the terrain and the weather and to the endorsements given it by prominent visitors drawn by the promise of the Royal Palm Hotel. Phil Armour, the Chicago meat tycoon, brought his yacht down, prepared to sneer at Wheeler's folly and sail off grinning to Nassau, but he was big enough to change his mind when he saw the place, wiring wife, daughter, and other chilled Chicagoans to come down to the sun. Political analyst Jed Packer came and pronounced the hunting first-class; he'd boosted more than one president into office, and folks extrapolated from that that he knew about game. Young millionaires came for their honeymoons; old ones came for their health.

The completion of the Royal Palm put the seal of approval on this venture called Miami. Whatever doubts had existed about Carlisle de Beaupré were forgotten once the scaffolding on the hotel was dismantled—a process as seductive and tantalizing as an unknown woman slowly removing a veil—and the marvel of design and construction was revealed. Situated where the river flowed into the bay, the U-shaped, clapboard building was six hundred and eighty feet long, with two massive wings perpendicular to the main body, its chief design feature a lawn-green mansard roof dotted with dormers. It was five stories tall, with a six-story center section housing F. Morrison Wheeler's immense private suite and topped by a lookout platform from which guests were treated to the views of the bay, a glassy aquamarine expanse veined with deep purple coral reefs. They could also look down upon the town and its ever-expanding gridwork of streets, and up the river as it wound its way from the distant, mysterious Everglades.

Fronting the long eastern side of the hotel was a veranda under striped awnings where the rocking chair brigade assembled to meet the bay breeze as it swept across a green lawn, which had been brought in sodded sections from Atlanta, complete with daisies, weeds, and ants, and which had been not so much planted as rolled out like carpeting. On the lawn stood an onion-domed gazebo with fretwork delicate as a bird cage—a gift from Viscount Linley-Ferard, who had helped finance the pavilion at Brighton to which this gift bore a resemblance in miniature—and a covered wishing well dedicated to the warrior Osceola, a public relations gesture performed less to placate the displaced Indians than to create a connection, however spurious, to the Seminole habitation of the past.

The hotel was painted a much mixed and much ballyhooed shade of yellow: duller than daffodil, more restful than canary, with something of the glow of apricot and the lucidity of lemon. Aaron Fine sponsored a contest to name the color, the prize two free gallons of it; the winner was the piano teacher Madame Carney with Sunrise Blush.

De Beaupré's design for the Royal Palm Hotel was closer in concept to modern colonial than to anything that would evoke the Spanish heritage of Florida. His sentiments were to leave Addison Mizener's look—a bastardization of Spanish, Moorish, and Mediterranean—to Palm Beach. De Beaupré saw the Royal Palm as belonging less to Spanish Florida—of which the only local evidence was the hideous stucco monstrosity of Fort Dallas—than to tropical America. His design would be a living organism on the continuum of native American architecture, though given his background in the classical vocabulary of the Beaux Arts school, the hotel was as grand in conception and execution as if the Petit Trianon had been rethought in wood.

In the past, if a structure he was building was meant for a waterfront site, de Beaupré would have placed it on a cliff or a rise set back from and above the sea. In addition to keeping the structure well above the temperamental tides and allowing it to catch the sea breeze, these locations afforded the owners as expansive a view as their money and self-esteem demanded. In the cliffside communities of Newport and Narragansett this worked well, but at the juncture of the Miami River and Biscayne Bay, the Florida landscape was flat. However, de Beaupré was clever enough to realize that despite such problems, the major asset of the Royal Palm was nevertheless its site. Without tall trees to frame it or hills to set it off, he gave the hotel itself the rises and falls, the angles and turns, that nature omitted, and he used the landscape in such a way that in the end he got as much credit for the view and the setting as if he had thought them up himself.

The garden was landscaped to simulate—in a more aesthetically acceptable and practical manner, of course—the very hammock land that had been razed to make way for it; when praised for respecting the natural splendor, de Beaupré modestly admitted that he simply knew what to remove. Since blasting had destroyed the original trees, however, hundreds of coconut palms had been brought full grown from Elliott's Key, along with yucca and banyan trees, artfully strung with vines of orchids. Tropical birds—parrots, toucans, macaws, flamingos—were brought in to nest and strut along the great lawn, though between the time the last pieces of scaffolding came down and the first Astor checked in, the birds had disappeared back into the wild.

There was a putting green for golfers, a private dock for fishermen and their yachts, horse trails into the hammock, and smooth green tennis lawns banked by a viewing section equipped with a network of screens and a tent for luncheons al fresco. A mile-long road of crushed oolitic limestone encircling the grounds made for noiseless carriage rides; at night it shimmered like a ribbon of pure moonlight.

In every way the hotel's interior was calculated to elicit successive gasps of wonder: the walls were painted egret white and made bright and gleaming by thousands of electric wall lights, table lamps, sentinel poles, and chandeliers. Sunlight rarely made direct access into public or private rooms—it would only fade furniture and carpets—but was filtered instead through glass of amber, ruby, cobalt, and emerald. Guests reached the upper rooms in electric elevators lined in mahogany and furnished with tufted benches under pier glasses. There were also a half-dozen sets of interior stairwells for the invisible comings and goings of the servants.

Private suites (of up to five bedrooms and three baths) and studio rooms alike were decorated with post-Victorian wicker trimmed down, de-scrolled, unfretted, with just enough talc white paint to make them shine and not so much that they were too stiff to give and groan with the weight of their users. The main dining room—a circular affair with tables fanning out like spokes from a marble fountain—gave out onto the bay and its tall, beveled glass doors were left open to catch the breezes. The limestone road ran past it so that a guest arriving after dark could enjoy the welcoming spectacle of fifty chandeliers and twice that many sconces illuminating a room of gold and rose and mauve.

There were writing rooms with special stationery for ladies featuring an embossed cut of a royal palm tree with a wreath around it and the inscription "Hotel Royal Palm, Biscayne Bay, Florida"; a billiards room of dark green walls and teak racks; a reading room stocked with leather-bound classics; an arcade of shops from New York, London, and Paris in addition to local ones; and a swimming pool where the most daring women bared arms and feet to bathe.

In the shadows of the Royal Palm, the tent community that had formed of railroad and hotel construction workers continued to grow. The tents they lived in were of an unappetizing green canvas almost high enough for a short adult to stand up in, with slatted wood floors and canvas windows and doors that rolled open and shut but with nothing to keep out the mosquitoes except cuss words. The rains of winter and the dampness of spring did nothing for the tempers of the dwellers in Tent City but plenty for mildew and rot and gnats. Still, humor somehow remained high, maybe because these workers could see the town taking shape around them, could see its future and their own place in it. And besides, it cost them nothing to be patient.

After the initial flurry of interest caused by the explosions, excavations, and revelations of the hotel, capped by the contest to name its hue, the people of the town partook but little of its pleasures. Fifteen cents bought them a swim in the pool, but once the novelty had been sampled, they admitted a preference for the bay. Still they were enormously proud of the hotel's lavishness—"It's like living near the Sphinx!"—and the wealth it attracted made them feel sure that their town was securely on the path toward success. Much to Clara's relief, even Rufus and Ida Finch got lucky; they took out ads in *The Metropolis* advertising trips to the Fountain of Youth and piloted oldsters to a natural mineral spring on the south bank of the river where the water went for ten cents a glass, two bits bottled. They told Clara they had plans to set up a little café there, and when a bridge was built to the south shore they'd expand it into an inn, then maybe a hotel.

The merchants who had rubbed their palms in anticipation of the buying power of the guests were both gratified and disappointed at the materialization of their hopes, for though business improved, it was mainly the servants of the guests who did the shopping, and the merchants knew that as long as the guests themselves kept to the hotel and its shops, the hoped-for boom in business would not occur. The town still had its frontier aspect, and if you blanched at the thought of going all the way out west, you could spend an afternoon on Miami Avenue and experience the same effect.

And what a sight these guests presented to the residents of town as, dressed in the latest of fashion, they moved cautiously on the dusty streets! The women's hats had brims so wide that their owners could walk with heads held high and still keep their faces in shade, because only manual laborers and shameless servants allowed their skin to be coarsened by overexposure. The hotel veranda stretched as long as it did just so that people could get the benefit of the warm tropical breezes and be shaded at the same time. Even veils could not mask the whiteness of skin thus protected, and augmented by powders that, in the inescapable heat, mixed with perspiration and caked to reveal the pinker tones beneath. The women took small, tentative steps, but what else could they do in skirts this tight at the ankle? And what tiny voices piped out from behind those veils! And what tiny, delicate hands in skin-tight lace gloves! The guests glanced uneasily at the town women they passed, repelled by the frank rawness of the skin on their hands and faces. Some of them were bonneted and others bareheaded, they noted with horror. So these were the native citizens of this place— these people in homespun, crude linen, these scrawny women in shapeless dresses who took long, unfeminine strides and who had bony faces and permanent squints. "How . . . fascinating, and how quaint," they were heard to remark before beating a hasty carriage retreat to the safety of the Royal Palm's civilization.

After porch rocking, golf and tennis, bathing in the hotel pool, and shopping—all of which Wheeler himself admitted could be done in any decent Southern hotel—it was the natural terrain itself that was the big attraction. Palm groves and wild orchids, mangrove swamps and rainbow fish, Indians and arrowroot mills, saw grass, bougainvillea, the Everglades—this was another world! The residents of the bay referred to these first winter tourists—not to their faces, of course— as "the swells." Anxious to demonstrate their advanced level of cultural refinement, the visitors could be heard peppering their chatter on Miami Avenue with many an *à bientôt* and a *tout à l'heure*. Often they seemed to reel back in astonished delight—"Look at this flower! Why, it is the *invention* of the color red!" "Did you see yesterday's sunset? It was as if there had never really *been* a sunset before!"—as if they were second in line after Ponce de León himself in discovering the place, and never mind that the Finches and the Gorams and the Sparkses and a dozen other families had been there a decade before, the Spanish two centuries before, the Seminoles close on to forever.

For the men, deep-sea fishing was the most exciting pastime, and this was where McLeod's expertise would come in handiest, or so Clara thought. And though he agreed to pilot the *Newport* on these expeditions, he was not available for the every Tuesday and Thursday kind of affair Clara had in mind. McLeod was forever coming and going—to the West Indies and Venezuela to scout for new seed samplings for the Van Lieu experimental station, to Key West to sell his own vegetables, to who knew where to do who knew what. Clara agreed with Geneva when she said that Mr. McLeod was as hard to pin down as dandelion fluff.

"You could make a fortune if I could get you to stick to a schedule," she told him. "You could have a fleet of boats. You wouldn't even have to be here, just lend your name and reputation—"

"Don't need a fortune," he replied with a shrug. "I know that makes me stick out like a sore thumb around here these days but . . ."

"What *do* you want, Quentin?" Clara asked. They had eaten dinner on the porch of her house; the sun was setting behind them and the candles had just been lit; there was the smell of strong coffee in the air and the faint perfume of the gardenia Clara wore in her hair.

McLeod hunched over the table to light his pipe, then sat back and looked at her, his blue eyes clear and bright and frank as day. "Why're you so anxious to have me around here so much?"

Clara met his gaze straight on. "I think you know why," she replied.

"Jesus, Clara!" he said in exasperation, then tossed his pipe on his dinner plate and leaned toward her. "When you look at me that way, you make me think that all the rest of this is just a lot of . . . of . . . that the only thing that really counts is—"

Clara shook her head to stop him from continuing and looked down at her hands clenched in her lap. After a moment of silence, McLeod picked up his pipe again. Soon he was lost in a cloud of smoke, and the moment for a new declaration passed as quietly and sadly as a boat containing a loved one disappears over a horizon.

The moment for compromise, he knew, had passed for both of them, and McLeod felt as guilty for letting his courage fail him as Clara did; to please her, he hired himself out occasionally as a tour guide and led boating parties in the *Newport* to the burned-out lighthouse on Passion Key, sending shivers down spines with the stories of the Seminole War of 1836 and how John Lloyd and his lady friend were trapped in the tower when the staircase was burned. There were boats from Jacksonville and Tampa, Key West and Pensacola and other ports on the gulf, plus schooners from the Bahamas docking regularly on the bay, though the steamer the *Murphy D.* was forced to anchor two miles down the bay because the water wasn't deep enough. Other boat trips organized by Clara led the tourists to crocodile breeding grounds, to the Miami River rapids, to the natural bridge at Arch Creek and the bug-infested mangrove swamp across the bay—the original settlers called it the Beach—that some fools from up north had bought sight unseen and now were trying to turn into an avocado ranch. There was even a carriage trip to the Reade Groves, which Clara led herself.

The ladies contented themselves with bicycle rides along the smooth mile-long limestone road circling the hotel, a road that Emmett Flye, hired by Wheeler to publicize the hotel around the country, described as "the most perfect in the state." Another of Flye's brochures called the town "America's sun porch." At the end of a long day, the ladies strolled to the hotel docks under large hats and umbrellas, their long skirts blowing in the breeze, to welcome their weary men ashore, graciously smiling alongside the odoriferous catch of tarpon, whip ray, and herring hog, thus captured for photographs that would appear in rotogravure sections of papers across the country.

The runaway growth of the town was not exactly what Clara had expected, and every day she saw—in the increased traffic on the streets she was used to walking, in the lines outside land sales offices, in the overcrowded docks and arriving trains and lack of housing, in the stream of boats steaming up and down the Miami River—how naive had been her vision of this ideal city and how difficult it was to control the city's growth.

In addition Clara was worried about money. Profits from the sale of the Reade Ironworks in Middleton were almost gone. What she took in from the boat tours she organized was barely enough to pay the guides. Income from the Reade orange groves had to be used first to pay the workers, then for increasingly high freight charges; what was left was reinvested in plants, seeds, fertilizer, equipment. The Miami Hotel was rarely booked to capacity during the tourist season— not when the luxury accommodations could be found elsewhere— yet it was still in the process of expansion and had not shown up in the black. Loans she had made to the Stargers, to Aaron Fine, to Tommy Schell and a dozen others remained outstanding for the most part, and she was now in the awkward position of seeing these people prosper while they still owed her money. She was not unaware of the irony that it appeared to everyone in town that the Founding Mother was a woman of considerable means.

To stave off anxiety about her dwindling resources, she kept reminding herself that it was the short picture at which she was looking; Miami was growing, no doubt about it. *Miami on the Move,* in fact, was the latest in a series of railroad brochures distributed along the line. There was enormous profit yet to be made if she could just hang on to her land. But the land she retained—at the juncture of bay and river, surrounding the Royal Palm and including Fort Dallas and its environs, the Reade Groves, and less desirable hammock and Everglade acreage—was her only asset, and the thought of selling it was repellent to her. She railed at what Wheeler and the developers who'd bought from him were doing—burning hammock land and dynamiting mangroves to build unappealing wooden homes far in advance of actual need—and found herself in the position of protectress of the land she owned, a position that further reduced her finances.

But the machine of progress was moving, and she continued to move forward with it as Clara Reade, businesswoman, lumber dealer, negotiator, real estate agent, advisor, money lender. She walked the town every day now and knew it as she knew her own house and yard. She would put on the sturdiest pair of brogans Smiley's stocked and start at the northern boundary line—the intersection of North Miami Avenue and Fifteenth Street—then head south, where she picked up the new limestone road being laid for the Royal Palm and strolled among the workers around the shoreline of Biscayne Bay.

As she and Wheeler had planned, the numbered streets ran east and west, the named cross streets alphabetically north and south. There was a street named Wheeler and another named Reade; since their initials came so late in the alphabet, the cross streets started at Z and worked backwards. East of Avenue T on Thirteenth and Fourteenth streets, most of the houses were two-storied wood frames that the railroad had built for its workers, leaving the tents to the Negroes. Painted white, they all had small front porches and dark gray trim, and their boxy silhouette would have looked familiar to anyone from Cheshire, Massachusetts, or Moline, Illinois. There were a few brick-veneer buildings on Wheeler and First Street—the new Bank of Biscayne, the Bull Rapid Furniture Emporium—and some balconied dwellings on Reade and Ninth, though most were plain pine clapboard saltboxes, roofed in rough shingles and stained dark to cut the glare.

The sidewalks everywhere were still planked and wobbly, and the streets in general, though forty feet wide in optimistic anticipation of increased traffic, were muddied by rainfall, pitted and rutted with horse and carriage tracks. Clara had sold barren acreage of coral and limestone to a buyer who had quarried the rock for the hotel road; he swore that paved streets in town were the next step.

Clara was used to seeing familiar faces during her walks and to greeting people on the street by name, since nearly all of them, at one time or another, had come through her office for advice, for money, to make a deal for land, to rent a storefront. She marveled at their high spirits and energy; why, even the most routine daily happenings were exciting just because they were demonstrations that the town was made up not of railroads and stores, but people: Mrs. Geoghan setting potted plants out in the sun on the balcony over her husband's Groceries and Grains, and drying sheets used on her boarder's bed, and shouting that her elderberry muffins were done and for sale; Ella Starger calling for her brother Simon, who lounged inside Bugsby's Billiard Parlor when he should have been rolling barrels of millet at the bakery, and Cal Sparks's youngest boy circling around her, too shy to speak; Farley Goram, who swore he'd never come to town, selling fresh-caught pompano off the back of a mule cart.

Clara was always glad for a chance to visit with Flora, who confided with pleasure that they had just filed their homestead claim. "The railroad let us count all the years we been squatting on the property and valued our land at five hundred dollars!"

Farley, wrapping fish in yesterday's *Metropolis,* didn't look at either of them and shook his head as he spoke. "Do you know what Thoreau said? 'We do not ride upon the railroad, it rides upon us.'"

"Can't live in the past forever, though," Clara said.

"Why not?" Farley asked. "People've lived in the past for thousands of years, and I don't see it did them any harm. Were they all fools?"

Ida Finch continued to make weekly trips to the north bank for her piano lessons with Madame Carney, and she would stop by and talk to Clara until it grew dark. "I played nearly the whole of the Prelude today! First time! Madame Carney says I'm coming along real fine and wants me to send away to Montgomery Ward for some Schubert too. Says I got just the right spirit and the right technique, and if I only had the right piano . . . " Clara sensed Ida's loneliness in her reluctance to end these chats—Clara was reluctant herself to end them—for though Clara may have had some nostalgic feeling for the peace and quiet the bay would never see again, Rufus and Ida Finch had looked forward to the noise and activity of their land being developed.

Rufus continued his supply-buying trips to Key West, where he also picked up the mail for everyone in town. But as stores on the north bank began stocking the same merchandise, people objected to the bother of getting in a boat and rowing across the river to get supplies; the postal franchise was the only reason the Finches stayed in business at all. All up and down Miami Avenue there was growing dissatisfaction with this roundabout system. Out of loyalty to the Finches and knowing she was fighting a losing battle, Clara argued for the status quo. And while opinion went against her, there was no agreeable alternative until the government granted a mail contract to the railroad.

"It ain't fair," Rufus Finch declared. He and Ida stood at Clara's office door. Clara sensed that they came to her not only to commiserate but in the hopes that she could somehow change things around. Ida clutched a new book of Schubert to her chest, running her hands over it as if it were a good luck piece.

"I give Wheeler half my land and I get nothing for it," Rufus said, picking at splinters of wood in the door frame as if he would dismantle the whole town that way.

"You've got the rides to the Fountain of Youth," Clara offered. "And what about the inn you're planning on?"

Rufus turned hot, angry eyes on her. "You're not talking to an idiot, Clara Reade." Then he shrugged and continued to pick at the wood. "Or maybe you are. 'Cause I ain't seen one customer buying land on my side of the river, and on this side they're lining up for it at dawn." A splinter pierced his skin and blood came.

"Things'll get better," Clara said.

Rufus licked his thumb. "Optimism comes cheap on the north bank."

"There's still talk of building a bridge across the river," Clara said.

Rufus shook his head. "There's talk of building a staircase to the moon too, and I don't see no one investing in property up there neither."

"The Florida Eastern Star's not going to let all that beautiful land on the south bank go undeveloped," Clara insisted. "You have to be patient. You have to—"

"We had a good little business going before you come to us with your bright idea!"

While Clara did not like being blamed for their troubles, she hesitated to remind them of their willingness to go along with her plans. "I'll do what I can," she said. "I mean it."

"Oh, if I could fill my purse with promises!" He waved his arm to indicate the activity on Miami Avenue: lights and streamers being strung on storefronts for the Christmas season, buggies filled with grain being unloaded at Carlson's Feed and Supply. A parade of tourists lodging at the Miami Hotel moved by the office, loaded down with packages. The iron rang out from Schell's livery; two Cuban vendors hawked tobacco leaves from bales slung across their backs. The very air seemed to shimmer with potential. "And we give the railroad half our land." Rufus shook his head. "What fools we was. It don't mean nothing to them, half our land."

Ida grabbed his arm. "Rufus, maybe Clara's right. Maybe if we're patient—"

He yanked his arm away. "I don't want you coming to this side no more!" He tore the music book from her.

Ida reached out empty arms as he strode from the office. "Rufus, no!" She looked once at Clara, then ran outside where Rufus was tearing the music book apart and throwing it in the street. It got caught up and torn under the wheels of a passing carriage as Rufus disappeared behind a wagonload of fertilizer.

Ida ran into the flow of traffic; a horse reared, the driver shouted at her, and cartons of eggs and a crate of oranges tumbled out. She dropped to her knees to gather what was left of her music. The shredded book was strewn along the street, papers swept in the air were trod underfoot and ground into the sand. A cart's wheel grazed her shoulder and knocked her down.

Clara came and kneeled next to Ida. "I'll speak to Wheeler about the post office. I'll do what I can to—"

Ida clutched the torn pages to her chest and struggled to her feet, turning grief-stricken, accusing eyes on Clara. "You done plenty," she shouted. "You built yourself a town!"

15.

"Are you sure you won't be my escort?" Clara asked when she posed at the doorway of Harry's room. "You look so handsome in your tuxedo." She could tell by the way he turned from her that she had said the wrong thing.

Harry, sitting on his bed in paint-stained mole trousers, was in the process of pulling on a pair of cracked and muddy boots. "I approve of the dress," he told her, "if not the occasion."

"It's business, darling," Clara said with a glance down at the unfamiliar sight of satin rippling to the floor. "Senator McElroy's one of the guests. I've got my interests to protect. Our interests, I mean."

Harry stood up, stomped his boots in place, and dug his rough chambray shirt into his trousers. "I just can't help but see the Royal Palm and all of the pomp attached to it as the very thing Miami can most do without."

"I agree with you," Clara said. "But do you expect me to walk away from it just because it's there?"

"Like me, you mean."

"No, I didn't mean that, I—"

"What about that paradise we were coming to, Mother?"

"We've got it, haven't we?"

Harry shook his head. "Have we?"

Clara moved closer to him and saw him retreat. "You're angry with me."

"No, I'm not!" he protested and gathered together his hat, neckerchief, and Bull Iron work gloves. "There's just so much work left to do on the Miami Hotel. The new roof isn't even on."

Clara nodded and murmured her understanding, but the truth was she didn't understand why he worked so hard or what the great rush was to finish; nor could she quite muster the nerve to ask him to explain, afraid that he might tell her something she had no wish to hear. "I miss you, Harry," she said. "It's been so long since we took one of our walks in the groves or . . . Well, you have Maria now of course and maybe when all this frantic activity dies down you'll be getting—"

"Are you so anxious to have me married off?"

"No, of course not," she said. "Not unless you and Maria . . . You haven't said so, but I thought you loved her."

"Yes, yes, of course I do!" He looked at her with something like pain in his eyes. He let her hold him in her arms, and with his eyes closed for a moment he was back in Middleton, back in that third-floor room, a fire warming the winter day, her voice telling of a wonderful place in the South where they'd go someday. He smelled the faint gardenia perfume she wore as he buried his head in her neck. After a moment he pulled himself away.

"You look beautiful," he said. He smiled and kissed her cheek and saw her downstairs to the waiting rig.

Why do I feel such sadness at this moment? he wondered as he watched her go. He could not say it, but he missed her too, and their love—exclusive, private and primary, fantastical—seemed now irretrievably lost to him. And the promises of those Middleton afternoons, though realized in so many ways, had not delivered something essential to his happiness: someone he dreamed of to take his mother's place as his soul's true companion, a woman to divine in him the simple purpose of his life.

Of course, he had Maria now. He was in love with Maria. I love

Maria, he thought. I love you, Maria, he thought; though he could not make himself say the words to her, he knew they were appropriate. It's fear, he knew, the muted voice he could not still.

Sometimes with Maria, walking in the orange groves or paddling upstream in his flat-bottomed canoe—she prattling on about a beautiful dress she'd seen on a Royal Palm guest who didn't do it justice like she could, or about how meager was the table she was forced to set, nothing but "possum stew and rabbit meat and turnips," while the finest cuts of meat were being eaten in the best houses in town—Harry felt hemmed in, stifled, dying.

"Moody" was Maria's word for it as his attention went wandering. "Harry Reade!" she'd cry. "You're a million miles away! Now stop it. You scare me when you get that look, like you don't know me at all!"

When was he going to do something? Maria wondered at those times. Or was he just going to let them drift along forever like this lazy, good-for-nothing river? Well, it wasn't good enough or fast enough for her, and if Harry Reade wouldn't take the lead, then it was up to her to do it. It'd be the best thing, really; better for both of them in the long run.

The Valentine Ball marked the end of tourism for the year, the official season over, the Northern winter forgotten and the heat of the South becoming a bit too much. Home beckoned: it would not be so bad in the North now, the women reasoned as they packed, and they looked forward, after months of linen and lisle, to the wearing of their spring furs. Even as they dressed for the ball, private railroad cars were being hooked up to the engine in preparation for a noon departure the next day. Blessed winter cold would soon be theirs.

In his private suite on the tower floor of the Royal Palm Hotel, F. Morrison Wheeler was to host a special pre-ball dinner. Wheeler stood at the window and looked down at the ground and exterior of the hotel, which had been strung with thousands of tiny electric lights that made night day. The John Philip Sousa Band, hired for the ball, could be heard playing "The Lights Always Shine on Biscayne Bay," composed especially for the occasion by Florida poet Robert Ellis Archer. A display of fireworks was scheduled for midnight; Frederich Oerlins, the Bavarian engineer who'd done the honors for the unveiling of the Statue of Liberty ten years before, had been hired and given carte blanche. But first Wheeler had something to settle with Clara Reade, something he would couch in the form of a request, of course, a gentlemanly nod to the polite sensibilities of a lady, but which he would get whether she agreed to it or not. But he wanted her in a receptive frame of mind for something else, the other, more delicate, thing he wanted, and to that end had invited her to come a half hour before the others. He checked the dinner table, trying to maintain his emotional equilibrium through the nervous edginess rising in his chest. I should have a wife attending to this table setting, damn her, he thought.

"I don't deserve such special treatment," Clara said as she stepped through the French doors and saw the elaborate preparations.

Wheeler, eyeing the simple, elegant lines of her gown and the smooth sculpture of her bare neck and shoulders, pooh-poohed such modesty. "There is no one more deserving than my esteemed partner."

Clara smiled and let herself be led to a small settee. As she arranged the skirt of her gown and looked out the window across the bay, she felt calm and confident in her association with Wheeler and marveled that she should be this closely allied with a man so close in spirit to her husband. But he differed from Cameron in several ways: F. Morrison Wheeler actually enjoyed his accomplishments, reveled in his own largeness. His imagination, unlike Cameron's, had scope and a quality of vividness. Most significant of all, as far as Clara was concerned, here was a man admired and respected, a feared titan of industry, who treated her as an equal while not ignoring her charms as a woman. He had the courtly, old-fashioned manners of another era, obviously learned late in life, and a true regard, neither patronizing nor obsequious, for what she brought to their dealings. This attraction to him—Clara could not, in good conscience, call it anything less—contained none of the ease and good humor, none of the tenderness or sensual longings she had for McLeod, and she thought ruefully that if McLeod had once taken a firm hold of the reins of his own destiny, all she would ever have noticed of F. Morrison Wheeler would have been his signature on a contract.

They discussed the progress of the town, the beauty of the hotel, the rise in business, and the expected seasonal slump with the desertion of the tourists. "I would like to ask a small favor in that regard," Wheeler said. Clara sat up straighter. "Nothing for you to do, actually," he added hastily. "Undo is more like it." She was staring at him and for a moment he lost the train of his thought. "I want . . . um . . . I want your permission to serve champagne tonight at the Valentine Ball. As a matter of fact, I'd like you to relax your 'no liquor' provision for the whole next three-month tourist season."

Clara shook her head. "I can't do that."

Wheeler brushed an imaginary piece of lint from the knee of his trousers just to keep from looking at her. "Naturally I respect the morality of your position, but why not grant me this one small concession?"

"You misunderstand me," Clara said. "I'm not trying to legislate anyone's morals. It's the future of the city that's my concern."

Wheeler opened his arms expansively. "Mine too. It's our city. You see? We have the same idea."

"But it can't be your idea to have a tavern on every corner," Clara said, "to have drunks shooting up the town. That isn't how we see the future of Miami."

Wheeler had to drag himself from the intensity of her gaze. He walked to a small desk half-hidden in folds of drapery and rustled through some papers, nodding and muttering to himself until he chose one. "This 'no liquor' clause you've had written into these land deeds, Mrs. Reade . . . " He smiled sadly and clipped on his pince-nez to read aloud. " 'No buying, selling, or manufacturing alcoholic drinks inside the city limits.' " He lowered the paper and looked at her over his glasses.

"It's perfectly clear," Clara said. "You signed it yourself when my land went over to you. Everyone who bought land from either of us signed it."

Wheeler slapped the paper on the desk; a fringed lamp fell over and threw his face into grotesque shadow. "What the hell does it mean, 'inside the city limits'?" he demanded. "The city limits had not been established. This document was drawn up before the city even existed!" He crumpled the land deed and threw it to the floor. "Worthless! Unenforceable!" He took a deep breath, then another, and pressed his hands to his chest, calming himself before he dared to speak again. "There are holes in that document wide enough to drive the Florida Eastern Star through."

Clara did not have to reread the document to know the truth of what he was saying, and she was shocked that he had backed her into a corner. She had let down her guard with him too soon; had this been his tactic all along? To ease her into a weakened position, then force his will on her? To protest further, she knew, to plead her case with no further legal assistance or documentation would be folly. For the moment—and though she abhorred the very idea of it—a show of conciliation seemed her only recourse. She hated being at his mercy, though, even if it was temporary, even if it was feigned. Her own guard went up. "If serving champagne during the tourist season is that important to you . . ."

"To us," he said as he took a bottle of champagne from a silver ice bucket and began to work it open. "Mrs. Reade, you have no idea how important." The bottle opened with a pop; he poured the champagne into two glasses and came toward her. "For now I may, with impunity, toast not only our success but"—he gave her a glass, hesitated, then emboldened by the frank look in her eyes, dared to go on—"your loveliness tonight."

He closed his eyes to sip, flushed with the victory of having opened the door to a possible future with Mrs. Reade. Clara watched him over the rim of her glass, not daring to scoff at him just yet but furious that he had changed tracks so quickly, that he had lulled her into an awful complacency—that she had let herself be led! The compliment he paid her seemed, in light of his small triumph over her, an insult, and she would not be so easily gulled, not the next time. That there would be a next time she had no doubt, but it had only taken this one humiliating defeat to see that though as a partner he was stimulating, as an adversary he was dangerous. She sipped her champagne, eyes lowered to hide her rage.

Wheeler, as if sensing that his business maneuverings had pushed her too far, too hard, and too fast, leaned toward her, his voice low now and, despite himself, breathless. "I'm afraid for you, Mrs. Reade. You haven't the right sort of protection. Things could get out of hand and . . . Don't you see how simple it would be for us to become . . . adversaries? I don't want that to happen. I want your cooperation, your trust. I want your friendship and . . . " He stopped. She was so beautiful in the dusky light; the setting sun made her skin glow pink against the blue satin of her dress. "Perhaps . . . perhaps I may hope for more?" Her eyes widened. Was that a ghost of a smile he saw on her lips?

Had he gone too far? Revealed too much? Would she dare reject his offer?

The French doors were suddenly flung open and the rest of the dinner guests entered: Senator and Mrs. Joseph P. McElroy of St. Augustine, whose support in the corridors of government Wheeler was apparently enlisting, and Elliot Iverson of *The Metropolis,* whose presence automatically gave a sense of public occasion to this dinner.

Despite the heat—the slowly revolving ceiling fans did little but stir the humid air—dinner ran to eight courses: clear green turtle soup, escalope of pompano à la Normandie, filet of beef larded à la Cavaur, sweetbread glacé with asparagus tips, quail sur canapé, ribs of beef, and claret jelly and tutti-frutti ice cream. A pair of tiny canaries perched listlessly in the golden cage centered on the table; the New York violinist Alvin Caper accompanied Miss Delia Rolle in a lackluster between-course rendition of art songs by Fauré.

The conversational topics ranged from the heat and rain to housing for the people pouring into the city, life in the North versus life in the South, how new roads into and out of town would serve the farms and orange groves, Dickens's unfinished *Edwin Drood*—"Imagine the possibilities!" said Mrs. McElroy—a long-range plan of municipal building based on the new city charter, new fashions, French cuisine, and the construction of a new railroad depot. Clara had been hostess at enough of her husband's dinners to know that the subject of state aid to the city would not be addressed directly.

Wheeler led the conversation and regaled the company with stories of his by-now mythic rise to success, but his nervousness, his distraction, betrayed itself in the unconscious way he fiddled with his fork and folded and refolded his napkin. Every now and then he threw sidelong glances at Clara Reade and darted his eyes quickly away if she caught him at it. It had been a long time since he had courted a woman's good opinion, and when he had, youth was on his side. Those moments alone with her, when desire had made him briefly, rashly, young, only emphasized the weariness he felt when the moments had passed. Now he felt the hot, dry fingers of old age pressing on his shoulders, urging him down, and the struggle to resist made him perspire in rivulets, but he was determined at least to appear cool, to demonstrate his vigor for Clara Reade's sake.

"If I'd wanted to be overcome by the temperature," Senator McElroy was saying, "I could have stayed in D.C. and turned on the steam heat."

"It's our proximity to the equator," Elliot Iverson said.

"And what is that peculiar odor?" the senator's wife asked.

"It's either the ozone burning up," Wheeler replied, "or crocodiles mating in the bay." Mrs. McElroy gasped in alarm, and Wheeler winked at Clara as if to say: I, at least, have nothing to be on guard about tonight, and what about you?

Iverson laughed with forced heartiness at Wheeler's remark. "As if none of us had experienced warm weather before."

Clara looked at Wheeler when she thought she could watch him unobserved. A veil of respect had been stripped from her eyes and he looked to her suddenly a bit absurd with his garish, youthful cravat and the faintly ridiculous curl to his white mustache. He's gotten himself up like this for me, she thought, but it did not flatter her. When she'd heard about his unhappy marriage, about the mentally disturbed wife and the embarrassment she caused him on the streets and in the salons of Palm Beach, she had felt sympathy for her partner. Now she had to ignore those feelings, and remind herself that she could not trust him.

As dinner ended, the professional dance team of Sischo and Skopp took to the floor and demonstrated the Southern fling; after a few spirited turns Skopp swooned in Sischo's arms and sank in the collapsing *souffle* of her pouf skirt.

"I'm too enervated to complain anymore," said Senator McElroy. Clara watched a bead of perspiration make its slow descent along the side of his face to hang like a teardrop from his chin.

"The evenings are not usually this warm," Wheeler said in a perfunctory way.

"Really, Mr. Wheeler," the Senator's wife said, "I don't see where you get the energy to make so many excuses."

Wheeler opened his mouth to speak and closed it a moment later. He would not beg their indulgences, not in front of Clara Reade, anyway. After a long silence, a waiter appeared wheeling a tray with a silver urn of steaming coffee. As if even the sight of this was more than they could bear, the senator and his wife rose, as did Elliot Iverson; they placed their napkins gingerly on the table in front of them and, amid much shuffling of chairs and bowing to their host, proceeded to leave the dining room. When Clara rose and gathered her things together to join them, Wheeler pressed his hand on hers.

"Please stay," he whispered, then turned to his departing guests. "Sousa's band is playing in the Grand Salon!"

"Send them my condolences," joked Senator McElroy as he wiped a silk scarf across his bald, perspiring head.

"Better yet," Iverson said, offering his arm to the senator's wife, "give the poor bastards the night off."

Clara and Wheeler sat in silence. The waiter cleared the table and poured coffee from the silver urn. Clara watched Wheeler closely; he seemed thoughtful but not worried about the senator's early departure. As a matter of fact, he had clearly not tried to engage the senator's attention, and when she said this aloud, Wheeler concurred.

"I don't need government charity," he said. "I've got plenty of my own money." Clara felt a twinge of pity for him—the insane wife, the absurd mustache, the bragging, and now this stubborn desire to make his final mark. "But we do need something." He turned to her and smiled wryly. "To quote the eminent Mr. Emmett Flye: 'something that will really put this place on the map.' "

"Of course business drops off when the tourists leave," Clara admitted. "But Miami doesn't have to grow in leaps and bounds. That's not the way cities come to be. There's a natural progression, slow; it should take years."

Wheeler leaned across the table toward her and spoke with growing urgency. "I don't mean to criticize, Mrs. Reade, but you set your sights too low."

"Too low?" Clara exclaimed. "Too low!" She strode to the window and looked down at the lights of the town. "When I came here this was a wilderness of palm groves and mangrove swamps! I wanted to bring in the railroad. People laughed at me. You laughed too, at first. But I went ahead and persisted and now there's a city. I would hardly call that setting my sights too low."

Wheeler pursed his lips and studied her for a long moment. Her skin was flushed with excitement. In the time he had known her she had grown thinner, closer to the essence of her truest beauty. And though he could never thank her enough for having sent that orange blossom, he would never quite forgive her for it either. "I did have just the tiniest bit to do with it," he said.

Clara sighed. "Of course I appreciate your contributions," she said. "And I'd be a fool not to be grateful."

"Of course you are Miami's biggest booster, my dear. That's as it should be. And I suppose it is a perfectly fine little city if all you're after is a hometowny sort of place built to serve the tourists at the Royal Palm Hotel. But"—I don't have that many years left, he screamed inside—"I want quick action," he said.

"Now you sound like all those fast-buck artists who want to 'create' Miami," Clara remarked.

"Be careful, Mrs. Reade," he said, trying to maintain his equanimity. "You're casting aspersions on Mr. Emmett Flye."

Clara shook her head. "He'd have elephants dancing down Miami Avenue to draw a crowd," she said.

Wheeler laughed. "If I thought they'd draw the *right* crowd, I'd let him. But that's not the kind of attention this place needs. We need something larger in scope; I don't just want Southern attention. Or even just national attention." He came up to stand next to Clara at the window and looked down at the city. "I don't want this place to be yet another vacation spot in the sun." He said this last phrase as if he equated it with something foul. "I want the world to look at Miami. I want its name to appear on the front pages of the *London Times* and the *International Tribune*. Otherwise it means nothing to me but municipal contracts and petty details, the kind of stuff that bores me stiff." He glanced at the city once more, then turned his back with a dismissive gesture. "And when something bores me like that, I usually put it out of its misery."

So this is to be a monument to his ego, Clara thought. Look how he quakes in his boots at the thought it might not be worthy of him. "It's too soon to be nervous about how the town will go," she said and noted how his shoulders stiffened.

Wheeler did not like her noticing his nerves, but he could not help worrying. Age stood in the way of patience; he could not, as he had done through his most prudent business maneuvers, sit back and wait. "Through all of what is to come, Mrs. Reade," he said, making his face an impassive mask and turning to her again, "I hope at least I will continue to have your friendship."

Clara lowered her eyes; all she could see of him were his black boots as they advanced toward her until one touched the hem of her gown. He took her hand in his and pressed it to his dry lips. She lowered her hand a bit, then a bit more, and Wheeler bent with it.

One day, she thought, I will bring you all the way to your knees.

Though she was needed at home, Maria began making frequent unannounced appearances at the mouth of the Miami River on one pretext or another. She knew Harry was rarely to be found at home, but it would not do to wander over to the Miami Hotel, where he was usually working if he wasn't at the groves; she'd done that once, and when her father had gotten wind of it, he had slapped her so hard she had lost a back tooth. At first she would not even ask for or mention Harry by name to Clara, but the way her eyes darted whenever a footstep was heard—usually it was Geneva in the kitchen or Edmund coming in with firewood—told Clara all she needed to know.

"Harry's the first real adult man I've ever had the fortune of knowing," Maria finally confessed to her. "At least one who's not a fisherman or a sailor or a wrecker or someone's uncle or idiot cousin." She pressed her palms together and closed her eyes. "And Harry's so handsome. He's got a future too and one that's not waiting for the next shipwreck like my father and brothers'." Maria sighed. " 'Cept I don't know if he even likes me at all."

"Oh, I'm sure you're exaggerating," Clara said. "Harry's shy with people he doesn't know well."

Maria stared, red-faced. "He said he don't know me well?"

"No," Clara said, "he hasn't really said much at all to me. But I'm sure . . ."

"Oh, me too!" Maria said to cover her fear and embarrassment. "Me too."

Clara reported these visits to Harry, and though his irritated response puzzled her, she refrained from questioning him. There was something about the way he listened to her talk about Maria that told her to keep her thoughts to herself, and though sorely tempted to know all, she remained simply the bearer of news and no more.

Harry had thought himself in love with Maria for a time, then he had pitied her for the devotion she showed him, but now he was finding it more and more unbearable. He had been flattered by her need for him, but lately her feelings had come to seem like a gluey substance pouring over him, weighing him down and making him sleepy. He had begun to regret the day he'd taken her in his arms and comforted her.

"You're my salvation," she had said to him once, her body pressed close to his.

"I don't want to be your salvation," he had replied.

"But it's a compliment, honey," she had insisted.

And he had wearied of her constant chatter about money: everyone had it but her and she wanted it, she deserved it. Look at that fancy rig, she would say as they rode through town. Wouldn't that feathered hat suit me fine? I'd know what to do with a house like that! Make a man proud to come home.

One day Maria arrived just as Harry was settling in the mule cart to leave for the groves. There seemed no choice then—he could not embarrass her in front of his mother and Geneva, who stood in the shadow of the porch with a bowl of unshelled peas in her arms, narrow-eyed; she knows, Harry thought, surprised—and he let her come along. As they rode through the hammock, Maria looked at him with the placid expression of someone waiting to be noticed.

"People're talking about a war in Cuba, Harry," she said. "Hope you don't have to be a soldier. My brothers oughta go. They'd be good at it, they're so mean. If there's a war, I bet this grove land is probably going to be worth a ton of money."

"Oh, I'd never sell it." Harry tethered the mule to a post next to the toolshed, helped Maria down from the cart, and dragged out a wheelbarrow from inside.

"I didn't realize the grove was yours to sell," Maria said, following him down a row of young trees. "I thought all the land belonged to your mama."

"We're sort of partners on it," Harry explained.

"I bet she's queen bee."

"I guess that makes me a drone."

"You're funny, Harry," she said without smiling as she watched him bend down to inspect the soil. "You'd never sell your part, is that what you mean?"

"But why would I?" He stood up and brushed off his hands. "The whole reason for getting the railroad to come here is so we'd have a way to get the crop to the marketplace."

"Isn't land worth more than oranges?"

"Why does it matter so much to you what the land is worth?" He kicked the ground and moved to the next aisle of trees.

Maria followed close behind him. "I'm interested in everything about you, Harry. I was thinking how rich you could be."

"I don't care about being rich! All I ever hear you talk about is how rich I'm going to be." He reached up into the deep green mass of leaves and ran his hands over a pebbly-skinned orange. "The crop's near to ready. That's what I'm interested in."

Maria felt a sharp panic wash over her, and her confusion as to how to bring him back to her made her desperate. "You'll be very busy, I suppose. You won't have time for poor pathetic Maria, I suppose." Harry sighed but could not bring himself to deny it; at his silence, Maria drew in a sharp breath. "I guess I know when I'm being insulted." She turned and ran a few steps. Harry did not follow and she turned back. "Why're you making this so completely impossible?" she cried, running to him, pressing herself close. "Don't you love me?" Frustration brought tears to her eyes. Would he never take charge? Her lower lip trembled at his silence, and she touched the corner of her eye with her little finger. "Not even a little?" she murmured.

Harry turned away; her arms came around his waist and she pressed herself to his back. Harry looked down at her hands locked against his rib cage.

"Oh, I know just what's going to happen to me. Nothing! Everyone's getting rich except my daddy. No one's wrecking boats no more 'cause they're all coming in by train. Your mother don't need him bringing no lumber to her 'cause they bring that on the train too. Now you're forgetting about me, Harry. I hope a war does come and I get killed by it. Otherwise I'll wind up like my mama! There's no other way for me. I'm scared! Oh, Harry, please, please . . ."

Her hot physical presence was stirring his desire despite his revulsion for what she was saying, what she was asking of him. She ground herself against him, her hot breath against his shoulder. Her hands continued to grip tightly around him. He was stimulated by this storm of emotion but shook his head and pressed his lips tightly together. With a sob she let him go, slid down his body to the ground, and lay there, panting, weeping.

"Get up," Harry said.

"Got no reason to," she sobbed.

Harry kneeled at her side. Her face was streaked with dust and tears. He reached for her hands to help her.

"Don't be nice to me," she said and brushed a wisp of hair from her face. "It just makes things worse." In her embrace of him she had clutched her hands so hard her nails had pierced her own palms. He was awed by the sight.

"You're bleeding," he said.

She looked at her hands and shrugged. "It don't matter."

"You can't walk back through the jungle," he said. "The mule cart's at the toolshed. Come on." His voice sounded tightly controlled even to himself, thin and high, excited and strained as a boy's. He held her arm and they walked down one of the rows to the toolshed; he could feel her body vibrating against him. The mule was standing in the shade, pawing the ground.

Maria pulled away from Harry. "I won't go." Her lips were pressed in tight determination, her eyes red-rimmed and glassy.

Harry put out his hand to help her into the cart. "You've got to go."

She gave him her hand, suddenly pulled him to her, and kissed him as she had never kissed a man, mouth open, ravenous. She fit her body into his with yielding flesh, her mouth nibbling, her arms wrapped around him, her legs moving between his. "I'll do anything for you, Harry. Just tell me."

Harry groaned and pulled away. His face was flushed, wild-eyed; hers was relaxed, nearly slack. "Please," she whispered, eyes half-closed.

It was dark and hot inside the toolshed. Harry spread a tarpaulin on the soft, sandy ground and closed the door. Maria took his hand and pulled him down next to her.

His mouth touched her skin, but whether it was her arm or her neck he couldn't tell. He felt graceless and clumsy, aroused and reluctant. His fingers were thick and trembling at the twenty-two buttons of her dress. He heard impatience in her shallow, measured breathing. He heard fabric tear; she assured him it was all right and with a groan ripped the rest of her dress open down the front. Her breasts were silvered in the near darkness. He rolled against her heavily, as full as after an enormous meal. The utter darkness made him dizzy. A sour, animal smell rose from the ground.

Maria moaned and lifted herself to him, crying softly. Harry fell on her, kissing her ears, her eyes, her neck. Her breath was hot on his cheek as she whispered his name over and over as if in incantation. A touch of his lips on the flesh of her breast made her cry out.

Harry clamped his hand over her mouth. She writhed against him, but she was not fighting. Her tongue licked his palm; she was sobbing, her body heaving beneath him, clutching him, rubbing her fists on his back. Aroused by her flesh, by her desire for him, by the intensity of her feelings, Harry bore into her and forgot his own rage.

16.

On a July dawn a few months later, the pale blue sky rubbed with tissuey clouds, the heat damp and heavy, Harry started on a familiar route through the hammock. He'd told his mother he'd be gone for a couple of weeks, that this was a crucial time at the groves, that there was so much early-morning work to do that it made no sense to come home every night and so he would be staying out there, that she was not to worry if she didn't hear from him as he would have his hands full. The most awful part of this story was how simple it had become for Harry to lie to her.

Harry knew that his life was going in the wrong direction; he felt it as acutely as if he wore his shoes on the opposite feet. And yet the pull of Maria's sexuality could not be denied. Much as he vowed to stay away from her, to make each bout in the toolshed their last, she had only to press herself to him, to whisper her need of his body, to remind him of their last coupling, and Harry succumbed to his desire.

He could not discuss it with his mother. She was busy with the town, with McLeod, with Wheeler; she would only try to soothe him and make him accept what he couldn't accept. She would try to solve for him things that had no solution but the one that he had to seek, the one that was yet unknown. The only person who would understand this was Dr. Tiger—his mother's antipathy toward the old Indian was yet another reason to keep from her the real nature of this trip—and so Harry set out to find him in the Everglades.

By mid-morning he had gone beyond familiar terrain and was hacking his way through a seemingly inpenetrable wall of jungle. The hazy sun pierced it only in rays thin and sharp as bamboo shoots; it was too dense for large animals or even birds, and the silence on this still windless day roared in his ears.

Dr. Tiger had always told him to keep the river on his left when walking upstream, on his right downstream, and now he kept an ear cocked for its rush of water. By standing very still and not straining to listen so much as allowing the jungle to wash over him, he had begun to be able to pick out individual sounds: the brittle crackle of a royal palm frond was different from the whispered rustle of a banana palm; the slithering shush of a garter snake in the leafy underbrush was different from the abrupt staccato rush of the rattler. Dr. Tiger had taught him to pick out the smooth, relentless, hollow roar of the river, even on days when wind shattered the leaves around him. From then on, no matter how unfamiliar the path, he was not afraid.

He had taken his mother's sack of provisions—it would have caused needless disagreement not to—but planned to feast instead on what he could find on his own in the jungle. Dr. Tiger had begun him on this course of self-sufficiency, and now he continued to teach himself. He knew it would take years to learn all there was to learn—it would take a lifetime!—for he had seen the old man's face light up with wonder time after time at the formation of a tree trunk or the speed of a rabbit or the flow of the river. It is endless, he had told Harry. It is as long as the world. He'd showed Harry how to trap, skin, skewer, and roast a rabbit, and though it was not his favorite exercise, Harry could not deny the relish with which he ate it. With practice he learned to extract with his penknife the center shoot from a palmetto and to bite off just the tender tip; the palmetto berries were too bitter for real pleasure but they would do him in a pinch, if it came to that. Huckleberries were better, though rarer, and wild grapes could always be found around ditches: their white flowers looked startlingly like a shower of snow. Harry had once tried to explain snow to Dr. Tiger but in vain; the old man listened patiently, then pressed a hand first to Harry's forehead, then his heart and shook his head. Elderberries were plentiful, Harry found, but better sweetened with guava syrup. Geneva encouraged him to carry a lime with him and now, like a native of the keys, he drizzled it on everything he ate.

"I don't fool myself," he told Clara, squirting a lime into his morning coffee before setting out. "I'm not native. And I don't think I could ever learn what Dr. Tiger knows."

"I'm sure you know a lot he doesn't, darling."

"Oh yes," Harry said. "I can quote Thoreau and parse a sentence and order dinner in French."

"Don't underrate yourself, darling. You're a fast learner. Besides, it won't always be a wilderness down here."

Harry looked at his mother, then down at his coffee. Hadn't she understood a single word of what he'd said? "Well, at least I'll never take this place for granted the way someone born to it might." He would go a step further instead, apply himself to the study of all of it. Every lesson about life, about patience and wisdom and the natural balance of the universe could be learned here.

He was thinking, as he walked, that he would have to put in a well near the groves for the long dry season. How would Dr. Tiger solve the irrigation problem? he wondered, though of course the Seminoles lived in the Everglades, which, as far as Harry understood, was half underwater already and irrigation was the least of their concerns.

But since his groves were just at sea level, he knew the digging would not have to go far; water was under everything. Of course he might dig into coral and that would require machine drills—McLeod had even mentioned dynamite—but if he tested the ground first and found a place where he didn't have to go too deep, then he might be able to eliminate that problem. There was a road to be built too, and before that could be done the black mangroves along the riverbanks had to be cleared.

He stopped to catch his breath and found he'd taken himself into a section of jungle so thickly grown he could barely dig his hand into his sack to pull out an orange and had to peel it inches from his face; the vines and leaves pressed so close, the peel stuck to his clothes when he dropped it. He had a sudden vision of losing himself completely, trapped by roots while vines grew around him. He rubbed his face with his hands as if to wipe off the miasma of fear that hovered about him. He thought momentarily of turning back, but the path behind him was no less dense nor more hospitable than the path in front.

He drew a deep breath and continued, concentrating now only on the next vine to be sliced through, the next branch to be parted. The muscles in his arms and shoulders burned with exhaustion, and when he stumbled out of the overgrowth into an open glade, he was giddy with relief. He sank to his knees and sprawled against a tree to rest. He chewed on huckleberries and ate another orange, the last of a cache he'd stored in his sack.

The problem with building a road through the mangroves, though, was the black mud, but he thought that if he could dig parallel ditches the width of a set of wagon wheels and line them with boards, he might be able to keep the mud from collapsing in on itself. Or maybe not boards, maybe pack the ditches with rocks instead, then lay more rocks all along the top of the road too. It'd be a bumpy ride taking the crop from the grove to the river, but this kind of road would probably be more permanent than boards, which might go soft in the rain.

He did not rest for long, for in the clear space above him he could see that the sun had disappeared and the sky become dense with white, swiftly moving clouds. Around him the leaves began to rustle as the wind picked up. There was an eerie chemical smell in the air, and the skin of his hands had taken on a faintly greenish tinge. He stood and listened for the sound of the river, then left the clearing and set out carving another path through the trees.

The farther he walked, the stronger the wind became and the darker the jungle, though it could not have been even eleven o'clock. All he could hear was the wind whipping through the trees, leaves whacking flat against trunks, the rattle of shivering vines. The wind was blowing so hard now he was forced to take the route he could rather than the one he would. Above and behind him came the sudden retorts of rifle fire; he spun, startled, and realized, as another shot rang out, that it was the sound of branches cracking in the wind. He tried to pick up his pace; the jungle resisted him.

The pain and exhaustion in his arms intensified, a lick of fire every time he sliced the machete across another hanging vine or elephant-eared palm frond. He was smacked by leaves, pricked by thorns, and stung by the sharp-pointed yucca. He felt overcome by the sense of the jungle strangling him, the thick, loamy air choking him with its richness. He was getting drowsy from it, and the wind felt like two strong hands pressing down on his shoulders, forcing him to his knees. He had an overwhelming urge to give in to it, but knew he must not stop. If he lost the will of forward motion, he lost everything.

He continued on blindly, following the blade of his machete as it hacked through the jungle until he came up against a tangle of vines so thick they resisted the blade. Beyond them appeared the high saw grass of the Everglades, and with a sigh of relief he pulled the vines apart to crawl through. Halfway in he realized he had underestimated their thickness and elasticity, and before he could pull out they snapped back, hitting him so hard across the chest that he was immediately gasping for breath. When he tried pulling them apart again, his machete fell from his grip; all he could see of it was a glint of blade as it sank beneath a pile of leaves. As he wriggled to get free of the vines' embrace, the wind knocked a pine branch loose and it scraped all along his right side. His shirt tore, the branch lodged up against his belly, and with each movement the pine needles scratched against him till he bled. The wind vibrated the vines, and though he knew it was absurd he could pick out a waltz melody in it; every beat brought a throbbing jab of pain.

The jungle around and above him grew suddenly still and dark; a thunderclap rang out so powerfully Harry feared the ground would crack open beneath him. In the flash of lightning that followed, the 'glades beyond the vines were lit bright as day but drained of color and tinged with an aura of spectral doom. The wind picked up again, a palm frond sailed across the expanse of white sky, twisted and angular, immense as a pterodactyl.

Whom could he call out to? Who would hear him? With the sound of water hissing on flames, the rain came down in long silver shoots. It beat painfully on his forehead, and the most Harry could do to protect himself was twist his head enough to keep his face averted. His hope now was that the wetness would slick up the vines enough to let him slip through, but instead they began tightening on him.

Harry groaned in pain and terror. It had become impossible to take a full breath. His strength was ebbing; he was losing all feeling below the waist. Shallow breathing was making him light-headed, and he was horrified to realize that his ribs were about to snap. He gripped the vines again and pulled. I'm going to faint, he thought and pulled again. No. I'm going to die.

What happened in the next moments was so strange that he could only compare the experience to the time he'd had scarlet fever and been overcome by daytime hallucinations. His vision was that of a child who has fallen asleep reading Grimm's and awakened in that moment between the time the sun has set and the lamps are lit, believing he has entered the world of the story.

His mother was sitting on the porch, beckoning impatiently as if he were being stubborn about coming in out of the rain. Harry floated easily across the yard and hovered above her like a hummingbird. She reached up to grab him, laughing, calling him a tease. "Come and get me," Harry taunted. He floated higher, out of her reach—the house a doll's house, a pebble on the shore, a speck on the back of his hand, Harry was eye-level to a cloud—and remembered that there was something he'd meant to tell her but, oh dear, not something forgotten but deliberately withheld, and the sky started darkening. "Forgive me, Mother!" he shouted. Her hand was cupped to her ear, and he knew his voice was floating up and away from her. The chance to tell her was gone, and Harry was choking deep inside the clouds, rainwater on his face, in his eyes and nose, pouring down his throat.

Then he was back in the jungle, blown out of the tangle of vines, moving more swiftly than he could possibly move on his own power, held aloft and guided by firm and gentle hands. Beneath him was a narrow path of beaten grass over sand and coral and crushed bamboo, arranged as carefully on the ground as the stitches of a lady's needlepoint. The pain in his side came with each breath he took, and he looked down at himself, surprised that there was no blood.

He did not know or care where he was being taken, did not ask himself how this path came to be in the middle of the jungle. He thought of Dr. Tiger's dictum to surrender to the jungle and gave himself to it. The air smelled of bread and roses and ether. The path was bordered now by a row of tall coconut palms bowing precariously in the wind; their clustered fruits knocked against each other high above and, as he passed, fell to the ground behind him and burst open.

The wind suddenly stopped. From far away he heard the cry of a loon. The light in the sky grew whiter; he could not look at it without shielding his eyes. He was set down gently in the belly of a wide flatboat that glided through the saw grass as swiftly and soundlessly as the clouds passed through the sky. He raised his head, but the pain jabbed at his side and he sank back down. He opened his eyes again and looked at the sky. A lone heron flew above and was gone. By edging his fingers slowly along the side of the boat and lifting with patience, Harry finally managed to see above its rim.

All around was saw grass, sometimes as high as four and five feet, and the boat followed a narrow path of water through it. In a clearing ahead, he saw a curve of land that seemed to float easily on the long stretch of the horizon and to hold in its grasp all the sea of grass that lay spread before it. In the center, the focus of this comforting embrace, was an ancient and majestic cyprus tree that towered above the others on the strand.

Harry tried to call out to whoever was maneuvering the boat, but the pain jabbed at him again; he gasped, lowered himself, closed his eyes, and began once more to dream. A wild garden bloomed before him of frangipani and Jamaica apple, breadfruit and oleander, oranges and bougainvillea dripping in clusters. And from the profusion of riotous color there emerged a group of Seminoles wrapped in colorfully striped cloths. At the center, surrounded by generations of his tribe, Harry recognized Dr. Tiger; no one was older than he, and the smallest was an infant cradled in a sling in a young mother's arms. Between these extremes of age were children and adolescents and a half-dozen adults. The women's sleek black hair was combed forward and swept up in a pompadour. They were covered in layers of cloth: a blouse and a vest and a capelet above, a wide belt, an apron and skirt and petticoats below. The men wore their hair in bangs, and the gaudy cloth had been worked into long shirts and scarfs for them. And they wore beads, beads on necks and ears and wrists and ankles; the older the woman, the more beads she wore. Harry saw all this with the clarity of a dream, the sense of being outside the event and allowed, according to the rules of the dream, simply to observe.

Above him was a canopy of trees; though the wind rustled them with sudden violence, Harry felt protected under their density. Then Dr. Tiger was at his side, though Harry had not seen him move. He was glad still to be dreaming, for he knew this had to be the key to the unconnected sequence of events, and he smiled because the dream was so pleasant. One of the group accompanied Dr. Tiger. She seemed hardly more than a child, but her small, delicate face was as sorrowful as if she had known nothing but tragedy in her young life. Her skin was coppery gold, her eyes a deep, dark mahogany. Dr. Tiger rested a hand on her shoulder. She looked up at him—she's asking his permission for something, Harry thought—then looked back at Harry and smiled. Her small, serious face changed completely with that smile—as if she had known only joy—and the discrepancy made Harry's breath come short with the shock of recognition that this was not a dream at all. She was real, this girl.

She put a poultice to Harry's ribs and applied gentle pressure to it. Harry resisted for only an instant—he saw his own fear in her eyes—and then let go. She lifted her hands and the pain was dulled. With Dr. Tiger's help she wrapped a long, wet cloth many times around him and bound it tight. Then she was holding a bowl into which she dipped a carved wooden spoon and brought it to Harry's lips. The steaming liquid was black as ink; a root stuck up out of it; Harry smelled mint and indigo. He looked into her eyes again, and her answering gaze reassured him so that he did not hesitate to take the liquid. When he had drunk all that was in the bowl, Dr. Tiger tied a piece of string around his neck on which were strung peeled cloves of garlic. The girl washed the cuts on Harry's shoulder with a cloth. Whatever medicine she used burned his skin and stained it blue. Above him the clearing was filled with swiftly moving clouds. Harry reached out for her. The girl's smile was sweetness and sympathy; she pressed gently on his shoulder until he sank down again. He breathed deeply and fell immediately into a dreamless sleep.

A violent clap of thunder woke him. He was inside a structure of poles and palmetto thatch; a small fire was crackling on a bed of stones, the girl crouching over the bowl of stew above it, stirring. Harry smiled to himself. Heavy rain was falling; he felt safe, protected by the palmetto, the fire, the girl. In the corner he saw Dr. Tiger lying on his side under a tall canopy of cheesecloth, asleep, snoring. Harry peered through the split-log floor and saw chickens and small black pigs nestling under the hut. Above him, the inside of the roof was lined with deer and panther skins. Outside, barely visible through sheets of silver rain, he saw three more such huts.

The longer the storm raged, the cozier it seemed inside the hut. The girl continued to feed him, to apply freshly dipped poultices, to bind his rib cage with lengths of cheesecloth and tighten them until he grunted. Each time he did so she laughed very softly and stole a quick glance at the sleeping Dr. Tiger.

She smelled to Harry not of sweetness but of something elemental, the earth and the river. Her long, narrow fingers were dry and smooth. She wore none of the ornamental breastwork on her jacket Harry had seen on the other women in her tribe. Her dress was modest—a long calico skirt of vivid red and orange that hid her bare feet and a short jacket that allowed Harry a fleeting glimpse of the smooth copper-colored flesh of her belly. She wore no head covering, and her thick hair was rich and coarse and black as a crow, knotted loosely behind her neck, held in place with a small animal bone.

One time Harry grunted before she pulled the bandage, before she even touched him, and she looked up, met his eye for the first time. Harry smiled. "What's your name?" he whispered.

She shook her head, and Harry saw that he'd put sadness and fear in her eyes. She crept back to the fire to stir the stew and did not look at Harry the next time she changed the bandage on his ribs. Harry tried not to bring that look to her eyes again and grunted only when he felt the pain. The girl seemed apprehensive though, and Harry became as attuned to a misstep on his part as if she were a bird nesting temporarily in a hand and wary of the fingers that might enclose it. Her skittishness eased in response to his gentleness.

Harry was content then just to keep his eyes open and watch her patient, graceful movements, hardly noticing the difference when he had fallen asleep and began to dream of her. He awoke in the morning to a band of sunshine creeping through the opening of the hut, across the split-log floor, and laying a warming arm across his shoulder; he was as comfortable as if he'd spent the night in his own bed.

In the corner Dr. Tiger stirred and emerged from his canopied bed. He crouched over Harry and looked first at his wounds, then into his eyes. "Heavy heart," the old man said. "Different boy."

Harry looked down. How could Dr. Tiger tell so much about him without Harry's having said anything? He nodded and Dr. Tiger touched his hand. Harry looked up. Dr. Tiger was smiling, motioning for Harry to look around him. Harry followed his gaze and saw only the stew pot above the fire and the three palmetto-thatched huts outside and a half-dozen coconut palms. And the sky. And the ground of coral and sand and scrub.

"I don't understand," he said.

Dr. Tiger kept smiling and repeated the gesture. "Look," he said. "See." He left Harry with those words and Harry pored over them, trying to extract a meaning. Look. See. Look. See.

The girl came inside. Framed by the door, silhouetted by the sun streaming through it, she seemed to him no bigger than a twelve-year-old, but everything else about her spoke of her womanhood. He drew down the blanket and looked at himself, his ribs bound, his skin stained blue. When he started to rise there was a twinge of sharp pain. He touched his side gingerly, and for the first time remembered the heavy vines in which he'd been trapped. The girl moved from the door toward him.

"You saved my life," he said.

The sunlight molded the side of her face in liquid gold. For a long moment she did not lower her eyes but met Harry's gaze and held it. A shudder ran down his back, a thrill of recognition. There was no flirtation, no real or false modesty in her look, no questioning, no judgment. She simply saw him. Harry had the urge to laugh, and the moment a hint of it curled his lip, the girl turned away and left the hut. She returned a moment later with a tall young brave who stood at the door while she changed Harry's bandage and fed him the ink-black soup, wordlessly urging Harry to lie back to rest.

The day passed, Harry in and out of sleep, watching the life of the tribe through the opening of the hut: the men moving across the clearing in the morning, hoisting spears and rifles on their shoulders and stopping to eat from a large kettle of stew, returning in the evening, some with game or turtles, others with only their rifles; the women sewing with large-eyed needles, or adding potatoes and carrots to the endlessly simmering *softie* stew; the old men stripping bark for a canoe, the old women threading beads and flattening ornamental coins on a rock. Over the whole scene there lay a quiet hardly broken by the whispering gossip around the stew pot; the young children were surprisingly quiet even in their wildest physical play.

On the second afternoon the girl came, touched the binding on his ribs, and helped him to his feet. Harry looked at the hand touching him, at her eyes seeing him, and answered her unasked question without speaking. She smiled, and Harry, proud of himself, smiled back at this perfect communication. He felt light-headed and a bit shaky and leaned on her for balance as they left the hut. He smiled again at how much taller he was; why, he could look down on the top of her head and see the delicate center part in her glossy hair.

The young brave was waiting for them and walked alongside in silence. He held his head and body with such grace that he seemed still even when he moved, his broad, flat face calm and expressionless. His thick black hair was shaved from neck to crown, leaving a wide spiky crest across his forehead. He wore the traditional long shirt, his legs and feet bare. One hand rested on a curved knife tied to a strip of rawhide that wound around his waist, the other held a long spear, its tip powdered red with curare.

They crossed the clearing and walked past a wide, deep field where corn, melons, squash, and sweet potatoes grew; the children of the tribe were entrusted with keeping away birds and animals, and Harry saw that a few of the older boys carried bows and arrows. Beyond the field a few women were engaged in an industry with which Harry was familiar: the manufacturing of starch from the coontie root. Comparing their primitive system to the machinery that even poor farmers like Farley Goram had begun using, Harry knew they would soon be priced out of business. The women at work, he noticed, did not look at him as he and the girl passed.

With the young brave never far behind, they walked through the hammock to the edge of a stream shaded by tall cypress and long dense curtains of Spanish moss. The girl sat on a wide cypress stump, and Harry lowered himself to a thick patch of bright green moss beside it. The brave squatted next to the fallen cypress tree itself, which had been stripped of its branches and partially hollowed out for a canoe. He took out the curved blade and set to work.

The silence was complete but for the splash of a catfish surfacing and diving, the rustle of an egret lighting near a myrtle bush, the measured dig and thrust of the brave's carving tool. Harry took slow, deep breaths, feeling the girl's eyes on him, the pain not so bad now, as if her bearing witness soothed it. The smell was of the earth, of fresh weeds and damp roots, vital, riveting, like the smell of the girl herself but intensified, primitive as Eden. He looked at her arranging strands of dried saw grass across her lap, fascinated by the swift movements of her fingers as she wove a chain of the grass and from the chains a mat. She seemed to him the essence of this place, the life and the future of it, sitting calmly, silently, the living embodiment of the earth and the water that surrounded them.

There was within Harry a deep physical stirring, a pull toward her, as if her presence alone could move his emotions as the wind moved the long strands of hanging moss, holding and guiding them in some perfect, uncharted, unknown dance. His breathing became shallow and measured; he dared not disturb the silence. His shoulders trembled; his hands flexed and unflexed on his thighs with the need to touch her. But it was more than mere touch he wanted, an eternity beyond the simple pleasures of the flesh he'd known.

Isn't this, he thought, looking at the canopy of leaves that arched over the small brookside glen where they sat now, isn't this all the life I ever wanted? His own dreams and plans for things—his whole concept of a future that he could somehow influence—suddenly seemed to him absurd, irrelevant. He wanted to . . . ingest this girl, to live inside her and take her inside him. And the feeling of how completely he was under her spell made him afraid that he would be overcome with emotions. He begged silently for her to speak, to break, even for a few moments, this impossible bewitchment.

"You are Harry," she said.

He leaned back against the cypress stump, sighing deeply, and listened to the sweet music of her voice, liquid and light, alternating with strange guttural awkwardness. Her name, she said, was Shinassa; she was the granddaughter of Dr. Tiger, the sister of the young brave, Billy Jumper. Her own parents had died during an influenza epidemic brought by a band of white traders who had wandered into their camp looking for crocodile skins. She learned to speak English from her mother, who had learned it from the missionaries at the mouth of the Miami River twenty summers past.

He asked her why Billy Jumper followed them.

"It is . . . unwise for Seminole woman to be alone with white man," she explained.

"I am not like all white men," Harry replied.

Shinassa looked at him; her grandfather had told her of this young white man who wanted to know the land as a Seminole brave would know it. She knew the man told the truth. "There was once a young brave took for his wife a white woman, a prisoner in the war. The children of this union . . . No member of my tribe will break bread with them. They are as, as no one . . . as nothing."

"But—"

Beside them, Billy Jumper threw down his blade. "Our blood pure blood," he declared. "Pure Seminole blood. We do not mix with white man blood or black man blood. It bring illness, war."

"Some people say it is the Seminole that brings war," Harry said.

Billy Jumper shook his head. "The white man say."

Harry looked to Shinassa. "How can I tell you I am not of them, not like them, not—"

"Every day we are afraid," she said. "White man take our land and build a house and say it is his land. And we will go to this bad place called Indian Territory. The braves will fight for our land, and if that bring war . . . " She shook her head. "It can be no other way." Her sense of fatalism struck Harry more forcibly than anything she'd said before.

He was permitted to stay until his ribs healed enough for him to make his way back to the bay by himself. His mother expected him to be gone a week at the groves; with the hurricane and the roads probably washed out, she would not worry about him for at least that time; he could stay here as long as they would let him. But his condition no longer required Shinassa's attentions, and he was removed from the hut and given a place to sleep on the moss under a cypress tree on the edge of the communal clearing. He ate as the others ate, from the communal pot of stew that simmered day and night in a kettle over an open fire. He did not know what he was allowed or not allowed to do, and he hesitated at first to move too far from the tree. Shinassa no longer tended his wounds or appeared in the clearing, and at first he wanted to look for her. The need to see her influenced every movement of his eyes, and he felt at peace only when he closed them and allowed himself to ride the rivers of feeling that flowed in silence, in absence. Look. See. Look. See.

One morning he was roused before dawn by a prod from the butt end of the spear of Billy Jumper. Harry scrambled to his feet, frightened, and backed against the tree. His clothes were damp with ground moisture; his arms and legs stiff and cramped. He did not feel a worthy adversary to this long-limbed, muscular brave. But Billy did not attack; he leaned his spear against Harry's tree and disappeared into the hammock. Harry grabbed the spear and ran to catch up.

They spent the day in Billy's dugout cypress canoe, moving slowly through the tangled mass of cypress and mangrove and hanging moss. So skillful a sailor was Billy that even as he dug his pole into the mud and pushed, the water around them seemed hardly to ripple. Billy had learned well from his surroundings; even as a fly lit on his eyelashes, he made no motion with his face. It was a skill he practiced, to be as still as a tree, watching for catfish, his spear at the ready. "Even water snake not quicker than Billy Jumper."

He stopped at the giant cypress tree, the roots of which dipped deep into the muck like a gnarled old hand balancing with great delicacy on splayed fingertips. Billy removed his wildly patterned shirt: he was naked now but for a triangle of deerskin hanging from a rawhide strip around his waist. His skin was the color of red mangrove that had dried in the sun. He stood still, spear poised, become part of the swamp itself. Harry sat very still and kept his eyes focused on the water for any kind of movement. The water here was blackish green and seemed not to move at all. The cypress were tall, their roots high above the water, some spaced so widely apart the boat moved beneath them. Tiny black crabs scuttled around them, catfish moved sinuously a foot beneath the surface of the water, as elusive as a thought.

Harry felt his concentration leave him over and over, his eyes blurring, his mind wandering back to the camp, wondering where Shinassa was, what she was doing, and then, with the subtlest movement possible, Billy Jumper sent a spear through the belly of a catfish, and Harry resolved to renew his efforts at concentration. He was exhausted at the end of the day, though he had done nothing but observe. When he reached his spot at the tree, the moss had been covered in pine needles, and over that was a mat woven of the finest saw grass. He looked around him, and though he did not see her, he knew she was there, knew she watched him even now.

The next day he rose and saw Billy Jumper waiting for him at the stew pot. The day after Harry knew to go directly to the dugout canoe. The day after that Billy Jumper showed him how to hold the spear and how to throw it. At his first try Harry heard the small throaty sound that was Billy Jumper laughing. At the end of these days of instruction, Billy Jumper would talk to Harry, his words always at odds with the calm studied patience of the hunter. His English words were angry ones, accusatory ones, full of information and misinformation, and though Harry did his best to correct him, Billy would have none of it. His knowledge of the white man and his ways was narrow, limited to stories passed down from the elders of the tribe: about missionaries who denied the existence of the Great Spirit, traders who took from them what they could not spare and gave them what they could not use, of the Spaniards who had been eager to take their land and the American soldiers who disgraced their women.

A hundred years ago there were over five thousand in his tribe, he told Harry. Some of them were not Seminole but Yamasee, Apalachee, and Calusa, refugees from tribes in Alabama and Georgia forced deeper south by the Creek Wars. Their numbers were further enhanced by runaway Negro slaves, many of them from fierce and proud African fighting tribes: the Dakar Senegalese, the Ashanti, the Gold Coast Coromantee. They were an agricultural and pastoral people, a people of peace who built their villages around oak clusters on hilltops to be closer to the sun. Nearby were crystal springs, cypress strands, grassy meadows where their several thousand head of stock could graze. They planted their fields with corn, peas, beans, and pumpkins; around the village were orange and peach trees.

They believed in the Great Spirit and a host of lesser spirits, in a sky-world above the earth and a subterranean world below it. They believed that the sun and the moon and the rainbow were earthly manifestations of beneficent spirits. They believed in a reality transcending ordinary existence and that under the proper conditions—sacrifices or ritual or prayer—an animal might speak, a stone might move.

The tribe had been decimated by three wars in which its most valiant men had lost their lives. Devastation followed devastation: capture, prison and torture, escape and recapture, humiliation and the insidious introduction into the tribe of new strains of disease. Their numbers dropped. They could not resist being forced off their land, forced to abandon their villages, pushed further and further inland to the farthest reaches of the Everglades. Dugout canoes were fitted with masts and sails, for the distances to cover were great. Their cattle and sheep confiscated, their land left behind, they turned to hunting and fishing and gathering. The large villages gave way to small family camps; instead of cabins they lived in thatched huts.

Billy Jumper was sorry the wars were over, he told Harry; he would never be able to prove to the spirits that he was a man worthy of his illustrious name until he could avenge the braves who had died before him. He wanted to marry a hundred women so his seed would populate a new tribe. He grieved to see himself at the dwindling end of his people, but that fact was undeniable: today his tribe numbered only two hundred.

One day Harry went to the canoe and Billy was not there; without hesitation, he stepped into the boat, pushed off from land, and entered the cypress strand on his own. He had not traveled very far when he saw the gnarled head and jaws of an alligator, the rest of its body concealed in the dark water and saw grass. Its hide was the blackish green of the water, speckled yellow at the snout. The head was half turned away, and Harry remembered Billy telling him that a gator was only vulnerable in two places: the eye or where the backbone joined the head. As Harry watched the gator moving around the boat, he reached for the spear.

The gator's mouth opened slowly, showing two glistening rows of long, sharp teeth. The sleepy hooded eyes stayed on Harry as the gator moved in infinitely slow circles around the boat. For a moment, Harry's concentration wavered—he saw himself killing it with a perfectly aimed throw and winning Shinassa as a medieval knight might slay a dragon for the hand of the maid in the castle—and suddenly the gator was not there.

Harry resisted spinning from side to side to find it. He remained still, cursing himself for that instant's lapse, and waited for the gator to reappear. The silence slowly separated itself into individual sounds: a frog's throaty trill and an answering one, an owl's hoot high in the darkness of the cypress overhang, the scuttling of a nest of spider crabs, a spoonbill's swishing swoop into the clearing, landing with a tinkling splash to stand on one leg and peer at him.

And then, as the canoe began to rise at the prow, Harry knew where the gator was. The spear vibrated, alive in his hand; it knew the target, ached to fly, strained against the guiding touch of his fingers. There would be one moment, one instant only. The boat reared up, Harry was thrown in the air, the gator half out of the water and—Now!— he let the spear go just as the gator arced back into the water, and it found its target in the pupil of the creature's left eye. The gator spun over, its striated pink underthroat pulsating, its immense tail thrashing as Harry tumbled into the water next to it. The gator thrashed blindly toward him. A slow pool of thick red blood bubbled around its head, the paroxysmic flailing stirring up a pink foam.

Harry swam to shore, dragging the canoe behind him, and squatted on an enormous cypress root while the gator breathed its last, then waded back into the water and hauled the carcass into the boat.

Shinassa, he thought as he poled his trophy home, see what I've won.

The next morning Dr. Tiger told him he must go. Having learned something of the tribe's fatalism, Harry accepted the news with a nod, knowing there was nothing more to be said, no questions to be asked. He did not look around him for Shinassa; he knew she was there, just as certainly as he knew she would not show herself.

Billy Jumper gave him the canoe he'd carved, and Harry guided it into the sea of saw grass. He poled forward without thinking, without looking back. He saw her in his heart, where he had been taught to look; he did not need to see her with his eyes. The cypress strand . . . the tallest tree of all . . . at its roots a beautiful young girl. Morning misted her skin smooth and translucent, delicate as pearl. He wanted to lick off each bead of moisture. He held her close, shivering, slipped his arms tightly around her, felt the fine bones of her rib cage, spread his fingers until he touched the swell of her breast. His lips caressed her ear.

Mine, Harry thought. He knew he would return.

Two days later he emerged from the jungle and walked the last mile along the river. An enormous sense of well-being came over him. A young palm tree had been blown down in the storm and lay across the path that led back to the house. Harry climbed over it and made his way easily along a path he himself had created weeks before. It was littered with broken branches and leaves. Worried suddenly about his mother and how she had fared in the storm, he started to run. As he neared the house he saw McLeod and Edmund, shirtsleeves rolled, sweating, hatchets in hand, piling splintered lumber on the bank. McLeod, seeing the alarm on Harry's face, intercepted him.

"Your mother's OK," he said, looking Harry up and down. "Where you been for two weeks?"

"Didn't she tell you?" Harry said, not meeting McLeod's eye. "At the groves. Oh, that toolshed rattled and leaked but—"

McLeod bent to heft a pile of wood. "You don't have to tell me, Harry. I just thought you could use a friend."

Harry stared at him, shocked. He knows, he thought, and he started to protest again, but then Clara appeared, a few rotted planks across her shoulders. She saw him and the planks fell around her. She rushed to him and held him close. "Oh, Harry, I've been so worried. Quentin was sure you were safe but . . ."

She led him back to the house to show him the damage the storm had done, while Harry told how he had been safe during the storm in the toolshed at the grove and had met some crocodile hunters who gave him better shelter in the 'glades.

"I was out in back pulling weeds from the flowers when the storm hit," she said. "And something just seemed to change in the air. A rabbit stood there frozen in fear. I never saw anything like it. Then there was a clap of thunder and he bolted. I spent the afternoon under the house with Geneva's cow for company and at one point I fell asleep and had a terrible dream that you were trapped somewhere and calling for me and—" They came to where the house stood, and Clara stopped. "Oh, Harry, look at this mess!"

The porch roof had fallen in a great heap into the yard, crushing the porch steps. The wicker furniture had been scooped up by the wind and bounced all the way out to the bay. Pine trees had been wrung off at the root and flung in all directions.

"One of them missed Edmund and Geneva's shack by about a foot," Clara said. "Geneva's been staring out to Eleuthera ever since, longing for home. Nothing much in the way of damage in town, amazingly.

Oh, the railroad depot's going to need rebuilding, but we knew that anyway. Good thing the Royal Palm's closed for the season. This hurricane's one attraction the tourists'll be better off not seeing. Quentin says we can replace the porch and rebuild the kitchen. Of course he really thinks we ought to move out of the house altogether and into Fort Dallas. Well, we'll see, we'll see." She looked around the yard once more, shrugged, and rubbed her hands on her apron. "We're saving any old planks that aren't in splinters. Lumber's about the scarcest thing there is, you know. Cal Sparks and Sons ought to do real well."

In all the activity that followed, Clara never got around to asking exactly how he'd weathered the storm. As long as he was safe, his mother didn't bother to ask for details, and it was just as well. Nor did McLeod press him to tell more than Harry was willing and Harry came to think that perhaps he'd been mistaken in thinking that McLeod somehow knew where he'd been. What had happened seemed to Harry so deeply, so essentially private that it had not even occurred to him that he had a choice to reveal it or not. He had known the first time Dr. Tiger came to him that he had something significant to tell him. But he saw too that this sense of inevitability did not come without its price. For most of his life, Harry had believed he would never keep a secret from his mother, had even sworn an oath to it. The circumstances of his father's death, his guilt over it—fading now but present in the form of a tight core that could still spread its acid heat through him—forced him to break that oath, but he had sworn it would be the last time. To have broken it once again was the only aspect of his experience with the Seminoles that was truly unsettling to him. How much farther from his mother would his true life take him? Could he reconcile the two, he wondered. And could he bear to leave his mother behind? He did not know and put off knowing, but the deep, dark light in Shinassa's eyes shone within him now and guided him toward the truth.

17.

Along Miami Avenue and Biscayne Bay, in stores and rooming houses, in cafés and at the docks, Cubans were becoming a familiar sight, not just the ones selling tobacco and sponges and rolling cigars in storefront shops, not just the sailors and fishermen and cooks, but the new arrivals seeking support for their cause—freedom from oppressive Spanish rule in Cuba. Their fight against slavery under a royalist government struck a responsive chord in the breasts of the people of America, where like battles for freedom had been fought and won at Lexington and Concord more than a hundred years before.

When José Martí, the leader of the revolution, visited the city on the last leg of his campaign to enlist American support, McLeod prevailed upon Clara to host a fund-raising dinner in the dining room of the Miami Hotel. Frail in appearance, exhausted, Martí—a man of international importance, a poet and journalist—burned with the determination to secure liberty for his homeland. With sardonic humor, speaking to an audience made up in part of Cuban exiles from Tampa and Pensacola, he urged revolution and decried pacifism: "Free countries are not created by wishful thinking in the depths of the soul." The Americans in the audience sympathized with the Cuban dilemma: this was the New World, after all, and the only alien power ruling by force on the North American continent was Spain.

Privately, some were confused. Hadn't Spain discovered Florida? Wasn't Ponce de León a name beloved by Florida schoolchildren? Didn't Spanish names abound in the state? And yet suddenly they were supposed to hate and revile all that was Spanish. The complexity of this issue was put aside in favor of the more pressing Cuban struggle for freedom, and hate Spain they did.

A few weeks after the banquet, Wheeler called Clara to his office in the Royal Palm for what his message promised would be a historic meeting. Clara assumed it would have something to do with protecting Miami—and his own interests—from what was happening in the Caribbean. But she was wary; though the city's interests came first with her, she was no longer sure she could say the same for him.

He had moved his papers off his desk and onto a big round table set up in the middle of the room. A large map of the Caribbean was tacked to one wall. A male secretary in shirtsleeves and a celluloid collar sat at a small table in a corner in front of a large Corona typewriter, and the sharp clacking sound accompanied their conversation. Elliot Iverson was sitting at the big table, furiously taking notes as Wheeler, pacing, red-faced and excited, beckoned Clara to take a seat.

"We needed another shot in the arm to get moving again, Mrs. Reade," he said. "And now we've got it!"

"Hearst's an old pal of mine," Iverson interrupted and glanced at Clara. "Knew him when I covered the criminal courts for the *New York Journal.* Why this kind of thing's right up his alley. I'll start sending dispatches right to his office. Soon as we whet his appetite, he'll send reporters and sketch artists and really get things moving."

"What kind of things?" Clara asked.

Iverson looked at Wheeler before he spoke. "Why, our war with Spain, Mrs. Reade," he said.

"But we're not at war with Spain," Clara replied.

"A good war sure never hurt a paper's circulation," Iverson said to Wheeler. "Look at the *Atlanta Gazette* before and after the burning, and you'll see what I mean."

"And I'm sure we all hope we won't ever be at war with Spain," Clara persisted.

Wheeler shrugged. "Yes, yes, yes, Mrs. Reade. But do try to see the advantages if there *was* a war."

"It never hurt to bring things to a head." Iverson turned to her with a conspiratorial wink at Wheeler.

Wheeler called to the secretary. "Make that letter to the war department a cable instead!" He turned back to Iverson. "We need to organize a lobby in D.C. I'm thinking of asking for twenty thousand troops."

"I'd make it twenty-five thousand," Iverson suggested. "Then maybe we'll get fifteen."

"You're not suggesting the United States attack Cuba?" Clara exclaimed.

Wheeler shrugged. "A war's going to start one way or the other. Who fires the first shot is simply a technicality. War is war, same on both sides. I know the people are supposedly fighting for their so-called freedom, but I also know the real reason people fight wars and that is greed, pure and simple. So let's not any of us try to fool the other about nobility of motives."

"You may be willing to implicate yourself in that venal summation of mankind's behavior, but leave me out," Clara said.

Wheeler looked at her with the same sadness she'd seen in his eyes the first time they'd met. "I may have to do just that, my dear."

"The United States has always maintained a position of neutrality," Clara said. "Besides, it's up to us to protect Miami, not lead her into danger."

Wheeler shook his head. "Don't you see it yet, Mrs. Reade? War is the answer to our prayers. The very thing that'll put this city over the top."

"How's this for the lead?" Iverson said and read from his notes, " 'Miami, once a sweet little vacation town, is marshaling its resources to become a camp for twenty-five thousand brave soldiers defending the shores of America.' "

Wheeler clapped his hands together and turned to the secretary again. "I want land cleared right away for the troop site. Ten acres ought to do it. Extend the north and west borders of the town."

"And of course we need a fort with a strategic location on the bay,"

Iverson said. "The best spot is where the bay meets the river." Both men looked significantly at Clara.

"On my land? Absolutely not. And the Finches will feel the same way, I assure you."

"Not if I promise to build a bridge to the south bank," Wheeler said.

Clara watched as he dispatched Iverson to talk to the Finches and the secretary to the telegraph office. His sheer drive was still impressive; no longer content to set a state in motion, he was ready to push the world around. But the price, she thought, would be paid with people's lives. He was not merely her adversary now but the whole population's. She had to save the city. Their partnership, the thrill of reaching a mutual goal realized, had come finally to an impasse.

When they were alone, she could look at him with nothing less than contempt. "So you create a war. That must give you quite a sense of power."

"You insult me, Mrs. Reade." Wheeler shook his head. "And you give me too much credit. I am simply taking advantage of a potent situation. Oh, I know I must strike you as perhaps being opportunistic, but"—he lowered his voice as he moved closer to her—"I believe I am a man of other virtues, which I am perhaps not too bold to know that you have come to appreciate." He advanced on her, smiling. "I think you have come to see some of them demonstrated in my co-operation with your various requests over the last few years. And we are so close now to making Miami into something we can really crow about. But I don't want this triumph only for myself, Mrs. Reade. A man . . . a man like me . . . can be lonely. Triumph can ring hollow when only the masses give their accolades." He came closer still, his eyes on hers. "I think you know what I am leading up to, Mrs. Reade."

Clara pulled her head back and looked at him in wonder. "God help me, I think I do."

"You won't need God's help, my dear." He reached out to lay his hand on her shoulder. "I am offering you a kingdom."

"If it's Miami you're referring to, it isn't yours to give."

"Isn't it?"

That Clara had ever found him anything more than a cold, ego-maniacal, contemptible schemer seemed now the height of improbability. With a sharp jerk of her shoulder, she threw off his hand. Wheeler's smile did not change.

"I understand perfectly," he said. "You need time to get used to the idea."

"I don't need anything you have to offer," she said.

Wheeler shrugged. She could see his smile had frozen on his face.

"Saving yourself for your fisherman?" he asked. Clara did not reply. "You're a fool, Mrs. Reade. But you will not make a fool of me, and you may rest easy knowing that I will not embarrass either of us by making this offer again. So if in the future you will just stay out of my—"

"It's *my* city," Clara said, "and I won't let you ruin it by creating this war."

"Ruin it? Oh, Mrs. Reade, Mrs. Reade. Don't you understand? I'm saving it."

The city changed more rapidly now than Clara would have thought possible. One week the large expanse of Wheeler-owned jungle west of town was being dynamited, the next week a Key West lumber mill sent fifty men to haul the felled trees onto barges. Clara watched with a growing sense of alarm. The land now stood bare and dry, and what was going to happen was clearly inevitable. Store owners, encouraged by the prospect of troop arrival—reported in *The Metropolis* as if it were the government's orders and not Wheeler's request—placed large orders with their suppliers for new merchandise, and the railroad ran extra freight cars. Like Wheeler, most viewed the impending war as a sales opportunity with a promised consumer population in the thousands.

Rufus and Ida Finch couldn't have been happier than on the day their new piano was unloaded at the depot and carried in the back of Tommy Schell's hired rig along Miami Avenue for all to see. When the cart stopped in front of Clara's office, Ida took her place at the keyboard and played Chopin's Nocturne for the gathered crowd. Clara watched from the doorway as Rufus approached.

"So you're going to get your bridge after all," she said.

"Yep. Things is finally going my way. Mr. Wheeler's putting plenty of money into this war effort, you know," he said seriously. "Not that

I ain't glad some of it's finally coming my way. Building a fort on my land's about the best thing happened to me yet. Too bad he didn't ask you to have it built on your side of the river."

"If Spanish gunboats were to come, they'd surely run aground on the reefs long before they got here," Clara said. "Besides, I don't want to have anything to do with the war. I certainly don't want to profit from it."

"I hope you ain't trying to insult me, Clara."

"I'm only speaking for myself."

Finch took off his hat. "Maybe I said some things to you I oughtn't to've, Clara." He put out his hand. "I apologize."

Clara took his hand and held it. "I hope Wheeler makes good on his promise for that bridge."

"I got it in writing," he replied. "And the dredges're coming in soon and'll scoop up enough sand so the fort can stand on a mound twenty feet high. Oh, what a view we'll have! 'Course I hope we won't never need the fort for real, but . . . " He looked out at the street he'd once so envied. "Town's booming, huh? Can't say the war's done bad by it so far." He glanced at Ida with pride. "Ain't that a sweet sound she makes? A Steinway upright, yessir."

The cry *"Cuba libre!"* was heard now every day on the streets of Miami. Readers of *The Metropolis* became avid followers of the developments of the revolution, experts on guerrilla tactics, advisors on military strategy, and speakers for the democratic way of life. When the revolution succeeded in tying up industry and commerce by commandeering the ports on the island, though, Miami residents were a little nervous: could this have an adverse effect on their business too?

At a meeting of the Businessmen's Association, Wheeler assured its nervous membership that as far as they were concerned, there was no cause for worry. "The world will hardly let its supply of sugar be compromised because a country wants its freedom. I've got too much of my own money tied up in the almighty peso to allow anything like that to occur." He turned to Senator McElroy next to him at the podium. "And I'm sure President McKinley believes likewise. Or," he added with a wink at the crowd, "he can be persuaded to."

The Hearst and Pulitzer papers had sent reporters to Havana. When they wired back the disappointing news that there was no war to write about, they were told simply to supply the stories and if they were good enough—incendiary, outrageous—the war would take care of itself. And though recent times had been boom for sensational journalism—the assassination of President Garfield, the Johnstown Flood, Custer at Little Big Horn—the stories that came out of those tragedies were nursery primers compared to what royalist soldiers were reported doing to innocent Cubans.

"The skulls of all were split to pieces down to the eyes," ran a story in *The Metropolis.* "Some of these were gouged out... The arms and legs of one victim had been dismembered and laced into a rude attempt at a Cuban five-pointed star... The tongue of another had been cut out and placed on his mangled forehead... The Spanish soldiers habitually cut off the ears of the Cuban dead and retain them as trophies."

"Cuba libre!" Wheeler snorted as he looked down at the placards and banners strung up along Biscayne Bay. "The only reason the United States'll get involved in this," he told Iverson, who was taking notes, "is because we can't afford to take the losses of our investments in Cuba."

"Don't you believe in the democratic cause, F. M.?" Iverson asked with a barely concealed smirk.

"Oh, absolutely!" Wheeler laughed. "If what you mean by that is the freedom to make my way in the Caribbean. I've been working with some men in D.C. on a new idea—a canal through the isthmus of Panama. Can't do that if Spain stays put." He saw Iverson writing that down and took the pencil out of his hand. "Just between you and me, Mr. Iverson, it wouldn't be the worst thing that ever happened if Spain invaded Miami. 'A besieged city.' Think what it would be like afterwards, how government money would pour in here."

The citizens of Miami were more than interested in the reports from Cuba; they were outraged. Even the most recent immigrants considered America's history their own history, and they'd be damned if they'd allow this tyranny to exist a two-day boat ride from their homes. But even as there came to be a sense of Miami's place in the scope of world affairs, fears mounted: Will they invade our very shores? Are we in danger? Some left town on extended visits to relatives. Others were made bold by the sense of the rightness of the cause.

When the Miami Minutemen were formed, Harry was one of the first to sign up, and he told Maria that he'd probably be going to Tampa soon where forces were being marshaled for Cuba. They were lying side by side in the toolshed, and faint strips of light came through the slats of wood. Maria was silent for a long moment, listening to their breathing; the darkness around them made her feel she'd disappeared. She looked down at her hands and saw her nails glowing in the faint light. "You didn't even ask me."

Harry laughed a bit harshly. "I think you'll be able to care for yourself without me."

"I hear the relief in your voice," she said.

"Please." Harry scrambled to his feet and pulled his clothes on. "This is the right thing to do."

Maria looked up at him, a silhouette darker than the darkness. "I can tell you hate me. That you have to force yourself even to look at me after. That you would rather get killed in that stupid war than talk to me nice again."

When he had returned from the Everglades, Harry had been determined to end things with Maria, but the force of her will and the heat of his own desire had prevented him from doing so. They had continued to meet at night. They usually spoke little. Harry sensed that words were dangerous in this relationship: he remembered having said to her, "You have me," and how that had been both their first step toward each other and the first step of his own descent. He could barely trust himself now to think, could hardly stand to articulate his feelings in his own mind. He despised himself, despised his flesh and his desires even as he was helpless not to satisfy them. Once he would have let his mind seek the peace of the Seminole camp and memories of Shinassa. But now, sinking in a morass of desire, he tried to keep those images untouched, afraid that his imagination would soil them. There was no doubt in his mind that he was a traitor to himself at the very core of his being.

Maria had struggled hard against the wall of his silence but without effect. She felt herself yielding to his misery, despising him, yet holding him closer than ever, desperate, terrified. And the tighter her grip, the more clearly she saw that he had eluded her. Their connection was only sexual, and both of them were surprised at how, in spite of their growing distance, they had continued to meet, continued to tumble together amidst the orange blossoms under a starless, heartless sky, and surprised at the intensity of desire during those few impassioned moments.

When Harry finally spoke—and the flame of hope flared for just that instant in Maria's breast—it was to say good-bye. He reached out now to touch her hand. She pulled away. "I'm sorry," he said. She didn't answer; all he heard in the darkness was the measured sound of her breathing, and for a moment he was frightened at its resemblance to a caged animal's.

Clara feared the day when Harry might be called to war, and though she had to admit he looked handsome in his blue and gray uniform, she refused to watch him drill with the others on the lawn of the Royal Palm.

"How can you hope to establish peace and liberty in Cuba by killing people?" she asked him.

"People are already being killed," Harry said. "The wrong people. Innocent people."

Clara sighed. "All right. I understand your point of view in the matter. But why do you have to be the one to go?"

"I'm used to the weather, for one thing. I could be valuable down there. I'm practically a native. They'll probably give me a commission. They need men who know the terrain."

"I need you here," Clara insisted. "The groves won't function with-out—"

"I appreciate your concern, Mother, but . . . " He looked away from her, unable to tell her that it would take something like this war to draw out the poison that had filled his soul, that he would not be worthy unless he could atone for these last months of cold-hearted pleasure.

"There's something else, Harry. Something you're not saying. You're throwing yourself into this without—"

"It's our duty to further the cause of freedom," he said stiffly.

"You've been taking those newspaper stories too seriously."

"I believe them, if that's what you mean. Don't you?"

Clara shook her head. "I don't trust it when someone tells someone else what his duty is."

"As long as it isn't you telling me, you mean!"

"Harry!"

He saw that he'd hurt her, but how else was he to make her leave him alone? "I'm sorry, Mother. I'm sorry. But . . . I have to do this. I have to go. Please don't stand in my way."

Clara knew she had to accept his decision; to continue to argue against his belief in the justness of the Cuban cause would be to alienate him. Yet something still nagged at her: is that really why he's going? His headlong rush seemed to her emotional, frantic, but then the whole town was becoming that way and maybe Harry was simply being swept up in it. She consoled herself with the fact that, no matter what *The Metropolis* printed, no matter what Wheeler wanted, there really was no war with Spain.

All that changed on February 15. On that evening, a mysterious explosion occurred in Havana harbor—culpability was never to be proved—and the USS *Maine,* sent to Cuba at the request of the American consul general to protect American nationals and American property, was destroyed. Two hundred and sixty men were dead in Cuban waters. Now neither the public nor the President had to be stirred up.

"Remember the *Maine*—the hell with Spain!" Sketch artists sent back paintings of the bombing: men flung into the air above a black sea lit red and gold with the flames of the stricken ship. The war continued to be fought on the front pages: "Spain Breaks off Diplomatic Relations!" "US Blockade of Cuban Ports!" "Torture Continues!"

With crowds lining the streets and waving American flags, seven thousand troops arrived in Miami to a hero's welcome. Wheeler stayed in his tower suite, grumbling over the eighteen thousand more he didn't get. Harry lost no time in joining up. The Miami Minutemen, he told Clara, was nothing more than a glorified drill team and would never leave the parade grounds, let alone see battle. During one of their practice sessions with second-hand guns and mismatched uniforms, a rifle had accidentally discharged. The inexperienced men, sure the city had been invaded, dropped to their knees and aimed at the bay. The sheepish laughter that followed only convinced Harry that if he wanted to see action, he had better join the regular army.

Overnight, Miami, a respectable-looking small city with white houses, garden gates dripping wisteria, and cupolas sporting heron-shaped weather vanes, became as it had been in its infancy: a city of tents. In no time flat the soldiers were muttering about Wheeler getting free labor, and they weren't half wrong. They'd been led to expect a tropical paradise—Flye's brochures had been distributed to all the recruitment offices—but one look at Miami shattered that illusion. The Royal Palm Hotel, featured heavily in the literature, which suggested that each soldier would have his own room and personal maid, was closed for the summer to all but the officers and the newspaper correspondents who were to make Miami, for two months anyway, the focus of international attention. Besides that, there was a town of fifteen hundred settlers—smaller than the ones they'd left behind—bordered by a nice-looking bay, an OK river if you liked rivers, and a nightmarish wilderness.

"I read the brochures, and they said this place was paradise. It's a hundred damn degrees at midnight! The only paradise is in my dreams."

"I may not have a girl, but the mosquitoes sure love me!"

Harry, unused to this kind of company, could tell nevertheless that his fellow soldiers' sense of humor was bound to run down; he shivered for what might happen to the town when it did and hoped the troops would be sent to Tampa sooner rather than later.

The troops spent their duty time digging trenches and laying water lines, but the water in the exposed pipes was too hot to drink and smelled and tasted like sulphur. Since the hard rock prevented them from digging deep latrines, sanitary facilities consisted of buckets and shallow pits, and more often than not the men simply took to the woods for relief. Dr. MacKenzie warned of the possibility of disease even as the stench rose from the hammock, but all the army did was dump barrels of lime in the open trenches and advise the female citizens to carry scented hankies when the wind brought the smell townward.

The storekeepers couldn't supply the troops with food, and so the army fed them tinned meat—"embalmed beef," as it was known in the tents. Their uniforms were woolen, and they suffered even on Miami's balmiest days. Though they complained of the prices of things, they paid whatever was asked since there was little to do in town besides spend money, drink illegally or take a dive bare-rumped and screaming from the docks into the bay. They complained about the heat too and about the mosquitoes and about the recently paved streets that the residents had gotten used to but the glare of which was blinding. Aaron Fine sold inexpensive dark glasses to them, and on the brightest days the town looked like a home for blind veterans. In a feature story called "Boys away from Home," Elliot Iverson quoted one soldier: "If I owned Miami and Hell, I'd rent out Miami and live in Hell."

The merchants were glad for the new business—Finch was even selling fresh spring water to the army from his failed Fountain of Youth and having it sent overland to stock the troop ships in Tampa—but even they were worried about containing these seven thousand men with nothing to do but wait on orders. The churches tried to entertain them, but as the weeks wore on, the fleshly pleasures of North Miami proved more attractive diversions.

North Miami, a small district that had grown up on the outskirts of town to serve liquor and supply other illicit pleasures in reaction to Clara Reade's "no liquor" clause, now swelled to accommodate the soldiers. Hundreds of drunken, restless men prowled the dark, unpaved streets looking for something to do. Who knew when they'd get the chance again? Who knew if they'd be called up to fight? Who knew who'd be alive in a month? A week? They wanted a last bit of excitement, the smell of female flesh, the taste of whiskey.

Murders occurred almost every day, and blood stained Dr. MacKenzie's front steps so bad he stopped having them swabbed down and said he'd wait for the war to be over to put in a new set. Townspeople started carrying guns as a matter of course, and no woman felt safe on the streets after dark. Tommy Schell stabbed a soldier he found pawing his wife in the stable where he kept his best rig and then had to refinish the carriage to get rid of the blood. The Ladies' League demanded to know how they'd come to this pretty pass, having to protect themselves from the soldiers when the soldiers had been sent to protect their freedom.

Negroes were in danger all the time. Geneva never left Fort Dallas, where Clara had moved, and Clara herself rode in the wagon next to Edmund, a rifle across her lap, to protect him from rampaging soldiers near the markets. One night a drunken sailor broke a bottle over a Negro's head and dug the jagged edge into his neck. When the dead man's family sought retribution, the sailor's friends banded together and raided Colored Town. Another Negro was shot when a soldier accused him of brushing up against a white woman.

But the soldiers and townspeople came together when the prisoners from the first captured Spanish ship were brought by steamer to the bay. Miamians watched the defeated Spaniards march in chains down Miami Avenue. Bidding was spirited between Fine and Brett Kingsley for the buttons on the soldiers' uniforms. Kingsley won and made a neat profit selling them to the crowd as souvenirs.

With the conflict escalating amid daily newspaper reports of atrocities, the prospect loomed that the troops would soon leave Miami for Cuba. Clara was terrified at Harry's insistence on going, but despite her detailed explanation of the way Wheeler and the newspapers were creating the climate for war, he would not be dissuaded. It was in this mood of fear and frustration that she sought out McLeod on the *Newport,* docked at the old Miami Avenue pier.

"I want you to talk to Harry," she told him. "I want you to convince him to stay in Miami. He'll listen to you. When I try, he tells me only a man would understand. As if I'm some kind of, I don't know, hysterical mother."

McLeod saw that Clara was uncharacteristically blind to the irony in this statement. "I've already talked to him," he replied, and to Clara's look of hope he could only shake his head. "He's as stubborn as you are."

"But—"

"Chances are he won't get sent down, Clara. And if he does . . ." He paused and could not help but dart his glance away. "Well, I'll be down there too," he said. "I'll keep an eye on him."

"You?" Clara searched his face, not wanting to believe what she'd heard, but McLeod simply met her eyes and nodded, and suddenly the love she'd felt for him, the love that by unspoken mutual consent had been submerged, resurfaced, flooding her chest so that she could hardly catch her breath.

McLeod pulled her to him as if his embrace could stem the tide of her feelings and comfort her, but she clung to him with a new intensity and something opened in him; in another moment he would weep along with her for everything they'd had and let slip away. "Jesus, Clara," he said in a choked whisper. "I thought we were all done with this."

"Don't talk, Quentin. Just . . ."

They held each other for a long moment, but instead of being calmed by the embrace, their emotions were pitched higher and higher. It was McLeod finally who pulled away and slapped his hands together as if to break the spell of passion and longing and regret that threatened to overtake them. "Government says no more pilot boats in the bay, so I got the *Newport* commissioned out to Cuba." He shrugged and tried a smile that only half came off. "It's not much of a job. Transporting a couple of military bigwigs back and forth."

"But—"

"Smooth that wrinkled brow, Clara. You're supposed to be proud of your men."

Clara found her voice in anger. "But it's all so unnecessary," she said. "Wheeler, Iverson—they're manipulating this whole thing for their own ends. Wheeler's the one who's asked for troops; it's his assessment of the situation that the government acted on. And now we're all caught up. The newsmen created this so-called war just to sell papers. Wheeler uses it as a way to build up Miami. It's nothing but a sales tool you're defending."

McLeod hesitated to speak, impressed and moved by the passion of her words more than by the sentiments they expressed. "You're full of theories today," he said quietly.

"It's the truth, Quentin," she pleaded.

He nodded. "It's also the truth that people are being shot on the streets of Havana because they want their freedom."

"Do you really think that by intervening and shedding blood we're going to stop bloodshed and disorder?" Tears welled in her eyes; she turned away even as McLeod embraced her.

"We'll come back. Both of us."

Clara looked out at the calm waters of the bay. "Will you?" she said bitterly. "I don't know."

Harry lay in the tent and listened to the men outside. They were usually quiet in the mornings, the effects of the evening's debauch leaving them limp and dizzy. Harry was as tired and enervated as they were. Unused to idleness, he worked around the camp during the day and stayed there at night despite the proliferation of mosquitoes in brackish ponds nearby and the rising stench of vegetable decay. The troops camouflaged him. He was one of them, a soldier, a man meant to fight. Maria could not reach him here; away from her he found that his desires cooled and his mind cleared. He knew he could—he must!—do without her, deny himself the pleasures of her flesh if he was to survive the battle inside. And he began to allow himself to think of Shinassa and the pure pleasure of the few short days he'd spent near her.

Maria wrote to him as if he had already gone to war, and though she insisted that she pined for him, she seemed to relish the idea of him in battle. He read her letters listlessly and never answered them; the sight of her handwriting was enough to make him turn his face to the canvas tent wall. "Darling Harry . . . when war comes . . . our love . . . be strong and brave . . . you and myself . . . a hero in battle . . . tomorrow . . . forever . . . love . . ."

When war finally came, it was short-lived and, at first, far away, on the other side of the world, in a place hardly anyone in Miami had ever heard of called the Philippines. It was there that Admiral Dewey and his fleet sailed into the Spanish-held harbor of the capital city of Manila. The next day the headline of *The Metropolis* read, "Dewey Smashes Spain's Fleet." The troops in Miami received their orders, were mobilized, and boarded the trains to Tampa for deployment in the Caribbean.

The city of tents was folded and packed away; ten acres of empty tins and newspapers and ragged pieces of khaki clothing remained. Protest as he might, Harry was ordered to stay in Miami with the minutemen and guard the city. Now that fighting in the Caribbean had accelerated, there was more than ever, the army said, the possibility that Spain might attempt a sneak attack. Miamians were nervous; only when the troops left did they realize how protected they had been and how vulnerable they now were. Harry didn't believe for a minute that Spain would bother about Miami, which, now that the troops had gone, seemed as far from the site of battle as Manila. Disappointed, he spent his days in the shabby blue and gray uniform he'd hoped never to wear again, drilling once again on the now-deserted parade grounds with the middle-aged merchants and underage boys who made up his unit.

Construction of Fort Finch on the south bank, despite Finch's willing participation, never went further than the huge mound of sand dredged from the bay and piled in front of Finch's store. Before the fort itself was even started, Dewey had made his move and the project was abandoned. Rufus Finch demanded that the sand be removed since it effectively blocked his view of the bay, but the army engineers were gone and his demands went unmet. The lookout tower of Fort Dallas would be sufficient for spotting Spanish ships, and Clara, who wanted all along to have nothing to do with the war, agreed to let it be used for that, its original purpose.

Fort Dallas had a long and not always honorable past. Built originally as a frontier plantation, it had limestone walls three feet thick, the rock quarried from a pit near Arch Creek by Negro slaves. Its owner, running short of money for his great scheme to build a town on Biscayne Bay, made what he foresaw as a brief foray to California, only to be killed when his own gun discharged as he dismounted his horse. The fort languished, overgrown with wild hibiscus and sea grape, then became a lookout post during the 1836 war against the Seminoles; during the war between the states, it was the refuge of deserters from both Confederate and Union troops, of Union spies and blockade runners. It was an army post again during the Second and Third Seminole wars, then was purchased by the Biscayne Bay Company sales agent, Quentin McLeod, who sold it to Clara Reade.

Reluctant as Clara and Harry had once been to leave her parents' house, storms had dealt it blows from which it could not recover; despite repairs and replacement parts, it simply became no longer habitable. The former officers' quarters inside Fort Dallas became their new home. Made of stucco and lime, it seemed permanent in a way that her parents' house never had, and they moved into it all the objects from Middleton that had been thus far kept stored: shelves of books, a few paintings, a Queen Anne chair upholstered in rose damask that had been used in the attic studio in Middleton, a set of silver goblets, Harry's baptismal robe, her best china plates. The one-story fort dwelling gave out onto a wide courtyard, once an arid expanse of sand and coral and scrubby dwarf pines, now planted by Clara as the yard of the old house was. Shade came from the oaks that ran along the outside wall of the fort, and Clara used the lumber she'd bought from Cal Sparks to construct a porch and to shore up the tower on top of the fort.

She enjoyed sitting on a little bench inside the tower to watch the sun set. The bay fanned out in an immense vista from the mouth of the river, coral reefs creating dark purple lines, the whole framed by stately royal palms that soared above the banana palms, the buttonwood, and the mangroves that grew in dense profusion along the shores. It was to this spot that she came to watch her town grow, trying not to think about the war two hundred miles south and of her fears for the safety of Quentin McLeod.

"You're too stubborn to die," she had joked with him the day he left and to herself had thought: too smart, too careful.

She knew he would have written if he could have but knew too that unless the mail was of military significance, it would not get through. From the day after he left she had not known for sure if he was alive or dead; not a day had gone by when she was not prepared for the worst. All she had for comfort were rumors—Why did people still like to gossip so about Quentin McLeod? she wondered—each rumor more awful than the next: he'd been wounded during the battle at El Caney; he'd drowned when the *Newport* was bombed in the harbor at Santiago; he'd been shot freeing prisoners in a detention camp in the hills; he'd died a hero; he'd disappeared a coward; he'd caroused in cantinas with a Cuban mistress; he'd contracted malaria and languished in an army hospital in Texas; he was an opium addict in Siboney; he was burned, swathed in bandages, unrecognizable, insane.

Clara felt she would go insane herself if she paid too much attention to all the news of him that came her way. She concentrated her attention instead on the growing town, glad that Harry, though unhappy and frustrated, was at least safe.

He spent the long days after the troops had gone inside the fort, feeling absurd, useless, powerless to do more. At night he often wandered the town, which had regained its old quiet and calm since the soldiers had gone, and always ended up at the field where the tents had been and the promise of battle had kept him buoyed for personal victory. The stench was still present but fading. The stagnant pond on the far side of the camp would dry up when spring came, houses would be built on these grounds, trees planted, and all traces of the occupation would be gone.

In the harbor of Santiago de Cuba, Commodore Schley attempted a maneuver similar to Dewey's in the Philippines and with similar results: "Spain Flees Cuba, Fleet Destroyed," *The Metropolis* declared. Harry read avidly the reports of ground fighting at Siboney, El Caney, and at San Juan Hill. His old bunkmate wrote and bragged about being flank to flank with Teddy Roosevelt and the Rough Riders. *"SURREN-*

DER!" was the *Metropolis* headline on May 1. The Spanish empire was shattered, *Cuba libre* a fact.

After a week of celebration, Miami tried to return to normal, but the storm of publicity had hit it as swiftly and surely as a hurricane, and the city would never be quite the same as it had been. But, as Wheeler hoped, it was finally "on the map."

For a month or so after the war was over, the Miami Minutemen continued to practice their drilling, drawing fewer and fewer onlookers as the heat wore on and the novelty wore off. Harry saw that they were becoming figures of fun in their tattered uniforms; he flushed with embarrassment when they took up their rifles at dawn and fell into formation. The more they drilled, the more precise their maneuvers, the more humiliating it all seemed.

Yet he was also somewhat reluctant to see these sessions end, for that would mean the resumption of life as usual, a practice extolled along the streets of the city as that thing most desired, especially as the summer ended and the tourist season loomed not five months away. But it was precisely "life as usual" to which Harry, alone among Miamians, did not look forward, for everything in the time before the war was touched by Maria, while all he could think of now was the brief time he spent in the Seminole camp. Hidden in the far reaches of the Everglades, the girl beckoned to him. Because she was there, Harry was able to hold on to the hope of a future that was radically different from his past; each day a part of him surrendered to that hope and moved inexorably toward her.

Early one morning Maria's brother Ned made his usual appearance at the fort to walk with Harry to the morning's drill at the parade grounds. Ned Sparks was lanky and pale, with huge freckled hands; he had Maria's smile—though not her beauty—and he asked for nothing but the return of good humor from Harry, whom he already treated with the respect due an admired older brother.

They made their way quickly through the alternating squares of sunlight and gray, muggy shade along Miami Avenue. Ned set the pace; just once he wanted to get there before Aaron Fine and Kevin Starger, who were invariably first to arrive. Only a few others were up and out this early, and the street's emptiness made Harry hungry and light-headed.

"I been practicing that new turn," Ned said. "Got it down pat. Wanna see?"

Harry shook his head; though he liked Ned, on this particular morning Ned's good mood rankled him. He had the high spirits of a boy who, though having missed his chance to go to war, would play at it as long as he was allowed. His enthusiasm made Harry feel tired and old.

"A new march step is definitely something I can do without," Harry said harshly, and though he saw Ned's face fall he couldn't help but continue. "The minutemen are going to be history pretty soon, you know."

"Oh, I'd like being in history," Ned said, then realizing what Harry meant, looked down at the ground and kicked a pebble. "But I'll sure miss the drilling, won't you?"

Harry shrugged. "I'm tired of it. I'm tired of marching to nowhere, and I'm tired of wearing this old uniform, and I'm tired—"

Ned laughed. "You sure got the morning cranks today, Harry. C'mon soldier, don't drag your feet. Let's go, boy. Hup! Hup! Hup!"

Ned high-stepped around Harry, doing smart pivot turns and about-faces. Harry waved his arms as if Ned were a pesky fly he was shooing away, but just as he tried one big swat, he fell to his knees.

Ned laughed and kept marching in a circle around him, raising dust in Harry's face. Harry swayed but made no attempt to rise, and Ned stopped. "You look like hell, soldier." He laughed, daring Harry with the mock insult.

"You too," Harry replied and tried a laugh that erupted startlingly into a cough so violent he pitched over on his side.

Alarmed, Ned kneeled and peered into his face. "Harry? You joking, Harry? You OK?"

"Never better," Harry said. He looked at Ned as if from a great distance. Why was he standing so far away, and look at how his arm was elongated, pulling out of his shoulders . . . And why was the air so thick? "Something burning?" His voice was faint, echoing.

Ned swallowed hard. "I'm getting the doc, Harry. You look—"

Harry raised his hand to protest, but Ned was already on the run. Harry dropped his head back. Above him the sky was white and steamy, the sun bearing down like a grudge. He closed his eyes for a moment; he knew it was vitally important to keep them open, and he intended to open them again in just a second, just one more second, but for now . . . for now . . .

He heard the slow pounding of his pulse, a sound sonorous and hollow, as if his entire torso were a cave and his heart hung on a pendulum, each swing weaker, heavier, each arc slipped, short. I'm dying, he thought, and lifted his head to be blessed.

18.

With the war over and the city returned to normal, it became horrifyingly apparent that more had been left behind than cleared acreage and the merchants' stuffed coffers. No one would ever blame the soldiers or the war; there was, in fact, no one to blame, for no one really understood what lay at the roots of the legacy. They only knew that often as not its outcome was death.

In a tiny article printed in *The Metropolis* after the battles had been won and *Cuba libre!* was the law of the land, it was reported that despite the heavy fighting, thirteen out of every fourteen American deaths were caused not by gunshot, not by explosions or drownings or machete wounds, but by diseases contracted in the overcrowded camps and on the unfamiliar island of Cuba.

A particularly virulent strain of yellow fever had decimated a few small villages in Cuba and appeared to be making its way across the Caribbean to Key West, where a hotel had been burned down after the discovery that half the guests had it. Nervous Miamians consoled themselves with the fact that Miami was still well above the fever line, then read in mounting horror that the fever had jumped north of them to Tampa. "Drink a glass of whiskey at sun up and sun down, and the fever will never catch you," advised Iverson in *The Metropolis*. From Tampa it snaked north to Jacksonville, and at first they breathed a sigh of relief, thinking the fever had skipped right past them, until someone remembered that smug joke coined when the railroad caused the first real estate boom: "Where's Miami and how do I get there?" "Go to Jacksonville terminal and follow the crowd." With people in Jacksonville dying by the dozens, the joke was no longer funny.

Harry's was not the first case. Even before the Treaty of Paris was signed, Perry National, a young singing teacher from Chicago, rooming on the third floor of Mrs. Geoghan's boarding house, manifested all the signs. But National, a bachelor, an orphan, and by nature shy and solitary, suffered in silence and died alone. It was only later, when other cases came to light, that National's death was recalled and the fever given as probable cause. Before that it had been too terrible to think about, even to consider as a possibility.

There were several theories as to how the fever made its way into Miami. Since, in retrospect, Perry National's was the first case, his whereabouts and activities were traced. Mrs. Geoghan remembered that a few days before he began canceling his pupils' lessons, he had boarded a sloop from Santo Domingo to buy fruit. "He had a weakness for exotics," Mrs. Geoghan explained sorrowfully, as if that was what had killed him, and it was concluded by some, then, that the fever came to town inside a mango from the *Madre de Deus*. The sloop was long gone, and now no Cuban ships were allowed to dock.

Dr. MacKenzie, espouser of the prevailing medical wisdom, pooh-poohed such notions and said the fever was invariably traced to stagnant ponds, to cesspools and filth and decomposing animal and vegetable matter, to intense heat, and to hot sun and was transported by mosquitoes. The population gasped; he could have been describing Miami's own worst view of itself.

Some people packed their bags, shut their houses, and took the first train out no matter where it was going. The Florida Health Department, used to these outbreaks, and fearful lest the fever continue to spread throughout the state, sent representatives to organize the Dade County Health Unit and place Miami under quarantine. Now anyone who wanted to leave had first to stay in a detention camp; if in two weeks they manifested no signs of the fever, they were allowed to go. If they became ill—and more than a few did—they were installed in Mrs. Geoghan's rooming house, turned makeshift hospital when her boarders discovered the cause of Perry National's death and evacuated, or on one of two barges afloat at the mouth of the river, where they either lived through the ravages of the fever or did not.

The camps and the quarantine did not prevent people from trying to steal away. A couple recently emigrated from a peach farm in Georgia panicked when their child showed early symptoms, packed all that they could carry on their backs, and disappeared after dark into the hammock. Months after the epidemic had peaked and receded, all three bodies were found in the limestone quarry near Pineland.

Officials from the health unit were bribed to sign immunity cards that would allow people egress. Armed guards—Spanish-American war veterans for whom the wearing of a gun was enough reason to take the job—were stationed at the railroad depot and along the docks to discourage illegal departures. Fatalists heaved a sigh of despair and accepted their approaching doom; town attorneys Dick Kinnan, Bob Dorsey, and Henry Spycker did record business drawing up last wills and testaments.

The period of isolation began in mid-September. Stores shut down; the streets were deserted at high noon. Occasionally, an anxious mother would be seen scurrying into Dr. MacKenzie's office or out the back door of the pharmacy where Virgil Moss dispensed quinine tablets and blood thinners, which were two methods of treatment. Uncomfortably hot baths were another, as were liberal doses of rye whiskey. Some citizens, unaffected but for a galloping anxiety that they might be next, were quick to subscribe to this last method and continued the treatments long after the quarantine was lifted; just in case, they said, sipping, just in case.

It was believed that the most susceptible were the panic-stricken, the overworked, and those newcomers to town unused to the tropical climate. The least susceptible were those whose minds were free from fear and anxiety, a rare state indeed given the reports of new outbreaks daily. To avoid the fever, citizens were advised to abstain from drugs, to bathe frequently in very hot water, to sleep high above the ground, and to remain in the open air as much as possible, but only between sunrise and sunset. There was a theory that night air was the most fertile for transmission, and people tended then to stay indoors, screened, shuttered, and shut up tight against the invisible marauders.

Clara would stand in the tower above Fort Dallas, exhausted from her vigil at Harry's bedside, a gardenia-scented handkerchief pressed to her mouth, and watch tiny, fluttering yellow flags dotting the doorways of the town below her, each a sign that the fever had hit. Smoke pots burned in the streets to ward off mosquitoes, and the atmosphere itself seemed to have a sickly orange glow, as if the fever had taken on animate, visible form in the dull flames, in the wisps of gray smoke and the smell of thick, burning oil. Below her, in the mangrove swamps along the river, fever cannons were set off in the belief that stimulated air currents would help to blow the fever away.

On the other side of the river where Clara was used to seeing the Finches on their porch and hearing Ida at her piano, she now saw an empty yard and a yellow flag hung on the door. Clara remembered Rufus Finch saying how optimism came cheap on the north bank. Not now, she thought, because in the face of the illness's proliferation, optimism seemed an insult. The same blackboard in front of Fine's General Merchandise that years before had been used to keep track of the votes to name the city was now used to list its dead.

People were afraid to breathe deeply, to eat and drink, to touch another's flesh, to feel a neighbor's breath on their cheek. They were wary even of their friends, yet imbued too with a sense of sadness at this state, for the onset of the fever was sudden and the man in the pink of health on Monday might be jaundiced on Thursday and dead on Sunday. The most dreaded sound was the slow, clanking drag of the wagons moving the dead to the docks. They rolled only at night, the bodies stowed in back under a tarpaulin, stopping only long enough for the victim's clothes to be piled in the middle of the street and burned. A few stragglers stood on their porches, others peered through their curtains, and some moved as deeply into their homes as they could to avoid the sight as the clothes became ashes and the ashes rose on a column of smoke into the night sky. An unspoken fear: would the ashes infect the air? The bodies were then transported by boat for burial on a deserted island to the south that came to be known as Death Key.

Once word got out that Harry had been struck, Fort Dallas was closed to all visitors and a yellow flag hung on the front gate. Though Clara chastised herself, there had hardly been time to notice the telltale signs, and no sooner had Harry been brought from the street outside Schell's Livery to his own bed inside Fort Dallas than he developed a frighteningly high fever. His breathing was labored and shallow that night, his lips dry and cracked by morning. Clara sat up with him, watched his face by the dull glow of the kerosene lamp, rubbed ice on his wrists, touched cool water to his lips with her fingers, fanned him until her arms ached. The next day she wove together long strands of fragrant grasses, hung them from a perforated pipe at the window, and let water slowly drip down the strands. Even the slightest breeze now wafted cool, fragrant air across the room to his bed.

That night his face was flushed, his fever higher, his tongue red and pointed and split. Delirious, he complained of being impaled at the hips, of a fissure dividing his skull in two. Unable to do anything to make him well, Clara stayed at his bedside and did what she could to make him comfortable. She assured him that he would be all right, that he was better than he'd been, that the fever was breaking, his color returning. To herself she was more realistic: the fever would run its course; Harry would either survive it or succumb. She could not fool herself about that, but neither would she let the truth erode her hopes.

By the third day his skin and the whites of his eyes had taken on the jaundiced color that gave the fever its name. He was restless, babbling, sleeping deeply and waking suddenly, moaning, and then, his stomach visibly convulsing, he began the bloody black vomiting, the hemorrhaging from his nose and mouth that was the disease at its climax.

Maria came every day and rang the bell at the front gates. When Geneva shooed her away, she camped outside and refused to leave. When she rang on the third day, Clara went to the gates, opening them only enough to see her. Maria was unkempt, her dress soiled, her face smudged, hair in disarray. Clara wondered that she didn't have the fever herself.

Next to Maria's head the yellow flag fluttered in the faint humid breeze. "I want to take care of him," she pleaded. Her face was tear-streaked, her eyes desperate and anxious.

Clara shook her head. "Don't you see the flag? We're in quarantine."

Maria raised her hands as if she would tear the flag down and shove Clara out of the way. "No. Please. I have to! I have to!"

Clara's grip on the gate tightened. "You'd get sick yourself."

"I don't care," Maria replied, shaking her head wildly. "I don't want to live if Harry dies."

"Don't talk like a fool," Clara said impatiently. "He's not going to die."

Maria's eyes opened wide, red-rimmed and bleary with tears. "How do you know?"

Clara sighed, exhausted. "Because I say it, that's how."

"He loves me," Maria insisted. "I can make him well. I'll force him to be well. I'll—"

Clara was unmoved; this display of emotionalism would do no one any good. "I've cared for him his whole life," she said.

"Then it's my turn now!"

Clara stared at her; was this love speaking or something else? "Go home. It's yourself you should be taking care of."

"But I love him!"

"Then pray for him," Clara said and closed the gate.

Clara was at Harry's bedside when Geneva slid a letter under the door. Even before she moved to pick it up, she recognized the military stationery and felt a sickening wave of fear. The letter seemed to shimmer in the shaft of morning light pouring through the window. In a moment she would pick it up, open it, and know, and she hesitated now, as if to prolong the last layer of her innocence. One by one they had been peeled away, leaving her raw and disillusioned.

If he was dead . . . No, she couldn't think that way and yet could not make herself pick up the letter. As long as she didn't know, Quentin was still alive, unhurt, exactly the same as he'd been the day he left.

Harry was sleeping now; the fever seemed to drain all his strength. She touched his warm, dry hand for comfort, then moved slowly across the room and picked up the envelope. It was light as a bird in her hand; it would tell her everything. She stood at the window thinking of nothing. Geneva was standing in the garden, holding a rake. Behind her the bougainvillea swayed in the breeze along the fort wall. Clara remembered McLeod picking up her umbrella with his toes on the day she'd arrived. No, she thought. No memories. Not yet. She tore open the envelope. The letter began, "My dear Clara." She gasped and leaned against the wall for a long moment, her hand covering her eyes.

"Miz Reade?"

Clara looked down into the yard to see Geneva on her knees in the garden; was she weeding or praying? "He's alive," Clara said, and Geneva jerked her head up and looked around her as if waking from a dream. For the first time in all the years Clara had known her, she laughed.

"My dear Clara," the letter began.

There were times in the last few months that I came as close to the great beyond as I ever care to again. The fighting in Cuba was bloody and bad, Clara, and I am sorry to have seen it. A man's got to harden up plenty to stay open-eyed and useful at a massacre. Boys and men suffered on both sides, and though I rejoice in the victory for liberty, I am more convinced than ever that this carnage is no way to win it. I have never been a religious man or had near as much to do with God as I probably should have, but now I can't help thinking that war's not His way. The foundation for peace is all wrong and people don't believe in it, not in their hearts, because they know how it truly came to be. Phew. This war's got me on my high horse, as you can see. I don't know what you might have been hearing about me, but the facts are that I ran generals in and out of port cities for part of the war until my poor boat got hit. That's right. The *Newport's* gone to its grave in the clear waters off Havana, and Clara, it was a sight as sad as seeing a friend go down. After that I got involved in some ground fighting at Siboney—it's where I saw the worst of it—and got myself a second wound, this one from a bullet; the first was from a piece of shrapnel from the torpedo that sank my boat. Both of them are just in my leg, nothing that's going to keep me much out of things.

I got billeted to this army hospital here in Corpus Christi and was set to come back to Miami in October, but it seems you all got yourself on quarantine. I will be honest, Clara. I am worried about you and Harry and about every other dear soul in town. I have seen the fever, once in New Orleans and once in Key West, and it is one tough customer. There's a nurse here now, tapping her foot and waiting for me to finish writing so she can put this into today's mail, so I will close off now.

When you think of me, see me standing at the gates of Miami waiting for that damn quarantine to be lifted.

Enclosed with the letter was a brochure on which McLeod had scribbled, "The nurse brought this in from the railroad station here, and I've seen others like it. What the hell does Wheeler think he's doing by promoting Miami as a vacation spot in these times? Everyone on the Gulf knows what's going on in Miami. Is he trying to fool the rest of the country? This kind of stuff's got to stop."

Clara held the letter to her chest and went to Harry's bed. There was some pink in his cheeks and she dared now to hope he was over the worst of it. One hand on her son's arm and the other clutching the letter, she told Harry what she had never told anyone before: "I love him."

After Harry'd awakened and was able to keep down a cup of broth, Clara read the brochure McLeod had enclosed. It was titled *Paradise Regained* and was profusely illustrated, its prose extolling the glories of the bay, "whose deep blue waters dance gaily beneath the almost perpetual sunshine and invite the home seeker to make his abode here," its weather, "where winter's chilling blasts are never known, but all the year the summer skies smile back at sunlit seas and flowers bloom their fairest just when the ice king's grip is firmest on less-favored lands," and the life-enhancing sunshine that made Miami "a restful land, where jaded body and brain may find repose."

Then, sure that Harry was resting, she dressed and rode her carriage to the Royal Palm. Wheeler had had the good fortune of being detained in Palm Beach for the duration of the quarantine, and the hotel was shut down. It was upstairs in Wheeler's tower suite that she found Emmett Flye. He was fatter than the day he'd come to her office seeking work, and he had the prosperous look of someone who'd made money fast and spent it so it showed: an onyx pinky ring, a diamond and ruby stickpin punching a hole in a silk cravat, and most outlandish of all, a gold front tooth. He still wore his suit too tight, and his shoes squeaked when he crossed the office to shake Clara's hand.

"I've just been with the Businessmen's Association," he said. "Now that's a group that needs calming down. They're afraid their precious tourists are going to pass Miami by this season."

"As well they might if they knew the truth," Clara said.

"I wouldn't worry about that," he said.

In Wheeler's absence Flye had been instructed to bury the news of yellow fever under an avalanche of boosterism. People who didn't fear getting the fever were panicking that if the news spread, it would be the end of Miami. That fear was well-founded. Hadn't the epidemic in St. Joseph's caused the virtual abandonment of the town? Hadn't Napoleon Bonaparte's imperial ambitions in the Americas been thwarted when the fever destroyed a force of thirty-three thousand sent to suppress the rebellion in Santo Domingo? Wasn't it the reason the isthmus of Panama had never been pierced with a canal? If plagues could twist history as they had, could Miami, having just triumphed over the effects of the war, survive intact? And even if the citizens stayed, would the tourists ever come back if they knew what had happened?

"What the tourists don't know won't hurt 'em," Flye said.

"But how can the Florida Eastern Star continue to promote Miami as the place where"—she took out the brochure McLeod had sent and read from it—" 'where the gates of death are farther removed than from any other state.' "

Flye smiled expansively. "Just because we've had a little trouble here doesn't mean we shouldn't advertise. As a matter of fact," he added confidentially, "it gives us even more reason to."

"Haven't you heard?" Clara said. "Miami is in the middle of an epidemic!"

"The middle?" Flye shook his head as he walked to the desk and routed through the papers. "I've done my research, Mrs. Reade. I know what's what. Yellow fever rises and falls in ninety days." He pulled a long sheet of paper from the pile and held it aloft. "Look at these statistics I got here on the outbreaks in New Orleans. Every single time it climaxed within the predicted limits. On the fifty-third day one year, on the fifty-sixth day another, then the fifty-seventh, and again the fifty-third. See? The average is always ninety days from the onset to the time the quarantine's lifted. So. Ours started in September, so we'll be free and clear of it by Christmas and ready for the tourists to come pouring in."

Clara looked at the chart, then up at Flye's smiling face. "This is truly contemptible," she said. "You are playing with human lives. Luring tourists here when there's a plague—"

"I don't know why you want to keep on using such terms," Flye said. "It's awful discouraging."

Clara shook her head in dismay. " 'Paradise Regained,' is that what you'd rather call it? This kind of ambition for Miami, this kind of commercialism at any cost—"

"Before you go passing judgment," Flye said, "consider the case of Job."

"I never thought of you as a Bible-reading man, Mr. Flye."

"Mmm, there's parts I like, parts I don't." Clara watched him place splayed fingers on his chest in a grotesque parody of a righteous sermonizer. "For example," he said. "Is not Job depicted as the ideal man? Yes, I think he is. Yet he owned thousands of sheep and camels and oxen." He looked at Clara and dropped his hands. "When you consider that, don't it give a new meaning to the word *commercialism?*"

Clara took a deep, controlled breath. "Mr. Flye. Money cannot bring back the dead. Or in our case even cure the sick."

"I know your son's got it, Mrs. Reade, and I feel for you. I do. But"— and now he assumed a new pose—fist on hip, chest puffed to strain the buttons on his vest. "Remember what the great merchant Desponde said to the Duke of Burgundy: 'Trade finds its way everywhere and rules the world. There is nothing but may be accomplished with money.' "

"It proves nothing to make history mean what you want it to mean."

Flye shrugged. "How about a more recent, personal statement then?" He picked up a piece of paper and winked at her. "You see how I want you on my side." He looked at the paper and smiled. "Dated just yesterday, as a matter of fact. A testimonial." He cleared his throat to read. " 'I think it is the greatest place I've ever visited. I came here tired and worn out, with little appetite. I began to feel the benefit of the climate before I had been here twenty-four hours. Nowhere in America—' "

"What lying fool said that, and how much did you pay him?"

Flye laughed. "Why Mrs. Reade, I'm disappointed. I thought you'd recognize the style. I wrote it, of course. Me, Emmett Flye. The best friend the city of Miami ever had."

19.

Harry felt he had traveled a dark and dangerous landscape transported by the fever and now, recovered, had awakened on a distant shore. And it was clear that he, having come this far, could no longer live in the country of his former life. All sense of duty and obligation to past emotions had been burned out of him.

He sat up in bed and felt the sun spread its warmth across his lap, thinking with fondness of the boy he'd been—so young, no naive, so misguided and easily led—but he'd aged a hundred years since then. Well, no, he thought now, smiling, smoothing the blanket around his legs; that kind of wild exaggeration was the boy in him talking, and there was no need for that any longer: the way was clear.

He spent his time now mapping out a program of recovery. He would not be arrogant or force his body to heal faster than it could, nor would he linger with his weakness or indulge his fatigue. He knew he had to rest and eat and slowly rebuild his strength. The life he would soon be leading required a kind of physical stamina he had been in the process of casually achieving when he'd fallen to the fever.

His mother came into the room with his lunch on a tray and put it down on the table beside him. She had not left his side during all the weeks of his illness; his gratitude at such loyalty bridged the gap that had kept them apart and made him love her as he had not in a long, long time. They might have been back in Middleton in the days of his childhood illnesses when each was the other's best and only companion. The joy he saw in her face at each new step of his recovery now told him, without her speaking of it, that she felt so too.

He was glad for this time they had managed to grab just as each had felt on the brink of being inextricably lost to the other, grateful that the schism that had opened between them had had this extraordinary chance to heal. Harry was sorry only that it had come on the eve of his departure from her life. Knowing that he would leave in a matter of mere weeks added a final note of poignancy to every exchange of even the simplest words. He was determined not to speak to her of his decision until his departure was imminent; for his mother to know that he was going, that they would never have time like this again in their lives, would only burden their last weeks together with unutterable sorrow.

Because she was without this vital piece of information, Clara was indeed very happy. Harry was well; together they had lived through a perilous time and emerged not merely alive but closer than ever before. She knew that to speak of it would make them both self-conscious, and so she merely reveled in his good health, in the small daily chores that took her to his room, in the simple sight of his dinner plate emptied, of color returning to his cheeks, of first steps and first laughter and a last kiss at night. She was able also to return to her life in the city; it needed her just as Harry did, for it too was recovering from a brush with death.

Two hundred and sixty people had suffered through the fever; fifteen had died, among them the youngest daughter of Flora and Farley Goram, the foreman of the work crew out at the Reade Groves, and much to Clara's personal regret, poor Ida Finch. It was when she returned to the fort from Ida's funeral—Rufus had had her body exhumed from its grave on Death Key and reburied on his own property—that Clara found waiting for her a letter from McLeod, telling her he would be home before Christmas.

· · ·

The only spot in town where Clara was guaranteed not to be assailed by customers, clients, or people seeking advice was in the tower of Fort Dallas. The breeze was fresher in the tower than in the town, the air cooler; the very height itself in this land of endless flat plains provided a sense of removal she could not get even in the quiet, shadowy depths of the hammock or on the empty vista of the bay.

A faint mist was rising from the hammock; the sun appeared to sizzle as it sank into the tops of the trees, when Clara caught sight of the Key West steamer coming in to dock at the bay. Even at this distance there was no mistaking McLeod at the prow. He had his hands on the railing, his legs planted wide apart as if he owned the world. Late afternoon sun lit up his white hair from behind so he seemed to Clara to be shimmering, incandescent. A sudden rush of desire for him made her flush and smile. She watched him as the boat moved swiftly past the fort, then turned, disappearing beyond the mangroves to dock out of sight on the bay.

She ran down the tower stairs, across the yard and through the gates to the palm grove. She could see boats bobbing on the bay. The clouds streaked the sky pink and orange and were reflected purple and red on the water. The rushing breeze enveloped her in the smell of frangipani. Clara saw McLeod as she approached; the colors of the sky were mirrored in his eyes, his skin was burnished the copper of the forest floor, and she was reminded once again of the way she had seen him the day on the river when she knew she belonged here— when he told her that she did—as part of the living landscape.

"An old Civil War vet carved it for me," McLeod said of the panther-headed ebony cane he now used to walk. "What a crazy old coot he was! Been in that army hospital for thirty-odd years, still has nightmares about being cut up by Grant's army and fed to the 'darkies' on his pappy's plantation in Oxford, Mississippi." McLeod shook his head and ran his hands over the intricately carved cane. "This is what he does all day every day. When he isn't clutched on to a hunk of wood and a carving knife, his hands tremble so bad he has to sit on 'em."

Clara listened to McLeod speak, so glad to have him back she could not pity him for the "souvenir" he'd gotten in Cuba. It was apparent when they walked back through the palm grove, though, that the wounds had done more than scar him and that the cane was more than an adornment. He had never seemed dearer to her than when he came into the fort and embraced her, at last, in the garden.

Later in the day, after he'd seen Harry and let himself be waited on at lunch by a newly smiling Geneva, he and Clara set out in her flat-bottomed canoe; he was silent and remained so all through the trip upriver. And she spoke, for the first and last time, of the horror of Harry's bout with yellow fever. "I held him. I slapped myself to stay awake. I held my hand over a candle and burned my palm to stay awake because I knew that if I let go of him for even an instant—" She put her hand to her mouth to stop the sob that rose in her chest. McLeod put his strong, warm hand on her shoulder and drew her to him. She rested her head against his chest and wept the tears she had held back until now.

Clara did not question him about what more had happened to him in the time he'd been gone, sensing that there was something in his silence that demanded respect. She watched him instead: the play of his back muscles when he leaned over to dip the paddle into the river, the glistening drops of water splashing on his forearms, the sun glinting on the lank white hair that hung over his forehead like a little boy's, the balancing grip of his bony knees on the insides of the boat, his lips pressed in concentration, eyes squinting in the sun. She felt it a rare privilege to be able to look at him this way, in such frank appraisal and pleasure. He only turned to her once, and she saw, in the quick shy smile, that he knew she was watching him and that it was all right with him.

"Oh, how I missed you," she whispered hours later as they lay on a blanket of moss in a shaded glen near the river, Clara's hand idly tracing the veins on the inside of McLeod's arm. McLeod murmured his reply into her thick hair undone and tangled on her neck. His cane dangled from the vines above their heads. Shafts of sun coming through the overhang warmed the skin on Clara's bare back, and she moved in closer to McLeod. The years had melted away, their stubbornness and disagreements gone. This is what is important, Clara thought. She twisted her neck to look up at him, to plant a quick kiss on his lips. A cloud crossed the sun, chilling her.

"We were fools, Quentin, to have spent so much time apart." He said nothing, his fingers threading through her hair. "I can't even remember what or why or . . ."

"I know, I know," he replied, yet there was something in him that did not know at all, or knew and did not like the knowledge. The war had unsettled him in ways he could not have imagined; things that had once seemed important no longer did. As much as he wanted Clara, had thought of her, dreamed of her, planned for the time he would see her again, there was yet a part of him that longed for a quiet place away from the bungled, destructive affairs of men, apart from the noise and harshness of cities, free of the ruinous specter of greed. And even as he held Clara close to him and smelled the sweet gardenia in her hair and licked the salt and sun on her skin, he knew that having once asked her to give up the city and leave with him, he could not ask her again. Knowing what her answer would be, he dared not. Knowing the loss of what he knew he would now never have with her, and the choice he was bound to make that would seal it, filled him with sorrow.

Clara sighed beneath his shifting weight. This feeling of safety in his arms would go on forever.

Harry was on his knees on the third story of the hotel, hammer in hand, back burning from a morning spent driving nail after nail into the teak lumber Cal Sparks had salvaged off a Spanish boat wrecked the week before on the Florida reef. The imprint of the royal seal of the king of Spain was still visible on some of the boards.

His mother was planning a New Year's Eve party in the banquet room downstairs, and the very rooms he was working on now were booked to be occupied in a matter of days. He had been out of bed for weeks now, his strength and color slowly returning, and he could have been gone already, but his conscience would not let him leave until this work was done.

He heard his mother's footsteps coming up the outside stairs, and in a moment she joined him, taking a seat on a canvas camp stool and looking at Harry and his work with a pleased expression on her face.

"I hate to admit it, but it looks like Emmett Flye's advertisements did the trick. Every place in town is booked for the season, even Mrs. Geoghan's boarders have come back, though I don't think she'll ever let that room out again. You know which one I mean." Clara looked down at the top of his head; his hair had grown long and wilder since his bout with the fever and needed cutting badly, but she did so love the way it lay in sweat-dampened curls at the nape of his neck. "I want to start a movement to dredge the bay. Make Miami a deep-water port. What do you think? Get shipping really going. I just hate being at the mercy of Wheeler and the Florida Eastern Star. Those freight rates are going up so fast! Well, you know. But it's the only game in town, so we've no choice but to go along with it. If seagoing ships could dock here, though . . . Oh, Harry, I've got plans. Such plans. It wasn't until you got sick that I realized how much we had and almost lost. We were drifting apart, darling." Harry turned his head away. "No, don't deny it. I can only say it aloud now because it's no longer so. It's awful to think that it took a bout with yellow fever to do it, but"—she reached for his hand as Harry scooted a few feet off—"these are great days, darling. Days that'll go down in history."

"You're beginning to sound like another one of those greedy boosters who . . ."

Clara said nothing for a long while, trying to understand this outburst. She looked at his profile; she knew every curve, every shadow, every line and never failed to find new beauty and expression in it, but now she saw trouble and distress. "Harry, what's the matter?"

"Nothing," he said, but could he say that he had lost his way in more than one sense? Could he tell her about Maria, about being shamed in sensual pleasure? Could he confide that his life had taken a wrong turn and he needed desperately to right himself? Harry had thought of little but Shinassa since his recovery. He could see so clearly the moment he would take her as his bride and tried not to think of what might have occurred in the time since he'd last seen her. His true life as a man was about to begin. He'd be glad to see the last of Maria but he dreaded having to tell his mother he was leaving.

He wished he didn't have to, that somehow she could divine by maternal instinct the new course—the true one at last!—his life was about to assume. He feared too that she would try to dissuade him and so had convinced himself that she did not need him, would not miss him, would be better off in fact without him. In steeling himself against her possible objections, he had grown angry with her before either had said a word. Perhaps all he needed to tell her was how he had found the way at last. "All right," he said finally, "I'll tell you." He

"Don't patronize me, Mother," Harry replied coldly. "I know how you feel about them, and it most certainly is personal to you."

"What if it is? That doesn't mean that I'm wrong. Can't you see the pain in store for you?"

Harry shook his head. "You don't know the pain I've been in."

They stared at each other like weary combatants across the chasm that divided their separate lands. "What makes you think her people will be any happier about this than I am?" Clara asked.

"I don't know!" Harry cried. "Maybe they won't be. Maybe—" He turned wide, stricken eyes to her. "Oh, please understand, Mother. Please don't fight me on this. Please help me."

This pain in him, the longing for her aid, drew her to him, and she embraced him fiercely. "Oh, Harry, I'm sorry. I'm sorry." But even as she held him and comforted him and pledged her support, she knew she could not do what he asked. These people had killed her parents. How could she give them her son?

Clara told McLeod of Harry's feeling for the Seminole girl and of her own fears for what the outcome might be.

"I've had dealings with 'em myself over the years," he said. "Never been cheated by one in a trade. Never known one to hurt a white man since the last damn war, which mostly was a case of them being kicked off their land and fighting back best they could. They used to live right here at the mouth of the river, you know. Even had their burial mound somewhere down by the bay. Then they got edged further and further in till the only land the government left 'em was a piece of hammock in the Everglades. The one thing I don't like's that they rub fish oil on their skin against the sand flies and smell pretty high in the summer. After that, their reputation's the worst thing about 'em."

Clara listened, tight-lipped. "They killed my parents, Quentin."

"No disrespect intended, Clara, but you don't know that for an actual fact. Around that time this area had more'n its share of drifters and ex-cons and Civil War vets that got their senses blasted out of 'em in battle. It could've been one of them did that to your ma and pa. Like I said, Indians get blamed for a lot of stuff they didn't do."

"I know what they did."

McLeod took her hands in his. "Does it really make you rest easier having that kind of certainty if there's a chance it's not so?"

Clara was unmoved by what he said and only more staunchly held on to her belief in the barbarous attack. But it was McLeod finally, much to Clara's dismay, whom Harry sought out for help.

"Give her time to get used to the idea," McLeod told him. "You've been thinking about it for months; she's only had a couple of days."

Harry shook his head sadly. "She can't even look me in the eye," he said.

The boat Harry took was McLeod's design—a narrow flat-bottomed canoe with high sides and a curve to the pointed prow—ideally suited to the shallow water and saw grass he'd encounter.

"The water's high in the 'glades now," McLeod told him, "and the only real hazard's stepping barefoot on oyster shells. They can be sharp as coral, so you best wear rubber boots when you're sloshing around in the muck. You'll be doin' plenty of that. The Seminoles sail their canoes from Little Tiger Town south to the Piney Woods to get some deer hunting done 'fore the water level makes the 'glades too shallow to cross. You head northwest once you hit 'em, aim for a high rise—Aleck Town it's called, or was called. You'll find 'em. More'n likely, they'll find you."

To Clara, McLeod said, "I'm not acting as mediator between you two, but I might as well tell him what I know about the Everglades, because he's going whether you want him to or not."

Harry and Clara said their good-byes the night before he left. The rawness of their emotions kept each quiet and gentle with the other. Clara felt for the first time that she had nothing to offer him that he would accept but maternal words of caution, and Harry responded as a dutiful son with respectful murmurs that he would be careful, would take precautions, would not take chances. It seemed to Harry that they spoke to each other as from a great distance. He wanted to shout out to her, "Mother, it's me! It's Harry!" How could she be so cold? How had she forgotten who he was?

Clara could not understand the rashness of what he was about to do. She wanted to shake him by the shoulders and wake him up to the consequences, the reality of his actions, the folly, the pain in store for everyone. She wanted to weep for the waste of it all, but her sorrow butted up against her anger; she remained dry-eyed and let her cheek be kissed by his cold lips.

The whole notion of love between Harry and this Indian girl still seemed to her unbelievable, an insult, an affront to the memory of her parents. She tried to console herself with the thought that it might all come to nothing; the tribe might reject him, the girl herself. Oh God, but it was horrible to hope for his unhappiness!

She spent the night awake, eyes open and staring at the cloudless black sky. An owl kept up a continuous hooting; she thought she would go mad with the loneliness of its unanswered cry. She fell asleep just after dawn, knowing that Harry would already be on his way.

20.

Though he started early, it was close to noon before he'd covered the five miles to the rapids that marked the edge of the Everglades. The water was not violent, but a gradual six-foot drop from the 'glades to the riverbed made it impossible to row against the current, so Harry dropped over the side of the boat and dragged it to the bank. From there it was a long pull uphill, using the mangrove roots for purchase.

When he had completed the ascent, Harry tumbled back into the canoe and stretched out for a moment, eyes closed, drifting. He opened his eyes moments later to see the swoop of a white egret in the sky above. He stood up and there, stretching outward before him, were the Everglades, an immense expanse of blue-black water. Growing out of the water everywhere was the keen-toothed saw grass, four, five, even six feet high. In the distance, dark dense green islands seemed to float on the horizon.

Harry stared for a long moment, awed and calmed by the sense of infinite space. Far to the west he could make out a pine island that rose high above the water level and was marked by a long, curving stretch of cypress strand. That'll be where she is, he thought. He stowed the oar and took out a long bamboo pole; then, one eye on the cypress, he adjusted his balance and began poling the canoe across the 'glades.

The going was rougher than he thought it would be. The mild flow of current toward the sea was against him, the sharp edges of the saw grass sliced into his heavy shirt and cut his hands, his arms and back ached from digging the pole into the mud, and the vast flat plain of water and grass offered no respite from the sun. All Harry could do to stay cool was keep dipping his handkerchief in the water and wrapping it around his head.

He did not lack for company, however; the clear water was alive with minnows and crayfish, cottonmouth moccasins and bullfrogs. He poled under the shade of a cypress strand hung with wild pink orchids and long strands of Spanish moss; as he curved around it into the sun, an immense flock of wading birds was revealed: spoonbills, flamingos, even a few great blue heron. Wild turkey squawked and strutted on a high ground of thick green wax myrtle bushes and he saw a deer arc in the air on a rocky hogback.

The saw grass seemed to take on a pattern of interlocking trails intricate as a spider's web, but Harry resisted following them, for he knew that their appearance of leading him somewhere was illusory. And when, late in the day, the water became too shallow for the boat, he ditched the pole inside, pulled on the high rubber boots McLeod had given him, and stepped into the water to pull.

The sun remained hot even as it sank; low clouds stretched out at the horizon gave the sunset a queer amber color he'd never seen in the sky above the bay. The cypress strand he aimed for faded slowly as darkness fell. As the sun disappeared, the amber drained out and the sky and water went silver and gray.

In the darkness, guided now only by the flickering yellow light of a small kerosene lamp, he allowed questions to surface in his mind. Would he find her? Would she accept him? Had she thought of him all this time as he had thought of nothing but her? Or was it all a fool's errand? Would he come to grief? He had no answers, only the will to go on, to let the intensity of his desire carry him toward his destiny.

"Accept it," McLeod told Clara.

"And if I can't?"

McLeod saw the determination in the rigid set of her lips. "Come on," he said. "There's something I want to show you."

He kept the boat close to shore as they maneuvered upriver, then along a smaller narrow branch called Tiger Creek, where they moved silently in the dappled shade of oaks and palms. Clara didn't question where he was taking her, glad to be distracted from brooding alone about Harry.

A startling shoot of white wild orchids soared up out of the blackest tangle of mangroves. A mass of what appeared to be brown moss at the base of a cypress tree came suddenly alive and proved to be a nest of hermit crabs scurrying for safety. There was a smell of rich loamy earth and flowers and a hint of rankness and decay below it. McLeod finally pulled the boat into a small, sturdy dock where the mangroves tapered off, and he helped Clara onto the smooth, grassy bank.

"It's just up this way," he said and set out, pulling himself up the bank with his cane. She followed him across a clearing bordered by fallen oaks that looked to have been split by lightning, until they reached a low stone wall with a battered gate, gray and splintered and swinging on a rusted hinge. A sign in flaked, nearly invisible paint said McLeod. No Trespassing. Gnarled old hibiscus bushes poured red blossoms over the wall alongside fragrant pink and white oleander. On the other side of the wall were palms with silvery gray fronds and great bunches of golden dates. Wild grape vines as thick as a man's wrist wound around enormous rubber trees. McLeod pointed to a field ahead of them.

"I've got about four acres in bloom," he said, gesturing widely with the carved panther-head cane. "Over there's shallots and squashes, sugar cane, eggplant, pawpaws, and a couple more exotics. The other side's fruit. I got mangoes and avocados, rose apples, Spanish limes, Surinam cherries, Puerto Rican pineapples." He stood still for a long moment looking out over his land.

"It must take a lot of work to keep this going," Clara said.

"Didn't live here for years." He shrugged. "Rather of lived on the

Newport," he said. "Even if I'd wanted to let it go to seed, I . . . Come on. I'll show you the cabin."

The cabin, set on a slight rise above his fields, was a straightforward and unlovely arrangement of pine boards and tar-paper roof, raised two feet off the ground like Clara's old house had been.

"Certainly can forget there's a city when you're out here," she said, and McLeod smiled, but she saw that something was held back in the smile and she knew there was more he had to show her.

Around the side of the house Clara saw heaps of dried-out coconuts piled on ground strewn with dried red thistle; a lone tamarind tree stood against the pines, a pale blue blanket hung in shreds from a clothesline, a water pump was solid with rust, its handle in the up position, its bucket overturned and bottomless.

The porch floor creaked under McLeod's first step. Clara hesitated to follow him, the sound was so plaintive and lonesome. He poked the door open; it groaned on rusted hinges. McLeod was leading the way, and she followed. In the dim light she could see that the room was no bigger than the one Edmund and Geneva had once lived in. The neatness—scrubbed floorboards and walls, the faint smell of cleaning lye still in the air—told Clara something she hadn't suspected of the fastidiousness of the man. There was a delicately carved rocking chair she could not quite imagine him sitting in, though, and a hand-carved mahogany desk with gently tapering legs that shone with turtle oil. Two or three kerosene lamps were mounted on the walls like sconces and another stood on the desk. On one wall was mounted the skin of a rattlesnake at least eight feet long. There was a table for eating covered with a lacy cloth more suitable to a city parlor, and a vase on it held a fresh bunch of anemones; Clara felt a thrill of pleasure at the sight of the flowers, for she knew he'd meant them for her. In the corner was a cook stove and a big pipe that carried the smoke outside. McLeod had a kettle of water on the surface and was preparing a pot of tea.

His back was to her, his shoulders tight, and he seemed reluctant to turn. But he had invited her to see the cabin, as he had invited no one for years and years. She hesitated now, doubtful for a moment, and looked again at the lace tablecloth, the delicate rocker. "What happened to her?"

McLeod's shoulders relaxed at the question; he'd waited long and patiently for the right person to ask it. He turned away from the stove and took a kerosene lamp in his hand. "Come with me," he said.

Clara followed him out the door, across the small clearing, and along a narrow path through the hammock that ran parallel to the river. He stopped under the widely arched branches of an ancient oak tree. Under its sheltering canopy was a wire enclosure a dozen feet square. Inside were two crudely carved gravestones: Ella Sharp McLeod, wife to Quentin, born 1860, died 1881; and next to it a smaller one, Evelyn McLeod, daughter to Quentin and Ella, born 1881, died 1881.

"Her time came nearly two months earlier'n we expected. I was in the West Indies gathering root stuff. When I came back..."

He looked at the ground, at the graves, as if he was still trying to explain it to them. "Such a tiny thing, her insides were all torn up by the baby. She lost so much ... so much blood. And the baby ..." Clara saw his shoulders come up again in a helpless shrug; he turned to her, his eyes wide open and glistening with remembered pain. "I shouldn't have ever left her, but ..." He turned to her. "I know why you can't let go of Harry," he said. "Not in your heart. Not while he's still ..."

Clara came to him and took his arm, and they walked in silence back toward his cabin, but she stopped short of crossing the threshold again, for she knew now that this time McLeod had left her as he had never left her before, that he had withdrawn from the city, from her, and would not be coming back.

Maria found a quiet spot in the hammock, far enough away from Fort Dallas so she wouldn't be interrupted, close enough to be found after the deed had been done. Let her see what her precious boy's done to me. Let her see, and see what she thinks of him then.

She picked the deep shade at the base of a pine tree. The fallen needles had turned brown and made a soft bed for her. She leaned back into the shade and arranged her dress neatly around her legs. He once liked this dress, I could tell the way he ripped open the buttons. She touched the tips of her fingers to her throat; he once kissed me here. It was very quiet; tiny shoots of sun streamed through the pine-needle overhang, dappling her hands and the whole front of her, warming the ground and releasing the smell of pine. I could live here, she thought. Sit real still right here and never, ever move. Turn invisible as a panther, all eyes and a mean laugh.

She had lain awake for a month of nights, or slept and dreamed she was awake and couldn't sleep. Her father and brothers were gone for weeks on end. Not that she treasured their company—beer drunk most of the time and ordering her around—but with no one home in that ugly house, she had only herself to talk to. Sometimes her throat would go raw with all the shouting out loud she did. She thought of it as her soul screaming for deliverance. She relied on the advice that came in that voice and believed it when it told her to seek out Harry Reade. He'll save you, he's handsome, find him, make him love you.

I love you, Harry. She liked saying it out loud to him, and when she had said it once she just couldn't stop, even when she could see he didn't like it. I love you, Harry. She'd never think of a thing like that herself, because she was really too shy and backward; she was the kind of girl who worked hard and never complained and took her lot in life as a good girl ought to and prayed and cleaned and cooked and tended her family, and someday she'd be rewarded in heaven, but before that there'd be a husband who loved her, and so she readied herself and wore her only good dress and waited for the man to appear. Was it a crime to want things? *He* thought so. But he was wrong. He didn't know how it really was 'cause he always had everything he wanted. She'd known Harry was the man for her the first time she saw him. And oh, how her life was gonna change! A nice house and pretty clothes and a good shiny carriage with a fine, long-maned horse— make that two of 'em, one special for Sundays.

Her brothers would never understand what love was all about. Love was being soft and sweet to a man and needing him so you could almost die from the hurt of it. Love was what a woman alone in a house knew about.

But he didn't love her. He tricked her instead. He made her think he loved her when he dried her tears and held her hand and spoke in the soft voice of an angel, but when she showed him how her insides ached for him he turned away, and when she gave herself to him he left her. Gone, gone, gone, and now there were only memories of him. No decent man would have her now. Harry had disgraced her and left her, and all ahead was loneliness.

She took heart thinking of her mother, felt closer to her today than she ever did, wasn't mad at her, loved her. She would be unlike her mother in one way. She would not slip away while no one was looking . . .

She lifted herself up on an elbow, dug her hand deep into the pocket of her skirt, and took out the kerchief. Pressing it first to her mouth, she thought that there was no doubt that the smell of the quinine was surely the smell of poison and death. When she unknotted the cloth and spread it open on her lap, the tablets spilled into a little pile in the depression made by her thighs. She pocketed the cork from the canvas canteen and began eating the tablets, washing each down with a swallow of water. She'd overheard Dr. MacKenzie saying that the right amount of quinine would kill the yellow fever and the wrong amount would kill the person who had the fever, though what the wrong amount was he didn't exactly say and Maria couldn't ask or even let on she heard. Quinine, and the thing would be done. There might be convulsions first, he said, and even blindness before it was all over, but no doubt the deed would be done.

Her chest was suddenly hot. She rose to her knees and drank the last of the water, swallowing hard to keep the tablets down. She lay down again. Pine needles scratched her face; she laughed. Stop tickling me! And where'd you hide the rest of them tablets? She was dizzy as she sat up again. The waves of nausea subsided and the burning fell to her stomach.

I will do this thing and it will be done. She opened the Bible in her lap. Thy will be done, Harry Reade, for you have destroyed me as surely as if you fed me these pills with your own hands. But I'll rise from the ashes of your cruelty. I will punish you. You will remember me to your dying day.

Bolts of black lightning shot across her line of vision. She was suddenly frightened and clutched her chest. Oh Harry, why'd you go and leave me like you done? Why didn't you love me? Why didn't you save me?

Her throat swelled; she could no longer swallow. The burning moved to her chest, to her breaking heart. Good, good. She reached for a branch of pine needles and let herself slowly down onto her back.

I love you, Harry. Good-bye.

· · ·

Clara came to see her at Dr. MacKenzie's. She was sitting up in a big bed in a back room set up like a hospital. The shades were drawn, the room dark as twilight. Maria was wearing a white robe; her freshly washed hair hung loose and covered her face. She had been in a coma three days.

"That you, Miz Reade?"

"Yes."

Maria nodded and smiled. "Come stand by me," she said, and Clara approached the bed. The girl's head was turned away from her and she reached for Clara's hand.

"You got to get him home now, Miz Reade."

"I can't do that, Maria."

Maria gripped her hand tighter. "You got to, Miz Reade," she said. "And I don't mean next week neither."

"Everyone is so sorry for your misfortune, of course," Clara said. "But—"

Maria's smile broke into laughter and she turned to Clara, brushing the hair from her face. Clara drew in a sharp breath; she'd never seen eyes like that, the whites red, swimming, bleary, enormous. "Why, I never been luckier!" Maria cried. "I'm gonna be a mother, Miz Reade. Doc MacKenzie says me and Harry . . ." She dropped Clara's hand and leaned back against the pillow; a lone bloody tear coursed down her cheek. "I like how that sounds, don't you? Me and Harry." She laughed again and more tears flowed. "Me and Harry. Me and Harry."

Part Three

21.

In his autobiography *Miami's Son* (Palm Isle Press, 1986), Cameron Reade writes this account of his birth:

I was born the night the century turned. There was an enormous celebration in progress all along Biscayne Bay. Viewing stands and buffet tables had been pitched on the lawns of the Royal Palm Hotel. A society dance orchestra was playing in a makeshift pavilion at the river end of Miami Avenue. Inside Fort Dallas, at my mother's bedside, were my father, who never left her side throughout the ordeal, and my grandmother, in whose house my parents lived at the time. Attending my mother in the event was Dr. Charles MacKenzie, who reacted with speed and courage when it became apparent that his patient, struggle as she might, could not bring me to term, that in fact the labor was protracted, the bleeding profuse, the birth a breech. My father held her hand tightly, my grandmother stood just outside the circle of a candle's flame, both hopeful yet helpless. Using a knife sterilized over this flame, the good doctor cut my mother open and I was pulled out by the heels—like Macbeth, I am not of woman born—squawking and red-faced and ugly,

I've been told, as sin itself. Fireworks celebrating the new century exploded in the sky above the bay and flashes of light lit up our scene of carnage.

I admit of course the unlikelihood of having a true memory of these moments, yet throughout my life, on certain dark nights of celebration, yea, even now on the eve of my eighty-seventh year, I can hear the sounds of a woman screaming, a man weeping, and can see in my mind's eye my emergence into light through a miasma of blood.

The facts of Cameron Reade's birth are different in at least two regards from what this account would lead his readers to believe. He was seventeen, about to embark for France and the Great War, when he found out that his actual birthday was not the century's own but the last day of the preceding September. It was his grandmother who told him that the deception had been perpetrated to protect the reputations of his parents, who were married five months at his birth, and also to protect his own, for the future. It pleased Cameron to learn that someone had known even then that there was greatness in store for him, but he was certainly not surprised by the information; it was as if the tide had gone out and revealed the sand around his feet. He merely nodded and said, half to himself, "That explains it then," adding, when he saw the inquiring look on his grandmother's face, "Their marriage, I mean." She shook her head sadly and kissed his cheek—he smelled that oversweet gardenia perfume she always wore—and Cameron felt, for one burning, horrible moment, that the information explained nothing at all, that this old woman had told it to him only to inflict pain. But why?

Being born on the eve of the new century, however, was a fact too neat to surrender simply because it was not so. As he reached his twenties, a war hero and already on his way toward his first fortune in real estate, Cameron was conscious of the use to which he might yet put the aura of being Miami's Son. He had his new bride stitch in needlepoint the legend "Grandson of Founding Mother, First Baby Born in New Century" and presented it to his grandmother the morning, twenty-two years after the event, that they were to sign the papers making them partners in the biggest real estate development the city had ever seen.

The other suppressed fact, which would not be acknowledged in his autobiography or anywhere else for that matter, was that his father was not present at his birth. This was not something Cameron had to be told; this was something he always knew.

In 1905 the first *Official Directory of the City of Miami* was published and included these new businesses and services: Thos. Schell Livery, Bicycles, and Automobile Service; H. Stram, Taxidermist ("Young Live Alligators for Sale"); Miss K. C. Ligon, Modiste; Getzoff and Zimmer Meat Market ("Yacht Trade a Speciality"); Ideal Bottling Works and Carbonated Beverages; Frisk Dynamite and Blasting Supplies, L. and T. Fleischman Building Materials ("Specialties: Georgia Pine and Cypress"), McDonnell's Saloon ("Jug Trade"), The Everglades Hotel ("Where the mocking bird sings you to rest every night, and the orange dispels its perfume").

There was also a telephone company (twenty-five cents for three minutes and not to be used during thunderstorms), a conservatory of music, two moving picture houses, streets paved either with blinding white limestone or wooden blocks that popped and floated away in a hard rain, a handful of noisy automobiles, and a skyline of church steeples and coconut palms.

Miami had finally lost the rawness and vulgarity of its early pioneer days and taken on the trappings and manners, the drawl, the easy gait, the appearance—never mind the panthers prowling in people's backyards, Dr. MacKenzie's cows grazing in the shadow of the Royal Palm Hotel, or a family of Seminoles changing clothes at the rock seawall—of small Southern town respectability: wide streets and shaded sidewalks, picket fences and magnolia blossoms, lamp posts and telephone wires, a city hall with Romanesque columns and a monument to a Confederate general, hands poised on sword hilt, guarding a fountain inhabited by iguanas and bullfrogs.

The corner of Fourteenth and Miami Avenue was the city's center, with the four corners taken up by the columned and domed Fort Dallas National Bank (capital: one hundred thousand dollars), Fine's Emporium (upgraded and expanded from General Merchandise), the Biscayne Hotel and Pharmacy, and Starger's Bake Shop and Grocery. An ice factory along the bay produced fifteen tons a day and made possible the existence of Rushmeyer's Ice Cream Parlor. Artesian well water was now piped through major streets and right into people's kitchens. The Rollison Company received a charter from the city for an electric streetcar railway and was backed by the Fort Dallas National Bank. The line ran a single car from the depot at Sixth Street along Avenue B to Twelfth and then west on Twelfth to the courthouse; passengers were heard to comment, "Now this is city living!"

Not everyone was pleased with the way things were going. When what he really wanted was a bridge, Rufus Finch's frustration made him walk around town, collaring people and trying to get them to sign a petition that the river be filled in and built on. Public senti-ment—not to mention the interests of the boat owners who took tourists all the way to the rapids and back—stayed with the river. Finch was still mad: not only was there no bridge, but the dredging of the bay during the war with Spain had muddied forever his one tourist attraction—the Fountain of Youth—and even though a few stores were built on his side of the river, the business district remained on the north bank. But when the Miami Avenue bridge was finally built, and developers came to him with offers to subdivide his property, he took the money and attention with a mixture of sorrow and joy. His trading post was torn down and Ida's old piano accidentally destroyed, even though Rufus had promised on her deathbed to keep it forever and in tune. The hammock on his property was dynamited, leveled, and readied to be platted out and sold. Finch was never quite sure he'd done the right thing.

There was a sense of transformation in the air, though factory chim-neys and engine whistles still struck an incongruous note considering that even a short ride from the center of town brought into view vast spaces and solitude, the silence of the hammock, and the sharp, rank, sweet smell of the Everglades.

For no matter how much the city grew, it was still only the civilized center of a vast area of uninhabited land—someday it would be called Greater Miami—and there was still plenty of room for pioneering. Not that it was much easier than it had been before the railroad came. Oh sure, you could get there easy enough now, and your fertilizer and lumber and such could be ordered, delivered, and paid for in a week or so, not to mention the calico and sugar and chewing tobacco you could buy right off the shelves of Fine's Emporium downtown, but that didn't change how hard it was to homestead in general, what with limestone running under even the best land, hurricanes that could wipe out a whole season's crop in an hour, and heat that made it impossible to work during a summer's day past noon. For every pioneer who came and stayed to work the land, there were three who gave it a shot and left.

But when Miami won the county seat of Dade, rich and poor, strivers and arrivers, citizens and boosters alike beamed with pride. Why, Dade took up an area almost as large as the entire state of Maine! the papers said, though in actuality it stretched only from the St. Lucie River on the north to Jewfish Creek on the south, which wasn't quite two hundred miles square. No matter what people's social position, chauvinism united the town: "Down here, friend," a resident was likely to tell a new arrival, "we call it Mah-Am-Mah."

Clara Reade found that her hopes for Miami were dashed over and over by the specter of Wheeler's domination. He built homes on the south bank and let them sit empty rather than wait for the demand to increase. New settlers were coming in on every train; he wanted things waiting for them. He made no secret that building ahead of demand was his policy; cost was lower today than it would be tomorrow, and selling prices would always be on the rise. In the name of progress, he sold land so cheaply that the prices at which others could afford to sell theirs appeared prohibitive. His customers were often the lovers of the quick buck who bought low and who often resold the next day and could still underprice everyone else.

Since in their original deal Clara had given Wheeler plots of land that alternated with plots she retained, there were still whole stretches that remained unsold and unsettled—hers—butting up against other areas—his—that now fairly bustled with noise and activity. Fort Dallas and the acreage around it still belonged to her; although it was the most valuable and desired in all of Miami, it was the one parcel she owned that she'd never sell. The land not a hundred yards north and west, though, belonged to Wheeler. As a result, stores and houses and factories ringed the fort. Clara could see the town she'd founded merely by climbing to the tower above the fort and looking down. She knew that Wheeler indulged in these inequities simply to demonstrate his control over the town. For her own sake and for the sake of the smaller businesspeople and early settlers whose interests she unofficially represented, she prepared herself to stop him.

She dispatched a note, sufficiently pointed to pique his interest, vague and general enough not to raise his back hairs. At first he put her off—"My apologies, Mrs. Reade," he wrote, "but my business activities are such that . . ."—and set the meeting for a month in the future. When the day approached he postponed it—"A sudden business emergency in Palm Beach requires my presence, and so . . ."— reset it for a few days later and then sent a telegram to cancel it completely. Throughout all of these delays and false starts Clara was the soul of patience, even sardonically amused at such transparent attempts to show her that he was not at her beck and call.

Wheeler felt like the spoiled child he'd never been, secretly pleased to manipulate her so obviously, with no one to tell him to behave himself. The fact that she did not give up only proved the extent to which she needed him. There was no question as to their relative positions of strength; his money and what it could do for the town had effectively foiled all her attempts to make her own influence felt.

Informed that the site for the first school had been picked by her and the Dade County Superintendent without consulting him, Wheeler donated the building materials and enough paint from the storerooms of the Royal Palm to make the school look as if it had been spawned by the hotel. He built the first Presbyterian church complete with a spire and a clock, a weather vane, and a stained-glass window—Christ tormented by Roman soldiers—imported from a crumbling cathedral in Tuscany. He paid for the new waterworks and the new electric light company and, by putting up the first five thousand, encouraged the Fort Dallas National Bank to back Rollison's streetcar railway system. He hoped, by modestly keeping his name out of these transactions and leaking the truth of his largesse to the public through Elliot Iverson and *The Metropolis,* to incur the love of the populace.

And though he promoted shipping in general—especially the use of his own low-draft freighters for cargo into the Caribbean—he effectively delayed the expansion of the docks, as he owned much of the waterfront. He certainly did not want shipping to increase to the point that boats competed with the Florida Eastern Star.

When he did finally allow the meeting with Clara Reade to take place in the tower suite of his hotel, he felt calm and relaxed and rather looked forward to spending this time with Mrs. Reade. The usual display of pleasantries was cut short by Clara, who felt he condescended to her with each new offering of tea and biscuits, each proffered bow, each sympathetic smile. She came right to the point: "The rate at which you're building, Mr. Wheeler, has to slow down. Things are getting out of proportion. All this spending! You have to give people a chance to breathe. You have to—"

" 'Have to,' Mrs. Reade?" He stood at the window looking down at the city and sighed with satisfaction. "Don't you see what this is becoming?"

Clara kept her seat despite his crooked finger beckoning her to join him. "You don't have to tell me what it could be," she said. "I lived here when it was only palm groves and mangrove swamps."

Wheeler turned from the window and faced her. "And that, if you don't mind my saying so, is your whole problem. You can't get that old picture out of your mind. Sentimentality, don't you see, is the enemy of progress. You see this city as something to be built only according to your own small plans, and those plans are circumscribed by nostalgia and, even worse, by a budget that is a bit, shall we say, mm, pinched?" Enjoying his position of superiority, he gestured magnanimously to the biscuit tin. "Another Peake Freen?"

Clara shook her head. "I just want to keep the city a size that suits the people in it and not one that accommodates your ambition."

"You say 'ambition' as though it were a personal eccentricity. But you're no stranger to ambition yourself, are you, Mrs. Reade? It's one of the qualities I have always found most intriguing about you."

Only her clenched fists betrayed Clara's feeling. "You know perfectly well that what you're doing makes my land worthless."

"Not when you've kept the area's prime location for yourself. Think what a smart developer would give you for—"

"Yes, they've scratched at my door, but I'm not selling Fort Dallas."

Wheeler shrugged and sat at his desk. "Suit yourself. But don't expect me to sympathize with your financial incapacities."

"I haven't said a word about finances. I'm talking about the future of Miami and—"

"Progress hates a vacuum," Wheeler said, adding, as if shocked by a sudden possibility, "Are you against progress?"

Clara sighed impatiently and met his stare. "I just don't see it as an end in itself."

Wheeler shook his head sadly. "I knew the day we met that we would come to this," he said and for a moment something like compassion flickered in his eyes. "Can you believe I never meant for you to suffer?" He glanced away, and when he looked back all sympathy was gone. "But I won't accept responsibility for it. I told you I would do things my way and I have."

Clara gripped the arms of the chair but restrained herself from rising. "And your way is to sell land so cheap you don't make a profit and build ahead of demand so no one else can make a profit either!"

Wheeler ran his hands over the documents on his desk as if he drew strength from them. "You overestimate my fortunes. I shrink in horror daily from the expenditures I'm required to make. Remember, it was I and I alone who financed the railroad. The expenses of the Royal Palm—which you have to admit created the tourist trade—were all mine. I paid for the new well. I paid for a waterworks and an electric light plant and a new railroad depot. It'll be years before I earn anything on these investments."

Clara stood up. "The city began with me," she said. "In my imagination and with my persistence." She strode to the window and looked at the streets below. "You may not like it, it may not fit in with this visionary stance you seem to have assumed, but without me there would be nothing down there but palm trees." She turned back, glad to see that she'd finally made the color rise in his face.

"With all of my financial risk taking, I see very little gratitude or cooperation on your part or anyone else's in this luckiest of populations," he said.

"I can't match your ability to donate churches and schools and streets and buildings, but I'll be damned if I'll sit back and let you take credit for the existence of Miami. And on top of that, you expect me to thank you for it."

" 'Miami,' " he said and laughed derisively. "It may be called 'Miami,' but whose city is it really, Mrs. Reade?"

Clara stuffed her gloves in her purse and started for the door. "You didn't find it. You didn't name it. The only thing you'll ever be able to prove is that you've bought it. If that's a comfort to you, Mr. Wheeler, you have my sympathies."

He managed to remain standing until the door slammed behind her, and when it did, he fell back in his morris chair, exhausted, his sense of victory shaken by the knowledge that she was right.

22.

In a new promotional brochure, Emmett Flye wrote that Miami had the world's greatest per capita consumption of cement, and for once he wasn't exaggerating.

Jean Lanctot, a transplanted Alsatian with a gray mustache and muttonchops and a thick French accent, bought two acres of limestone rock pit from Clara, ran a rail line out to it, and arranged with the governor to hire convict labor to quarry and crush the rock. So great was the demand in the city that Lanctot invested in a machine that could crush, screen, and wash in one ear-splitting operation; hearing loss was the system's only liability. Within a matter of months the Lanctot Quarry was employing two hundred men and shipping fifty carloads of rock into Miami every day. The new courthouse and jail were built from it. The streets of town were paved with it, as was the country road between Little River and Arch Creek and also the narrow causeway across the prairie.

Now ambitious young architects came to lend their talents and make their names. In the business district they designed new stores built with long second-floor porches that jutted out over the streets and served to protect shoppers from the sun. Simple wood-frame construction gave way to the combination of wood and masonry, which naturally grew in size and prominence to suit the elevated mercantile status of the inhabitants.

In the residential areas, not just houses, not just streets, but entire neighborhoods were now created. The Victorian influence dominated, with the Queen Anne variation—nearly a national style at the time— being particularly popular. The standard elements had been rethought and reworked, though, using native Dade County pine painted in the pastel shades picked up from the flowers that grew in the hammock, and the preferred roofing was fish-scale shingles. Whether this look suited the tropical environment or not was hardly the point; Miami's prominence on the national landscape would be in direct proportion to its high-pitched roofs, turrets and spires, brackets and bay windows and potted palms. No more a frontier outpost, these buildings announced, no more an isolated little town way down south but the newest of the New American Cities.

Though urban purists thought it premature for these areas that scored both sides of the river to be called suburbs, the neighborhoods did take on that look, with streets wide enough for passing carriages and neat, boxy front lawns bought in sod squares from the landscaper who'd supplied the sprawling greens for the Royal Palm Hotel.

On both sides of the river, the houses were more lavish the closer they were to the bay, and a bay block itself—the stretch of Northeast Second Street at Biscayne Boulevard for example—was the toniest, with elaborate, even eccentric mansions fronting the water. Except by speculators, land in itself was not particularly valued; the residents had come for the water, the weather, the view, and the business opportunities, not to be farmers or real estate agents. Houses were often only a carriage width apart, status achieved through the placement and proliferation of porches, crenated molding, and curlicue lathework.

A few blocks from the bay on Northeast Second was a house square and simple and stripped to its essentials in the English Craftsman style, interpreted in America by Gustav Stickley—as if in direct rebuttal to the Victorian excesses of its neighbors—and it was in this house, number twenty-one, that Harry Reade lived with his wife and their son. Until the baby was born, they had lived in his mother's home in Fort Dallas; it was Maria's fond hope that propinquity would endear her and her child to her mother-in-law, but she was soon to see that Harry and Clara's relationship was not the close and affectionate one it had once seemed to her to be.

When the arrangement proved unworkable—a fierce coldness on Harry's part, a bewildered hurt on Clara's—they struck out for quarters of their own. In their initial discussion as to where they might live, Maria firmly rejected Harry's wish to move outside the city.

"I've had enough of country life, thank you!" she said in a manner meant to be light-hearted and chirpy but which only drew from her new husband frowns and sighs of dismay. " 'Sides, Harry darling," she added, sidling up to him, "my eyes..."

Harry edged away from her, nodding, guilty, unable to face her and, finally, acquiescent. The quinine had caused permanent damage to her vision. Objects far and near swam in and out of focus. Direct sunlight made her cry out in pain; even the simple heat of the day caused profuse tearing. Indoors and out she wore round black spectacles that looked to Harry like the tarnished coins put on the eyes of dead men. He only saw her eyes at night, after all the lamps were out, in bed, when she would pull him to her and cling as if drowning. Then he saw them, lit by moonlight, vivid, streaming, sly as a cat's.

Despite everything—her perfidy, his despair—he entered the marriage determined at least to behave decently, not to allow a mood of acrimony to pervade his household as it had pervaded the household in which he'd grown up. He would not become his father. He had come to accept finally that Maria was no more or less responsible for their situation than was he, nor did she seem any happier with it. But he made it clear that he would not dedicate his life to atonement nor to satisfying her demands. She had spells of gaiety while awaiting the birth of their son, but Harry came to know—had suspected even at the time—that it was a mood close to hysteria and presaged a high-strung fretfulness that would be never far from the surface.

She became, for a short while, more beautiful—the weight she gained during her pregnancy gave her a look of womanly ripeness unseen in the girl she'd been—but it was an abstraction to him, unconnected to desire. After the baby was born, she remained stout; because she rarely went outdoors anymore, her skin was white, with a pearly, unhealthy sheen. The avidity of her need for him proved not to have stemmed from passion but was a manifestation of a deeper, untapped longing that asserted itself at times of stress, when the only way Harry could calm her was to take her to bed. Not for long could either of them keep up the pretense that they had ever truly wanted each other.

He tried to keep himself busy at the Reade Groves—Wheeler continued to raise the freight rates and Harry had to work longer hours simply to maintain the same profit margin—and spent as little time in the house on Northeast Second Street as possible. When he was there, he avoided Maria and the child by finding things to do, repairs to be made, shelves to be built, shingles replaced, papers filed, orders filled, carriage wheels oiled, anything, anything, to keep his hands and eyes and mind busy.

"Why don't you hire someone to do that?" Maria stood at the door of the toolshed, the light behind her back, though Harry, kneeling on the floor of the half-finished shed, could still see those flat black discs that covered her eyes. "It don't look refined to be on your knees like that. Mr. Jennings next door'd never be on his knees. He keeps a nice white shirt on and hires someone to do this kind of thing."

"I'm not Mr. Jennings."

"Are you purposely trying to embarrass me in front of my neighbors?" she demanded. Harry banged a nail into the floor. "When I met you I thought you were a gentleman."

Hammer in hand, forced to answer, Harry merely said, "I like doing it myself."

"Well, I still say it don't look nice," she said, in a perfect imitation of a patient, dutiful wife. After a long silence broken only by the rhythmic smack of the hammer, she said, "Your mother was here."

Harry hesitated for an instant, hammer poised in the air, then continued banging. "Did you tell her I was home?"

"Of course not, Harry," Maria replied with an exasperated laugh. "You told me not to. But I still don't see why. She's your mother, not a bill collector."

"I have my reasons," he said. "That should satisfy you."

"Well, it don't," Maria said. "You hardly ever see her except on business. I'm sure she misses you."

Harry looked up at her with an amused expression on his face. "Why the eagerness for me and my mother to be friends?"

"Why are you looking at me like that?" Maria asked and fussed self-consciously with her skirt. "It's only natural for a mother and son to be friends."

"Are you sure that the future of your own son doesn't have anything to do with it?"

Maria slapped her skirt into place and crossed her arms. "So what if it does?" she demanded. "A mother wants the best for her child. You wouldn't understand that, though. You don't have any feelings for your own son. It's . . . it's unnatural."

"Be quiet. You don't know anything about it." He waited, poised above his work, for in a moment he would be alone again, but Maria stood her ground.

"Harry?"

"What?"

"Your mother could help us," she said.

"We don't need any help."

"Everyone in town is getting rich but us. Everyone in town is starting a new business but us. Everyone in town has land and—"

Harry brought the hammer down on a nail, then again and again until Maria gave up and went away, and still he kept banging.

On the day of his wedding his mother had appeared in the doorway of his room, in the field of vision in which a remembered image of Shinassa had stood but a moment ago. In her hands was a stack of papers tied with a ribbon.

"Your wedding present," she said and laughed at his hesitation. "Oh, go on and take it, sweetheart," she said and thrust it toward him. "This is my last chance to spoil you."

Short of turning away from her completely, he could do nothing but accept it. He was aware that Maria lurked at the half-open door far down at the end of the hallway.

Loosened, the ribbon fell to the floor and coiled around his feet. Harry stared uncomprehending at the top sheet of paper and, as he riffled through them, at the second and third and all the rest with equal confusion.

"Deeds to property, darling," she said. "The Reade Groves. Some wooded acreage along the river. A cotton field. I tried to make it an assortment, like a box of Louis Sherry Chocolates." She laughed at his open-mouthed stare. "Don't be too pleased. Some of it's mangrove, some of it's wetland, a lot of it, as a matter of fact." She watched him restack the papers, reach for the ribbon, and retie them. "I should have given them to you years ago but . . ."

He set them down on his bed and stared at his hands. "I can't accept them," he said. "I'm sorry I'm not more grateful."

The papers sat on the bed between them and seemed to Clara as forlorn as a message in a bottle that will never be received. "Why do you want to punish me?" she asked. Clara waited a long moment, staring at him, but he would not look at her. "She's pregnant with your child, Harry."

"I know that."

"I couldn't do anything other than what I did," she insisted. "Don't you see that?"

"I see it."

"And you did the right thing by coming back. The honorable thing. You couldn't have done anything less. Not my son. I know you."

"You're right. You do."

"And yet you blame me."

Harry sighed and looked at her for the first time. "I'm going to say this only once, and then I don't want to talk about it ever again. I love Shinassa. Being with her, I understood why I existed in the world. I had no doubts or fears. I was sure. I even came to believe that you would love her someday too. But you know me better than I know you. You knew I'd 'come to my senses.'"

"I didn't make Maria pregnant, Harry," she said and saw the face she loved so well twist into an accusing sneer.

"You wanted me to come back! You handed me over to her!"

Clara shook her head. "Would you have wanted me to send her away and pretend that I didn't know where you'd gone?" she pleaded. "She almost killed herself with those pills."

"And was it your job to make me see the error of my ways? To be the instrument of my reform? Do you sleep easier now knowing you did the right thing?"

Clara pressed her lips tightly together. "You've become very hard."

310   · *BISCAYNE* ·

Harry shrugged. "It's how I intend to get by in this"—he glanced down the hall at Maria—"in this marriage."

"But you'll have a child, darling. That makes up for a great deal."

He silenced her with a look; the cruelest thing was yet to come. "My father had a child," he said and saw, with grim satisfaction, the look of horror on her face. "So you tell me what it makes up for." He picked up the property deeds and put them in her hands. "The wrong can't be righted with a gift, Mother. I'm a married man now." It took all his will then to turn away from her, so she would not see the tears in his eyes.

He tried not to think about the past; when he did—in the last moments before sleep or the first upon awakening—he saw it as two diverging paths, one which he had taken, one which now trailed off into darkness. It was almost unbearable to remember the happiness that had been so briefly his, yet to think about it, to close his eyes and be there with her, was the only happiness he knew.

He had lived with Shinassa as man and wife for only a month and in that time had come to know what it meant to love a woman with his spirit and to show her that love with his body. This love was so different from the physical pleasures he had taken with Maria, the two acts seemed unrelated except in the crudest sense. He and Shinassa came together with gentle tenderness; each touch of her flesh on his flesh was so filled with feeling, his spirits so lifted, he would sometimes weep with the sheer exalting joy of it. They seemed to float together, the surfaces of their bodies dissolving into one another, hour after hour with nothing held back, no secret unrevealed, no love unspoken, no desire unquenched.

She had welcomed him back as if sure not only of the fact of his return but of its precise moment. There was no question then but that they accepted each other. Because Shinassa was without parents, the strictures within her tribe against intermarriage were relaxed, though he would still have to prove himself worthy. Billy Jumper was his champion, Dr. Tiger his mentor, and if the others remained wary, these two at least were convinced. His feelings for Shinassa made it seem beyond question that they would spend their lives together. His mother, he knew, would come to love her as a daughter; he was sure of that. Once she saw Shinassa and knew her beauty and gentleness, there could be no doubt in her mind that this was right.

Harry would lie in bed now, Maria at his side, and in the darkness of the room imagine drifting with Shinassa in a bark canoe through acres of water hyacinths, in and out of the shade beneath the overhanging canopy of cypress and Spanish moss, the sun dappling their naked limbs, exhausted with pleasure . . .

It was McLeod who came with the news about Maria. "I'm just the messenger," he'd said. "I haven't come to take you back. That's up to you." And his mother? McLeod had shrugged. "She said she'd trust you to do the right thing."

He walked alone in the hammock while McLeod waited in his boat and Shinassa waited in the hut. He could not go to her; if he did he would not be able to decide. And he realized with a chill that by that simple act he had already decided; the moment McLeod had appeared, the decision was made. His mother knew him very well indeed to leave it up to him when the way was foreordained. He was not the kind of man who would forsake his duty; that kind of man did not deserve to stay with Shinassa.

He climbed into McLeod's boat without looking back and left the Seminole camp for the second time. This time he knew he would not return. The image of Shinassa accompanied him unbidden all the way back and all through the moments of his wedding and the days and months and years of his marriage. Whenever he closed his eyes, there she would be, her rich black hair spilling down her strong back, the smell of cinnamon on her skin, and a keening sound would escape his lips when he opened his eyes and her image vanished.

Since he'd come back from the fighting in Cuba, McLeod's ideas about how to live had undergone a drastic reappraisal. It was what happened to his leg that caused it. The original injury— shrapnel piercing the skin below the knee and snapping the tibia— had been untended for almost a day after it had happened, complicated the day after that by a bullet grazing the knee itself. The army doctors in Havana cleaned the wounds, set the break, removed the shrapnel and the bullet fragments, and sent him to Corpus Christi until the yellow fever epidemic in Miami was over. The doctors in Texas sent him back to Miami with assurances that the infection, not yet healed, would heal soon. In his determination to be as he was before—in his assumption that he soon would be—McLeod changed none of his behavior. When the leg ached he downed shots of bourbon to dull the pain and emptied the dregs of the bottles on the open wound to cauterize it. When it didn't heal he tried boiling bread in lees of strong beer and applying it as a poultice; he tried mustard and linseed and vinegar wrapped in a skin of India rubber; he tried catechu ointment and morphia liniment and convinced himself he was healing when he wasn't.

Persistent pain, night sweats, and fever finally mocked his bravado. With Clara's encouragement and the advice of Dr. MacKenzie, he traveled to Chicago to have the leg rebroken and reset. Before the procedure he was warned that he might be left with a slight limp; afterwards the doctors told him that the infection had moved into the bone itself, now pulpy with gangrene. Perhaps if they'd got to it sooner, perhaps if he'd been younger . . . As it was there was nothing more to do but amputate. McLeod raged at them, scorned their diagnosis and their advice, challenged their skills, accused them of cowardice: there's always something more to do, goddamnit!

The operation was scheduled for the morning, but McLeod left the hospital that night. It was March; there was ice on the ground; the pain was a lick of fire from his knee to his eye. Nevertheless, he made his way on foot from the hospital to Lake Michigan and stood alone on the shore, tiny in the face of so much water and sky. Burning with fever, he saw the sky running red, so bright he had to squint. Shimmering palm trees were outlined against it, blindingly white. Sails cruised by on the sharp-edged crystalline waves. The longing was so strong to walk home on the path of sunlight, it almost made him forget the pain. He dipped his foot into the water; the shock of the cold brought him back into the dark and cold of the Chicago night, back to the fire in his leg, back to the operation.

Maybe another kind of man would have had an easier time of it; maybe another kind of man would have settled into his handicap and braved it out best he could. But something in McLeod faltered at such acceptance. It took him years to get used to the fact that his right leg stopped at the knee. And though he could strap the false leg on in a few seconds flat, he never got used to the stiff-gaited limp it gave him.

Just as they had been when he'd first come south, the bay and the river were again the greatest attractions for him. Nature held his attention the way it had when he'd first seen the Miami River and worked for the Biscayne Bay Company; in a funny way he was grateful that what had happened to his leg had taken him back to that. He was happiest, as always, out of the growing city, off its noisy streets, away from courtrooms and council meetings and municipal planning sessions. Out on the bay, his back to the city, there was no sense of years passing to tell him how he'd aged, no skyline to show him how his concerns were out of step with the modern world, nothing to mock his loss of youth and vigor.

He wound up spending most of his days on board the *Starfish,* the boat he'd built to replace the *Newport,* now lying at the bottom of Havana harbor, poor old thing. As captain of his own charter service, he had a loyal crew of three and a growing reputation for being just about the best guide a fisherman would want to have in the waters of Southern Florida. His first customers tended to be middle-class family men or salesmen staying at Mrs. Geoghan's rooming house and other places like it, but as word of his skills spread, his clientele changed to the millionaires and state senators staying at the Royal Palm or on private seagoing yachts. For a while McLeod had his back hairs up about the rich, but his reputation led them to him and, being a democratic soul, he couldn't turn them away. "The rich got rights like anyone else, I guess," he told Clara.

Once he started taking them out on the *Starfish*—sometimes for as long as two and three days, down to Carysfort Reef to bring back amberjack or barracuda—he found he liked them and felt at ease in their company. Unlike the salesmen and office workers he was used to, they'd already got to where they were headed and had no particular axe to grind. Usually they were more relaxed with a rod and reel in their hands—and more likely to haul a decent mess of kingfish or Spanish mackerel out of the bay—than those below them on the social and financial ladder who kept a death grip on everything.

For their part, the rich went with McLeod because he was the best at what he did and because he never flattered them or asked them how business was or told them what he thought of the American political situation. He could spot the fin of a game fish a quarter mile off and guess the species and the weight within a pound or two, suggest which rod to grab and how long a line you'd probably need and whether to use a hook or a float. And for the long mid-afternoons when the fish stayed deep and nothing was biting but mosquitoes, he was full of tall tales told with a face confidence men envied. He once urged novice fisherman William Vanderbilt to go into the dairy business with him and market all the free milk they could squeeze out of a herd of sea cows. Vanderbilt was ready to sign till he saw the crew laughing. And while McLeod was talking he'd be frying up the morning's catch and serving it with creole hot sauce; once you'd tasted it you'd want to write to the chef at Delmonico's, tell him he ought to be ashamed of himself. His reputation was such that when Teddy Roosevelt came to Miami, the first thing he asked for was a day at sea with Quentin McLeod.

He spent some time tending his gardens at his upriver cabin, which he still kept as neat as in the brief bright days when he'd lived there with his young wife, but the only other place on land he ever set foot was Fort Dallas or the Reade office on Miami Avenue and there only to come for Clara, make her put down whatever she was doing, close up shop, and come out on the *Starfish* with him.

He had seen his own death, and with acceptance of it, he came to know the true value of his time and how he intended to spend it. Even a life with Clara seemed no longer a missing element; nothing was missing. All was as it had to be. He loved her still and never doubted it but knew as he knew the rise of the sun that it was her city that kept her from him; the competition undid him totally. Even as he helped her bring back Harry from the Seminole camp, even as he stood by her at Harry's wedding and watched a new and terrible sadness descend upon her, he could feel his own grip on her slipping, slipping, and with no way for him to grab a firmer hold, she would soon—and without her own awareness—elude him forever.

23.

A year after Harry's return, the Seminoles began to come to town a Sunday or two each month. They used a large rock pit along the bay's seawall to change into pants and hats, white-man style, then set up their wares outside one or another of the five churches, selling deer meat and alligator skins, and shopping in stores with the profits. The first time he saw them, Harry was on his way from services and they were outside Fine's Emporium loading their packs with sugar and calico and beads. He flushed, he felt weak, the blood pounded in his ears; he heard one member of the First Baptist Congregation say to another, "Them Indians is getting too familiar. Caught a pair of 'em sleeping in my backyard this morning."

"You kill 'em?"

"And waste good buckshot?"

Harry disappeared into the safety of the group that passed the store, and when he dared to look back the Indians were gone. After that he made it his business to learn their schedules so he could observe them. He would pick a spot a good distance away, in the shade, half around a corner, beside a stack of cornmeal in back of a delivery wagon, and he'd watch, his face hidden further by a broad-brimmed hat, his breathing shallow, hoping, terrified, that he would see her. He never did.

"Thank God the harvest is over," Maria said as she moved from the sideboard with Harry's plate of eggs. She was still dressed in a wrapper, her hair half-undone from sleep, though it was past ten o'clock. "Now you won't be out at all hours, and we can have dinners like a real family. I tell you, Harry, with you gone so, my nerves . . ."

Harry pressed his lips together—he never listened when she rattled on with such self-deception—and looked at her as she set the plate down in front of him. He remembered how frightened he'd once been by the specter of her injury, and for a short time at the beginning of their marriage, fear and guilt had made him compassionate. But now, seeing her pampered and coddled, her beauty faded and coarsened, living on macaroons and sherry and laudanum for her "nerves," he could hardly stand to bear witness to the disintegration. She seemed to exist solely as a punishing reminder of how life had failed them.

Much to Harry's mute dismay, she had insisted on naming their son for his paternal grandfather, and since Harry would not reveal the truth about his feelings for that man, the name Cameron—one which both Harry and Clara thought they'd never have to hear again—was heard daily. Harry found himself recoiling from the boy who bore it, and he could not help but admit that the unfortunate association of the name was not the only reason, for though he bore his grandfather's name, everything else—the deep-set eyes, the dark hair, the tilt of his head, the questioning, skeptical air—were all the boy's mother's, and Harry felt, absurdly, he knew, that Maria had conceived the boy by some bizarre parthenogenesis.

As an infant, as a boy, more and more, Cameron came to seem to Harry totally his mother's son, afraid of his father, wary and shy in his presence, hurt, needy, and finally, later, resentful, sullen, disdainful, silent. Harry observed this happening as from a great distance. These two, this mother and her son, could not actually and truly be related to him, he told himself; some essential affection simply was not there. He longed to be away, and yet duty bound him just as it had bound his father to him and his mother. Conflict made him restless. In the peacefulness of the Reade Groves, in the quietest moment on Northeast Second Street, he was edgy and discontent.

"Eat your breakfast," he said merely to stop the incessant flow of her words. "I don't like to see you looking so pale."

She poured a cup of tea for herself. " 'Course I'm pale," she said as she took her seat at the opposite end of the table. "Can't stay out in the sun much, can I?"

Harry's throat grew thick; he could hardly swallow the eggs. "I won't go on apologizing to you for the rest of my life."

"Well, that's fine!" Maria jumped to her feet; her tea sloshed over the sides of the cup. "I'm cooped up in this stale little box of a house all day. Nothing to do, nowhere to go, no one to see." She took a deep breath and resumed her seat. "No money to spend."

"Ah, now we come to the point," Harry said.

"Huh?"

"First the hysterics, then the request for money."

"You think you know me so well."

"I know your habits at least."

She tried a little conciliatory laugh. "As if all I did was ask for things, Harry! My God, but you're a suspicious soul. Don't I run things nice here? Don't I keep this place neat and nice?"

"Do I complain?"

"Hmph. I guess that's about all the praise I'm likely to get." Harry stared at the eggs congealing on his plate. "You do admit it, though. Well, that's something because—" He suddenly smiled to himself and she saw it. "Oh, you think you know me so well, do you? But I got some surprises left." She paused as if to let the rancor seep out of her tone. "Honey," she began again, "I been thinking. I been thinking that I wanna have something to do, only it's gotta be something indoors and you admitted I kept the house nice—"

"Well?"

"I been thinking . . . I wanna run the hotel."

"The Miami?"

"Yeah."

"It's got a manager."

"Oh, he don't know nothing! You been there lately? He's drunk and the rooms're empty. And with tourists pouring into town like they are and a hotel being right in the family, only sorta rundown, it seems such a shame."

"But why you?"

She hesitated, as if weighing whether or not to be straight with him. "To make some money out of it," she said finally, daring him to laugh. "You think I'm always gonna live like this? When your own mother lives like the queen of the city?"

"Don't compare yourself to my mother," Harry said. "Remember how you used to live and count yourself lucky."

"Oh, I do," she said, though it grated on her sense of self-importance to be reminded of where she came from.

Harry shrugged. "Go ahead then."

" 'Course it'd take fixing the place up."

He laughed. "I hope you're not relying on me to give you the money," he said, "because I just don't have it to give."

"Don't have it! With all the time you spend at the groves? I don't believe you."

"It's true whether you believe me or not."

"But how? You said you had the biggest crop ever last year."

"Do you have any idea what it costs to run the groves? Salaries, equipment, the new irrigation ditch, repairs to the road. The freight charges alone are killing me. That's if the railroad even delivers the crop before it's spoiled. So go ahead and manage the old place, but if you want my money to fix it up, you really ought to go to the Florida Eastern Star. They're the ones who've got it."

She hated the satisfied look on his face, like he was glad not to give her any! Like he was happy seeing her poor and in misery and here she only wanted to advance herself. If she didn't know how much it'd hurt, she thought she might just break down and cry at the unfairness of it all. "There are husbands in this world who love their wives so much they'd give them anything." She spoke in a singsong cadence that was a parody of the more seductive rhythm of their early courtship.

Harry moved his plate away with a sigh of exasperation. "And now the monthly dirge for our lost romance. I think I'll beg off playing my part, if you don't mind."

"You hate our life together, don't you?" she said in a coarse, accusing whisper. "Well, you got no one to blame but yourself. It's your doing that I am the way I am."

Harry wiped his mouth with his napkin and threw it on the table. "All right. You've registered your displeasure in a life that most women would find a source of comfort and joy." He looked at her, compassion long buried under an avalanche of distaste, and could not help but add, "But you're not like most women."

Maria pursed her lips in what was to Harry a pathetic reminder of the pout he'd once found alluring. "You used to mean something different when you said that."

"Don't be disgusting," he said.

"Is that what you think I am?" Maria laughed harshly. "Well, what about—"

"No!" He stood up and walked to the windows, clenching and un-clenching his fists. Talk of love had pushed him to the edge of his patience; mention of Shinassa would send him over. "I've been a decent husband," he said. "And I won't have you—"

The door opened and little Cam skipped into the room. "Mother, can I have—" He stopped short at the silence. His mother's face was flushed around her specs. His father was standing at the window, his back hard as a wall. Cam clenched his fists and dug them in his pockets. Why'd he always make her feel bad? He took his seat at the table and watched his poor mother stealing hurt looks at his father's back.

Harry and Maria sat down and breakfast continued in a roar of tiny sounds: the rustle of Harry's newspaper, the clink of Maria's spoon as she stirred and stirred her tea, the rhythmic thud of Cam's heels beating on the rungs of his chair. Long after the food had turned cold on everyone's plate, they continued to sit.

And so Harry continued to work hard at the groves and continued the impersonation of dutiful, obliging husband. Whether Maria was a fool not to see what he was doing or simply smart enough to look the other way—for her own sake, what good would confrontation do?—their family life continued its charade of normalcy. As long as he slept beside her, even for the last hours before dawn, as long as the three of them ate breakfast together and Maria could kiss his cheek at the front door for their neighbors to see, all had the semblance of being well. And then a realization struck him with the clarity and bite of a hard bracing slap: despite himself, as if mocked by a destiny he could not escape, he had recreated the same family into which he had been born.

Though she could not pinpoint the exact moment she had stopped loving Harry, Maria knew that all her tender feelings for him were long gone, replaced by a cold, resigned acceptance of their life together. And as long as he didn't leave her, as long as he continued to come home at night and sleep beside her—it didn't matter that he hadn't touched her in years—she would continue to accept things as they were. Replacing the yearning for him that had once made her heart beat fast and her breath come quick was anger and contempt and a kind of wheedling dissatisfaction with the very qualities in him she used to find so appealing. His shyness, his fastidiousness, his patient gentlemanly responses to even her most extreme behavior, had all congealed into something alien and remote; no matter what she did, she could elicit no warmth, no pity, no regret.

She had once thought that the mere existence of a son would get her all she wanted, but it just didn't turn out that way. Son or no, she was going to have to work for every damn dime. Not that she didn't love little Cam; she certainly loved dressing him up cute and hearing compliments on how well behaved he was and what a sweet pair they made in their one-horse rig as they rode along Miami Avenue and how nicely he pronounced words and what good manners he had. By five she'd trained him to jump from the carriage first and give her his little hand to help her down.

He looks the spitting image of me, she thought on more than one occasion, and he is a born gentleman. The funny thing was that Harry didn't even know how like him Cam really was: same manners, same seriousness, same watchful eyes; why sometimes she had to shout at the sweet boy just for looking at her in that Harry sort of way. He'd understand someday why he couldn't be anything like his father and why she did what she did to see to it that a thing like that never happened. Harry and Cam's being close, knowing each other, would have stood in the way of her long-range plans. As the years went on, she swore that what she did she did in the name of mother love.

She needed first to be independent of Harry. Their marriage had taken her out of her father's shack in the hammock, but a plain house on Northeast Second Street with neighbors a spitting distance away was not far enough. Little Cam would take her further. Let Harry keep to himself. Let him love an Indian. Let him drink himself into a stupor every night of the week. What did it matter when she controlled the heir?

Cam was quiet around his father, and Maria did all she could to make him hate Harry short of ordering him to, which she was sure she could've done successfully, Cam being the obedient child he was. That she didn't was more a sign of her cautiousness in not overplaying her hand than a demonstration of any concern that the child might be frightened by such commands. She'd just wait until he grew up— patience would be her constant companion—until little Cam was old enough to be the agent of her revenge. Until then she didn't have to do more than note Harry's absences and let Cam's hurt feelings take care of the rest.

Her mother-in-law was going to be a big help without knowing it, and Maria began a pattern of regular bi- and sometimes tri-weekly visits, always bringing Cam, coaching the boy on the way there on just how to behave and how to kiss Grandy nicely and how to hug her around the neck and tell her she smelled like sunshine.

And Cam would do so, much to Clara's delight, and the visits took on a comforting regularity. Clara felt Harry could not drift too far away while his family stayed so close. The two women would sit on the wide porch of Clara's house inside the fort, each in a ladderback rocker, Maria's dark glasses firmly in place, sip Geneva's cool lemonade, and fan themselves with palmetto fans. Cam was the fulcrum on which all conversation spun. Clara loved to watch Cam no matter what he did, and Maria watched Clara watching him, smiling whenever Clara smiled. "I think it's so nice how he loves his grandy so," she said, as Cam chased a rooster around the yard and finally caught it in a great whoosh of dust. He emerged from the battle holding the reluctant beast in his arms and stroked it and marched back and forth in front of the porch, finally letting the squawking thing free and falling asleep at his mother's feet.

"Isn't he the sweetest thing you ever seen?" Maria whispered as the two women smiled down at the sleeping boy.

"He's growing so fast," Clara said.

"Like the city of Miami itself, I always say." Maria leaned over to stroke Cam's head, then looked up at his smiling grandmother. "He's

Miami's true son, don't you think?" Maria didn't wait for a reply but leaned toward Clara and spoke in an urgent whisper. "This town's growing so fast, it takes my breath away. And I wanna be part of what makes it big."

"But—"

"I know I started off small, and I'm humble as can be, but don't it seem right that us early settlers get in on the big deals?"

Clara still found it unsettling to look at Maria—she hadn't seen her eyes since the day she'd visited her at Dr. MacKenzie's—and she smiled instead at her sleeping grandson. "The Reade Groves are doing so well," she said. "Harry's had the biggest crop ever."

Maria essayed a dry laugh. "Well, I don't have much to do with the groves," she said. "What I was talking about is my idea of managing the Miami Hotel and sending it on its way to future glory." She stroked the hair of the boy sleeping at her feet, then looked up at Clara again. "You think it's a good idea?"

Clara hesitated. "It's not much of a hotel," she said. "We built it back at the beginning just because there was no place for people to stay. Now though, there are hotels that make it look . . . well, you know."

" 'Course I don't just wanna check people in and out, I wanna fix it up," Maria said. "Build on to it, add rooms and porches and pretty furniture, expand the lawns, put in a new garden. You know—attract the tourists."

"That's going to cost a lot of money."

"I know you helped lots of people starting up new businesses." Maria sighed. "I hoped . . . you'd help me."

"But have you talked this over with Harry?"

"Yes, but he don't want me to do it."

"Well, perhaps he knows best."

Maria hesitated but couldn't stop her lips from trembling and, even though she knew it'd burn her eyes something fierce, burst into tears. "My life's not going at all the way I hoped. Oh yes, I know, I got myself out of my daddy's shack in the hammock and don't have to make no possum and coon steaks for him and my brothers, but I still don't have a cook the way you got your Geneva and that I know Harry can afford only won't. Even next door to us, Mrs. Jennings has her Blanche to help around the house. But Harry says he just isn't bent on making money the way everybody else in Miami is, and nothing I say—and I say plenty!—can make him see the light. He don't even feel sorry about my eyes—he don't!—and it's all his fault too. Running off to live with an Indian. To this day, I can't get it out of my mind. Harry even smells different since he come back. And he touches me different too; it's enough to give me chills. I don't wanna think about him and that filthy Indian girl, but there it is, the thought's there and what'm I supposed to do about it? If you store things up, they eat at your insides and you die screaming. Harry's the one run off and did something bad. Why should I be the one punished while he gets off scot-free? Why'd my eyes have to go? Why'm I the only one has to cook for a whole family when everyone else has help? 'Course I do have Cam and that boy is one big comfort. There isn't a mother loves her son more'n I love Cam. Half the time I wish Cam'd be in bed with me instead of Harry, with him smelling different and touching me with those cold, careful fingers and moaning in his sleep. I can just imagine what he's dreaming about!" Tears streamed down her cheeks, and she dabbed at them with a wadded handkerchief. "He don't want me to make a success out of the hotel. He wants me to stay home all the time. He don't want us to grow big with the city. He don't want no part of Miami. Just the groves. The groves! The groves! The groves! Can't even stand the sight of oranges no more." She took off her glasses and Clara saw her eyes, red-rimmed, swimming in tears, enormous, desperate.

Clara turned away to look down at the peaceful sleeping form of her grandson. "Of course I'll help you," she said. "Of course. Of course. Only . . ." She looked up at the weeping girl and, for the first time, was truly frightened for Harry.

24.

For years a virtual recluse, Maria became a familiar figure in the city: a young matron, neatly hatted and dressed, driving a modest rig, distinguished from the other young matrons who moved along the streets laden with packages or sat gossiping in Fanny's Tea Room on Biscayne Boulevard, only by those flat black discs over her eyes, from which tears seemed always to be flowing. She spent long work days inspecting all the hotels in the city, her little boy in tow, both of them serious, unsmiling, exclusive. Of course Maria did not intend for the Miami to compete with the really grand hotels, but at each she found something to note: the all-white dining room at the Halcyon, the caged birds at Lime House, the violinists in the lobby of the Perdido, the grillwork elevator at the Royal Palm. She saw that making the Miami the sort of hotel that would attract the well-to-do tourist would require more work and certainly more of her mother-in-law's money than she had initially foreseen. But Clara never said no to any of her requests—Maria always had Cam

with her, sitting him down in his grandy's lap when she did the asking—and the Fort Dallas National Bank never said no to Clara.

In preparing the hotel for renovation, Maria interviewed each of
the town's architects, but each withdrew from the project when faced
with demands for a design that apparently made sense only in her
own mind. The architects compared stories about her afterwards, and
one in particular drew appreciative laughter for his imitation of Maria
Reade saying, "It's gotta be swank, and believe me, I know the diff!"
The most talented, in Maria's estimation, was the one who was, finally,
the most amenable to her ideas. He was also the one most in need
of the work.

The last acre of hammock within the downtown—apart from the
land around Fort Dallas—was part of the hotel grounds, and Maria
had it cleared to create a new front lawn. The one and only time Harry
came to the site was the day the first trees were dynamited out of
Maria's way. He watched from across the road, thinking that years ago
he had sat on the hotel's back porch and watched the parrots and
toucans. He imagined now he could hear their outraged squawks
under each new explosion, and several times he saw flashes of brightly
colored feathers, but whether the birds were flying away or hurled
aloft by the force of the dynamite, he could not tell. When the blasting
was over for the day, he crossed the road to gather pieces of crabwood,
Madeira, and mahogany. Maybe carve them into something, he thought
idly, maybe just . . . have them. As he loaded them in the back of his
cart, Maria picked her way across the fallen trees to him.

"Are you trying to embarrass me by picking up all that junk?" she
demanded.

Harry shrugged as he got back into the cart. "I'm just taking some
souvenirs."

Maria shook her head. "You and the past," she sighed. "You're
so . . . so . . ."

Harry flicked the reins and was gone before she could finish.

A week later, the ground was free of trees and the mound of dirt
exposed was ready to be flattened. Maria had watched for a while,
calling suggestions to the Negro diggers, and now stood with her face
to the bay, her hair done up neatly under a pink straw skimmer with
a girlish ribbon hanging down her back, her new French-style dress
starched and fresh-looking even though the day was steamy. A late-

afternoon breeze scented with brine and mimosa rustled her skirt and stirred vague longings in her that made her think back to that first day Harry had come to the Sunday service. Oh, the hopes she'd had!

She looked back at the hotel and the gang of workers swinging shovels and pickaxes into the mound of dirt that would become the front lawn of the Miami Hotel. Who would have thought life would have gone along this way? Why I'm . . . She searched her mind for just the right word to express her current state and could come up only with "happy," though she immediately felt disappointed with it; "happy" didn't take in the largeness of accomplishment at having triumphed over Harry's lack of interest and support. The only thing that still bothered her was the way he managed simply not to see her anymore. "Sometimes I think your daddy's the one with the vision problem and not me," she said more than once to little Cam.

Her mother-in-law, rather than sell any more of her land to raise the money for the reconstruction of the hotel, arranged for a loan with the Fort Dallas National Bank. Maria had known she'd help. After helping all those strangers start up new businesses, she could hardly turn down her own son's wife, now could she? A large tract of wetland was put up as collateral, and Maria understood how that made perfect sense.

There was no chance that the hotel would fail; hotels all over town were turning away tourists for want of available rooms. And by next season the Miami would be one of them, and the loan would be paid off in large piles of silver. She pictured herself standing at the top of the steps, pockets bulging, proudly saying, "Sorry. Full up."

The Miami wouldn't be as grand maybe as the Royal Palm or the Halcyon, she admitted, but grand enough. Why do it at all, she'd said breezily to Clara as they left the bank the day the loan was approved, if you don't do it right? Clara hoped to win some peace for her son and some measure of a future for little Cam by satisfying Maria. She remained a distant benefactor to her daughter-in-law and, though she asked to be shown all the plans, was not present on the day that the newspapers referred to as the Day of the Excavation.

Maria was still standing alone at the edge of the bay, dreaming of the future, staring through dark glasses as her shadow stretched out along the sand gone gold with the setting sun, when she heard the first scream.

A small crowd of shoppers and tourists had gathered, and she pushed her way through the crush of bodies, steeling herself for the sight of blood. What she saw piled atop the dirt was what seemed to her—and had to the Negro laborers at first—a trove of buried treasure: chinaware, glass bottles, clay pipes, flintlock guns and pistols, lead shot, glass beads and tiny mirrors, iron kettles, cloth, silver and copper coins, white ironware, Oriental porcelain, flower-painted delftware. But then other, less valuable things had appeared beneath and now lay in a separate pile. A hush fell on the crowd when they saw what had been last unearthed: animal bones, scalps, and finally, chillingly, human skeletons. The Negro laborers who'd done the digging sat on empty boxes of dynamite and trembled.

Rufus Finch edged his way next to Maria; no longer safe in keeping his money in a sock under his bed, he came regularly to the north shore to attend to banking business. He took one look at the pile and shook his head sadly. "Seminole burial mound."

Maria couldn't have been more delighted if they'd struck gold. Much to the shock of the assembled onlookers, she burst out laughing and rallied the workers. "Nothing to scream about, boys. It's just dead Indians." When they made no motion to resume their digging, she doubled their pay. Some of the Negro laborers still refused to cart the bones in wheelbarrows to a storage shed; to them spirits of the dead were powerful and Indian spirits even more so. To Maria bones were bones, and Indian bones mattered even less.

That the government regarded the Seminoles as savages was a fact scrawled in blood across the pages of Florida history. Given the larger picture—the Seminole Wars over, the treaties agreed to and signed by both parties, and Everglades swampland legally set aside and reserved for the Indians—this disturbance of their burial mound was hardly worth anyone's attention.

"Don't be rough with those skulls," Maria cautioned the workers who accepted her offer. "We'll make a little museum out of 'em." She picked one up and hefted it in the palm of her hand. "Hmm. Lighter'n I thought it'd be," she said to Finch and shrugged. "Maybe open a little shop in the hotel and sell 'em for souvenirs."

At dinner in Fort Dallas with Clara and Harry a few days later, Maria was willing to concede, when pressed by Clara on the silent Harry's behalf, that the situation was a bit unsettling, though privately she rejoiced in her good luck at being able at last to pay Harry back in kind. "Like I told the reporter from *The Metropolis*"—and here she read from a copy of the paper left handily on Clara's sideboard— "'The decision as to whether the skeletons and other artifacts will eventually be displayed behind glass or sold as souvenirs will be delayed until the Miami Hotel is nearer completion and Mrs. Harry Reade can more formally assess the retail opportunities.'"

She put the paper down with a beleaguered sigh. "But after all," she said to Clara with a glance at Harry to make sure he understood the reasonableness of her position, "it's done and it can't be undone and there's no harm to any living soul."

"It was a grave, for God's sake," Harry said quietly.

Maria looked at Clara with the tiniest smile of complicity. "I don't see how anyone can expect me to feel sympathy for a whole tribe of people who bury their dead bodies in one big hole instead of side by side in separate boxes like decent Christians. Do you, Mother?"

Later, while Maria was readying little Cam for the carriage ride home, Clara said to Harry, "I only invested in the Miami Hotel to help you. I hope you understand that."

Harry did not look at her; his reply was merciless: "It was too little and it was too late. And of course it did backfire in a most unhelpful way, didn't it?"

Clara could say no more, though she longed to point out that initially he had approved of her help—at least, in his silence, he had not disapproved. But she saw now that she had wronged him yet again, unable to strike the right note of conciliation whenever the Indians were involved. And it chilled her too for Harry to think—but could he actually think it?—that she had entered into a true bargain of the heart with his wife.

The original three stories became five, with a wrap-around porch on each supported by fluted columns. French doors opened out from rooms filled with elaborately carved Eastlake furniture that the architect had found in a wrecker's warehouse in Key West. The furniture had gone down inside a ship on the Florida Reef, but most of the water stains, the architect assured Maria, would be undetectable under a dab of artfully applied paint. And the creaks? The creaks, the architect replied with as much withering contempt as he could muster, are an attribute of antiquity and demonstrate an object's value.

A low kitchen wing was added to the back of the hotel where there wasn't a view of the bay to block. The wing unbalanced Harry's original plan for the hotel, however, and now it looked as if it were limping. In addition, humid air hung between the ell and the main body of the hotel and prompted Elliot Iverson, a resident in the same dark, viewless back room since his arrival in town, to avail himself of Wheeler's offer of accommodations at the Royal Palm.

"Despite my desire to live undistracted by the beauty of my surroundings," he told Maria, "the smell of fried turtle is too high a price to pay for the privilege."

The front entrance gained a set of aeolithic columns rescued from the fire at the Desirée Arms, and it didn't matter to Maria that they were three feet too short for the expanse they needed to span; they definitely qualified as "swank." A broad sunken piazza, carved out in front of the hotel where the burial mound had been, was adorned with a promenade and shaded seating and pebbled in multicolored coral. Unfortunately, water from the limestone stratum beneath kept seeping up and making it impassable during the height of the tourist season. Maria's pride and joy was a statue of Cupid in the center of the piazza, created by the famed Italian sculptor Carlo Tambini, known at the time for realistic busts of New York society matrons; little Cam posed for the statue, and Signor Tambini, she felt, really did capture his likeness. "At the price we paid him," she told Clara, "he better have!"

The lobby was low-ceilinged—there was nothing to be done about that short of gutting the entire structure and starting from scratch— and carpeted with another treasure from the wrecker's warehouse. The faint aroma of mildew never left it, though, and Maria herself could be seen of a midnight surreptitiously dousing it with rose water. A forest of potted palms stood on the carpet along with islands of overstuffed sofas, matching ottomans, and fringed floor lamps. The walls were covered in damask and hung with gilt-framed paintings of the Madonna and other adored mothers. There was an all-white dining room, a pink tea room, a reading room with books bought by the yard from a supplier in Boston, a ladies' lounge furnished in Heywood

Wakefield wicker, and a smoker complete with leather Chesterfields, brass spittoons, and copies of the *Police Gazette*.

Rush as the workers did, the hotel was not ready in time even for the Valentine Ball that marked the end of the season. Maria was philosophical about the loss. "You can't force a good thing," she told Clara, who was beginning to understand Wheeler's complaints about finances. Then, casting a critical eye on the piazza, Maria added, "Gives us time to drain it once and for all and really get things right."

Clara Reade's famous "no liquor" clause—still written into land sales—managed to keep alcohol consumption and its attendant evils off the city streets, but once the town had been incorporated and legal city limits posted, it took only one smart operator to cross the city line and open the Easy Come Easy Go Saloon. Gamblers and prostitutes settled in North Miami, and with them came the schemers who were out to get the most for doing the least and who moved on before people had a chance to count their change. Liquor was imported in old gunboats from Key West and the Bahamas—even Cal Sparks made a few midnight runs—along with fringed settees and Larkspur lotion and murals depicting ladies in poses of lascivious abandon.

The sailors who docked in Miami said that for sheer lewd excitement, Hell's Kitchen could not compare with North Miami. Saloons stayed open round the clock. Roulette wheels ran in the middle of North Miami Avenue. Chinese opium dens flourished. Negroes and Cubans and whites brushed up against each other with thinly veiled hostility. Violence simmered just beneath the surface; on a single night there might be as many as three killings. Both *The Metropolis* and the newly founded *Herald* kept saying that something had to be done. Ministers shouted from their pulpits that Hell lurked in view.

Harry had often heard his mother say that if there had to be a Gomorrah, at least her "no liquor" clause had managed to keep it outside the city limits. Now he thought her a bit naive despite her years and experience. She saw what she wanted to see and remained ignorant of that which would disturb her idealized view of her city.

Simon Price, Miami's first marshal, spent a lot of time there; too much, some said. But though Price might have been drunk enough to need a hand in mounting his bicycle, he'd ride fearlessly into the fray, brandishing his pistol and shouting, "Stop in the name of the law!" After a few years of this he could be heard to grumble that if he'd known he was going to be this busy, he'd have stayed standing over the hopper at his father-in-law's brewery in Van Etten, New York.

Harry spent the night of the burial mound's unearthing in the long, crowded bar of the Seminole Arms Saloon, drawn there by the hideous irony of the name, and on subsequent nights went there again and again, unable to bear that house on Northeast Second Street where he was constantly reminded of all he had lost. Nobody in North Miami asked him why he was there, where he was from, or how many days more he planned on staying, just so he paid for his drinks as he downed them.

One night McLeod found him and joined him at the dark table in back where Harry sat alone. Each seemed faintly embarrassed to see the other there.

"If you're coming to take me back—"

McLeod shook his head. "I been out to the Seminole camp," he said and saw the hope light up Harry's tired face and how what he said next darkened it again. "Dr. Tiger's dying. Well, that's all right, they say, seeing as how he stopped counting the years at ninety, but ... the worst of it is that he's got his mind set on leaving the camp. Says there's no place here for him to die since the burial mound ..." McLeod shrugged; this was more painful for him to say than he'd thought. He raised his hand and signaled for a whiskey. "He wants to go to Texas. After the wars, the government relocated a whole bunch of Cow Creek Seminole and Mikasuki over there in Corpus Christi. The old fool was going to walk. I talked and I talked and I talked to him and he agreed to let me take him in the *Starfish*." Harry had sunk lower in his seat; the overhead light threw deep shadows down his face. He ain't a boy no more, McLeod thought. The whiskey came and he downed it in one quick swallow.

"You came for me once before," Harry said. "I went with you then. I won't go with you now."

They sat in silence for a long moment. Finally, McLeod stood up. "I got to get a get on," he said. "Gonna try to make Elliott's Key before tomorrow. Dr. Tiger's itchy to give this place his back."

Harry didn't linger in the Seminole Arms. There were other spots in North Miami that didn't know him, and as time wore on he completed the circle of accommodations and began again, only to find that the Seminole Arms had become Sally's Red Hotel, that the alley that once led to the Chinaman's had been repainted and turned into the New York Burlesque House, and that O'Toole's gaming tables were transmogrified into Ada Wilder's Silver Dollar Saloon.

After a few years of this kind of life—at the groves all day, at the bars all night—Harry's looks began to change. Too little sleep and too much strong liquor scored and shadowed his face. He no longer was out of place in these bars; he'd become just another man who looked natural with his fist around a shot glass.

In his seventy-fifth year, F. Morrison Wheeler had become a grizzled old warrior weary of the battlefield but reluctant to retreat. He felt himself besieged from all sides, set upon by hostile forces on every front when, if the world were a just place, the populace would have been strewing rose petals at his feet and crowning his head with laurels. Instead, new claims against railroad policies were filed daily, and lobbying in the state capital for an increase in harbor facilities grew stronger every week, with explicit criticism of the railroad's effectiveness.

Despite his knowledge that Clara Reade was merely the personification of the forces that worked against him in the city, he longed to see her on her knees before him. For years she and the other citrus growers had fought him on the rates the Florida Eastern Star charged to transport their crops. All right, I am not an unreasonable man, he told them and dealt out certain controlled concessions. But was he thanked? Was he praised for the conciliatory gesture? No. They said it wasn't enough. And when he stood his ground, they brought charges against him to the Interstate Commerce Commission.

Much to Wheeler's embarrassment, the commission was shown documentary evidence—bills of lading, shipping receipts, import tax stamps—that proved the F.E.S. had given preferred rates to crops grown on F.E.S.-owned land in Cuba. As Wheeler's lawyers shuffled papers and studied their shoes, the commission decided in favor of the citrus growers: shipping rates on the F.E.S. would not only be lowered but hereafter overseen and regulated by an impartial board. Rage as he might, the power was wrested from his hands.

"I'm not a vengeful man," he told his ailing wife's nurse, as if to convince himself of the truth of it. "But is a little appreciation too much to ask?"

"I appreciate you," Miss Fisher replied.

Wheeler gave one of his rare, barking laughs and held the nurse's hand. "Thank you, my dear," he said and kissed the hand he held. "Your concern is most..." He didn't really have to make their arrangement legal; as his wife's nurse, she had a perfectly legitimate reason to live and travel with them. She could even have stayed on as she was and not become his mistress; everyone thought she already had.

Life with his wife had become unbearable; there was no love and no interest, only an unfelt obligation earned by the relentless piling up of the decades. But Pauline Fisher—lovely, pliant, with incredibly skillful hands—was four decades younger than he and Wheeler was certainly not blind to how that might appear to the public eye: an old wife discarded, replaced by a new wife stolen from the cradle or by a hard-bitten fortune hunter who could only make him look ridiculous.

He thought of his pious mother, of their little cabin on a rocky hill with Bible samplers on the walls, and of the boy he'd been, standing waist deep in wild flowers as the Adirondack and Ohio sped by above him. Had he come so far from that innocent time that he could consider making any but the moral choice?

The hell with everybody; he decided to marry her.

Night after night thereafter his bride-to-be leaned her pretty head on his shoulder and tatted lace for her wedding lingerie while Wheeler devised a plan. It was a medical fact that his wife needed constant care; even the professional Miss Fisher agreed that no nurse, no matter how dedicated, could attend to all the needs of such a patient. And so she would become a permanent resident at a sanitarium he owned in upstate New York. The lady in question, mentally unbalanced and often violent, was, when lucid, nobody's fool, but she and her lawyers found themselves no match for her husband and his.

Heavily sedated and generously financed, she was sent to that sanitarium while a New York court declared her incompetent. The Florida State Senate—at the urging of the man whose railroad helped make the state what it was—met in emergency session to pass an amendment making the insanity of a spouse grounds for divorce. Forty-eight hours after it was passed and the divorce accomplished, the marriage of

Pauline Cox Fisher—it was not the first marriage for the bride either—and F. Morrison Wheeler was sanctified by all that was holy, the amendment was reconsidered and repealed.

The people of Miami did not take kindly to such fiddlings with the law, nor to the photos of this old geezer nuzzling his young bride on the rotogravure page of *The Metropolis.* Wheeler ever after blamed his reversals in Miami on a perception of him as immoral and above the law, and of course nothing could have been further from his intentions! How, he wondered, could they persist in so misunderstanding him?

Before long he came to wonder too why he'd done it at all and what good he ever expected to come from this marriage. It was humiliating to think that he derived so little pleasure from an arrangement that had caused so much trouble. In the end, he came to know something about himself that perhaps he had always deferred knowing: personal happiness was fleeting, emotional sustenance illusory, fulfillment through another person simply out of his reach. His only true satisfaction came in his exercise of power.

The board of trade met to discuss a cause dear to the hearts of merchants, growers, and passengers alike, all of whom had come up against the unfairness of the monopolistic Florida Eastern Star: the future of Miami as a deep-water port. Wheeler declined the invitation to attend—in fact thought it the height of arrogance and insensitivity even for them to have asked, though of course would have been outraged if they hadn't—and followed the proceedings instead with a purloined set of daily minutes. Each day brought new insults to his industry as grievances old and buried were brought up for close public scrutiny. Testimony piled up not simply in favor of the deep-water harbor but against the F.E.S. in general. There were dozens of speeches; Clara Reade's particularly stung: "A public utility monopoly possessing political power is a menace. Miami will make no more progress as long as it remains under the control of special interests."

Wheeler's wife brought him a cup of chamomile tea with a few drops of laudanum to stop his trembling.

"What does she know about progress?" Wheeler muttered. "And how dare she refer to the F.E.S. in that degrading, euphemistic way?"

"You ought to stop reading these reports," his wife advised.

Wheeler hardly glanced at her. "Just keep the kettle boiling."

The outcome of the meetings was as he feared it might be: the drafting of a petition urging Congress for appropriations to dredge the bay and deepen the harbor to create a port that oceangoing ships might navigate. "But this is a railroad town!" he cried and crushed the report between two red fists, knocking the teacup off its tray. He poured himself two fingers of brandy and then two more. "The damned governor himself's on their side!"

In a quiet, brandy-tempered rage, he issued orders to have fences erected all along the bayfront land he owned, and he watched with grim satisfaction as the children who spent the day swimming where there was a break between the mangroves and the docks—sandwiches in a bag hanging from a tree to foil the ants—were left high and dry, and the boats that carried the goods of the ungrateful had no place to berth. The harbor waters were filled now with schooners unable to load or unload their cargo. Those goods went bad on board or on the docks, and the stench of their rot drifted in sickening waves over the city. Balmy breezes indeed!

The Miami Herald, whose editor was more sympathetic to the cause of the smaller businessman than the railroad-oriented *Metropolis,* reported that Wheeler was bottling up the harbor and that, according to Clara Reade, the land he fenced was not his to fence at all but designated in the original deed as a public park. *The Metropolis,* whose editor now lived gratis in Wheeler's own Royal Palm, published a photo of his host and his host's wife aboard their private yacht anchored four miles south of the Miami River, and reported that the great man called the claims of Clara Reade "utter nonsense." The *Herald* conducted an exclusive interview with Mrs. Reade and printed her assertion that the fences had less to do with whether or not the public was entitled to a park and everything to do with Wheeler's continued attempts to prevent a deep-water harbor because of his fears that it would become competitive with the railroad.

"What does she know of my fears?" Wheeler cried.

After the printed words came a series of events that startled a populace now used to threats and counterthreats: the fences Wheeler erected were cut in the night, the next day rebuilt by Wheeler's men, the next night cut again, then rebuilt and cut again until Wheeler, wearying of the whole business and regretting the extremity of the measure he was about to take, instructed his lawyers to bring a one-hundred-thousand-dollar lawsuit against Clara Reade, naming her as the force behind this movement to damage private property and to harass him. "It's time to end this once and for all," he told *The Metropolis.*

The city council, upon careful study of the original land sales between the Biscayne Bay Company and Clara Reade, and Clara Reade and F. Morrison Wheeler, citing the key phrase, "dedicated to the public good," decided that the land was indeed meant to be a park. Not only was Wheeler's suit against Clara dismissed, but she had the satisfaction of being present when the fences were cut down for the last time.

"They think I'm finished," he told his wife.

"Oh no, Freddie. Not you."

"And what's worse, they're not afraid of me anymore. They think I'm an old man. They don't know what I can still do."

"*I* know, Freddie. And that's all that is important."

In order to reverse the downward slide of the public's perception of him and the Florida Eastern Star, Wheeler grudgingly acceded to the suggestion of Emmett Flye that he don the mantle of humility and landscape a portion of the bayfront to give this damned public its damned park.

On the day the park was opened, he stood beneath a canopy of palm trees on the narrow strip of land along the bay and addressed a crowd made up of railroad workers and businessmen and citizens and reporters eager to watch him eat crow.

"Four acres of palm grove and coral beach," he said with a magnanimous sweep of his unlit cigar. "Its purpose is inscribed on this brass plaque set in a bench of native limestone supplied by our own Mr. Lanctot." He put on his spectacles and read. " 'So the citizens of the loveliest and fairest city in the South may come and rest and contemplate the beauty of the bay.' " He glanced at the docks behind him, at the boats and stevedores and immense piles of cargo ready to be shipped, and looked back at the crowd. Though his whole being cried out, Call the damned thing Wheeler! he said, "I give you Biscayne Park."

His tone of voice masked his rage, but the cigar in his hand snapped in two. He held the pieces behind his back and dropped them as he left the park grounds, smiling, smiling; his wife at his side, he waved one last time for the photographers, then climbed into his carriage and fell back on the cushioned seat. The carriage moved slowly along Biscayne Boulevard toward the hotel. When Wheeler closed his eyes, he could not help thinking the unthinkable: that the battle was nearly over, that he was ready to withdraw.

He stayed in his tower office at the Royal Palm and rarely went outside. His color faded. His hands trembled when he was tired. He did nothing all day but sign papers and listen to his wife and her cronies playing bridge in the adjoining room. But he was to be spared nothing, for when the dredging of the harbor began, it seemed he had the best view in town. He refused to leave the city and, short of that, could find no adequate means of diversion and so found himself, despite himself, enacting the role of the perfect audience. Day after day he stood at the window, his lips set in a hard, determined line, watching. Each breath was slow and measured, as if he knew exactly how many he had left. The sound of machinery groaning, the sight of water and sand spewing fountainlike day after day for months, for a year, seemed to mock him with their air of festivity. In the town below him, the people were in a celebratory mood, forgetting even as they cheered the dredges and the barges that carried sand from the bottom of the bay out to the coral key called the Beach, how powerful a force he had been and could still be.

Behind him, his wife was chattering about their upcoming vacation trip to Key West, but Wheeler had no time for a vacation. Old age pressed heavy hands on him; he did not want to end his life standing in the ashes of this humiliation.

His wife came to stand beside him. "The hell with their gratitude," she said. In the few years of their marriage this wife had demonstrated a surprisingly acute grasp of the working of his mind and had, in addition, amassed a small but efficient repertoire of phrases calculated to pacify him. "Don't they see that they'd be lost without you?"

Looking out the window at the dredges spewing sand, then at the busy intersection of Miami Avenue and Fourteenth Street, the four corners taken up by Starger's Bake Shop, Fine's Emporium, the Biscayne Hotel, and the Fort Dallas National Bank, Wheeler was struck by the particular aptness of what his wife had just said, and he thought that the only way to prove once and for all that he owned Miami would be to destroy it.

25.

Clara had already closed her office doors and was waiting impatiently for McLeod in the shade of the second-story porch above her, watching the carriages and well-dressed people hurrying along Miami Avenue. She spotted that shock of white blond hair before McLeod saw her and ran the few steps to meet him, took his arm, and steered him back into the flow of traffic toward the dock.

"Why so eager?" he asked.

"As if you didn't know," she said.

McLeod shrugged. "Usually I got to spend at least a half hour of wheedling to get you to come on the *Starfish* in the middle of the day."

"Stop teasing me."

They continued moving down Miami Avenue, their pace no faster than McLeod's limp allowed, as Closed for the Day signs were hung in shop windows, the flag was hoisted on the Fort Dallas National Bank, doors slammed, bells rang, and shopkeepers and their impatient wives joined the crowd. The mayor had declared a holiday this day that the dredge was to complete the work on Government Cut—the channel that would finally connect Biscayne Bay to the Atlantic Ocean across a seven-hundred-foot strip of land at the southerly end of the long, thin peninsula called the Beach—and the whole town was gathering at the docks for the short boat trip across.

As he walked, McLeod was aware of people moving out of his way, staring at his leg, and he stared right back, eyes burning, daring them to keep it up. Clara's pleasure in seeing him turned to consternation on his behalf. Because they walked slower than anyone else, the docks were almost empty by the time they got there, and the broad sweep of the bay beyond was already dotted with hundreds of yachts, schooners, rowboats, and steamers.

McLeod's crew had hoisted the sails when they saw him coming and had the sheets in hand. Clara looked out at the bay so she wouldn't see McLeod step down gingerly onto the *Starfish,* one hand on a brass railing for support; though he never complained of it, the pain of the effort showed on his face. He never asked for help or sympathy, and woe to the unthinking, well-meaning soul who offered it.

Clara waited until he called her name, then made a great show of having to wrestle with her long skirts as she boarded and took her place near him at the tiller. The sky was the color of milk poured in a blue glass bowl. It might rain later on and the sky might clear for a while; there might even be a purple sunset. But it was as humid now as any July day and Clara was glad to be out of her office and on the open bay. It was a great day for Miami, no matter what the weather. She looked above her as the sails caught the wind; they were off.

As they cruised along the surface of the bay, they passed many sailboats and steam yachts, some coming down from Pineland City, others up from the other keys, all headed east toward the Beach. Gone were the days when the bay was the settlers' private waterway. Now one had to be aware of all the other boats on the waters, and there were several new obstacles. Once the dredging had deepened the harbor and the mangroves had been cleared away, a complex series of interlocking docks were built hundreds of yards out into the water. The Biscayne Bay Sailboat Association had constructed a clubhouse that sat on pilings in the bay. From a new dock at Twelfth Street ferries made their way four times a day across the bay to Barrett's Casino and Bath House on the Beach. Schooner traffic in general was on the rise and pleasure boats manned by novice sailors got in everyone's way. On a windy day, especially when the green bay water was tipped with white caps, there were invisible traps—reefs, pilings, sand deposits left by the dredges—that ripped rudders clean off unfortunate boats. Engineers hired by the city council had put in makeshift rows of heavy pilings as guides for schooner pilots unfamiliar with the area, but now sailors like McLeod, used to making their way by sighting coral reefs and by the changes in the water surface that signaled depth changes, were apt to be the ones to get into trouble. More than once McLeod had had minor accidents with these pilings and the hull of the *Starfish* bore the scars.

"There was Crocodile Hole, remember, Clara?" he said, pointing to a spot on the shore where the ice factory stood. "And there was the entrance to Indian Creek. I can just about make it out now by the roof of Schell's Livery." He squinted to look further up the coast. "Didn't there used to be a whole line of royal palms there?" He shrugged and glanced at Clara. "I guess they come down to make way for Biscayne Park." He pointed farther north. "And there's Nigger Landing. Used to dock the *Newport* there. It was about where the Fifteenth Street Foundry is, I guess." He strained his eyes against the sun glaring off the water, pointing to other spots along the coast. "The House of Refuge Landing's gone, so's the one at Baker's Haulover. Oh well . . ."

Clara watched him, half listening; his words were caught up by the wind and whisked off out of her hearing. She didn't care, content just to watch him, reminded of the day she'd met him and how she'd watched him then too. He was at once the same—the white cornsilk hair, the bright blue eyes that caught the sun, the mischievous smile, the sense that he held, still, some secrets she would never know despite knowing so much—and very different. He was less eager to quarrel now, content to let things stand as they were, withdrawn from the fray; he had put a distance between himself and the world, as if he'd become an observer out here on the water, absent from the game itself.

Clara was moved by him in a way she had not been when they'd first met nor even later when physical passion had raged in her and she could hardly look at him without wanting to wrap her body around his. He had seemed to her immortal then, as unchanging—as un-changeable!—as the land itself, and the fact that he'd been wounded, damaged, added an aching tenderness to her love. She smiled at him in a way that spoke of their long and intimate knowledge of each other; McLeod caught her at it and turned red.

"Mighty bold look for a Founding Mother," he said and put his hand on hers with the shyness that often overcame him in moments of intimacy.

Clara leaned toward him; she didn't want these words floating away on the breeze. "I guess maybe you'd better marry me," she said, her lips close to his ear. When he didn't answer she pulled back to look at his face. "You do want to, don't you?"

McLeod wouldn't meet her eye. "Well, I always did . . ."

"There's a *but* coming. I can hear the thud."

"No *but*. Let's just . . . wait till after this channel's dug."

"Is that a promise?" she asked with a nervous laugh. There was a pained expression on McLeod's face, even though he managed to nod at her. "Maybe I better get it in writing," she said, but his response was suspended as they neared the Beach and all his concentration had to go to steering them in and around the other boats bobbing offshore. The crew started taking in the sails. Clara sat still and tried to keep out of the way. She was embarrassed by his refusal of her but wanted to take him at his word, that it was only a delay. She busied herself adjusting her hat in the wind and forced herself to think instead about the digging of the channel.

On shore, the tall iron dredge was being hauled into place. A row-boat came abreast of the *Starfish* and a young sailor helped Clara climb down into it. She faced land and watched the thousands of people clambering ashore and milling about. McLeod joined her and sat heavily on the seat next to her. The rowboat was pushed off and they were taken the ten yards to shore; neither of them spoke. Clara's face burned under the cool breeze and she longed to lose herself in the crowd and the excitement of the day's momentous event.

The board of trade had known from the beginning that to dredge the harbor was merely to tantalize Miamians with what might be, for even if the bay could be made deep enough to carry ocean liners, the route to it would pose a greater problem, involving as it must, not merely the scooping of sand but underwater demolition of coral reefs from the Miami River all the way to Key West. Once the bay had been deepened, what was required was a route from the bay directly to the ocean, and so the engineers had set their eye on the peninsula across from Miami, a narrow strip of coral reef covered with mangrove swamp that had for years been referred to simply as the Beach and, when Miami itself was named, as Miami Beach. While this peninsula served as a breaker against the Atlantic tides, it also stood in the way of direct access to the ocean.

Since the days of the original settlers, the Beach had been viewed as both boon and a source of frustration. People were attracted to it primarily because of its situation: one coast faced the bay, the other the ocean. Families rowed out for the day, the men and children to dip in the ocean waters, the women to hunt turtle eggs in the sand, declaring them superior to hens' for baking, though a bit on the salty side. Wreckers visited the Beach in search of treasure or at least usable timber. But all of them were daunted; so densely overgrown with mangroves was it, so infested with mosquitoes and sand flies and crawling with alligators, rattlers, and rats that even the hardiest of the coon and possum hunters soon gave up their trips. There were few who saw any future in the Beach at all except as a barrier that protected Miami during sea storms.

The first people who tried to profit by it were some Northerners who didn't know any better and bought the land from the government for thirty-five cents an acre. Fighting mosquitoes and sand flies all the while, their hands and faces swollen with red welts, they cleared the land of mangroves and, despite the continued presence of rats and bears, planted coconuts all the way from Cape Florida to Jupiter. As any of the settlers could have predicted, the nuts were eaten by the rats and what the rats overlooked was smothered by new growths of strangler figs.

The mangroves grew back too. Other attempts were made to cultivate the place, but none succeeded until the Rivers and Harbors Committee of the Congress, having woken up to the importance of Miami as a harbor—"It pays to lobby" was the wisdom of the people of Miami—appropriated three hundred thousand dollars to deepen the bay, then dredge a channel that would allow ships from the Atlantic Ocean to cross Miami Beach right into the new harbor on Biscayne Bay. In a neat side benefit, the Beach turned out to be the ideal dumping ground for the thousands of tons of sand dredged up from the bottom of the bay. And so, without exactly planning it, a real sand beach was created on top of the coral reef that was at the base of the land. That's when the Barretts built their casino and bath house and started a ferry service, and the idea of Miami Beach as a resort on the ocean took a firm hold in the imagination. It was a hundred yards in front of Barrett's that the mayor now stood being photographed digging a gold-plated shovel into the ditch by the dredge and tossing the symbolic first clump of sand.

"I've declared this day a holiday," he called out over the wind and the roar of the ocean waves, "in order that all the citizens of Miami may witness the mingling of the waters of Biscayne Bay"—his open right palm indicated the bay, and the heads of the crowd turned to it as if they'd never seen it before—"with the turquoise blue of the Atlantic." This sight was less familiar to the residents of Miami, and the sight of the ocean going on and on, joining them to the waters of the world, inspired awe.

"What a thing it is to await the force of nature to come," the mayor continued. "This meeting of ocean and bay will occur with a tumultuous roar; it will be cataclysmic. The heavens themselves will herald the event with claps of thunder as monumental as those that must have torn the sky when Moses parted the Red Sea."

The sky, in fact, showed no signs of this, but remained as milky blue-white as on any other humid day in July. An eye was kept on a promising cloud, though, as if it were merely waiting its cue to be coordinated with the promised heave and thrust of the steam dredge and the movement of the bay, whose flow people now interpreted as a desire to meet its ocean counterpart.

A few women Clara knew from the Ladies' Aid Society burst into tears at the mayor's inspirational words, and their husbands, comforting them with reassuring pats, seemed moved near to tears themselves. Clara thought that, in its way, this coming moment was every bit as significant as the moment years before when the first train had steamed into Miami.

The dredge, looking like a great prehistoric beast of iron and wood, with pulleys and chains and metal teeth, was ready to begin. The thirty-five hundred citizens were advised by the digging crew to open their parasols or stand back if they didn't want to be covered in wet sand. With a great groaning creak and a metallic retort sharp as a pistol shot, the dredge was fired up. There was a relieved smattering of applause from the crowd, as by parents for a child who has recited as rehearsed.

In moments the hammering thrust of the dredge was as steady as a heartbeat, and the fine sand spray glistened in the sun as a shower of snow. Bets were taken as to how many thrusts it would take, how many hours, how high a pile of sand it would build before the waters commingled.

As the dredge continued its work, the mayor and the chairman of the board of trade walked the periphery of the crowd, accepting congratulations. They shook Clara's hand, muttering about her being the Founding Mother and how a statue of her ought to be put up in some prominent place.

"This an election year?" McLeod asked him, and the mayor laughed nervously and congratulated McLeod, whom he'd never met, before he continued on his way.

"A deep-water port and access into the ocean!" Clara said, in awe herself now that it was actually about to become a reality. "Think of it, Quentin! No more being a slave to the F.E.S. Make Miami a port city and break the railroad's monopoly once and for all."

McLeod shook his head. "Poor thing."

Clara laughed. "You mean 'poor Wheeler.' "

"I mean poor Miami."

"You're as excited about it as I am, admit it," she said.

"Sometimes I wonder why we didn't just leave things like they was," McLeod replied. "Sometimes I wish I could wake up and find the whole city sucked back into the jungle and all of it just like it was when I first got here."

"Now you're being sentimental, and I don't believe you even mean it."

McLeod sighed. "Well, what's done's done, I guess. Can't control things every time they take a turn you don't like." He looked at Clara. "But I wouldn't go feeling sorry for Wheeler just yet. A man like that don't get to be a man like that by being pitied. It suits him to let this channel happen, and when it suits him to blow you out of the water, Clara, he'll do that too."

"I'm not such an easy target," she replied. "Both of us developed the town. Everyone knows that."

"Everyone!" McLeod exclaimed. "Everyone? Oh, honey, I know the mayor just called you the Founding Mother, but look around you. How many of these people do you actually know? How many of 'em actually know you? To them you're nobody 'cept a name on a street sign."

"Well, you may be content to be a relic of the old days, but—" She stopped and looked at him. "I'm sorry," she said and began again. "But I want to make you see it as I see it. Miami's got a real future now with the harbor deepened and the new docks and this connection to the Atlantic. We were here since the beginning. We can't turn away from it now, just when it's ready to take off. Why, you could have a fleet of boats. You could—"

"I don't want a fleet of boats!" He laughed. "I'm just a fisherman with an hourly rate and rods to rent and I like it fine like that."

Clara smiled and took his arm. "Now we both know you are being overly modest." She felt him stiffen and draw away from her.

"That's what you think I am?"

"No," she said, suddenly angry, and pulled her arm away. "I think you're trying to force me into some kind of choice and at the worst possible time!"

"You made your choice, Clara," McLeod said. "You made it a long time ago."

Her anger left her as soon as she saw the sadness on his face. "No, Quentin. No. I . . ."

He looked out at the bay. "I don't know, Clara. Maybe you're right. Maybe I am a relic of the past."

"If you're one, I'm one too."

He looked at her and then at the crowd watching the steam dredge. "No, darlin'. That's one thing you're not."

"But—"

There was the sudden sickening sound of grinding metal. The dredge had stalled, and though its operator struggled with its gears, the great beast stopped pumping and, with a staggered series of grunts and gasps, died. The silence was total. The crowd seemed to be holding its breath as its eyes moved from the machine itself to the five-foot expanse of sand that still separated bay from ocean. Five feet! The mayor, standing near Clara and McLeod, and only a moment ago proud and chesty as a bantam cock, was suddenly deflated, paralyzed with confusion; the ceremonial shovel with which he'd thrown the first clump of sand dropped from his grasp.

Clara was never to question what drove her to do what next she

did—though McLeod had an answer as soon as he saw her do it—
but she rushed forward, grabbed the mayor's shovel, and started digging where the dredge had stopped. The crowd, for a moment as
paralyzed as the mayor, now came to life. Men tossed hats and coats
aside and dropped to their knees to dig with their hands; women lifted
their skirts above the ankle and kicked the sand with their feet. The
roars of laughter and excitement seemed to fill the sky, and not ten
minutes later, amid warning shouts and cries, the crowd stood back,
exhausted, covered with sand and grime, soaked and filthy, tremulous,
and watched the first tiny beads of bay water inch past the toes of
their shoes toward the ocean.

They held their breaths. The first drop of bay water to touch the
ocean water produced in the crowd a gasp that might indeed have
come from the sky itself. Clara was pulled back out of the water's path,
spade still clasped tightly in her hand. The crew of auxiliary diggers
took over. Minutes passed, sand flying, and the width of the stream
increased until the bay water was actually pouring into the ocean. The
crowd moved back farther from the advance, and then the water suddenly breached the barrier and gushed with incredible force, drench-
ing those in the front up to their knees. Two of the diggers were
knocked off their feet, flailing wildly for safety they didn't find till a
rowboat picked them up two hundred yards out to sea. The crowd
gathered around Clara, offering congratulations. She heard her name
being passed from stranger to stranger. Elliot Iverson wanted an exclusive interview for *The Metropolis,* photographers took her picture
holding the spade, reenacting the moment she grabbed it, shaking
hands with the mayor, digging, smiling, waving to the crowd, and all
the while she kept her eye on the waters widening the channel.

At the end of the day it measured five hundred feet across, and
already half the boats in the bay had made the journey through just
to say they had. The port city of Miami had become joined to the
oceans of the world. Clara was taken back to Miami on the mayor's
schooner. McLeod and the *Starfish* were nowhere to be seen.

26.

The home Clara had made for herself had been added to over the years and now sprawled across the yard inside the walls of Fort Dallas. The stucco had been colored with a solution of whitewash and terra cotta so that the whole glowed the pink of a baby's blush in the sun; hibiscus climbed around the doors and windows and oleander spilled off the roof and along the fort walls.

Edmund tended the flourishing garden, and each of Geneva's meals was blessed with the bounty of Dr. Tiger's seeds: peas and beans, eggplant and okra, golden squash blossoms and scarlet tomatoes. Though Clara still occasionally found Geneva staring out to sea, pining for her island home, Edmund was usually in song, his eyes lifted to the sky in praise of God or bowed to a flower, thankful all the time.

When only Clara and Harry had lived there, a second floor was put on; when Maria moved in and had Cam, a separate wing was attached and a second floor added to that too. The old enlisted men's quarters on the north side of the yard was turned into a storage area, housing a few pictures, rugs, and pieces of furniture from the house on E Street in Middleton and what was salvaged after the hurricane from her parents' old house on the bay. The wide expanse of the yard itself was planted with patches of periwinkle and mimosa in addition to the vegetables, and shade trees and climbing vines shaded stone benches along winding paths of crushed coral. Bougainvillea and clipped Spanish moss dripped over the fort walls; just over the western side a clapboard house was built for Edmund and Geneva and the children they now produced every April with clockwork regularity. "Edmund want all our babies born in the sign of the Ram," Geneva told Clara. "So they be hard-headed like he." If it was up to him alone they would have had more, but Geneva put her foot down at five. Clara was glad they had as many as they did; Fort Dallas would have been a lonely place without them once Harry and his family moved to their own place on Northeast Second Street.

When Maria and Cam visited Clara, which they did punctually every Thursday and Sunday, like the only heirs of a wealthy ailing spinster, they usually came alone. "Harry says he's sorry. He's at the groves," Maria would tell her with a pause before *says*. Or, "Harry's back's bothering him." Pause. "Supposedly." Just when Clara thought that Harry had overstepped even her own patience with this pointedly insulting behavior, and that the hurt she'd done him didn't warrant this much punishment, Harry would show up with Maria on his arm. On one of these occasions, he was drunk.

"H'lo, Mother." He kissed her cheek—the smell of whiskey came with it—then looked her right in the eye as if daring her to call him to accounts.

They ate lunch at a table set up under an oak tree in the garden. Maria, on this rare occasion of his presence, clung to Harry and cooed sweet words to him all through the meal, even though she felt his body grow rigid when she pressed herself to his side.

"You left a little tiny speck of shave soap, honey. Here, let me . . ." She licked her little finger and rubbed it in circles on Harry's earlobe, smiling, giggling, then leaned back in triumph and looked at Clara as if she'd proved their intimacy.

Clara noted that Maria seemed to have forgotten how once she had poured out her litany of complaints about Harry; that outburst probably had been what was necessary at the time to suit her ends. Much as Clara might have liked to believe in the current image, she had gotten to know Maria too well and had never had much faith in Harry's capacity for charade; whether he wanted it to be or not, whether he spoke it or not, the truth was written on his face.

When his father was present, Cam seemed to want to be away from both of them, despite his mother's cooing commands. "My boy's so shy," Maria would say until she had cajoled Cam to her side. He ate quietly, alert for the sound of tension in his mother's voice, impatience in his father's. Clara often noticed him eating in silence, spoon poised in midair as he kept secret watch on both of them. Oh those eyes, Clara thought when she watched Cam watching Harry; how they judged. And what did they really see? When Clara looked at Harry, all she saw was how the sorrow in his heart was etched on his face, how it had erased his youth and added heaviness to his body, had shortened his temper and eaten away at the lightness and charm that had characterized him in the years before he married Maria. She feared that Cam only saw an angry, disappointed man who kept him at arm's length.

The boy seemed to take his mother's constant offhand praise and shows of affection for granted, but let his father carelessly smile on him and how he blushed and fidgeted. He didn't dare approach Harry at those moments, but rather lingered by his mother, though in fact he seemed as unconscious of her as she was of him.

During each of these visits, Maria would take Cam by the hand and, on one pretext or another, contrive to leave Harry and Clara alone. It was her hope that some magical reconciliation would be accomplished while she was gone and that when she returned her own life would have been altered without her having had to do more than cleverly arrange the meeting. On this occasion, armed with a huge net, she took Cam to prowl the garden in search of butterflies.

Clara and Harry sat in silence at opposite sides of the lunch table. A spray of purple orchids in water had wilted in the heat. The sun coming through the leaves above them made the whole table top shimmer as if it were underwater. Flies buzzed over the remains of fried pompano and Cam's half-eaten slice of huckleberry pie. In the near distance was the plaintive sound of Edmund picking out a tune on his mandolin. Harry had loosened his collar and leaned one arm on the table, the other he tossed over the back of the chair. An unlit cigarette dangled forgotten between his fingers. Clara folded and unfolded her napkin, breathed deeply of the air fragrant with mimosa, looked at Harry, and hoped, like Maria, that something magical would happen between them.

"Harry?"

He hesitated before responding, as if weighing whether or not to respond at all. "Yes, Mother?" His voice was cheerful but flat. He stared at his hand lying on the table.

"How are things at the groves?"

"Wonderful."

"I see that prices of seedlings are up."

"Mmm."

"The new freight rates should help offset that."

"Yes."

She was dismayed by the speed with which he flung the answers in her face, each a slap that said, Take that! And that! But to look at him, to see the pain and true weariness of his expression, melted her anger. "Are you working too hard?"

"No."

"You don't look well." He looked up at her with a slight smile on his lips, as if it gave him satisfaction to look this way. Rebuffed yet again, Clara persisted. "Is there anything you need? At home, I mean."

"No."

Oh, these words, these words! she thought. He said all was well yet the very blandness of his manner—his face taut, his eyes red-rimmed, evasive—showed her an image of a man drowning and at the same time flaunting his refusal of all offers of help. "Harry, won't you talk to me?"

He shrugged. "But we are talking."

Her patience suddenly worn out, she threw her napkin down and stood up. "Are you often drunk in the middle of a Sunday afternoon or just when you come to see me?"

Harry picked up his tea and sipped. "Don't you like my visits?"

Clara slumped against her chair. "Oh, Harry . . ."

He looked up at her with a sweet smile. "Yes, Mother?" His duty completed in this short Sunday afternoon visit, he wouldn't reappear for a month or more, but the regular visits of his wife and son continued.

How differently Cam behaved when he and his mother came without Harry. Though there was always a sense of watchfulness about him,

Cam usually ran right out of his mother's grip, across the yard and through the high wooden doors to find Edmund and Geneva's children, his playmates. Before each visit was over, though, Maria made sure that the child spent enough time with Clara so his grandmother wouldn't feel neglected. Sit with Grandy, the child was told. Give Grandy a kiss. Tell Grandy what a pretty dress.

Cam was always well behaved and neatly dressed; his disposition was equable and there was even a sweetness about him, but Clara felt there was never enough time to make a careful study of him. Though she noticed little things—that he was shy, wary, skeptical of everyone, even of her, that he only half listened to his mother's words and wouldn't let his father know he heard him at all—he seemed somehow an abstraction, an idea of a grandson and not anyone she really yet knew. Clara felt, in fact, that she could not know him, that everyone apart from his parents remained alien to this boy.

Clara was well aware of how Maria handled her, using Cam as the sweetener when a favor was about to be asked, and thought sometimes that Cam, whom his mother ignored but for the automatic caress, the rote words of affection, noticed it too.

As far as the Miami Hotel was concerned, there seemed no end in sight to the improvements that needed to be made, despite its now being open for business. Her daughter-in-law's manipulations were as obvious as the sun, but Clara didn't care; to accede to them seemed a small enough price to pay for the presence of her grandson at her side, his arms around her neck, his lips on her cheek. And if when she closed her eyes and ran her fingers through the curls at the base of his neck she thought of her own lost Harry, what was the harm?

Maria identified Clara's feelings about Cam as envy and let Clara know that if she was dissatisfied with her generosity—the threat implicit in every visit, in every request, in every compliment and kiss— she could turn Cam's mind against her as easily as she could pluck a bougainvillea blossom from the vine.

"I feel so bad for Cam," Maria said some weeks after a visit at which Harry had been present. She looked up at Clara.

"Why is that?" Clara asked, as she knew she must.

Maria sighed. "Well, it just seems that so very many people are coming down here, down to Miami, and buying up all the land right out from under the people it really belongs to."

Clara laughed. "That reminds me of something Harry used to say about the land not belonging to anyone."

Maria sighed. "Oh, Harry." She brushed at a fly that was buzzing at her ear. "I guess we all know that land belongs to the people with the deeds." She glanced at Clara for confirmation; a nod did it. "But don't it seem wrong that any stranger can just waltz in and buy it up right out from under our noses? Oh, it just kills me that my daddy never bought nothing. What's he gonna leave little Cam when he dies? An old wreck of a boat? And poor Cam's growing up, and soon he'll be a man, and even though his parents was pioneers and his grandy's the Founding Mother herself, he won't have nothing. He'll be poor as I was." A sudden course of tears flowed out from behind her dark glasses; Clara was fascinated at Maria's use of those tears. "I'd hate for us to have to go 'way somewheres. But I won't have my little Cam suffering poor. If only he owned some land, some little place he could call his own. He'll be a man soon enough, and . . ."

"But he's only nine years old," Clara said.

"Still . . ."

"Well . . ."

Maria never knew just how close Clara came that day to refusing her, just to see the precise form her revenge would take. But if she tested Maria and the threat proved real, the revenge as crude as she suspected it might be, Clara would have to wait until Cam grew up to find out what he might do on his own. Her hunch was that, as the years passed, he would finally turn that skeptical eye on his mother, if he hadn't already done so, and Clara wanted to be around when that happened. She thought of the stack of land deeds that Harry had refused on his wedding day and saw a neat kind of justice in giving the boy what was rightly his.

"Perhaps I might give Cam a little something to safeguard his future," she said.

Maria feigned surprise. "Oh, I didn't mean that you . . . Well, maybe just a little bit of a safeguard . . ."

When these visits ended and Maria and Cam left, Clara often walked out of the fort doors and into the hammock surrounding the walls of Fort Dallas. The area had come to be known as Fort Dallas Park; as a preserved area of hammock land within the city limits, it was a pastoral reminder of how that mile and a half square of downtown Miami had once looked. Clara and a landscape architect worked on reshaping the park—cutting, trimming, unearthing and replanting, bringing in specimens of exotics from the experimental stations and the Van Lieu Groves—and as streets and houses were developed around it, it had begun to take on the planned look of a real city park.

Clara had begun this project long before Wheeler had been compelled to dedicate Biscayne Park to the citizens, and Fort Dallas Park, though never actually so named or officially put forth as public land, had become itself something of a tourist attraction. When Clara stood in the tower above it half hoping to catch sight of the *Starfish,* she would often see picnickers in city clothes strolling along the paths, swinging wicker lunch baskets, running idle fingers through bushes and branches, kneeling to peer closely at a ring of moss hair fern or reaching up to shiver a shoot of white baby orchids; their cooing delight, their cries for companions to come and see their discovery, always drew a smile of gratification from Clara. Though she did not want the place overrun with guests, she could not, in good conscience, turn any away.

The stone walls still protected the house itself from visitors, yet one day the cowbell at the entrance rang and moments later no less welcome a guest was announced to Clara than F. Morrison Wheeler himself. Before she could tell Geneva that she must have gotten the name wrong—Wheeler, a virtual recluse since the last court case, would never stoop to come here—she peeked through a window curtain and saw him sitting on a stone bench by a bank of lavender in the yard, smoking a cigar.

He rose when she approached. "Charming, Mrs. Reade," he said, gesturing to her flower gardens and the park beyond. "I had no idea you'd added such charming little touches here and there." He puffed a perfect O on the cigar. "Perfectly charming."

They sat and Geneva brought iced lemon water and an abalone shell for an ashtray. Wheeler commented on the scent of mimosa in the air, though he puffed his cigar all the while; on the brightness of the pinkwash on her house, though he shielded his eyes from it; on the twists of the grapevines on the porch columns and the shoots of sun pouring through the lattice, as if she'd ordered them personally from heaven above. Then he turned his attention to Clara herself.

"You're looking quite well too, Mrs. Reade."

Clara sipped her drink. "I feel fine, thank you." She waited, faintly amused at these obvious diversions, for him to get to the point of his visit.

"I have never felt better myself," he replied and ran a newly ringed hand over his still thick white hair. "It's truly amazing how marriage to an amiable woman can calm a man and make him see clearly things that he saw only through a fog before."

"I don't believe I've met your wife," Clara said, and couldn't resist adding, "Of course I've seen her at public functions. She was with you at the dedication of Biscayne Park, wasn't she?"

Wheeler smiled tightly. "I'd like to say that we'll include you at our next dinner party, but I'm afraid that our last dinner party was literally that. Yes, Mrs. Reade. We're . . . moving on."

"Leaving Miami?" Clara exclaimed. "So soon?"

" 'Go south, old man.' That's the current wisdom. We'll be traveling light, as the young people say. I'm only taking one souvenir." He ran a finger under the twin curls of his white mustache. "Would you like to guess what that one thing is? Never mind. I won't prolong the suspense. I'll just tell you." He resettled himself on the bench, flicked the ash from his cigar and looked at her. "I'm taking the railroad. That is, I'm extending it all the way to Key West. We begin laying the tracks at the end of the month. I've been advised against it, of course. Wheeler's Folly, they say. But those opinions mean nothing to me when I think of the tentacular connections to be made. Key West to Cuba! Key West to all of South America! And with the Panama Canal, Key West to the Orient!"

"Don't tell me we've driven you away," Clara said with mock concern. "We didn't mean to hurt your feelings, Mr. Wheeler. We just wanted to even up the sides."

"I never thought of sarcasm as your purview, Mrs. Reade."

"Just protective coloration," Clara replied.

Wheeler grunted and leaned toward her. "Here's what I predict when I extend the railroad to Key West: a huge upsurge in work at the rock quarries, at the supply houses and sawmills in Miami. Sales as never before in the retail stores along Miami Avenue. Employment up. Prices higher than ever. The depot will be a hive of activity as men and material for the new rails are shipped from the north. Business in Miami will boom as never before. Tourism will soar. And then, as the tracks move south, as all the activity passes Miami by, precipitous, inevitable, crushing decline."

Clara swallowed hard. "Miami can survive without the railroad."

"Can it? You're not so sure yourself. I see doubt flooding your eyes."

"If you'll put out that damned cigar—!"

Wheeler smiled and tamped the cigar in the abalone shell. "No more railroad-related jobs means a significant drop in population. And once Miami's lost her status as the terminus for the Florida Eastern Star, tourists will naturally want to stay on the train. Why stop here when they can go to Key West? To Havana? To Caracas, Venezuela? Think of it. Tourism halved. No, quartered; decimated. There goes the economy. And I'm afraid I won't be able to help. As a matter of fact, I'll be needing all my capital to pay for laying the new tracks. I wonder how the Fort Dallas National Bank will fare without my deposits. You see, Mrs. Reade? When the railroad leaves, Miami will become just another whistle-stop on the way to Key West."

Clara leaned away, studying him as if he had been revealed to her for the first time as an alien being. "You'd do all this just because people asked for fair treatment?"

"Fairness is apparently in the hands of the Interstate Commerce Commission." He shrugged. "Oh, don't worry too much, Mrs. Reade. I've no doubt but that some shabby remnants of the city will remain. But not Miami as it is. Not Miami as it might have been."

Clara's hands lay clasped loosely in her lap. She felt extremely calm; the fear would come later. "So you try to destroy Miami because of your pride. Must everything go your way?"

Wheeler scrambled to his feet, furious that she had not yet bowed her head in defeat and despair. "I think I'll dismantle the depot and take it with me too. That's two souvenirs of Miami."

She laughed at the pettiness of this remark. "I had no idea anyone so successful could be so bitter and unhappy."

Red-faced, Wheeler turned away and took several deep breaths. When he turned back to her he had composed himself enough to smile. "I won't insult you by wishing you luck," he said and brushed ashes from his vest. "No. Don't get up." He backed a few steps away from her, reminding himself that he was exiting victorious. "I know the best way out."

Wheeler's prediction seemed like the sour doomsday wishes of an embittered old man rather than the shrewd foresight of a business tycoon. "Of course he wants Miami to fail," Clara told Elliot Iverson. "But we're not going to stop using the railroad. We are simply adding to our options with the deep-water port. No matter how you look at it, though, Wheeler is leaving with his tail between his legs." She stopped to laugh. "Should we have expected his congratulations and best wishes for a swell time of it?"

With the initial work on Government Cut completed—though it would be two long years of impatience before all the dredging made both channel and harbor suitable for deep-water craft—optimism ran high. The extension of the railroad was itself such a Herculean task that the Florida Eastern Star resorted to a national employment drive— the Miami labor force, used to the last man and boy, was woefully inadequate—recruiting men from all over the forty-seven states, offering free transportation and high pay, with scarcely a mention of the dangers that would eventually be encountered with tracks being laid on coral reefs often no wider than the track span itself, with the Atlantic lapping at the eastern shore, the Gulf of Mexico not ten feet away from the western.

When the tracks started construction south, business and employment in Miami took the expected turn up. Citizens saw this as yet another example of how blessed the town was. It's the sun, they said half in jest, as if its rays conferred something like a Midas touch; there would never be an end to its shine or to their good fortune.

Workers came from as far away as Greece—mainly sponge divers— and from Ireland, Italy, and Sweden via the immigrant population in New York. Bells were installed at the docks and the depot that rang at six A.M. to rouse them, and once again Miami was filled with the sounds of construction; it was a familiar, even a comforting sound, for it spoke of activity and profit and growth. The saw mills operated night and day; their work force tripled. With increased demand for lumber, homesteaders sold trees for a pittance, glad to get the land cleared of the useless things and make a couple of bucks in the deal. Living quarters were put up fast and cheap, mainly bunkhouses clustered around a mule lot, a commissary, and a barn with a makeshift medical table to treat the frequent injuries to unskilled laborers working the saws. The rock quarries, commissioned to supply limestone beds for the tracks, never stopped grinding and crushing; Aaron Fine sold paraffin earplugs for the noise and cheap dark glasses to guard against limestone dust and the powerful glare. The Starger Bake Shop kept its ovens fired twenty-four hours a day, making flat bread and hardtack rolls that Kevin, their youngest, delivered in the family mule truck. Food and merchandise suppliers were forever running short, finally contracting with the government to buy in bulk. The depot was busier than ever; with daily shipments coming in on extended freight runs, even the most unskilled worker could find day work loading or unloading.

Some of the imported laborers found the track work too dangerous and demanding—hang the pay, what good's it do you if you're dead or got a hand blown off or gone blind?—and deserted the ranks, only to find themselves homeless and jobless, stranded in Miami. Not that the city itself pleased them either: the Swedes thought it too hot, the Irish too dry, the Italians too flat, olive trees or no. Pretty soon Miami—most particularly the honky-tonks north of the city line—was filled with the unemployed, and violent crimes increased.

The tourists put up with the inconveniences, secretly pleased to be the witnesses to the next great boom in the city that had become famous for them. It was only when the tourists left and the streets emptied some that citizens became aware of a peculiar new sound in the air: silence. The clanging and sawing and blasting and shouting had faded southward. When the tracks reached the vast citrus fields around Homestead, a new depot was hastily erected, and the day came when it was clear that all the activity had not been another blessed boom for their city but the prelude to disaster.

A hundred or so citizens were lined up at the depot—contrary to his threat, Wheeler left it standing—with big welcoming smiles on their faces for the three-eleven postal run from Palm Beach. The train appeared under the usual cloud of steam, clattered toward them, slowed for the curve at Fifteenth Street and then, with a high-pitched toot from the steam whistle, tossed the day's mail onto the platform and passed on through.

The Florida Eastern Star, except for the regular passenger runs at noon and six, no longer stopped at Miami.

The people of the city were as bereft as if deserted by a lover. The remaining workers gathered their few possessions from the bunkhouses and left town too, moving south to the new temporary headquarters of the F.E.S. at Fort Pierce. Even as they saw it happening, people couldn't believe it. Even as the streets emptied and stores closed down at two for lack of customers, they said not here, not in Miami. What they meant was not in paradise, nothing can go that spectacularly wrong here. But it had. Merchants struggled along, wondering what to do with all the stock they'd bought. And the worst was yet to come.

On a morning in February, not three weeks after the Valentine Ball had signaled the end of the best tourist season they'd had yet, the Fort Dallas National Bank didn't open at precisely nine A.M. as it had done punctually five days a week for the past eight years. At ten A.M. Clara joined the short line on the bank steps—the Miami Hotel had to have new linen, according to Maria, and she also needed an extension on the loan—while curious passersby eyed the line nervously. By noon it was official: overextended on the electric streetcar system no one seemed to want to ride and on other investments in various other businesses that were no longer able to pay off, the bank had failed.

The Reade office on Miami Avenue looked as if it had been vandalized: account books sprawled open across the desk, file cabinet drawers had been yanked out and now hung open, gaping, dumb. Clara closed the office door against the street noise and pulled down the shade to block out the late-morning sun, wishing there was something she could do to block out the tumult in her mind. Life went on outside despite the catastrophe. But Clara could not spend yet another day listening to the complaints and woes of other people. It was as if, in her role as Founding Mother, she was not to be allowed to have troubles of her own.

She knew she'd overextended herself but had gotten used to never saying no to a request for help, for advice, or for a loan, and she rarely stumped for repayment, advancing large sums to Maria for the hotel, to the Stargers for their bakery, to Aaron Fine, to Schell's Livery; the list of people who had benefited from her generosity filled her ledger books and file cabinets. She turned back to the room and leaned for a moment against the door; the glass knob jabbed her in the small of her back and she pressed hard, harder, wishing she could scream out with the injustice of it all.

She sat down heavily in the creaking swivel chair behind the desk and turned on the small green-glass-shaded lamp. Contracts, leases, bonds, liens, letters of credit, bank statements—everywhere she looked was the hard evidence that had forced her decision to do what she was about to do to save not only herself but her city.

Yet it was still difficult to believe she had come to this. She added column after column of figures, measured assets against debits, sums owed and sums owing, payments collected and uncollectable; again and again the results appalled her. Try as she did to find an error in her favor, all she found was that her arithmetic was correct to the last few miserable dimes she had and the last outstanding dollars she could not collect. If that was not reassuring, at least it was unarguable.

The office door opened, and for a moment she was blinded by the wide shaft of bright sunlight spilling across the floor and over her desk; she recognized the silhouette of her son and his wife. "Come in and close the door," she said.

Maria held Harry's arm as they came into the office. "Thank you," Maria said. "I appreciate the dark."

Clara was relieved that they hadn't brought Cam. Her comments to them would not be easy to make or to hear and her grandson's presence would only make things harder. Clara knew she ran the risk now of losing the boy—of having Maria remove him from her—but it had become financially ruinous to continue appeasing her daughter-in-law. And if someone had accused Clara of getting the tiniest bit of satisfaction out of finally defying Maria's hold on her, she wouldn't have been able to deny it.

Harry stood in the deepest shadows of the room where the lamplight did not reach. Only his hands, loosely clasped in front of him, were visible. Maria paced slowly about, eyeing the mess of papers with a smile on her face. Everything Clara did in this office interested her; in one way or another, it would all be Cam's someday.

"I was hoping . . ." Clara began, then hesitated. "I was hoping I wouldn't have to tell you this." She indicated the papers on her desk. "That it wouldn't be necessary."

"Oh, you can confide in us," Maria blithely assured her. "Can't she, Harry?"

Harry did not respond. Clara couldn't see his face and wondered if he knew what she was about to tell them. She took a deep breath and let it out slowly. "I'll get right to the point," she said.

"I always think that's best," Maria said.

Clara nodded. "When the Fort Dallas failed, I only got forty percent of my money. I've been over and over these figures. You see, I was already—"

"Oh, you poor dear," Maria said and took a few steps toward her. "We had no idea, did we, Harry?"

"—I was already overextended at the bank," Clara went on. "The only thing I can do now is start to cut my losses."

"You know best," Maria said. " 'Course you got to think of yourself and your loved ones first."

Clara looked to where Harry stood; his hands had clenched into fists. He knows, she thought. He's ready. "I can't continue to support the hotel."

The words hung in the darkened room for a moment. Maria took a step toward the desk. Clara looked up at her; the lamplight lit her from below and the long shadows of her glasses over her forehead made her appear horrified. "I don't understand," she said with a little laugh.

Clara spoke evenly, without emotion or energy. "I can't pay the salaries or the supply costs; I can't pay for any more construction. I can't stock the kitchen. And I can't pay back the bank loan."

Maria glanced over her shoulder at Harry; her voice was icy. "Dear, tell your mother I don't think she's being the least little bit humorous."

Harry's voice came from the shadows. "I think you'd better listen carefully to her."

Maria hesitated, then sank slowly into a straight-backed chair. "I'm listening," she said and took out a handkerchief to wipe her eyes.

"You'll have to close," Clara said.

"Close? The hotel?"

"I'm sorry."

Maria laughed harshly. "You're sorry?" She glanced back at Harry again. "Your mother's sorry." She turned back to Clara. "I'm sorry too, but sorry's not sorry enough!"

"I'm doing the best I can," Clara said. "You're not the only one this has happened to."

"Still just thinking of yourself, huh?" Maria said. "Why don't you foreclose on some of them people who owe money to you?"

"They've been hurt by this too," Clara replied. "I can't extract money where there isn't any."

Maria jumped to her feet. "But I'm your daughter!" she shouted. "I come first! You're supposed to protect me!"

"There's no point arguing this," Clara said. "It has to be done." She picked up the inventory sheets. "The furniture is paid for, so that can be sold. The linens, the kitchen equipment are a total loss. But the books in the library are paid for and can be sold too. I don't know how much we can expect to get, but . . ."

Maria paced in and out of the light, looking from Harry to Clara. "This is some kind of trick the two of you cooked up on me."

"I had nothing to do with it," Harry said.

Maria laughed. Her face in the light was red and shiny with anger. "Like hell you didn't."

"For God's sake," Harry said. "Do you think my mother enjoys doing this?"

"Cutting me off? Ruining me? You bet she enjoys it!" She spun on her heel to face Clara. "Why's it have to come outa my hide? Why don't you sell some of your precious land if you're so desperate for money?"

Clara bristled at the spite in Maria's voice. "I intend to sell some of it," she said quietly.

"Some of it?" Maria said, leaning across the desk, shouting in Clara's face. "But I bet you keep plenty of it too. Meanwhiles I go under right before your very eyes!"

"Stop it!" Harry said and grabbed her arm to pull her away from his mother. "That's enough!"

"Let go of me!" She slapped him across the face, gasped with surprise that she'd done it, then did it again.

Harry pushed her hard, and she stumbled back against the office door. Her dark glasses fell to the floor, and for a horrible moment her burning, streaming eyes glared at them from out of the darkness. "You're killing me," she said in a low guttural voice.

Harry picked up her glasses and handed them to her. "I'll take you home."

She put her glasses on and reached for the doorknob. "I don't want you taking me home," she said and flung open the door. Punishing sunlight washed over her and filled the room; Maria gasped and covered her eyes with her hands. Harry reached for her, but she eluded his grasp and was gone, the door slammed behind her, the room plunged in darkness once again.

Clara could hear Harry breathing hard, could see his hands twitching nervously. She'd gotten so used to his icy indifference that she was surprised. "She'll be . . .," Clara started.

Harry shrugged. "I know what she'll be."

Clara waited a moment, as if the air had been so stirred by Maria that it needed time to settle. She went to one of the open filing cabinets, pulled out a sheaf of papers, and sat down at the desk again. "I've had an offer I want to discuss with you," she said. "To make sure you approve of it."

"You don't need my approval for anything," Harry said.

Clara glanced up at him, then back down to the desk. "I'm considering an offer from a developer—George Washington Haywood's his name—to subdivide Fort Dallas." She ran her hands over the papers, picked one up, determined, despite the rising swell of emotion, to continue with the business at hand, but suddenly tears were spilling down her cheeks. "I should have managed things better," she said. "I should have . . ."

Years of living with Maria had inured Harry to the sight of tears, but he had not seen his mother cry since he was a boy and the sight struck a responsive chord in him. He had once believed that his embrace had the magic to dry her eyes and bring a smile to her face. Now he had a sudden longing —so strong his chest ached with sorrow at the impossibility of it—for the simple faith he'd once had in such a cure. But even the thought of it had the effect—if just for a moment— of lifting the curtain on all that had come between them. He walked the few steps around her desk, put a hand on her shoulder, and pressed his cheek to hers. It took all his strength not to sink to his knees in front of her and bury his face in her lap. "Sell the orange groves instead."

Fresh tears flooded Clara's eyes; the suggested sacrifice of his beloved groves proved him to be the son she had believed she had lost. She put her hand lightly on his; the feel of him next to her was as familiar as if he'd never left her side. "That's the last thing I'd sell, Harry."

"Oh, Mother . . ." Harry turned away. Why now, why, when he was so sure he'd hardened himself against her, did she have to touch him so? He wanted no part of it; any softness in him only brought back the pain of the love he'd lost. He stood up and moved across the room. When he was sure of his voice, he said, "Whatever you think is best."

"Will you come and meet the developer?" Clara asked. "He's coming—"

"I don't want anything to do with it," Harry said. "You just . . . do what you . . . what you have to do."

George Washington Haywood—"My ancestor was father of the country," he was fond of telling people, though this relationship was never documented, "and I aim to be Daddy to Dade County myself"—could not have been more pleased by the bank panic that caused Clara Reade to summon him. "If she wants to talk," he told his assistant as the carriage stopped outside the fort, "she's ready to accept my offer."

He jangled the bells above her great wooden doors and waited, digging his fingernails into the crumbling stone walls, thinking that maybe a pair of columns topped by stone eagles ought to replace these old-fashioned doors as the main entrance. No sooner were they admitted inside by Mrs. Reade herself than Haywood began exclaiming on the virtues of the property.

"The most fascinating spot in the city! Very impressive the way the house is surrounded by fine old tamarinds and mango trees. You can almost smell Miami's history right here." He stopped and made a great show of inhaling and exhaling and, with a pointed glance, making sure his assistant did the same.

"That's a fine picture of a pioneer home, Mrs. Reade. Not luxurious for luxury's sake but sound and sensible and, well, just right." He smiled and touched his hand to his heart. "No matter what happens between us, I hope you'll decide to stay on. Our Founding Mother. Our first citizen."

Clara nodded her appreciation, imagining that there was nothing that would please him less than her continued presence. They walked on through the elaborately planted gardens around the main house, Haywood commenting effusively on each blossom and palm frond and shard of coral. When they reached the far gates that would take them into the park, Clara attempted to stop his soliloquy.

"I already own the place, Mr. Haywood," she said impatiently. "The more you recite the property's virtues, the less chance you have of getting me off it."

"Why, Mrs. Reade!" Haywood sputtered. "I was simply pointing out for my assistant's benefit the glories of the terrain. The bougainvillea draped on the garden walls, for example. Have you ever seen . . ."

His chatter was relentless and Clara stopped listening, paying more attention to the flies buzzing around an overripe pineapple left by a picnicker on an oak bench and the croaking of frogs in the mangroves at the river's edge and wondering which would be harder to do: leave the house altogether or continue to live there and have to watch Fort Dallas Park metamorphose around her into Fort Dallas Estates.

They walked side by side around the park, the assistant a few paces behind them taking notes, Haywood exclaiming with pleasure over the labyrinth of orange and lemon trees, the giant oleanders and hibiscus, the paths lined with coconut trees and banana palms. "My customers want the best of Miami living," he was saying. "They don't care about where the railroad terminal is and how much rock's quarried but about the sensual pleasure of life by the bay. And I wouldn't change a thing in this park; not a twig, not a coconut, not a—" He paused, murmuring to himself. "Have to clear out some of it, naturally. Have to put in roads to each house, of course, since they're all going to have automobiles. Might even want to put in a path or two that lead to the river. Build a few docks while you're at it, but—" He waved his hand as if to dismiss such petty alterations. "I see a great future here, Mrs. Reade. A model of the kind of developments Miami ought to be full of someday. Built with all the respect the natural terrain demands. You never want to let that go. You're a pioneer in this, Mrs.

Reade. The smartest kind of partner a developer like me could hope to have."

Clara knew that with the city's economy in its present precarious condition, Haywood was getting the better of the deal. But she had to sell her majority interest, and she had to do it soon. She could not hear of the coming desecration of her property more than once. To watch Haywood give the park what she could only think of as the once-over, assessing it only in terms of how many trees he'd have to cut down and how many houses put up to generate the most money, hurt her more than she'd imagined it could.

" 'Course Fort Dallas Estates'd be restricted. Can't have some riffraff moving in just because they've got the price of the ticket, so to speak. And private property means none of these tourists traipsing around and leaving their old pineapple rinds anywhere they please. Thought I didn't notice that, eh? I never miss a trick, Mrs. Reade. You'll see." He stopped to inhale again and dug the toe of his shoe in the ground. "Good soil too—I've had it analyzed, you don't mind?—full of veg-etable mold and disintegrated lime. No telling what you could grow. Though I doubt my sort of people're interested in that kind of thing. Might even want to pave whole pieces of it for their automobiles. Macadam roads're all the rage up north. Now, Mrs. Reade. My assistant's got the papers all drawn up, so . . ."

Clara hated his certainty that he'd made a deal on his terms. "Let me explain something to you, Mr. Haywood. It's no secret that I need money. I wouldn't be going into business with you otherwise."

This was the first sign that she'd actually made the final decision to go with him, and Haywood was hard pressed to contain his enthusiasm. "Really?" he murmured. "I had no idea you were in financial straits."

Clara shrugged; the transparence of his professed ignorance didn't matter. "It's public knowledge," she said. "But there's more than just profit involved and I want you to know that."

"Oh, there always is," Haywood agreed. "And I'm sure you've got only the highest motives—"

Clara continued to ignore his cynicism. "What Miami needs now is jobs to keep people here. Construction of Fort Dallas Estates is going to give hundreds of workers employment. Otherwise I wouldn't do it."

Haywood laughed. "Sure I can't talk you into adding Reade Groves to the deal? Give more people work."

"The groves? No. Never."

"Never say never," Haywood advised. "You thought you weren't going to subdivide Fort Dallas once upon a time, didn't you? You did the smart thing, though. That's why people look up to you."

They'd made their way to the front porch of the house, where Haywood's assistant set the papers out for her. Clara sat down in an old wicker chair and looked them over; with minor changes, they were identical to the ones she'd already spent days studying. The papers were dappled with the sun coming through the climbing hibiscus; for a moment, the print swam before her eyes.

"Have you taken the Grand Tour yet, Mrs. Reade?" Haywood asked. "A woman of your accomplishment oughtn't to hide herself in this backwater. They're crazy about Americans in Paris. With a couple of gowns from Patou and a few choice gems, you might just be able to buy yourself a baron. Think about it."

Clara saw Edmund and Geneva and their children on the far side of the yard, all dressed in their Sunday whites, in the shade of the high branches of an ancient oak, watching her. She could almost hear a long sorrowful sigh as she picked up the pen.

"No," she said to Haywood. "I'm staying." She scratched her name on the contracts.

After he'd gone, she went back inside. The house was quiet. Only the palm fronds brushing against the roof and the sharp whistle of a redwing broke the silence. She walked through the rooms and without thinking found herself climbing the stairs to the tower. The breeze was fresh and cool today, scented with mimosa and oranges. She sat on the bench and looked out over Fort Dallas Park and just beyond it to the city.

Oh, how she had looked forward to the town growing and becoming its own entity. And she knew—she could trace it step by step—exactly to what degree she was responsible. She knew that the moment she had sent an orange blossom to F. Morrison Wheeler she had set off a chain of events that made the division of Fort Dallas an inevitability.

My city, she thought, and then she thought, no. McLeod was right. She would be nobody particular to the new people but a name on a street sign or the lady who lived in that big house in Fort Dallas Estates or someone in an old copy of *The Metropolis* called the Founding Mother. But wait, some new arrival was bound to say, nobody actually founded Miami; it was always just here, wasn't it?

For a long, sad moment she stared at the city spread out below her. And like a mother who pines for her child's infancy even as she glows with pride at its assumption of adulthood, she missed the wild thing it had been.

27.

When the Miami Hotel was forced to close (it became first a boarding house, later a hospital for veterans of the Great War), Maria salvaged enough from her stock of unearthed Seminole artifacts to open a small gift shop on the corner of Wheeler and Twenty-fourth Street. Cameron was twelve years old at the time and saw immediately that the act of starting up the business had depleted his mother's resources; he would have to take charge himself. Her eyesight had worsened; before she left the house for the streets, she put on not only her dark glasses but a sunbonnet and a heavy black veil and she carried a parasol. Cameron drove the rig—at first sitting on a stack of cushions for which he outgrew the need over the next two years—ignoring the stares of the curious and the hoots of his schoolmates. He helped his mother from the rig to the shop, was in charge of the keys, the sweeping up, the dusting. He set up the stock so she could find things by touch and arranged for periodic visits by the neighboring storekeeper, Mrs. Davis, until he returned from school.

Reade's Gifts and Souvenirs was not close enough to the bustling downtown section to benefit either from the regular window shoppers or the guests at the Royal Palm and Halcyon hotels, and it was a little too close to North Miami and Colored Town to attract respectable locals. But the Eighteenth Street steamer docks serving Key West weren't too far away, and a few decent guest houses had sprung up along Wheeler Avenue to furnish a slow but steady stream of traffic.

They got by. To replenish the stock, Maria struck up business relationships with some of the Seminoles who traded in town on Sundays, buying from them bead and metalwork and alligator skins, which Cam added to the crockery and arrowheads and semiprecious stones unearthed from the burial mound. The skeletons were not on display in the shop; his mother had gotten offers from private collectors and from a museum in St. Augustine, but she decided to reserve them for the time when they'd bring the highest price.

"Ghoulish," Cam said.

"Squeamish," his mother replied with a laugh that always made Cameron shiver, as if she had something wicked in store for someone; it could only be one person.

Not long after they had opened for business, Harry came into the shop. Maria, kneeling on the floor behind the counter searching for a particular piece of pottery, rose to her feet when she heard the familiar voice, took off her apron, and adjusted the expression on her face. Cam watched his father for some sign of recognition of these efforts and saw a familiar, resigned smile, as if he had been reminded of something he'd almost forgotten.

Maria's shoulders sagged. Each time she and Harry came into each other's presence, all they seemed to see was what wasn't there. "Visiting royalty," she murmured to Cam, loud enough for Harry to hear.

Cam shrugged; the older he got, the more detached he contrived to appear, and once he'd got that guise down pat, he was able to see them more clearly for what they were. That his mother used him— as sounding board and companion, weapon and insurance policy against the future—had been apparent to him for years. It never ceased to amaze him now how little credit for intelligence she gave him. Didn't she know that he could see what she was up to? At a certain point he had come to see that nothing really took place in the present between his mother and father, that all their emotions were connected to things that had happened in the past, things unknowable, irrelevant, dead.

Cam and Maria both watched Harry now as he made a slow circuit of the shop, touching this or that object, running his hands lightly over others. His interest seemed both to please and bother his mother, Cam noticed; she was humming to herself and tapping her fingers on the glass display case.

Harry had made a complete circle of the shop and was back at the door, about to leave, when an object caught his eyes: a mat woven out of Everglades saw grass. Maria approached and shaded her eyes against the light from the street.

"Pretty, isn't it?"

"Yes," Harry replied, his eyes fixed on it, his fingers hovering over it as if afraid to light down.

"Never seen one just like it," Maria said. "You?" Harry shook his head. "Cam bought it off some Indian gal outside the Presbyterian church."

Harry turned and looked at Cam. Cam, idly spelling his name in dust on the glass countertop, stopped and looked up, but his sly smile froze on his face: he was shocked at the transformation in his father. He looked young as a boy and as if he were about to burst into tears or laughter, his lips half-parted, his eyes wide; but the eyes weren't young, they were old, old and filled with sorrow. Cam had been hanging on to these small expressions all his life, signs that his father saw him, really saw him; a smile, a frown, a joke were moments he treasured and feared would never come again. And now he was astonished to see that his father wanted something of him. But what? What am I supposed to do?

"Cam'll wrap it up for you," his mother said.

Fingers trembling, clumsy, Cam rolled the mat in brown paper and tied it with a string. His heart beat faster; so intense was his father's stare he dared not look at him when he handed him the package.

"Thank you." Harry pressed a dollar into his hand—his touch was like fire!—and moved toward the door with the package in his arms.

Maria seemed delighted with the transaction, as if finally Harry had behaved as she hoped he would. "Plenty more where that came from!" she called out after him. "You know them Indians better'n I do!"

After that, though Cam occasionally caught a glimpse of him riding quickly down Wheeler Avenue past the shop, his father never came inside again. The visit haunted him; he began to think of his father differently than he ever had. As soon as he had thought that things were settled, that he knew everything about him, his father had revealed something new, and Cameron suddenly felt frightened. The balance had shifted: it was his father who suffered, and somehow it was his mother's doing! Cameron was not a boy who gave free rein to his imagination, nor did he have much of a natural feel for interpreting people's behavior; he needed facts, direct observations, experiences.

When Harry was at the house on Northeast Second Street—he spent several nights a week in a cabin at the groves—the air was thick with unspoken recriminations. Certain words spoken by Maria were enough to set off explosions of deliberate, damning silences: words like "your mother," "that Indian," "shame," "disgrace." Cam had become curious about his father's quiet sadness on these occasions, and now, after his visit to the shop, a door had opened on the secret of this sadness and Cam was helpless to do anything but walk through. All he could see was the mute plea in his father's face.

And so on Wednesdays when his mother closed the shop early, in the evenings after dinner when she lay in the hammock on the back porch with the shades drawn, drowsy with her lemon tea and whiskey, on Saturday all day, on Sunday before and after church, Cameron followed him. The first time Cameron went to the groves, he took the original mule path instead of the new paved road; as he walked he tried to formulate a plan.

When he got to the groves, he walked down aisle after aisle toward the sound of men's voices and, when he found the source, hid himself behind a tree. The harvesting crew was at work atop a series of ladders, each with a burlap sack slung over his shoulder, reaching deep into the waxy green foliage for the fruit, plucking it—sometimes so hard both tree and ladder shook—then dropping it into the sack. A two-mule truck moved slowly down the aisle, and the crew emptied the full sacks in its back. Next to the truck, almost as high as the men on the ladders, was his father astride a horse. He was talking animatedly to the mule truck driver, calling out to the men on the

372   · BISCAYNE ·

ladders, wiping sweat from his face with the back of a suntanned, muscled arm.

Cameron scrambled to a tree that had already been picked over and squatted down at the base. Watching with no possibility of being seen, Cam felt as if he'd never really taken a good look at his father: the comfortable way he sat in the saddle, the ease in putting on his hat and adjusting it to the back of his head, the looseness of movement. Absent from his face were the lines of tension and the hard, thin set of the mouth. The eyes were wide open even in the sun, and he laughed as a picker tossed him a bright golden orange and caught it by rising slightly from the saddle and extending his arm just the right distance, like he must have done a thousand times before. I resemble him, Cameron thought, even though his mother had always said he looked only like her, and knew all at once what his grandmother saw when she looked at him.

He wanted to grab his father by his shirt front and demand an explanation, for both the look of sorrow in the shop that day and for this new look of pleasure, but he remained in hiding, not shy so much as instinctively sure that his father would be unable to tell him anything, that in fact, if he wanted to know anything, he would have to figure it out for himself.

Curiosity drove him; once he knew the answer there would be plenty of time to know what he ought to do.

He looked forward to these times with his father, came to think of them as time spent together; he wished his father would only do the same for him, watch him in secret, learn about him, know him. He realized that he had always taken his father at face value, believing that what he saw was all there was, but now, hiding, observing, he began to see that there was more to know and that his father was, perhaps, knowable.

He was thrilled at the prospect of the exposure of some hidden knowledge, something that might cause in him an explosion of feelings. The search gave a shape to his days. Curiosity became hunger. Though at the start it was enough just to have seen that look of sorrow and wanting, now that was merely a detail. He wanted reasons, explanations, solutions, and something else . . . It was hardly a surprise at all to trail his father to North Miami and watch him make the circuit of saloons, get drunk, drunker, until he passed out in an alley and slept there. It wasn't enough to see him stand at the Miami River rapids and stare out toward the Everglades. What was he looking for? Why was his gaze so steady, his eyes so sad?

He put the search aside finally, knowing his father's habits and nothing more. He never spoke to him, never suggested that he knew something; he felt, in truth, that he knew nothing. But the curiosity and the fear would not be put to rest. Someday, Cam thought. Someday he will come to me and I will know him.

For most of the next few years, Cam and his mother sat side by side in the narrow dusty store that forever smelled of the camphor dust in which the Seminole artifacts had been stored. She'd taken to splashing whiskey regularly in the tea and lemon she sipped all afternoon— "It takes the sting off these poor eyes"—and would spin out her plans for Cameron's future while Cam himself worked on his lessons, biding his time, murmuring dutifully whenever she asked if he could see the future ahead as clearly as she could.

"You're going to be the richest man in town. You're going to show everybody who ever slighted me just who you are and just what you're going to do about it. I don't regret a thing, though. I loved your father when I married him, curse his soul, so I'm pure. I'm only sorry I ever gave you that name. What a mistake! And you know why? He hated his father, that's why. That's the great joke of it all. Hated him. Held him in his arms as he was dying and hated him every second. What kind of man is that, hates his father, I ask? No wonder he treats his own kin the way he does. Broke his mother's heart too—that's if she even had a heart to begin with, which I doubt seeing's how she threw me out in the street. OK, OK. After all, I took her precious baby boy, didn't I? I s'pose from her point of view, I can't be punished enough for that. But to throw out her sweet darling grandson, who only loved his grandy—that's something I never bargained on. Oh, that is one mean old lady, I tell you. Hated her own husband, and from all I ever heard he was a fine upstanding man of business and rich as God and gave her everything, and what was there to hate? And look at me! Left with nothing but a little store and some junk from those stinking Indians! I tell you, honey boy, you are my salvation. Oh, when I think of what you're going to be. The richest man in town . . ."

By the time sunset came, the tears were flowing unchecked, and

Cam, as he had done many times before, pulled the shade down on the door and turned the Closed sign to the street. No one bought beadwork from a sobbing woman. Will these tears ever end? Cam wondered, staring out the window. When will the day come when I may turn my back?

The project of converting Fort Dallas Park into Fort Dallas Estates wound up giving work to several hundred men clearing the land, digging irrigation ditches, working the dormant lumber mills, planting, sodding, moving, building the houses and docks themselves. Although neither Clara nor anyone else could have known it at the time, the Fort Dallas Estates subdivision not only saved the city the loss of a good part of its working population but paved the way for the next wave of Miami's development. In a neat irony lost on no one, her actions ultimately required the Florida Eastern Star to reschedule their freight service back into Miami; Wheeler was defeated by Clara Reade once again.

The transformation of Fort Dallas Park was accomplished with the speed and efficiency that was coming to characterize all the building done in Miami. If Clara was unhappy about the breakup of her park, she did not show it. She made a large enough profit eventually to pay back her creditors and, with the retention of a certain percentage of shares in the estates corporation, had even managed to exercise some control over the way the subdivision was carried out. She told Mr. Haywood that if Fort Dallas Estates was going to be the view from her tower, it damn well better be a pleasant one.

The first house was built on the largest lot on the riverfront and took four years to complete because the reclusive owner, a self-made millionaire in Brazilian rubber, insisted it be made of oolitic limestone on the outside and mahogany on the inside. Later residents were not quite so particular. In quick succession came a wealthy widow from Maine with severe asthma, whose wheezing kept the birds from coming closer than a hundred yards of her; a plumbing contractor and his family; Dr. MacKenzie and his wife, though he kept his Miami Avenue office; three retired bachelor brothers; and a theatrical producer from New York, who used his cottage only during the winter.

The estates were still separated from Clara's house by the fort walls and from the town by deep rows of pine trees. The only entrance was at the end of Avenue C, marked by fluted columns of Lanctot limestone. There was an aura of exclusivity to the little community that other developers imitated in the new subdivisions that sprang up outside the city: Riverside Heights, Miramar, Biltmore, Grove Park.

Years earlier, on the morning of Cam's ninth birthday, Clara had sent a carriage for him. Maria had dressed him with great diligence; she herself was not to be the recipient of Clara's largesse, and she wanted to be sure that if Cam was, he looked the part. It was always simpler for Cam to submit at these times and to keep his thoughts private than to engage his mother with his differences and be subjected to her tears. He was not a calculating or devious child, but he did seem to have the knack for knowing what was expected and what would get him his heart's desires. When in doubt, he held his tongue; when sure, he often did the same. He was a model boy, as well he knew, and would have done any mother proud, yet his behavior had more than once brought out his mother's rage.

"You're just like your father! You're too quiet! Oh, talk to me, Cammy. Honey, talk to me." Tears, tears, tears, Cam thought even then, dutifully patting her shoulder, wishing he could be gone.

Clara had welcomed Cam that birthday afternoon in the garden; behind her, Geneva was coming out of the house holding a small coconut cake. They ate alone, the old woman and the young boy, at a glass-topped table in the shade of a giant oak. Cam thought of his grandmother as old though she was just a bit over fifty at the time. But Cam was less interested that day in his grandmother than in the tray she had placed in the center of the table. Some great bulge of paper poked out from under a bulky white napkin; finally Clara removed the napkin to reveal a stack of papers tied with a blue ribbon that barely concealed the thick rubber band beneath.

"Do you know what a deed is?" she asked.

Cam looked carefully at her; unlike his mother, she actually seemed to be listening for an answer. "It has to do with owning things," he said.

She smiled and he saw he'd done right. "That's very good," she said. "A deed means that you own property, that the property belongs to you, that you can do with it whatever you like." She undid the ribbon and pointed to the top piece of paper. Cam had had his fill of cake;

Clara slid the paper toward him. He took the paper in his hand. Clara was not smiling now but had an expectant, concentrated look, as if extremely curious to see his response.

"Do you see whose name is printed there?"

Cam knew but pleased her by looking again. "Cameron Reade," he said.

"Happy birthday, Cameron Reade. You're a landowner."

Riding in the carriage that took him back home Cam had felt he had crossed a threshold, that in a way he did not fully comprehend, he held in his lap the passport to his destiny. His grandmother was the only person in his life who did not appear to want something from him, who only wanted to give him things.

Maria had gone through the deeds quickly, her breathing shallow, then went through them again. After the third time, she fell back onto the sofa.

"Do you know what these are?"

"Deeds," Cam replied proudly.

"Deeds. Yes. Your generous grandmother has given you a hundred acres of wetland! A hundred acres of that miserable Everglades muck! That's what your generous grandmother's given you!"

Cam could see her eyeing the deeds as if about to rip them to shreds; he took them from her and held them to his chest.

"Wetlands! She's trying to unload her waste products on you!"

As time passed, relations between Cam and Clara became the least complicated and the most satisfying of any Cam had known. He sensed that her liking for him was inextricably linked to his father, and it pleased and comforted him to know that he was part of a line of succession, a link in a chain that went on and on and not some aberration of his mother's overwrought imagination.

On his tenth birthday his grandmother gave him the deed to two hundred acres more of wetland farther north and forty acres of adjoining hammock, and so on and so on, through all the birthdays and Christmases of his childhood, the parcels of land held in trust until his twenty-first birthday.

The giving of them, although regular and set, never lost its air of occasion and that was due both to Clara's sense of ceremony and Cam's gratitude. Each gift meant more than land; each gift bound them to each other as far into the future as they could see.

28.

Land sales in the city picked up in volume. People who'd bought lots early and built houses on them now sold off parts of their yards for double and triple what they paid for the whole piece just three years before. The new owners built on their smaller lots and pretty soon there were whole streets with big houses and no yards at all. The Stargers, their bakery in debt when the bank failed, sold all their street frontage property but for a piece the width of their house. Now they were so crowded in on both sides, they could lean out the window to water their neighbors' potted geraniums.

Complacency was unknown in Miami. If there was one fact everyone agreed upon, it was that this was a city in the making, not yet finished, not by a long shot. Though it had nearly everything a city ought to have, there was still the sense that nearly everything about it remained to be seen. Its history had barely begun to be written, its society yet to be established. There was as yet no small-city tradition for newcomers to fall in with, unless you counted optimism as a tradition and maybe it was.

Lord knows everyone who came to Miami was optimistic. Why, the very thing that Carlisle de Beaupré, architect for the Royal Palm Hotel, had once found so depressing about the terrain—its endless flatness unrelieved by hill or valley—was what would make possible the tentacular spread that lay just over the horizon line of Miami's future. Few people in Miami accepted such limits as geography did seem to impose on the future of the city, and Clara found herself agreeing with the general grumbling: yes, Miami has great weather; yes, the tourist population's on the upswing again, but once the land's all used up, that's that, isn't it? Clara and the others found this conclusion pretty hard to swallow, especially in light of what was sitting right to the west of the city: that damned stretch of—well, it wasn't exactly land, now was it?—the Everglades.

If you looked at it from the tourist tower at Musa Isle, though, it did sort of look like land: dense growths of cypress, Spanish laurel, and swamp myrtle watched over by bald eagles and ospreys and pelicans, smelling sweet as roses and milk, an endless prairie of luxuriant green and gold grass, just broken up a little here and there by silvery black patches of—they had to face it—open water.

The Everglades, as well Clara and everyone else knew or were told soon enough, was, in fact, more like a lake than land: fifty miles wide and two hundred and fifty miles long. But it was also less like a lake and more like a river in that it flowed. And it wasn't actually much like either of them when you considered the fact that it was only six inches deep.

In the gubernatorial election that year, Napoleon Broward struck just the right campaign note when he made the drainage of the Everglades his chief issue: all you do is dig out a series of canals from the swampland to the bay, open the sluices, and let 'er flow! As soon as Broward took office, the state's Internal Improvement Board offered the citizens of Miami the land along the proposed drainage canal at two dollars an acre to raise money for the dredge. When that was raised, a canal would be started at the rapids of the Miami River.

The publicity given the canal resulted in a score of realty dealers coming into Miami and speculating in hundreds of thousands of acres deep in the Everglades at a dollar and a quarter an acre, on the theory that once the draining began, all the 'glades would become habitable land. To promote their project to the public, they advertised heavily in Florida and in the Northern states that traditionally sent the most tourists. When the curious came down, the realtors hired steam launches stocked with picnic baskets and took prospective buyers on boat rides to see the 'glades firsthand. People unfamiliar with the area were treated to such exotic local sights as thick mangroves reaching out from the banks, alligators swimming in the shallows, and long-legged water birds clumsily taking flight at the sound of the launch.

The river forked at Tiger Creek, and the boat docked at a piece of land between the branches—Musa Isle—where an observation tower had been built. Any farther, the realtor explained as they disembarked, and the boat would be at the famed Miami River rapids, a phenomenon created by the excess water from the Everglades gurgling through a natural rocky gorge. Dynamite would someday put an end to that little hazard, and the river would be gentle as a baby's bath. The picnickers were encouraged to visit the shop at the tower's base, where they bought guava jelly and coconuts and picture postcards—the favorite was of Big John Frazee, a three-hundred-pound alligator wrestler, posing with a bare foot planted on the loser's gnarled snout—then climbed up the tower steps for a bird's eye view of the 'glades, while the realtor continued to explain the meaning of it all.

"The whole eastern side of the Everglades is rimmed by a rock ledge—think of a big cereal bowl—and all this water you see is actually above sea level. What that means is that once the canals are dug, there'll be nothing to stop the water from flowing straight into the ocean and leaving all this land as fertile as the plains of the Nile."

The pitch worked; the good word traveled. Some people even bought wetland acreage without coming to Miami to see it and, according to a survey done by the Everglades Land Sales Company, only two percent were displeased with their purchase once they did.

It had been years and years since the idea of canals had been rejected in favor of the railroad, but that was when they were meant only for interstate transportation. Now, though—now that they would create new land—canals were an irresistible idea, one that took a grip on people's imaginations and wouldn't let go. And everyone who owned some piece of the dream was encouraged to develop, subdivide, or sell.

"You have to sell, Mrs. Reade," G. W. Haywood told her.

"I don't like being told what I have to do, Mr. Haywood," Clara replied.

"I mean that you have a civic responsibility to develop the land."

"Now I'm being manipulated, and I don't like that either."

Haywood smiled. "It's one thing to give gifts to your grandson. But we're talking now about development, Mrs. Reade. Development on a scale this area's never even dreamed of."

"My grandson can develop it," Clara said.

"Your grandson's only fourteen years old! All he's developing is— never mind. Let me put it this way: don't you think it's selfish, when all this land could be put to good productive use, to hold it all back?"

When the disappointed Haywood had left, Clara closed her office and emerged onto Miami Avenue, squinting in the sun. Two blocks down the avenue, she saw a crowd gathered at a real estate sales office; she crossed the street to avoid it. It was as she mounted the sidewalk on the far side that she saw that the focus of the crowd's attention was not a realtor but a man standing on the back of a buckboard wagon. The buckboard stood in the shade of the second-floor balcony of a land sales office. The crowd was made up of women shoppers, children on their way home from school, traveling salesmen in loudly patterned suits, a few men from the boarding houses and barbershops nearby, and store owners between customers.

Curious, Clara moved slowly back across the street and into the crowd. The man raised a hand for the crowd's attention, and Clara recognized the gesture. It was Harry. She moved with some difficulty through the crowd, watching Harry's mouth move in speech, though she was so intent on staring at him she hardly heard what he said. She stopped behind a man in a bowler hat.

"I am not unaware," Harry was saying, "of the perceived advantages in the new life that Miami envisions for itself with the draining of the Everglades. But I for one do not intend to sit by and—"

One of the salesmen in a yellow checkered suit clapped his hands together and winked at the group of schoolboys. "He *stands* there and tells us he won't *sit* by!"

Used to being heckled, Harry did not let the man's interruption break his stride. "—and let people think that the great changes in the landscape will not bring upheaval and disaster as well."

"Next thing he'll tell us the sky is falling!" This time the salesman's jibe was greeted by hoots of appreciative laughter.

Harry raised both voice and hands to continue. "That broad blanket of saw grass moderates the cold air coming in from the north. Without it, frost and—"

"That muck?" the salesman said. "Who needs it?"

"Yeah!" replied a schoolboy taken with his own daring. "Who needs it?"

Harry shook his head in sorrow. Had these people ever seen the 'glades in their unspoiled prime? Did they understand that people lived there? But how could he make them see what no longer existed? What he himself had only dared to reexamine only a few months ago . . .

He had put off this walk through the hammock to the 'glades, had told himself repeatedly that there was nothing he could do to stop what was happening, until he began to suspect that he was only waiting for the situation to get bad enough for that to be true. As he made his way, machete in hand, he was relieved to see that the hammock itself was unchanged, but he knew such a state would not last long, not at the rate things were going. He read the daily papers and listened to street gossip. He'd seen what artfully planted explosives could do to an acre of trees and vines and knew that whole sections of the very ground he now walked would soon be homesites.

Entire cities were planned for the vast expanse of newly exposed land. Developers sold underwater acres as dry land—streets and homesites laid out on graphs—even before the canals that would drain them were dug. The first canal, a hundred and forty feet wide and thirteen feet deep, had already been plowed sixty miles into the interior of the Everglades. When the restraining dam had been removed, water poured out of the Everglades like a torrent, the water table dropped, and like the promised miracle, land had appeared where no land had been. If some land was newly flooded, it wasn't much to speak of. And if the water of the river and bay had been muddied, that seemed a small price to pay. The *Herald* and *The Metropolis* got together and were campaigning to change the name of the Everglades to something more significant, something with scope, something exotic: the Florida Nile was one suggestion. Prairie Garden, maybe. Empire of the Sun.

Harry had watched the bay being dredged and had not been disturbed in the same way. But the bay did not hold the same kind of
associations for him that the 'glades did; and the bay, for all the dredging and deepening, was not in danger of disappearing off the face of
the earth.

He could hear the river on his left as he walked, but the sound had
been altered by the dynamiting. Harry understood that it was only a
matter of the current flowing faster and thicker, that the sound was
merely denser, but the whole effect was of a rash, desperate rustling,
the water protesting even as it picked up speed in its headlong rush
from the 'glades to the sea.

Harry kept on walking until he could see slats of sky between the
trees. Even before that, he smelled the dead fish. The stench became
stronger the closer he came to the limestone ridge that protected the
hammock from the wetland; the insidiousness with which the smell
first mingled with and finally overcame the perfume of flowers made
it seem even more foul. Harry hesitated now to walk these last yards
ahead toward the glimpses of blue sky. There was still time to turn
back, to busy himself with other things so he would not have to see
what really had happened. He realized, as he stood there, that the
thought of decaying fish had not occurred to him; in fact he had not
allowed himself to imagine the worst. He was suddenly afraid.

He turned away from the 'glades toward the river, following the
outline of the ridge to just below the fork at Tiger Creek, then waded
across to Musa Isle. It was still too early for tourists or land buyers in
the steam launches; the gift shop at the tower's base displayed a Closed
sign. Harry peered through the screened window and saw rows of
painted coconuts, piles of alligator skins, and a tall brass spittoon in
which snowy white egret feathers were displayed for sale. With a
growing heaviness in his chest, he climbed the tower steps, but even
when he stood at the top, gripping the rail, assailed by the smell of
decay brought on the prairie breeze, he kept his eyes closed for one
long moment more of innocence.

He opened them, and stifled a gasp of astonishment and grief. What
had once been an endless plain of saw grass and water was now
revealed as land parched and dry as a desert: jagged points of eroded
limestone, dry and dead bone-white under the sun. Where the grass
had once undulated gracefully in the soft prairie breeze, there was a

cracked and dusty mosaic etched with sharp rivulets of iron-colored water. Along the ridge that curved out widely on either side of him, the tall exposed mangrove roots were gnarled, dying, slowly turning into tinder. The sky was chalk white behind the blue and seemed to Harry to be pulling away in shock.

Not that everything had died, of course, although a totality of destruction might have been simpler, in its finality, to comprehend. But life here, Harry saw, went on, reduced. There was still greenery in small isolated islands ranged out to the horizon. The sun glinted randomly in wide ovals of shallow water and in the thin meandering streams pulled inexorably to the sea. There was movement near him along the caked and muddy floor: lizards and iguanas darting from puddle to puddle, stranded, turning anxious heads to the sun. Much of the remaining life had gathered in the shrinking ponds and gator holes: natural enemies like panther and deer to drink, competitors like otters and coons to seek cray, herons and egrets to peck out their sustenance from the dwindling supply of fish. The concentration and incongruity of such gatherings would make easy work for hunters. Vultures glided silently above and perched heavily in trees, waiting. Far in the distance, Harry could see smoke and licks of flame where the parched wooded areas had ignited and were burning out of control.

Harry's hands held tightly to the tower railing. He felt numb, exhausted by the sheer scope of the devastation. His lips and throat were dry; a fine powder seemed to coat his face and hands. All he could hear was the broken sound of his own breath.

The awesome silence was shattered by a steam whistle and then the gaggle of excited voices as the first launch of the day pulled into Musa Isle to discharge its passengers. Harry turned to see the proprietor of the gift shop waiting for him at the top of the tower steps, his hand extended, open-palmed.

"That'll be five cents," the man said pettishly, obviously expecting an argument. "Just 'cause you come 'fore I opened don't mean you don't pay."

On the way back to the groves, Harry tried to push from his mind the picture of the arid stretches of what had once been wetland, to remember instead that wide stream he'd sat by with Shinassa when it was all afloat with water hyacinths, the sun streaming through the cypress, dappling their skin, sparkling on the water.

But the refuge he sought in memory would not hold up to the reality he'd seen; he saw it now, dried up under the punishing sun, the cypress withered, the hyacinths turned to pale dry flecks brushed by the breeze into nothing. He forced himself to think about Shinassa, not as she was then, but as she would be today. What had happened to her and her tribe, he dared to ask himself, when this devastation had struck her land?

The answer soon became apparent, for as the drainage continued and more 'glades life was extinguished, unprecedented numbers of Seminoles found themselves stranded, their most fertile land drying up, their livestock dying, their ponds and streams turning to muck while their lowlands were flooded so that they had to wrap their feet in thick webbing to keep from sinking in the mire. And those proud Seminoles who once poled their flat-bottomed canoes along miles of labyrinthine saw grass, who survived the white man's diseases, who resisted going down the "trail of tears" to Indian territory, found they could not live as the very land around them suffered *apstarte*—slow death—and so they made the long, dreadful trek across the 'glades into the city. Some sold their wares on the streets; some found jobs as servants for the white man; some lost themselves in the saloons of North Miami.

Tourists, on the other hand, thought it was awfully clever of the chamber of commerce to arrange this daily street show for them and were glad to buy some beads or a little mat woven from Everglades saw grass by a real Indian maid and sold to them by the very maid herself. Forman and Napolitano, who used to work for Buffalo Bill, brought down their own Wild West vaudeville revue and set up in a theater on the border between North Miami and Colored Town, then hired some local Indians for their Tableaux of Living History. And just as the unearthing of their burial mound had left the Seminoles no place to die, Harry saw that the drainage of the Everglades took away their last place to live.

He walked the streets of Miami looking for Shinassa, his heart pounding at the sight of every young Seminole maiden, until he realized she would no longer be a young girl. And what would he do if he saw her? He felt himself living all over again the pain of his betrayal of her. The specter of the Seminoles' banishment, of the destruction of their land, was more than he would bear in silence. Never had he felt more like the Seminoles' worst version of the heartless, marauding white man than when he saw the Indians on the streets of the city, their sorrow and contempt made invisible by the white man's blindness to it.

Harry no longer watched them from the shadows; what did it matter if they saw him now, when all white men were the same? He wished he had the power to give them back their homes, to return them to their land, even as their land became uninhabitable, drained out from under them. And perhaps Shinassa never came to Miami, perhaps her home had been spared, and if it had been, couldn't he try to make sure it stayed that way? Couldn't he at least protect the homes of those Seminoles who remained in the Everglades? And where once, atop the tower at Musa Isle, he had thought there was nothing to be done, he now saw that though the drainage and destruction could be neither stopped nor reversed, some land might still be saved.

He began by talking to the man next to him at the Holy Mackerel Saloon in North Miami about how the Everglades ought to be saved from annihilation, and if it took a few drinks to give him the courage to speak this unpopular opinion to larger groups of people, what did it matter as long as it got said? A few women outside Fine's Emporium listened, a few men around a billiards table didn't. A few poker players threw some chips his way just to shut him up; begging for charity was bad luck. He kept talking: now at a ladies' gardening club, now to the tourists from Key West debarking at the Eighteenth Street pier. A reporter from the *Herald* heard about him and asked what he was going to do with the money people were giving him. The question inspired Harry to start the Everglades Preservation Society. His goal, as he formulated it to a small but growing number of like-minded supporters, was not to waste time trying to stop development, because that was an impossible task—even as they spoke, whole towns were being built on former wetland—but to raise money to buy up as much Everglades land as they could, to preserve it as it was, to convince the state government to help them. He got signatures on petitions to bring before the city council. He allied his little organization with the National Audubon Society; Audubon himself had camped at the Miami River in the last century painting his famous *Birds of the South*. He drew up proposals for bills that, if enacted, would keep hunters from killing off wildlife indiscriminately, especially plume birds slaughtered in their nests simply to supply the millinery industry with feathers.

Taking as much time as he could away from the groves, he continued to make speeches: in saloons, outside churches, for the Ladies' Aid Society and the Improved Order of Red Men, before the county bar association and on street corners. He was often jeered at and scorned for backward thinking, for Utopian idealism, for not knowing opportunity when he saw it, for being un-American, for being a fool in general and a nuisance in particular. Harry persisted, driven by the need to redress the wrong he had done Shinassa all those years ago.

His speeches rarely varied but for the location, and on a particularly hot and humid September afternoon, he chose a spot on the sidewalk a few blocks down from the Reade office. For the same reason he had always avoided this area before, he had now chosen it: he wanted his mother to hear his speech.

"It will be impossible to replace the Everglades once it is destroyed," Harry shouted at the crowd in front of him. "Progress can't be counted in dollars!"

"It'll do till something better comes along!" someone shouted, and this time even the lady shoppers joined in the laughter.

"Do we improve our souls by destroying the natural landscape?" Harry asked them. "Animals and birds are already dying for lack of food, fish for lack of water. Now, I agree that life here is more comfortable, more hospitable and civilized than in the past. We should be thankful for the fruits of progress, and we are. But let us not go too far. The Everglades Preservation Society is in the process of acquiring land to protect it from devastation. We need your help. We need to awaken people to the true nature of—"

He stopped suddenly at the sight of a woman being helped out of a carriage across the street. She was exquisitely dressed in a long white linen suit and a wide-brimmed hat with a pale veil. It was the hat that so arrested Harry's attention, for curled around the crown, framing the woman's face, blowing delicately in the hot summer breeze, was

· *Barry Jay Kaplan* ·   387 a clutch of white egret feathers. The sight unnerved him. The crowd, suddenly quiet, watched as he leaped down from the buckboard and shoved his way past them and strode across the street, heedless of traffic.

By the time Harry reached the carriage, the woman was standing on the sidewalk fussing with her veil, her companion a few feet away adjusting the buttons on his gloves. Harry was dimly aware of the crowd's attention, but all he could see clearly was the egret feathers on the woman's hat. They seemed to him the living example of all he was talking about; he would have been no more outraged than if the dead bird itself were draped across her shoulders with rhinestones where its eyes should have been.

"Madame," he said and waited until the woman turned to him. "Do you realize that the bird who supplied the feathers for your hat was most likely shot in its nest?"

The woman eyed him steadily. "What a disgusting thing to say!"

Without another thought, Harry reached up and pulled the hat from her head. She screamed, staggered back, her hair come undone, her face in shock. Harry, shocked himself at what he'd done, the hat dangling absurdly in his fingers, took a step toward her to return it. The woman recoiled as if he meant to assault her further. Her companion, up till now a mere shadow to Harry, became all at once a hundred and eighty pounds behind a fist, and Harry found himself sprawled against the building, the hat snatched from his hand, his lip split and bleeding. Tiny egret feathers drifted down on him like gentle Christmas snow.

The crowd wasn't laughing but staring at him now from across the street. No one came to his aid. Harry closed his eyes to let the dizziness pass. He touched his fingers gingerly to his swollen lip and felt the wetness. He pictured the look of astonishment on her face when the hat came off; it was worth the bloody lip.

But had anyone really listened to what he'd said? Had they paid any real mind to him? He touched his lip again; his whole face throbbed now. Had the woman with the hat understood? Would anyone listen to something they didn't want to hear? It was as true for strangers on the streets as it was for his own mother. Why did he think Clara would listen? What claims had he on her attention, let alone her loyalty? The guilt that fueled his crusade had made him insensitive, impatient, and rash.

He took a deep breath and hauled himself to his feet, staggered and snaked his way through the traffic of carriages and slow-moving automobiles to the alley across the street where he'd left his carriage.

"OK, OK," he whispered to the horse and stroked its neck, more to calm himself, he knew, than the horse. He was gathering together all his charts and the petitions for which he was still soliciting signatures, when a hand gripped his arm.

"This is very impressive, Harry," Clara said, glancing at his papers. "All this research. You really seem to know what you're talking about."

Flattered, even embarrassed by this, Harry could not help but smile. "They didn't think so," he said with a glance at the street. "I'm still a very nervous speaker."

Clara dismissed his modesty with a smile and a light touch on his arm. "You're very persuasive," she said. "I agree with a lot of what you're saying. I know you're surprised to hear that coming from me."

"Well, I hoped you would agree."

"I wish there was some way I could help you."

Harry flushed. "I'm not asking for your help," he said, but the very fact of her presence, that she'd heard his speech—wasn't that a sign that perhaps she'd changed?

"This has to do with . . . with the Indian girl, doesn't it?" Clara asked.

Harry's shoulders sagged; no, she hadn't changed at all. "If you could only look at the issues clearly and put aside our personal differences just this one time—"

"There's nothing personal in this, Harry," Clara said simply. "I want to help you, honestly I do, but I just don't own the wetland property anymore."

Harry continued to stuff the papers into his briefcase. "Sold it to the first developer who asked, no doubt. Ah, the great march of progress."

Clara shook her head. "I tried to give that land to you once, do you remember?"

"I'm only sorry I didn't get to you before G. W. Haywood or whoever it was bought it from you." He snapped his case shut and looked at her. "Of course I would only have been appealing to your conscience and not to your pocketbook." He turned to pull himself up into his carriage.

"I gave all the land to Cam." Harry turned to look down at her. "Every birthday, every Christmas, for years. That whole stack of deeds is in trust for him until he's twenty-one." Harry's hand dropped to his lap, but he turned away from her. "It's him you should be convincing," Clara said softly. "Your son."

29.

Harry arrived there at dusk. Though the houses that flanked it were lit up, inside his own house all was dark. In the fading light Harry could see paint chipping off the clapboards, a shutter hanging askew from a loose hinge. He tied his carriage horse to the box elder and walked to the porch. The floorboards groaned under his step. He knocked softly and waited. A carriage pulled up in front of the house next door; Mr. Jennings got out and tethered the reins to an iron jockey on the lawn. Harry edged deeper into the shadows. He'd moved out to the groves permanently; he was no longer a part of this life. He knocked again, waited, and finally opened the door and entered.

No lights were on. The parlor, the staircase, the long hallway that led to the kitchen in back, all were in shadow. No windows were open; the air smelled musty and dank. He stood awkwardly in the dark at the entrance to the parlor, deciding whether to go in and wait or take this silence as an opportunity to rethink the whole notion of asking

Cam to join his crusade. He hardly knew his son; would Cam use this as an easy way to reject the father who'd never accepted him?

He became aware after a moment of a living presence in the dark, cavelike room—the deep breathing of an animal stirring awake—and saw the dim outline of a figure sunk deep in an overstuffed chair.

"Who's there?"

"It's Harry," he said. "Why are you sitting in the dark?"

There was the rasp of a match being struck, and two pinpoints of light appeared reflected in black glasses. The match was set to a candle on the table beside the chair; the room was washed a pale, sickly yellow.

"I hate electric lights," Maria said hoarsely.

Harry lowered himself onto a straight-backed chair near the entranceway. "I've come to see Cam."

"Didn't think you came to see me," she said and laughed, then stopped abruptly. "What do you want him for?"

"That's between him and me," Harry said.

"He's out. He don't come home for hours and hours yet."

"I'll wait."

"Leave him alone, Harry," Maria said. "He don't want nothing from you."

They sat without speaking, Maria's heavy, measured breaths the only sound, until Harry heard the floorboards creaking on the porch, then the door opening and the click of the hall light being switched on. Harry looked at Maria; she shrank in her chair as if the light were a weapon.

"Whose carriage is that outside?" Cam stood in the entrance, the light behind him. "Is he—?"

Harry turned and felt the light on his own face and knew the boy was staring at him. "Hello, Cam."

The boy swallowed hard and nodded. "H'lo."

"Your father was just going, Cam."

Harry studied his silhouette. "You're very tall," he said. "My father was a tall man."

"He gets his looks from me," Maria said. "He don't want to hear about your father."

Cam walked across the room and sat on the arm of his mother's chair and looked back at his father.

Harry saw expectancy in that look, curiosity, something that seemed to invite him. "Will you do something for me, Cam?"

"Do something for you?" Maria said harshly. "Why should he? You've never done anything for him."

"Of course I have no business asking," Harry said patiently to Cam. "I hardly have the right to be here at all."

"That's right," Maria said, "you don't." She put her hand on Cam's arm. "You don't have to say a word, sweetheart. I know you're upset." She looked at Harry. "Why don't you just go away now?"

Harry looked at Cam; the boy's face seemed open, attentive. "It's about the wetland your grandmother's put in trust for you."

"He doesn't have to listen to you!" Maria cried and leaped to her feet. "He listens to me!"

"I need your help, son," Harry persisted.

"How dare you call him that?" Maria embraced her son as if she would protect him from physical punishment. "I don't feel so good, Cammy," she said. "Will you help me upstairs?"

Cam's eyes darted to his father; after all this time following him, watching him, waiting to understand his need, waiting to be asked, Cam found his appearance here today both expected and startling. Something had begun. He could be patient now. He held his mother's arm and began to help her upstairs.

Harry saw the mute plea in the boy's eyes, as if begging to be asked, as if he'd waited all these years for it. He signaled to him that he would wait outside. Maria doesn't need him, Harry thought; she uses him as a weapon against me. As he waited in the carriage for his son to come, Harry remembered how obedient he himself had been to a father he neither loved nor respected, and he marveled at the simplicity, the inextricability of this bond. Despite the years of neglect there had been such hesitant expectancy on the boy's face . . .

"I told Mother I had to get something at the store," Cam said as he joined Harry in the carriage. "I always have to lie to her. It's never really worth telling the truth." His face was flushed; his fingers drummed on the metal trim of the carriage seat while his eyes searched his father's face. "Don't worry." He pulled himself up. "She can't see us. Even if she was holding the reins, she wouldn't be able to see us."

Harry made room for him on the seat. "I'm surprised to hear you talk that way about your mother."

Cam's eyes narrowed and he drew back. "You scolding me for it?"

Harry shook his head. "Just surprised." He clicked the reins and they moved slowly down the alley and into the street.

After a few blocks negotiating the traffic, Cam said, "You ought to have an automobile."

"Why is that?"

Cam indicated the Fords and Reos chugging past them. "Because it's the coming thing."

"That's no reason to get rid of a good horse," Harry said.

"But you could get there faster," Cam insisted.

"I guess I'm old-fashioned," Harry said. He kept his eyes on the road; the horse was skittish of the automobiles' noise. "Have you ever heard any of my speeches, Cam?"

Cam did not want to tell him that he'd heard the speeches many times. He simply said, "Some."

"Did you understand what I was saying?"

"Sure."

Harry laughed. "You may be the only one who *is* sure. I try to get people to see the folly of what they're doing, but all they can see are the profits." He paused, then went on. "What I want to ask you . . . is about the wetland your grandmother's been giving you."

"That land is worth a lot of money now," Cam said. "Mother says we won't have to live in that old house once I sell. But I don't really care about that." He glanced sideways at his father, waiting.

Harry was determined to speak bluntly to the boy, for he knew he had no right to appeal to him emotionally. He told him about the Everglades Preservation Society, about the opposing points of view, about what would be gained and lost. He hoped logic and good sense would be enough to convince the boy.

Cam breathed slowly through his mouth as his father spoke; so the moment was here at last. He felt himself moved to the verge of tears. "What do you want to do with my land?"

"I want to protect it," Harry said, "so it'll stay where it is and not come floating down the Miami Canal into the bay. I want to make sure that the people who live there now won't lose their homes."

"But I thought it was just Indians," Cam said. "What does it matter what happens to them?"

"These particular Indians helped me once when I was hurt, saved my life as a matter of fact, so I'm . . . grateful to them."

Cam looked at his father. I know all about you, he thought. I've followed you for years. I've watched you working the groves, and I've watched you get drunk and sleep in alleys, and I've watched you staring off at the Everglades, and I've watched you watching those Indians on Sunday afternoons after church. And he thought, this is what it's all been leading up to, when you lay your need bare at my feet, when you give me the means to your salvation. There was nothing his father could tell him now that Cam could not learn by continuing to observe him in secret. So comfortable had he become with this method that the very thought of asking any question directly made his face flush with embarrassment; he'd learned so much about him already and had exposed so little of himself. And hadn't he discovered the most important thing of all? His father needed him.

Cam looked away to conceal the triumph glowing in his eyes. His face remained set, lips pressed together, and he felt the deep satisfaction of knowing that finally, after all these years, his father was really concentrating on nothing but him. At last, Cam thought, at last I have him for my very own. The joy and power of such possession thrilled him. This is my reward.

"All right," he said in an emotionless voice. "When I'm twenty-one, I'll do whatever you want with the land."

Cam heard his father breathe a long, low sigh, then felt a hand patting his knee. "Good boy."

Cam started at his father's touch but didn't dare to look at him. Good boy? He wondered if this was indeed an apt description of him or if, in fact, he wasn't some other kind of boy entirely.

Clara made her way upriver in her small steam-driven boat, steering into the shade of the red mangroves on the south bank, her eyes on the water. She had put off going for as long as she could, at the same time knowing that at some point she would have to.

She maneuvered the boat into narrow Little Tiger Creek and was immediately plunged into a darker, quieter, cooler place, the banks so close to each other the trees formed a nearly solid arch above her. A little farther on, she saw the opening in the mangroves and guided the boat into the small, weathered dock. The flat, grassy bank had grown wilder since the time she'd been there, but as she walked up the gentle slope of the clearing, she noticed that in most other ways the place had been more carefully tended: the fallen oaks had been removed and the battered gate at the low stone wall repaired; even the sign had been repainted. The smell of oleander was strong in the afternoon sun, and she picked a blossom as she entered the yard. The cabin had been reroofed, she saw, and there were a few new floorboards on the porch; the delicate old rocker had been set there in the sun, and Clara guessed he used it himself now. Her eyes darted to the narrow path that ran parallel to the river and led to the two graves. She stood for a moment in the shade of an oak tree, gathering her courage.

McLeod appeared from around the side of the cabin, his face obscured in the shadow of his straw hat. His limp, no longer resisted, was more pronounced; his body had curved into it. Clara called his name. He looked up and straightened himself as she walked quickly across the yard, though he couldn't help leaning on his cane. He pushed the hat back on his head, and Clara saw that same slow, secret smile of his, but she noticed something quizzical in it too, as if a vital connection to his pleasure in seeing her had been frayed. She came up to him, and he took her hands in his.

"I'm glad to see you, Clara," he said huskily, then laughed, clearing his throat. "Don't believe I've used my voice much lately. Once the fishermen come down, I don't do nothing but use it, so I like to give it a rest when I can."

Clara shrugged to let him know she hadn't noticed anything different. "I've missed you," she said and heard the apology in her voice.

"Oh, me too," he replied with a little shake of his head, like a boy who'd forgotten his manners. "Me too."

"I've been wanting to come up, but there's been so much to do in town what with the canal and all . . ."

"Hey, you gotta see the garden." He beckoned her to follow, and she went with him out back where he showed her how his plantings had fared—the shallots and squashes, the eggplant, the pawpaws, and the mangoes and avocados and plums—picking a few things as he went and packing up a basket for her filled with Surinam cherries and rose apples and Spanish limes. When they came back around front, he pointed to the fence covered with purple and white hibiscus. "Finally fixed the hinge of the gate. You notice it don't play a tune no more when you open it?" He laughed and glanced at her, then led her in silence to the porch, where she sat in the old rocker as he took a seat on a small bench against the wall.

"I'm exhausted!" Clara said. "I spend half my days arguing with the Internal Improvement Board over the route the canal's going to take and the other half selling off pieces of land to raise the money to get the operation going. And if there was a third half I'd have to spend it watching that Fort Dallas Estates doesn't get overgrown with homesites. That Haywood fella's greedy, I tell you. He'd put 'em up like dominoes if I let him."

Though McLeod seemed content with not speaking, Clara couldn't stop herself from this forced enthusiasm, as if simply by keeping it up she could infect him with it and never have to say why she came.

"You got a right being exhausted," McLeod said softly.

Clara heard the politeness and the disinterest in his voice. "When I first came here, you were the one who had the idea about canals. Remember?"

"I was younger," McLeod said. "I didn't know anything." Clara laughed nervously; McLeod put his hand on her arm. "What's going to happen to my place when the canal's opened up, Clara?" Clara stopped laughing. "Come on now," he urged. "I won't break."

"They're dynamiting the rapids next week," she said. "River passage'll be smooth and easy after that, they say. Up the river, right into the 'glades." She stopped, a bit breathless, and they both looked out at his yard and the fence and the hibiscus and beyond, to that narrow path that ran parallel to the river.

He knows, she thought. He's known all along, and the fact that he hadn't said a word in protest made her see that it would always be more and more this way with him. With each year he would be a little less the dashing figure on the docks, a bit more the beaten giant, as time and the life of the city passed him by. She couldn't lie to him.

"It's probably . . . It's going to be flooded out, Quentin."

"Yeah." He nodded. "Yeah."

She saw now that what she had loved about him, his close identification with the land, was the very thing that locked him to the past and made him unable to do more than wonder and accept that things had come to this.

He planted his cane on the floor with a great thump and stood up. "Tell Geneva I expect a pie out of all those cherries," he said. He hesitated only an instant, then turned and walked away around the side of the house.

For that instant Clara denied it had all happened. Only a moment ago the words had been unsaid; only a moment ago she had held his hand in hers. She leaned forward in the rocking chair; she wanted to call to him; she wanted to get up and run around the side of the house and find him and hold him again, but she remained sitting in the old rocker, looking out at the yard and the rays of the setting sun lighting up a corona of white hibiscus at the gate.

Saddest of all was her realization that it was people like her who were responsible for the sorrow of people like him.

Harry was well on his way to a bourbon drunk in the Salty Dog—elbows planted on his usual table in the back, face cupped in his hands, hands pressed to his ears to block out the sounds of the crowd—and thinking about his son, how he'd looked the day he'd come into the house. Harry felt then that he'd unwittingly played on the boy's innocence and his never-before-acknowledged need of his father's approval.

Harry tried to rid his mind of the image of his son's face, the boy's eyes swimming with pride at the gift he was giving. Only bourbon was able to blur it. He looked up from his drink now and scrutinized each of the half-dozen house girls arranged around the back room. One more drink and he'd go talk to that little Cuban one near the piano, but one more, in fact, took the edge off his appetite for her. He pulled on his jacket, went to the bar, and slid two silvers through a puddle of spilled whiskey.

"Gone," he said huskily to the new bartender, hardly recognizing his own voice.

" 'Night, pal."

The streets outside were dark but for dull squares of light spilling from hotel windows and the open doorways of saloons. Tourists only came this far out on North Miami Avenue if they were looking for a girl or a rough time or were just too ignorant to know better, though there weren't many who couldn't see what this place was even if they'd never seen a place like it before.

He buttoned his vest, ran his hands through his hair, and straightened his jacket. His son was right about automobiles: he ought to get one.

Banjo music was twanging from somewhere out in the direction of Colored Town; a woman's high-pitched laughter ended with a slap. The night air was dense and humid and stuck in his throat. Harry felt drunker than he had in the bar. Just thinking about how far it was to his cabin at the groves made him want to hunker down right where he was.

Maybe go to Fort Dallas, he thought with a little laugh. Sleep in my nice old bed. He smiled to imagine the surprise on his mother's face. No. He shook his head and ran a few steps; he hated thinking about her when he was drunk. Couldn't go there anymore anyway, didn't seem like home. Not welcome in the house on Northeast Second Street either. Can always go back to the Salty Dog, he thought, rooms upstairs not so bad. Get that little Cuban girl for a pillow. Hell, what's it matter? Fall down right where I am, sleep in the alley. Done that before. Just have to get up in the morning and start all over again anyway.

He stopped, breathless, and leaned against a building in the shadows. No stars tonight, the sky a velvety dark brown like the fur of an animal. Storm by morning, he thought.

He decided he'd go and find his son. Poor Cam. He wanted to say he was sorry for everything he'd never done. And then maybe . . . maybe . . . He couldn't even imagine what might happen. Would anything? Would he be a real father? Have a real son? What would it mean? Did it matter? Wasn't Cam better off? Wasn't he all Maria's anyway? No. That's the coward's way out. Stop the chain right here. Be a father. Start. Start now. Start by going to him.

It was nearly dawn when Harry arrived on foot at Reade's Gifts and Souvenirs. The door was locked; a little hand-painted sign said Open at Eight. The streets were empty; the sky hung low. He wasn't drunk anymore, just bone tired; his skin felt raw and sensitive to the touch. He sat down on the bench next to the shop door and leaned his head back against the glass, breathing, sinking.

He dreamed he was standing on a wide, flat plain, not quite a desert but still a place where nothing grew. The horizon line was barely visible, the sky nearly indistinguishable from the ground. Endless, endless space. Something about it was familiar, but he couldn't find the words to say what it was. It didn't look like anything he'd ever seen, exactly, but the feeling persisted that he had been there before and, more, that he knew what was about to happen: from the edge of the barely discernible horizon something was about to appear, and he knew just what it would be. In fact, it was the same thing that had appeared over and over. In fact, nothing had changed or ever would until he could turn his life around, and at the moment he realized that, the dream took on the bleary tingle of a nightmare because he was rooted on this plain, he could not move.

"Mister! Hey, mister!"

Harry opened his eyes. The sun was winking at him at the roofline of the Everglades Land Sales Company across the street. Standing above him was a young Indian boy about Cam's age, dressed in the knee-length calico shirt typical of the Seminoles, deerskin leggings and moccasins; a grass-cloth sack was slung over his shoulder. Harry stared at the straight black hair and the serious expression and for a moment thought it was Billy Jumper. He rubbed his eyes and stood up to stretch, running his hands over his face, trying to erase the dream. His heart was beating fast.

"This your store, mister?"

Harry shook his head, staring at the boy.

"When they come?" the boy asked.

"Soon," Harry replied.

"You want to buy blanket?" the boy asked. He was kneeling down, opening the sack, drawing items out of it and arranging them in front of the store. "I give good price. You decide quick. Mother come soon. Raise price."

Harry shook his head, but the boy kept unpacking the sack: straw mats, beaded necklaces and bracelets, brightly colored handkerchiefs and shawls, the same merchandise Maria bought from the Seminoles to sell in her shop. "I've seen all this before," Harry said wearily.

From behind him came a woman's voice raised in anger, and Harry saw the boy glance up and quickly begin to repack everything he'd taken from the sack. The woman passed in front of Harry, continuing to scold the boy until everything had been replaced, then she turned to Harry, head slightly bent, not quite looking at him the way all Seminoles did not quite look at all white men, her tone of voice changing to one of apology.

The sun rising over the roofs across the way lit up the side of her face, sculpting it like molten copper. Harry stared, mouth dry, not surprised so much as relieved. The intervening years dropped away from him as easily as a coat slipping from his shoulders. It was so simple to accept what he saw before him, and now that it had happened it seemed right, natural, inevitable that it would turn out just this way.

He said her name. She stopped speaking and raised her eyes to his, her lips parted. She's been waiting too, Harry thought. He said her name again. It was as if he'd been saying it every day, as if they'd been together and happy every day, every day, all these years.

She said nothing, only nodded her head slowly, stared at him, studying his face, then moved a step back toward the boy and took his hand.

"Little Tiger," she said, not taking her eyes from Harry's. "This is your father."

30.

When word of the assassinations of Archduke Francis Ferdinand and his wife, the duchess of Hohenberg, reached Miami, the *Herald* defined the people's attitude: "What's one archduke more or less?" The Kaiser had had his summer sailing interrupted by the event, but otherwise Berlin was said to be peaceful as a tomb. On a lazy spring day in Miami, the troubles brewing across in Europe seemed not merely an ocean away but incomprehensible and minute, and yet through the complex tangle of European politics, one piece of news suddenly rang out clear: "All Europe on Verge of War!" cried *The Metropolis* not a month later. The residents of Miami wondered how this could have happened without their knowing more about it; it was so sudden, why, with no alarm sounded, no warning at all.

Optimism struggled to keep its toe in the door. "A general European war is unthinkable," *The New York Times* wrote. "Europe can't afford such a war, and the world can't afford it, and happily the conviction is growing that such an appalling conflict is altogether beyond the realm of possibility."

The next day Austria declared war on Serbia and, like dominoes falling into place, Germany went tumbling against France, Britain against Germany. Americans still couldn't quite make it out. All this Sturm und Drang over the murder of an archduke no more significant than a character in an operetta and not even a native of any of the countries involved?

A series of newspaper headlines told the story:

"Bloodthirsty Royals Prepare Fifteen Millions to Face Death."

"Monarchs Wreak Havoc on Doomed Lands."

"Subjects Are Mere Pawns of Rulers."

As the long, frightful, endless casualty lists were printed in the daily papers, people began to understand the full implications of Sir Edward Grey's remark: "The lamps are going out all over Europe. We shall not see them lit again in our lifetime." And while Americans continued to follow the conflict, thankful that Columbus had discovered their continent an ocean away from Europe, the war didn't seem to have much effect on the average person except for the fact that product shortages in the war-torn countries increased American exports and prices rose accordingly.

But other changes were more insidious, and it soon came to be seen that economics were only part of the effect of the war on Americans. As screaming headlines told of atrocities, U-boat sinkings, charges and countercharges, the steadfast belief in America's ability to solve all problems was shaken. Doubt and dismay replaced the easy confidence of a few years back. Nothing seemed so simple anymore. Optimism, exuberance, hope—they were not lost exactly but upset at their very foundations.

A flight school had been set up on a cleared strip of land below Palm Grove and named for flying ace Glenn Curtis; attendance took a wild swing up when the army started sending college boys to train. In light of the war in Europe, Miamians no longer thought of flight as merely sport. What did General Pershing mean exactly when he said that he considered one airman worth a whole cavalry division? He couldn't possibly mean to send Americans? It was unthinkable. But Government Cut had opened Miami to the oceans of the world, the war with Spain to international interests, and the citizens now had to face the vulnerability of such a prominent position. When the college boys were replaced in the flight school by trainloads of Marines—the Marine Air Corps was born right then, right in Miami, right back where Hialeah was being built—the war in Europe suddenly didn't seem far away at all.

One of the most popular songs of the day was "I Didn't Raise My Son to Be a Soldier," but as the war in Europe grew fiercer, more and more Americans found themselves in sympathy with the Allies. This feeling developed into real outrage against Germany when numbers of German spies were discovered sabotaging American industry and manipulating American opinion through the press. The name German measles was changed to liberty measles, sauerkraut to liberty cabbage, and dachshund to liberty pup. Teddy Roosevelt was all for "America for Americans," and in Miami the Germans were quick to join patriotic clubs and give loyalty addresses. The Stargers were accused of putting ground glass in their loaves and sending sketches of OX-Jenny aircraft to Germany to help defeat the Allies. "I am loyal to my city, to my state, and to my country," Fritz Starger wrote in a letter to the editor of the *Herald,* but protestations were expected and not necessarily believed.

Miami was a city preoccupied with war. And though its first skyscraper went up that year and eighty-seven new stores opened, and the tourist season, helped by the presence of the Marine Air Corps, was the best ever, nothing could shut out the painful reality of that April morning in 1917 when the President of the United States asked the Congress to declare war on Germany. The war in Europe had come home.

When her grandson came and told her that he'd enlisted, Clara was on her knees in her garden, struggling with a recalcitrant sassafras root. She stood up without his help, brushing dirt from her dress, and dabbed her face and neck with a gardenia-scented handkerchief as they walked to the porch. She sat down in her old wicker rocker, Cam on the step near her feet. The bougainvillea cast a pink glow in the shade. Clara was disturbed by both his request that she take in his mother and the news that his father had signed the enlistment papers.

"You can get your father to do just about anything you want, can't you?"

Cam shrugged, a smile on his face that anyone but his grandmother would have mistaken for boyish pride. "He's just guilty. He doesn't care anything about me. It'd probably be a load off his mind if I got killed in battle."

"Don't talk nonsense, Cam. Your father loves you."

Cam laughed. "I'm not the one talking nonsense."

"Fathers always love their sons," Clara said.

"Did my father's father love him?"

Clara hesitated. "In his way," she replied and wondered, even now, if it might be true.

"That's not what I've heard."

"It takes time to understand," Clara said. "As you get older you'll —"

"I don't care," Cam said. "I don't want him to love me. You're the only one that counts."

Clara was afraid of avowals like this, afraid of both the lie and the truth in them. "You think you can get just about anything from me too," she said.

Cam saw she wasn't smiling, and a burn of fear went through him: would she desert him too? "I don't want anything from either of you."

"Oh yes, you do," Clara said. "Maybe even more than you realize."

Cam thrust his hands deep in his pockets and paced up and down in front of her with the long-legged stride of a boy just grown into a man's legs. "I hate being told that you know something about me I don't know myself. It's probably not even so."

He was so unlike his father at this age, with none of Harry's romanticism or imagination, that Clara wondered what of her son she truly saw in this angry, fiercely independent boy; was she inventing a resemblance by imagining depths in him that, when understood, would reveal another Harry? "Maybe I don't know you as well as I think I do."

Cam stopped pacing and turned to her; he felt cold and scared all of a sudden, like a child who's run away and realizes he can never go home again. He fell to his knees and put his head in her lap. "Don't give up on me," he said. "You understand me better than anyone." A sudden swell of emotion filled his chest; he hesitated to continue, fearful that he was losing control of his voice. "But . . . I want to grow up and be something. I want to be away from Miami, away from . . . them." A sob caught in his throat. His grandmother's arms came around him;

he drew in the scent of gardenia with each breath, and it calmed him.

Clara touched the curls at the nape of his neck. "I don't want to lose you, Cam," she said, but she understood him well enough to know that trying to keep him in Miami was no guarantee of not losing him and wondered if Harry had thought the same thing when he signed the papers. "Don't worry about your mother," she said finally. "She can come and stay here." Cam held her tighter. "Miami's going to need men like Cameron Reade after the war. I'm depending on you, Cam. When you come back, we'll do great things together."

"OK," he said with a little laugh.

Clara held him at arm's length and looked into his eyes. She could not lose this link from the past to the future. "Is that a deal?"

Cam nodded. "It's a deal," he said. As his grandmother embraced him one last time, he touched the enlistment papers in his pocket: at last he was free to become a man.

Women dominated the city now. No able-bodied man was free of censure if he hadn't enlisted—thirty-eight hundred had—and those who didn't qualify, because of age or infirmity or for reason of some peculiarity like having flat feet or being too tall or too fat to fit into regulation uniforms, were tolerated as not very admirable examples of their gender. Maria hung a star in her bedroom window to show she'd sent a boy to war. Voluntary food rationing was instituted: wheatless Mondays, meatless Tuesdays, porkless Wednesdays. Major growers donated seeds, and all families were urged to plant backyard gardens and all farmers to plant fallow ground with velvet beans to enrich the soil. Housewives created loyalty menus using peanut flour and grits to stretch meals out. Motorists subscribed to gasless Sundays, the more patriotic of them—bigger show-offs, some said—hitching a team of horses to their front bumpers to make their point, most of them missing church services altogether. Enough money was saved on Sunday's gas to feed all the American soldiers in Europe for two days. Rallies were held to sell liberty bonds and liberty stamps to fill liberty books—"lick a stamp and lick the Kaiser" was the slogan children shouted to sell their stamps—bandages were rolled, and woolen blanket squares and sweaters were knitted (it was a summer war, though, and most of the boys used the sweaters more to plug up leaking foxholes than to keep warm). When the Ladies' Auxiliary learned that the charcoal needed for the filters in gas masks could be gotten from burning peach pits, they set up huge bins at the railroad depot and collected tons of them to send to the factories in Newport News.

The city's population, lowered by the men who went to war, was raised by families who wanted to be near their soldiers in training at the flight and gunnery schools. In addition, there was an almost embarrassingly high increase in tourism. The whole idea of a country at war prompted people to aspire to a certain austerity of mood, but the tourists came down to Miami in record numbers when their European vacation plans were necessarily put aside. Hotels were booked solid, and the pastors of the Saint Agnes Episcopal and the New Mount Zion Baptist churches appealed to their congregations to rent rooms to tourists who couldn't get to the Riviera this year but who needed their time in the sun nevertheless. Most of them were first timers on the Bay of Biscayne, and though they came begrudgingly, they found the pleasures of sun and beach more than a match for their European counterparts. Nearly all residents profited in one way or another from tourism. The price of a loaf of bread went from five to six cents, a cup of coffee from five to ten, prompting the opinion that a profit of two hundred and fifty percent was being made on every cup.

The time to make a quick killing in land sales and subdivisions stopped. Though realtors and developers saw the war as an unwelcome interruption in the Golden Age of Progress, avarice and ambition were put aside in favor of loyalty—or a reasonable facsimile thereof—to the country's war effort. Wartime was a time of waiting, of assuming a position and holding tight to it until the war was over. Construction ground nearly to a halt, plans were shelved. It was a time for patience, for taking the long view.

Clara had dreaded taking her daughter-in-law in to live with her, and during the first few weeks her worst fears came to pass. Maria walked the house and grounds only at night, her slippers shuffling along the floor, her fingernails tapping on the windows or scraping the walls. Her vision had deteriorated; she rarely went out of the house, imagining the stares and whispers of people for whom she had no use anyway, but why give them anything to gossip about? She passed the time with bottles of sherry and boxes of chocolate-covered cherries, drowsy, dreamy, dozing off on the settee clutching a fringed pillow to her chest, then waking, half-sick, playing gramophone records to cheer herself or give herself a reason to cry, singing to her three caged canaries, in whom she invested qualities of loyalty and devotion she found lacking in all human relationships.

She liked to open the little door on the cage and put both hands inside. At first she did it with little pieces of lettuce nestled in her open palms. After a few minutes of her quiet talk, the birds would come and peck at the lettuce. They nipped her too, although she knew they didn't mean to hurt her, and as the months went by and they came to trust her she recognized the nips as little bird kisses and didn't mind it even when some of the kisses were deep and drew blood and got infected. She liked holding their little warm bodies in her hands and stroking their tiny heads and feeling with the tip of her fingers their tiny, tiny heartbeats.

Sweet little things, she thought. They love me more'n anyone; never turn on me, never do me wrong, not like everyone else. She hadn't wanted Cam to enlist—"Don't leave me!" she'd screamed at him—but he'd gone anyway, and she sobbed and moaned those first weeks at Clara's, talked to no one but her canaries, except to complain to Clara whenever she was nearby how her plans and her dreams and her hopes had gone awry, how she'd been sabotaged and undermined and betrayed by mother and mother-in-law, by husband, and how even her own son had let her down.

"I knew first time I ever set eyes on Harry that there'd be nothing but suffering and holy hell on earth for me. I should never have married him. I should have killed myself when I had the chance. And now it's come to this."

Though she kept her office closed for business, Clara spent as much time away from the house as she could; there were bond rallies and Red Cross projects enough to occupy her. But she would not, finally, allow Maria to force her out of her own home; nor, she decided one day, would she listen to another one of her tirades.

"Now you listen to me, miss. Just dry your tears and accept your fate. I won't make excuses for either of our sons, but I won't take your part against them either. And I won't allow you to carry on this way one more night. There is a war going on, for heaven's sake. There are more important things for you to be doing than all that weeping and feeling sorry for yourself. I won't have it in my house; it's as simple as that."

Something in Clara's tone convinced Maria to mend her ways; that and the threat of being kicked out. In any event she joined the Women's Christian Temperance Union and helped prepare comfort bags for the boys, which included socks, bandages, and a Bible. Relentless singing of "Onward Christian Soldiers" now replaced her rantings as she sat in a dim corner of the parlor, her black glasses in place, her head tilted to one side, knees pressed firmly together, with a Braille edition of the King James Bible on her lap and her fingers running lightly across the pages.

"The Lord's watching over Cam," she explained to Clara. "I saw it in a dream clear as day: Cam is in his uniform walking through a forest looking strong and brave and proud, carrying the flag of our country in front of him, leading his men through the gunfire. And walking with him is Jesus in his robes. Not the mild Jesus, not the gentle Jesus, but the strong Jesus who defied all dangers, who brought courage to the meek and daring to the shy. He takes my Cammy's hand and says to him—I could hear him, Clara, I could hear the true sweet words as if he was in bed with me while I dreamed—'Walk with me to victory.'" Maria dabbed at her eyes and smiled beatifically. "Cam's gonna kill the Kaiser, isn't he? Make our country a safe place for all Americans, isn't that right? Isn't that the meaning of my dream?"

Upon his return to Miami a decorated war hero, Cam took a small bachelor's apartment in a downtown residential hotel, explaining to his mother that, were it possible, he would gladly take her out of Clara's house and with him to live, but of course she had to see that for a young man on the way up—this was not precisely how he put it to her, but the meaning, even to Maria, was clear—this was impossible.

Maria accepted the sealing of her fate. She had her Bible and her canaries; neither, as she told Cam, would ever turn on her or do her wrong. Cam merely nodded at the wisdom of this insight and let the distance between them yawn. Her presence in Clara's house became a hazier, less public one. Days often passed without her being seen or even heard by the Cuban couple who had replaced Edmund and Geneva when they had retired and returned to Eleuthera. When she died in bed of malnutrition, her birds shrieking for seeds, her body was not discovered for two days. The birds were frantically rattling their cage; she was wearing Cam's Silver Star on a ribbon around her neck. Maria had always attributed Cam's heroism to the intervention of Jesus as seen in her dream, a dream that had become famous in her circle of Ladies' Aid volunteers and church workers and which, after the medals had been won, gave her the reputation for the second sight that comes of extreme devotion.

The last time Cam saw her alive, she was bent over the canary cage, her hands inside, the birds pecking at the cuffs of her blouse as she murmured in a high, eerie voice, "Who does Mama love? Who does Mama love? Who does Mama love?"

Three years after the end of the war to end all wars, the peacetime land boom in Miami soared to proportions so vast in scope, so far-reaching in design and effect, as to dwarf all the land clearing, canal dredging, Everglades draining, and civic construction that had come before it. As thousands of new arrivals appeared, the familiar faces were swallowed up in the crowds massed on the streets.

They came by train and on the inland waterways by boats and by the Clyde Line from New York and the Baltimore and Caroline from Philadelphia. Automobiles with license plates from Nebraska, Kansas, or Illinois drove in caravans down the Dixie Highway and across the Tamiami Trail, sofas and tents strapped to their roofs, in response to full-page ads in local papers exhorting them to "Leave winter behind for a Workless Existence in the Land of Eternal Youth." Who could resist such a call? And if accommodations in Miami were expensive and hard to come by at first—whole families were sometimes forced to sleep on porches for twenty-five dollars a week—a walk in the soft evening breeze as the sun set in the Everglades was enough of the promise fulfilled to keep them going.

The city responded to this jump in population with an epic surge of building. Lumber came from as far away as Oregon and Alaska. The skyscraper was the new, preferred form of structure downtown. As examples ten, twelve, eighteen stories high came to be built, the city-scape was drastically altered; slabs and spires of apartment houses, hotels, and offices stabbed the sky; the majestic royal palms cowered; entire city blocks were plunged into shadow. Workers on scaffolds looked down at a harbor with ships' masts as dense as trees in a forest.

But the turbulent transformation of a small tropical city into a major metropolis was as nothing compared to what was happening to its environs. The city seemed to heave up from within itself, spreading its boundaries in a shapeless, uncontrolled frenzy: a September referendum annexed to the city Buena Vista, Allapattah, Lemon City, Little River, Silver Bluff, and Coconut Grove. A plain stucco or wood house would be built on the prairie a few miles outside of town and a simple access road dug. Then a half-dozen other similar dwellings would go up between the first one and the city's border. Pretty soon there was so much traffic the dirt road would have to be paved with asphalt, and then there would be an intersection marked by a drugstore and a grocery and a sign with a name: Pine Landing or Prairie Junction or Sea View. Then two-story bungalows would be built, then eight-room cottages with wraparound porches and a Baptist church maybe and a combination post office and tea room, and the wide, flat, empty prairie would have become a suburb. In no time flat it would spawn other ones farther out in the wilderness in one direction, closer to the city in the other. On a perfect day in May you might drive along open fields, smelling the perfume of the orange groves and marveling at the gloriously open expanse of prairie grass and oaks; take the same route next October, and you would have to maneuver around the interurban trolley tracks and wait for a signal from a beleaguered traffic officer to let you pass through town.

Real estate was the number-one topic of the day, and for a while it seemed that nobody in Miami ever thought of anything else. Brokerage licenses were issued to everyone—dairymen and farmers, bankers and haberdashers—on an average of sixty a day, and even that rate could barely keep up with demand. Everyone sold; everyone had a scheme.

Millions were spent on promotional stunts: one developer took prospective customers out to his Moroccan Villas on the back of an elephant; another hired the entire chorus of the Ziegfeld Follies to dress as gypsy girls and walk the paved streets of The Gardens of Seville—a landfill along the limestone ridge of the Everglades, complete with a replica of the Giralda Tower—while the Volunteer Fire Department snapped their fingers and beat beribboned tambourines. Advertising campaigns were waged to cement in the mind of the public the idea of Miami Beach as America's winter playground. There were even plans to reshape Biscayne Bay as the new Venice. Developers sank wooden pilings in the shape of the islands-to-be and filled them in with sand dredged up from the bay floor. Star Island was formed this way, followed by Hibiscus Isle, Fair Isle, and La Gorce.

In the maelstrom of subdivision and community planning, Clara Reade stood apart; in her idlest moments she sensed herself facing the abyss of old age, the excitement and adventure of her life behind her. The ways in which she was used to handling herself in the city were no longer either possible or appropriate. Though financially comfortable through her share in the subdivision of Fort Dallas, she did not have the wherewithal to make such large gestures as were being made in today's Miami, nor did she own any land but the groves and Fort Dallas that anyone would be interested in buying. Her life seemed to be a journey that, instead of heading toward completion, was turning back on itself as she searched for the one thing that would satisfy the gnawing sense that there was something significant yet to do.

She was not completely forgotten in the new Miami; organizations regularly presented her with plaques and awards, invited her to sit on committees or attend dinners, or sought her endorsement of some new city project or other. But she saw that she was as inextricably trapped in the past as a bug in amber. Her status as Founding Mother, once a source of accomplishment and pride, had entombed her in the history of Miami. Certain people, upon meeting her for the first time, were silly enough to present as a compliment their surprise that she was not a doddering old crone; some were even rude enough to express astonishment that she was still alive at all. Clara accepted their congratulations with wry good humor; age had taught her to be tolerant of people's ignorance. She understood that these new men with their millions, these new women with their short skirts and bobbed hair, simply did not know Miami as she did, had not seen it race from wilderness to metropolis. Twenty-five years from the time the railroad arrived had been long enough for it to become what they thought it had always been: a national center for citrus growing, an international harbor, a world-famous resort, the capital of the New South.

The old Miami was not simply the one of clear waters and rough roads but the one she associated with Harry and the first years they'd spent here. Harry. Her precious son. The gap between then and now, between the boy he'd been and the man he'd become, seemed immense and unbridgeable.

Not long after he'd left Miami with Shinassa and the boy, Clara had gotten a letter from him.

Dear Mother,

You must put your mind to rest when it comes to thinking of me. I could not bear it if I thought you continued to judge me harshly or worried over me when there are so many more important things that demand your attention and when your fears would be unfounded in the event. Truly I am doing at last what I have dreamed of doing for the last fifteen years. I am happy here at the groves. I have everything I want, everything I came to Miami to find. And, having found it, the lost years are as nothing. I know it may seem a wild and radical thing that I have done, but I hope I do not exaggerate when I say that not to have done it would have meant the end of me.

Shinassa was so young, so innocent, such a girl when last I saw her, yet it has not taken us very long to catch up on the time lost, to accept who the other is now. She explained that I did not leave her as completely alone as perhaps I left myself, for she had the son of whom I was deprived. In that way she felt I was always with her. And of course, according to her tribe's customs, she would have no other husband but me. During all our years apart she thought of me as I thought of her. We both like to imagine that our thoughts of each other met in the sky above the 'glades so that we have never been completely apart, so that those dream moments—always for me the happiest—were not unmet, were not empty.

The three of us are a bit cramped living in the cottage I used to live in alone, but I am planning an expansion; I suppose in that respect I am like everyone else in Miami. As you must know, it is difficult for any of us to come into the city now. Shinassa is shy of it; a proud and decent woman, she does not relish being regarded by people on the streets as an outstanding tourist attraction.

As for leaving Maria, I consider Shinassa my true wife and always have. Though Maria may be loath to admit it, our marriage was an unfortunate necessity and had long since become a blur of disappointments and recriminations. I regret her sorrow; I regret my own. Staying would not have made things better.

Again, I am well. Please try not to worry. Accept what has happened. When you think of me, see me in the groves with a straw hat on my head, eating a Reade Beauty and smiling.

Clara kept the letter on the table beside her bed and read it many times, hoping to find that place in herself to accept the turn his life had taken. She took him at his word and did not worry about him but found that, having dropped the idea that he would return to her, that things would be as they had always been, she no longer knew how to think of him except as existing somewhere in the past, an adored son who'd been lost somehow. She could not see him, could not claim him, but could only embrace a memory of him.

31.

At Cam's twenty-first birthday celebration lunch given by Aaron Fine, for whom Cam now worked, he was given an extra month's pay, a specially baked German chocolate cake, a silk lounging robe, and a few books from the salesclerks he supervised. After all those years of giving him parcels of land on his birthday, Clara felt that her gift of a gramophone was a bit of a letdown. Then champagne was served and Aaron Fine announced that he was taking Cam out of the haberdashery department and putting him on the main floor in the position of department manager. Cam thanked his employer with proper gratitude and solemnity, allowed his hand to be shaken and his cheek kissed by his fellow employees, and Clara wondered if it was possible that she was the only one who saw how remote he seemed from the festivities.

Clara placed her hopes for the future—Miami's as well as her own—on her grandson. "I see Cam as a man of his time," she had once told Maria. "He's got just the personality for success. Oh, I admit that he doesn't have the imagination some have,"—she was thinking here of

Harry—"but that can work in his favor. People will see him as solid and sensible, with the right kind of energy and drive to get things done. It'll make those others, those so-called visionaries, seem flighty and irresponsible." Maria had laughed at this, relieved, eager, and happy to watch Clara paint this picture of her young son.

Clara reasoned that people trusted Cam the way they might not have if he were a more idiosyncratic young man. She was sure that when the time came he would make a place for himself in Miami, even if he had to move everyone out of his way to do it.

The prospect excited her; she knew she'd be in on it in some way, that when Cam made his move, he would take her along with him. It would be her last great adventure in shaping the city of Miami, and the possibility of it, shimmering on the horizon, seemed to her the thing that would allow her to finish the great journey she had started when she and Harry had come to the Miami River so long ago.

Clara kept Cam under close scrutiny all that birthday afternoon, during all the festivities, promotions, and gifts. She detected throughout a quality of enthusiasm missing in him, but so subtle was it that his performance in the role he'd assumed could not be faulted. And what role does he play with me? she wondered.

After coffee was served, Aaron Fine, who had never married, even hinted that he could imagine a time in the future when he would have a new sign made—Fine and Reade—and how happy such a merging of two old Miami names would make them all.

For three years Cam had stood behind the counters at Fine's Emporium, where he had ascended to the post of assistant sales manager, a temporary post, Clara knew. Cam was extremely popular there, handsome in his white suit and red tie, his hair slicked back neatly and a glow on his freshly shaven cheeks. Women liked to buy gifts for their husbands and sweethearts from him; men trusted him not to let them go too far wrong in selecting the right tie to impress the boss. But Clara saw the undertone of his old restlessness vibrating just beneath the skin; it made her think of her Ford revving its engines and confirmed to her that though he began his adult work life at Fine's, it was not at Fine's that he would wind up.

At the end of the day, Cam asked Clara to accompany him to his apartment to help him select the right place for the gramophone. Clara sensed something brewing in him as he took long, loping strides ahead of her up the stairs. By the time she entered the room, the gramophone had been set down and forgotten. Clara took a seat on the rattan sofa, confident that she would soon know why he wanted to see her alone. "They spoil you rotten," she said with an indulgent laugh.

Cam was pacing the room in front of her, but her remark stopped him. "Oh yes. I'm supposed to be grateful," he said fiercely. "Every day, what do I do but help some old biddy choose a pair of argyle socks for her old coot of a husband, saying 'yes sir' and 'no sir' to my boss. What a joke. What a mean, miserable joke! He thinks he's doing me a favor giving me that promotion? He's digging my grave!" He clenched and unclenched his fists and began pacing again.

"I knew it was bad," Clara said. "But I—"

"I've never been so unhappy, Grandy!" he cried. "I'm trapped here. Living in this hotel, working in that store. Mr. Fine means well, I know that, but—" He stopped and faced her. "I'm not a merchant, am I? Aren't I bigger than that?" He smiled and sat down next to her on the sofa.

"As if I haven't known it all along," Clara said with a sigh of relief. "As if I haven't always expected you to do great things."

"I've seen you watching me, wondering when I'm going to get started. You don't know how crazy it's made me to stand by and watch all this activity going on in Miami and not be able to take part in it but—" He turned impassioned eyes on her and took her hands. "I love this city, Grandy. Just like you love it. God, but I'm sorry I wasn't here at the real beginning like you were. You've got no idea how I envy you having had that experience. But you know what the amazing thing about Miami is? It just doesn't seem to have any end in sight! As prosperous as it is now, it can be even more prosperous. And I'm going to be part of making it that way." He dropped her hands and stood up. "Wait." He ran across the room and into his small bedroom.

Clara leaned back, expectant but content. In just these few moments she saw in him the kind of enthusiasm that had been absent since his return from the war, the kind she'd been seeing in the idealistic, optimistic, impassioned young men who'd stormed Miami's downtown as if on a religious mission. It was the kind of enthusiasm Cam would need if he was to make his mark in the city. No, she thought, watching him emerge from the bedroom with a black leather portfolio, he was not the kind of boy to ascend the ranks of a department store, and

· *Barry Jay Kaplan* ·

417

she was glad of it. He would have to do something that was all his own.

He dragged a low table to the sofa and set the portfolio on it in front of Clara, talking all the while. "You've seen the kind of building that's been going on since the war. Well, that's nothing. Wait till you see what I'm going to do. All these developers come in from I don't know where; they don't know anything about Miami except palm trees and palmetto fans. It takes a native like me—like us—to really know the secrets of this place." He hesitated, hands hovering over the portfolio, then smiled at Clara and opened it.

On the first page was a drawing of a ring of palm trees and the legend, "Palm Isle, Florida. Developed by Cameron Reade."

"Let me show you, Grandy," he whispered. "Let me tell you all about it. It's going to be the most fantastic development that Miami's ever seen, and you're the first one to see it."

He watched, his breath slow and shallow, as Clara turned the first page. "I've been planning it for years," he said. Indeed, before Clara was the most elaborate subdivision Miami had yet to see, with wide and stately boulevards, elegant, inviting plazas, generous sites for homes, lavish tropical vegetation, underwater sanitation and fresh water tanks concealed within minarets, in a style not quite Spanish or Italian but a romantic and extravagant Mediterranean mix unseen in these overdone fakes polluting the landscape that looked to Cam like nothing more than backgrounds for moving pictures. The designs for Palm Isle made it appear as if the development had grown out of the terrain itself: it was not a desecration of the landscape but a celebration of it: a style that would immediately be recognized as pure Florida.

Clara looked at page after page of plans and drawings and listened to Cam's excited voice describing the population balance of Palm Isle, with houses for rich and poor alike, a membership-only country club, a pool, a movie theater, a concert hall. "But Palm Isle's going to be a lot more than a resort," he said. "It's going to be a whole city in itself. I've planned every street, every house down to the last hibiscus bloom. See how all the elements fall into a kind of harmony with each other? And with nature too!" He looked at Clara when the last page had been turned. "I've already talked to the Miami representatives of Franklin Standard Life Insurance Company," he said, "and the Mortgage and

Securities Company of Atlanta. They're interested in my ideas, and what's more, they're interested in me. Not that it didn't take some doing. War hero or not, they turned me down cold until I said that you were my advisor, that I wouldn't make a move without you, that we're partners! Well, you should have seen the look on their faces then. Being the grandson of the Founding Mother didn't hurt, I'll tell you that. What I lack in experience, you make up for, Grandy. I've had some talks with them but I didn't show them this. I wanted you to be the first to see it." He reached into a pocket of the portfolio and drew out a sketch for a life-sized statue of her in native limestone. "It'd be put up on a little island I'd create a hundred yards out from the mouth of the river. I've got the publicity all worked out for it too: 'The Founding Mother welcomes you to Palm Isle'—that sort of thing."

The next half hour was bliss as Clara listened to all the details concerning Palm Isle. The plans and drawings were thrilling, the statue of her both embarrassing and satisfying. Cam's excitement brought her back to the days when she and Harry had done just this kind of planning in anticipation of the railroad coming in. The completion of her journey was about to take place; all that she had waited for in the last years would soon come to pass. He needed her, Cam said; he couldn't do Palm Isle without her. This was indeed what she had hoped would happen, the very thing to bring her into the future of the city.

"And when you get right down to it," he said, "it's all due to you."

"Me?"

"All that land you gave me. From the pine forest to that cypress strand—that's going to be Palm Isle."

Clara looked at him, surprised. "But didn't you tell your father you'd give all that to the Everglades Preserve?"

Cam laughed. "What if I did? Today I'm twenty-one years old and I'm entitled to do with it whatever I want. Five hundred acres are going into the development of Palm Isle."

"Oh, Cam . . ."

"I expected you to be skeptical," he said. "I'd be suspicious if you weren't."

"But the Preservation Society is depending on that land."

"That's land you *gave* me!" he cried. "Land my father manipulated me into promising him when I was too young to know any better!"

"Still..." Clara could not help thinking how disappointed Harry would be.

"I know what you're thinking. That I'm landlocked, isn't that right? That nobody's going to buy land in Miami unless they have access to the water, isn't that it?" He clapped his hands. "But that's no problem. The only thing that stands between me and the river is the Reade Groves. As soon as you sign them over to me, I'll build canals across the prairie, through the groves, right to the river. See? I've thought of everything! *Now* what do you think of your grandson?"

For a moment Clara wondered if he simply did not see the implications in what he asked of her. He was young, after all; he had had very little experience in the world he wanted to enter. "But don't you see that you'd be taking the groves away from your father?"

"So? Are you worried about him?" Cam asked. "He'll get by."

"Are you trying to destroy him, Cam?" she asked. "Is that what this is all about?"

Cam's anger suddenly flared. "Do I have to spell it out for you?" he said. "For God's sake, he deserted both of us!"

"I don't see that as something we have in common," Clara said in a voice softened by shock. But she realized too that Cam was not so far wrong to think of them as co-conspirators against Harry. And with that came the knowledge that he was not a naive boy with big ideas and a blind spot, but a calculating, vengeful man with the aim of a marksman.

The road was smooth but unpaved, and as she drove deeper into the grove, dust rose around the car until she had to slow to a crawl to see anything in front of her. On either side of her, rows of orange trees in full blossom stretched to the horizon. She hadn't been out here since Harry had left with the Indian woman and her son and was not even sure where the new house was. Wasn't there supposed to be a road that crossed this one somewhere?

She stopped the car. The scent of orange blossoms was as familiar as if she'd been here yesterday. She inhaled deeply; she wanted to smile, but instead a cloud of sadness settled on her. She'd tried not to think of Harry too much, but not a day had gone by when she had not recalled his face and heard him speaking to her; it was always the Harry of the past, the Harry of their first years in Miami when he was so happy, so full of hope. But hadn't he written her that he was happy now? It's I who insists that things aren't the way they ought to be, she thought.

In addition to overseeing the Reade Groves, Harry had joined Artus Van Lieu and a few other independent growers in their experimental station to deal with soil and crop testing. If the rest of the state of Florida was any indication, the future of the citrus industry was even more enormous than anyone could have predicted. In grove land bordering the river, plants from all over the tropical world were being tested. The United States Department of Agriculture responded to Harry's invitation and pledged its support in hard dollars. A small library building was put up at the southeast corner of the grove near the river; there five hundred volumes and nearly twenty-five hundred pamphlets were collected having to do with agriculture and citrus growing. Areas were set up for research and investigation that would receive plants from foreign countries and try to acclimate them to Miami soil and weather conditions. Though the Reade Groves always got his first attention, Harry helped pioneer the growth of pineapples, which did well in sandy soil and held firm in shipping, especially the Spanish Reds and Egyptian Queens. His nursery thrived as well; the first year after the war he shipped ninety thousand citrus trees to start a grove in Cuba. He improved the hammock land adjacent to the grove by judicious trimming and the planting of other tropical trees and shrubs with less density. He provided picnic tables and laid out rough trails and opened the area to visitors. He expanded the small cabin in the grove and finally built a new one on poured concrete columns so that it stood raised off the ground and, with its porches and large windows, got the full benefit of the scent of orange blossoms blown in on breezes from the 'glades. All this was public knowledge. Clara read about him in the papers; she kept up on his life that way.

What would she say to him when she saw him? Could she tell him that she was giving away all he'd worked for? He must know how valuable the land was, though. He could not have isolated himself so much that he did not know what was happening in Miami. Palm Isle would not come as a surprise to him, she was sure of that. And wouldn't he be proud of his son? Wouldn't he?

And then, as if conjured from her own thoughts, she saw him walking down one of the rows of trees, dressed all in white with a straw hat on his head that threw his face in shadow, but she would know him anywhere. Without thinking, she called his name. He looked up and continued toward her. Despite the heavy-looking satchel he carried in his right hand, his stride was long and loping as a young man's, but her tentative welcoming smile froze on her face, for as he approached the car she saw that it was not Harry but a young man unmistakably, shockingly recognizable, and her smile faded completely in a burning flush of shame. But for a certain squareness to the face and a coppery sheen to his skin, he seemed not like a Seminole at all. The one thing she had never expected was that he would look so much like his father.

"It happens all the time," the young man said. "I'm Tom."

The resemblance to Harry was even more striking up close: the same curve to the mouth, the same curly hair, the same green, heavy-lidded eyes, the same out-thrust, pugnacious jaw. Though it pained her, Clara forced herself to hold his gaze; she wanted to watch his expression when she identified herself. "I'm Clara Reade."

Tom drew his head back, a flicker of apprehension in his eyes. "I wondered if you might show up one of these days," he said, his tone wary. "If you didn't, I'd probably have come looking for you."

"I'm easy to find," Clara replied.

"I know," Tom said with a friendly laugh. "The Founding Mother."

Clara joined in the laugh. She didn't question what else Tom might know about her, what his father might have said, how he had explained what they'd done or how he'd rationalized their actions, excused the pain they'd both caused and both borne. Clara knew so little of Tom. Until this moment he had only been an idea in Clara's mind, a word on a stranger's lips to which Clara remained deaf. "So you're in school?" she asked with a nod at his satchel.

Tom nodded. "University of Tampa. I'm studying to be a lawyer."

"I thought we had more of them in Miami than we knew what to do with."

"Not ones as good as I'm going to be."

Clara laughed. "Confident, I see."

Tom shrugged. "Stubborn is more like it," he said. "I just can't seem to quit something till I've got it licked."

"I'm the same way," Clara said. Their eyes met and darted away, as if a cloak of unwanted intimacy had fallen on their shoulders. Clara looked down the rows of trees. "I'm a little lost," she said. "Can you . . . ?" She indicated the car. "I mean, would you like to drive?"

"Sure," Tom replied, threw his satchel in the back, and as Clara shifted over, got in behind the wheel. As he maneuvered the car down the road, he pointed out some of the newer trees. "Harry's been replanting in rows laid out by a surveyor's transit," he explained. "You ever see any rows so perfectly aligned? He's out here on his knees at dawn, inspecting the saplings for mealy bugs and citrus mites. I keep telling him not to take it so personally, but . . . well, you know Harry."

Clara looked out at the even rows of young trees and smiled, not so much at the dizzying symmetry but at the obvious affection in Tom's voice. When she mentioned this, he laughed.

"I hated him at first. My tribe taught me that white men were the cause of all the ills of the world. 'Course, it was hard to be disabused of that idea since it happens to be true." He turned to her, and Clara could see that there was a trace of humor in his eye. "Harry showed me at least that it wasn't *all* white men."

"How did you come to call yourself Tom?"

"I was born Little Tiger. My mother still calls me that, but after all the years of being ostracized in the tribe for having a white man for a father, I wanted to have a chance for a better life in the white world. So I cut off my hair and told people my name was Tom Reade. Harry disapproves. But it's easy for a white man to have romantic ideas about the purity and nobility of the Seminoles. I'm a realist myself."

"What'll you do after law school?"

Tom laughed. "I've had a job offer," he said. "Cam asked me to work for him on the Palm Isle project."

"I didn't know . . ."

Tom shook his head. "I told him I'm going to work for the Everglades Preservation Society and wished him a hard time."

Clara nodded, unable to speak.

"There's Harry!"

Tom stopped the car and honked the horn. Harry was standing atop a ladder a few yards down one of the rows, his arm deep in the foliage of an orange tree. When he straightened up and saw Clara and Tom, he smiled and waved as if it was the most natural thing in the world to see them together, then climbed down the ladder and came to them at the car, holding an orange in each hand.

"It was your great-grandfather," he said to Tom, "who told me that the sweetest fruit grew on the south side of the tree." He tossed an orange to Tom and held the other in his open palm for Clara.

"I got lost looking for your new house," she said as she took it. "Then I met . . . Tom and—"

"It's just back there," Harry said with a glance over his shoulder, then opened the door of the car. "Come on. I'll show you." Clara hesitated and looked up at him. "Tom'll take care of the Ford. Don't worry."

Clara took his offered hand and stepped onto the familiar sandy ground of the grove. "You've done wonderful things here, Harry," she said as they walked.

"Just trying to protect your investment," he said with a little laugh.

"Your son was telling me all about your crusade against the citrus mites."

Harry glanced back to where they'd left Tom. "He's a good boy," he said. "He and his mother haven't had an easy time of it, but—"

"And you?"

"Easy? I don't expect things to be easy. Do you?"

Clara shook her head and Harry looked at her, took her hand in his. He was smiling, and his apparent ease eased something in her; she felt a tightness in her yield to the simple pleasure of being with him, and when she did, the happiness she felt made her realize how long she'd missed him. He appeared to have gotten younger in the years since he'd gone off with the Indian woman, as if the dark colors of misery had been washed clean out of him.

A couple of crewmen passed by holding a ladder; she heard a mule braying as she and Harry walked slowly through the lushness of the grove, surrounded by clouds of white blossoms floating on a sea of deep waxy green leaves, the air misted with their astonishing perfume.

"Listen," she said.

"Know'st thou the land where the lemon trees bloom,
Where the gold orange glows in the deep thicket's gloom,
Where a wind ever soft from the blue heaven blows,
And the groves are of laurel and myrtle and rose?"

She looked up at him. "Remember?"

Harry nodded. "When we first came to the grove. And didn't you say it was like Christmas trees decorated with balls of gold?"

Tears flooded her eyes; she had to look away and fumbled with her handkerchief. "I should start back soon. I hate driving in twilight. The road's all covered with frogs."

"Oh no. Please join us for supper. Shinassa's made a pumpkin stew. Please."

She looked at him, and it was as if she suddenly remembered something long forgotten and the last shred of resistance to him fell away. "I'd like that," she said and hooked her arm through his. As they walked down the row of orange trees now, she knew that the moment she had sought these last years, the moment of completion, had finally arrived.

Epilogue, 1988

Cameron Reade was dreaming of oranges; when he woke up there was the sour taste of them in the back of his throat. He groped for the water on his bedside table and knocked over the glass. The television set was on; it disgusted him to think he'd fallen asleep in front of it, sitting up too. Next thing I'll be drooling and telling my life story to the night elevator man, he thought.

He gathered his robe at the neck and went to open the window, forgetting that there was central air conditioning and the windows were hydraulically sealed. On the thirty-seventh floor an open window was an invitation to danger; a half-dozen gulls and herons had smashed themselves into the glass since the building had gone up, and each time elaborate scaffolding was hung from the roof so the blood and feathers could be cleaned off. Cam hated being this high, but after going to the trouble and expense of acquiring the bay rights, creating four city blocks of landfill, and constructing the Reade Building, he'd be damned if he didn't occupy the penthouse suite.

A sightseeing boat was leaving the mouth of the river as another was returning; of course the real mouth of the river, where his father and grandmother had landed nearly a hundred years ago, had been erased by the landfill. The water of the bay seemed thick and rough today, with layers of aquamarine and pink and deep green, and over all of it there was a thin purplish sheen from the chemical spills that happened so often lately; true colors never gleamed with such radiance.

He closed his eyes; he had no appetite for the look of things anymore. He was proud of being clear-headed and unsentimental, and he would not let old age chip away at that any more than he would let it bow the straightness of his back. For the sake of publicity, his publisher was trying to turn him into a lovable old curmudgeon, but Cam had scrupulously avoided that pose on every page of his autobiography and would continue to do so at the ceremony today. After today, nobody would hear from him again.

A copy of *Miami's Son, A Personal History of the City* by Cameron Reade lay on his night table. His name and his grandmother's could have been linked sixty-five years ago when he asked her for that land. She should have let him have it. Well, no one alive today knew the real story behind her decision, and their names were linked now, in spite of her.

"Palm Isle was the success I knew it would be," went the now-official version, "despite the baroque legal entanglements that made it impossible for my grandmother to free up the Reade Groves. She struggled mightily to help me, but the courts were slow in dealing with our case and in the end I was forced to take other measures. By setting up an elaborate purchase of small homesteads, starch mills, and a piece of a limestone pit, by filling in swamp areas and deepening Arch Creek, I was able to route a wide canal from Palm Isle to Biscayne Bay itself, to pave a wide concourse along one side and range waterfront homes along the other."

Yes, he'd succeeded in building the most lavish development of the twenties, and Palm Isle became the signature of an ever-widening network of real estate developments that had made him one of the richest and most influential men in the South. And this was despite the difficulties her lack of support and cooperation caused him, despite the contempt she showed him, ignoring him, going off to his father and that other son, breaking his heart. He hated even thinking about them, and in fact that had been the hardest part of writing the book:

while he wrote history to suit the way he wanted his story to be remembered, their faces kept coming into his dreams.

Oh, the whole thing was getting out of hand! He should never have written the damn book. He had certainly never intended to demonstrate gratitude to his grandmother in it, not after what she and his father had done to him: hogging the land he needed, preserving the swamps, saving orange trees, for God's sake! But he didn't dare air his grievances, couldn't really, without sounding like a petulant, unforgiving, bitter old man. He'd be damned if he'd write it down for the world to see how they'd hurt him, how she'd let him down, how he'd unwittingly forced her back into his father's arms, how he'd been abandoned and unloved by both of them.

Founding Mother, Miami's Son: his publisher had loved the angle. Except Cam knew that where he had bestowed his title upon himself, she had earned hers. He ran cold fingers over the book's slick cover; at least he'd had the good sense to leave his father out of it. No glory there, not in *my* story.

Staring at the book, Cam thought, can I have done all this, come all this way, simply out of loneliness and envy?

His secretary came, and they took the express elevator to the garage in perfumed electronic silence. The tinted windows of the Lincoln kept the sun out of the car during the short drive to the dock; there they boarded his yacht for the quarter-mile trip out to the island. Two boats were circling his own, spewing arcs of colored water.

The small island on which the statue stood had been created from sand dredged from the bottom of the bay and arranged around pilings, then planted with a dozen pines whose conical shapes seemed to worship the little monument. The statue, still draped in canvas, had been meant as a publicity kickoff for publication day, but as word of the unveiling spread, people seemed more interested in the statue itself and the fact that it represented a direct link to Miami's origin.

Oh, the past, the past, he thought. I'm drowning in it.

"I can still call the whole thing off," he grumbled to his secretary. "Just tell them I died. Isn't that what they're really waiting for?"

The secretary shrugged. "Rumor has it you're too mean to die."

Cam laughed. "I assume you mean that as a compliment."

Boats were already docked at the island when Cam disembarked. His secretary held an umbrella over him as a line of well-wishers passed before him and people to whom he'd never been introduced remarked how nice it was to see him again. The president of the historical society handed him a pair of oversized scissors, led him to a platform, and helped him cut the rope that bound the canvas to the statue.

The canvas fell like a cape shrugged off impatient shoulders. Cam looked up at it, blinking in the sunlight. Of native limestone, the statue depicted his grandmother in a long dress that blew in the wind, one hand clutching a carpetbag, the other raised to her forehead to shield her eyes from the sun, one foot slightly forward. Cam heard the murmurs of approval behind him. He looked up at the statue again: its head high, its eyes looking ahead as if peering into the future. Had he ever known her so young? Oh, Grandy. Cam wondered if she could possibly have imagined all of this the day she and his father came to the river, so full of hope and dreams.

The reporters edged closer to him, pads and pens in hand, the photographers hovering in the background. Cam sensed the irritation behind their patience: waiting for the old man to dry his eyes and say something they could use in tomorrow's papers.

"Do you think your grandmother would have liked what's become of her city?"

Her city, Cam thought. In spite of sixty-five years of giving everything I had to it. Her city. He glanced at the statue with contempt and gave it his back. The hell with her, he thought. "I think it's exactly what she and my father hoped would happen," he said and watched with a measure of righteousness as they jotted his sentiments on their pads.

Late that day as his boat returned him to the mainland, he looked back at the island. The statue was lit now from beneath so that his grandmother appeared to skim along the sleek black surface of the bay. With a deep, satisfied sorrow, Cam knew that even if *Miami's Son* convinced everyone of his version of Miami's history, he had simply not been clever enough to convince himself.

He rode back up to the thirty-seventh floor of the Reade Building, knowing just exactly how he had conspired in the ultimate triumph of Clara Reade.